Ripper

Other Books by Lexi Blake

EROTIC ROMANCE
Masters And Mercenaries
The Dom Who Loved Me
The Men With The Golden Cuffs
A Dom Is Forever
On Her Master's Secret Service
Sanctum: A Masters and Mercenaries Novella
Love and Let Die
Unconditional: A Masters and Mercenaries Novella
Dungeon Royale
Dungeon Games: A Masters and Mercenaries Novella
A View to a Thrill
Cherished: A Masters and Mercenaries Novella
You Only Love Twice, Coming February 17, 2015
Luscious (Novella) (Sweet Seduction Box Set), Coming May 1, 2015
Adored: A Masters and Mercenaries Novella, Coming May 12, 2015

Masters Of Ménage (by Shayla Black and Lexi Blake)
Their Virgin Captive
Their Virgin's Secret
Their Virgin Concubine
Their Virgin Princess
Their Virgin Hostage
Their Virgin Secretary
Their Virgin Mistress, Coming April 14, 2015

The Perfect Gentleman (by Shayla Black and Lexi Blake)
Scandal Never Sleeps, Coming July 7, 2015

CONTEMPORARY WESTERN ROMANCE
Wild Western Nights
Leaving Camelot, Coming Soon

URBAN FANTASY
Thieves
Steal the Light
Steal the Day
Steal the Moon
Steal the Sun
Steal the Night
Ripper
Addict, Coming Soon

Ripper

Hunter: A Thieves Novel, Book 1

Lexi Blake

Grinnell Public Library
2642 East Main Street
Wappingers Falls, NY 12590
www.Grinnell-Library.org

Ripper
Hunter: A Thieves Novel, Book 1
Lexi Blake

Published by DLZ Entertainment LLC

Copyright 2015 DLZ Entertainment LLC
Edited by Chloe Vale
ISBN: 978-1-937608-35-4

All rights reserved. No part of this book may be reproduced, scanned, or distributed in any printed or electronic form without permission. Please do not participate in or encourage piracy of copyrighted materials in violation of the author's rights.

This is a work of fiction. Names, places, characters and incidents are the product of the author's imagination and are fictitious. Any resemblance to actual persons, living or dead, events or establishments is solely coincidental.

Sign up for Lexi Blake's newsletter
and be entered to win a $25 gift certificate
to the bookseller of your choice.

Join us for news, fun, and exclusive content
including free short stories.

There's a new contest every month!

Go to www.LexiBlake.net to subscribe.

Chapter One

"I'm not really an expert at missing persons, Mrs. Taylor," I said to the small woman sitting across from me even as I wondered what she changed into when the moon was full. I was betting it was something sweet and fluffy. She had that look about her.

With shifters, it's always the eyes that give them away, but I couldn't really explain it to you. You have to learn to read the signs. There's something about the way they move and the depth of color in a shapeshifter's eyes that's different than a regular human being. If you watch a shifter long enough, their body movement will also give them away. They move with more fluidity than we do. But again, it's something you have to be trained to see.

"I was told you were a private investigator." Mrs. Taylor's chin came up and I would have bet money that she spent some of her time as a deer. There was a grace about the way she held herself.

I was out of practice, but my every instinct screamed prey animal. Sometimes at night I have strange dreams which, given my unique background, shouldn't be surprising. One of those dreams has to do with the police training exercises they put newbies through. They have you walk through a fake city street and little cutouts of people pop up and you have a split second to decide if you shoot or not. You want to shoot the bad guy, but not the mom carrying the baby. If Mrs. Taylor popped up, I would make the instant decision to not shoot. My father held a different worldview. He would shoot them all on the off chance the baby had a gun. You could never, never be too careful in my father's world. This was precisely why I had gotten out.

"I'm a licensed private investigator, but I mostly help insurance companies investigate accidents." I answered her, but most of my brain was working on how I would get her out of my office. I had some serious solitaire to play. Not to mention the fact that it was already one thirty and I hadn't eaten lunch yet. I take lunch seriously. My brothers often joke that I eat like a hobbit. I had missed elevensies due to a line at the Hurst Police Department, and I wasn't about to miss lunch.

Big brown eyes went all watery on me and I noticed that she had her purse in a death grip. It was a sure sign she was ready to explode.

"Maybe I could refer you to someone else." I searched my brain for a name to give her. I didn't get a whole lot of actual, in-person clients, so I was a little at a loss as to how to handle this one. My job mostly consisted of retrieving police accident reports for liability claims adjusters. I went out and took pictures of intersections and determined light sequences. Sometimes I interviewed witnesses when they were hard to find or refused to talk on the phone. I followed the "potentially less injured than they say they are" and took pictures of them doing various activities they shouldn't be able to do. My favorite? The dude who was suing for two million due to complete loss of leg function dancing with strippers. I have it framed. I took on the occasional divorce case, but I tended to side with the women, so I preferred female clients. It worked out because most men in a divorce case didn't go looking for a female PI.

"No," Helen Taylor said as the tears started to fall. "It has to be you."

I glanced around for anything I could use as tissues. I suppose most seasoned PIs keep a box on their desk, but I wasn't that seasoned. I was twenty-six and had only been on the job for six months. Atwood Investigations was a one-woman operation. I didn't even have a secretary. It was all Kelsey Atwood, all the time. I had lucked into the contract with Driver's Insurance and I was riding that sweet wave of lower middle income because I didn't have the energy to be ambitious. My mom was high school friends with the local district manager, and by chance the company's former PI on retainer had recently retired. Unless you wanted someone to walk into a suburban police department and request a report, I failed to see how I was the only one to do the job. I was about to go to the bathroom for a roll of toilet paper when the blonde woman pulled out her own little pack of tissues and daintily blew her nose.

I was sympathetic, but resolute. I didn't want to get involved in something messy. This client deserved better than I would be able to give her. She needed to be someplace that could really liaise with the police. I told myself a thousand different reasons why I wouldn't help this woman and almost all of them were noble. Of course, only one of them was true and it wasn't self-sacrificing.

I wouldn't help her because she was a shifter and I wasn't going back to that world.

"Please," she said, her feminine voice tremulous. "She has been gone for five days. She's never been out of touch for that long. We talk twice a day, Joanne and I. I work the nightshift as a janitor at a school. She calls every night to make sure I get home after my shift. Something bad has happened to her."

And I totally sympathized. It must be terrible to not know where your daughter is. I tried not to think about my mother being in that situation, but I knew she had been. My father would take my brothers out for long periods of time and not tell my mother where they were. He'd only taken me on a trip once, and my mother had been hysterical by the time I'd called. She'd had the right to be, though I never talked to her about it. My brothers and I still kept those secrets from her even after all these years. It was better she never know.

Helen Taylor slid a photograph across the desk. She was small, but she had elegant-looking hands with long fingers. I bet she was really beautiful in her animal form. "Joanne missed her sister's first dance. She would never let Nancy down like that. She's a good girl. My girls…they're all I have."

Her speech moved me. It really did. I'm not heartless, though sometimes I wish I were. I looked down at the picture she had given me not because I wanted to but because, somehow, I was required to. I had two brothers and I knew where they were. It seemed wrong when my siblings were safe to not acknowledge this woman's pain.

Joanne Taylor was a bright and smiling face in the picture. She was surrounded by her beaming mother and her little sister, who stared up to her like she was the sun in the sky. In this picture, Joanne was roughly seventeen or eighteen years old. She was wearing the black robe of a graduate and had her cap in one hand like she'd just gotten through tossing it up in the air. She was blonde like her mother and had big brown eyes. She looked like a girl with a lifetime ahead of her.

"When was this taken?" I heard myself asking before I could stop the question.

Helen Taylor sat up, obviously eager to answer my questions. "Two years ago. She's a sophomore at SMU today. Oh, she's so bright. She got a full scholarship. She's studying to be a teacher. I work at the school she went to. She wants to give back, you see."

That was great, but it didn't solve my problem. I sighed. I was going to have to be blunt. "She sounds like a wonderful girl." I slid the picture back across the desk and into Mrs. Taylor's unwilling hands. She took it back but flipped it over and over, like she didn't know what to do with it. "But I don't take cases like this. Besides, I work here in the suburbs. I don't work with Dallas police. I don't have any contacts."

It was a lie. My brother worked for the Dallas police as a contractor. I wasn't about to mention that fact.

"But your brother James has plenty of contacts," the woman said, looking confused.

I took a deep breath in and wondered who the hell had sent her. She knew so much about me. I didn't exactly advertise, and certainly not in the supernatural world. "James works specialized cases for the police. He tends to work alone."

That wasn't a lie. Jamie preferred to work alone. The one partner he'd taken with him on a job had spent a little time in a mental hospital after the case. He only occasionally worked with his best friend, who happened to be a Texas Ranger. My younger brother, Nathan, had the good sense to get out altogether. He worked retail at a software store while he put himself through night school. He made less money than the rest of us, but he didn't have to deal with this shit.

Mrs. Taylor stood. She looked confused, like someone had told her to expect one outcome and she'd been given something entirely different. She turned toward the door that would lead her into the parking lot and I thought I'd made it. I would close up shop as soon as she was gone and eat my turkey sandwich and go home. I looked forward to a nice, quiet evening sitting in front of the TV while I made lists of things I needed for this weekend's renovation project. I was changing out the faucets in my little house. I found working on updating the three-bedroom ranch my grandmother had left me soothing.

All those plans were blown to hell when Mrs. Taylor turned around. Her brown eyes flared as she stared at me. "No, I won't be brushed aside. You're the only one who can help me and you will."

I would have bet a lot that she didn't rebel like this often. I was the lucky one who got to take the brunt of her frustration with a system that had probably ground her down for years. I threw up my hands and stood to face her. "Why? Why am I the only one who can help you?"

"Because you're a hunter."

I slumped back into my chair. She'd managed to say the one word that was sure to send me to the bottom of a bottle. I had promised myself I would break off my relationship with Jose Cuervo, but it looked like I would be having a one-night stand with my ex tonight.

"I am not a hunter. Not anymore."

"You people think we don't know you," Helen said with a certain righteousness that put me on edge. "But we keep track of you. We have to. We have to know who is coming for us. My husband was killed by a hunter. He was so gentle. He changed into a buck. We played around the forest together. He was gunned down in the street because your kind can't stand that we exist. He was thirty-five years old."

God, I hoped it wasn't my father who had done it. My stomach felt sick, but I tried to keep it together. "I didn't have anything to do with that."

Mrs. Taylor took a second. When she spoke again, she was quieter, more sympathetic. "Of course, you didn't, Kelsey. I don't blame you. I'm sorry if I made it sound like I did. I know how your father raised you. It's a testament to who you are that you aren't like him."

I wasn't so sure of that. I was a lot more like my dad than I wanted to admit. "How do you know so much about me?"

She sat back down and looked quite motherly. "I work with

someone who knows you. When I told her my problem and how the police won't help, she said you would. She said you were the best."

I only knew one person who she could possibly be talking about. "You work at Olivia's school."

She smiled at the sound of Liv's name. That wasn't surprising. Most people who knew Olivia Carey brightened at the thought of her. I, on the other hand, was going to kick her ass. "Yes, she's such a nice young woman. She hadn't joined the school when Joanne was there, but I look forward to Nancy getting her for English next year. She works late sometimes and I talk to her while I clean her room."

"What did the police say?" I asked, though I was pretty sure I knew what they had told the freaked-out mom.

Helen's face twisted and I knew she was pissed as hell at the police. "They said she'd probably run off with a boy. They said it happens all the time. They took a report, but that was all they were willing to do."

And it was all they would do for the daughter of a janitor. In my experience, justice was for the people in Highland Park. The police had bigger problems to deal with than chasing down some poor co-ed who by all statistics likely had simply run off with a boy.

"What do you want me to do?" I asked because she had me. I would do the job because if I didn't, I would be adding Joanne Taylor's sunny face to the rotating players in my nightmares.

"I want you to do what you do best." Mrs. Taylor opened her purse and took out an envelope. She laid it on the desk. "I want you to hunt my daughter."

Chapter Two

I let my mind drift as I drove along 183. At this time in the afternoon, it was a fairly easy thing to do. In another hour or so it would be a suicidal prospect as the entire freeway would be moving at breakneck speeds with little distance between cars. That was driving in DFW during rush hour. Now, in the early afternoon, driving through Irving to Dallas was peaceful. If you live in the DFW area, you get used to driving. Some people might think that a thirty-minute drive was a big deal, but I did it at least four or five times a week and every time my mind drifted despite my best efforts. I could have the radio on or off. I could try to play mind games to keep my brain away from dangerous places, but nothing worked. I'd tried audiobooks once, listening to the last Harry Potter as I drove around the Metroplex in my old Jeep, but I had to back up and listen to the same chapter four times so I gave up. My mind wandered.

Now I let it drift to revenge fantasies. It was far better than the usual horror movies that played out in my brain. I was going to kill Olivia Carey and become the villain I always knew I could be. I imagined the throngs of weeping students at her memorial. They would leave little teddy bears at the sight of her horrible murder, which would occur wherever I happened to find her at that freaky school she worked at. If she was in her classroom, then that was my killing ground. Same thing with the cafeteria or the library. I wouldn't discriminate.

Nor would I let a thing like love get in my way.

I loved Olivia Carey. I've often thought that life would have been easier had I been born a lesbian. It was one of the universe's wicked mistakes that I needed a penis to make me happy sexually because in all other ways, Liv was the girl for me. I don't know how normal friendships work. I never had a real friend before Olivia, so I don't know if the intense bond we share exists between other girlfriends. Liv and I hadn't bonded over pedicures and crushes over boys. We bonded because she saved my life. I don't mean that in a "how would I get through without you" way. I mean that in a "stop the bleeding and convince me not to ever try that again" way.

Did that really give her the right to fuck with my life? I knew she thought I was wasting my talents on police reports and catching cheating hubbies. She thought I should put my skills to use helping the helpless and shit. She'd watched one too many superhero flicks. I wasn't that girl no matter how much she wanted it to be true. I would help Helen Taylor because she'd gotten through a chink in my armor and I felt a responsibility to her, but I would be fixing that fissure as soon as possible. Liv needed to understand that if I decided she was my weakness, I might have to dump her ass. She could find a more suitable friend and I would be happy alone without anyone's expectations to live up to.

"Fuck." I banged my hand against the steering wheel as I took the exit and then I winced because that hurt. I was smart enough to know that I was never going to kick Liv out. I could bitch and moan all I liked about being a loner, but I needed her. The thought of a world without Liv left me cold. I even tried to get along with her deadbeat boyfriend, Scott, and I hated him with a passion. I dreaded the day I had to stand beside her as her maid of honor while she threw away her life on that idiot because she was way too loyal to her college love. Sometimes I thought Liv collected people the way others collected stray dogs though, I should point out, she collects those, too. Once a person got into Liv's circle, she would never kick you out no matter how bad your taste in music or how surly your outlook on life was. Sadly, that last bit could be me or Scott.

Like I said, I'm honest with myself.

It was almost four o'clock when I pulled into the parking lot of the Montrose School for Special Children. I wondered if it bothered the students to be considered "special." I was sure the outside world heard that moniker and assumed special needs. These kids had special needs, but they had nothing to do with what you normally associated with the term. These were the children of supernatural citizens. The teachers here knew how to handle teen werewolves when the moon was full. They had classes to teach young witches how to control their power.

I hopped out of the Jeep, noting that Liv's little hybrid was still in the half full parking lot. The school went from kindergarten through high school. It was a small school, but they had lots of afterschool activities. At this hour, it would mostly be the high school kids left attending their Spanish club meetings or the mandatory "Dealing with Demons" seminar they held twice a year.

"Hey, Kelsey," I heard someone say.

I glanced over and saw a young werewolf walking toward her car carrying a stack of books that I was surprised she could see over. Ellen Yardley was a student of Liv's and I ran over to grab a couple of those books hindering her sight.

"Thanks." She was a lovely seventeen-year-old who would graduate in the spring. "It's not the weight that bothers me, but boy, are those things unwieldy."

I laughed as she opened her trunk. "Is your teacher trying to kill you?"

We dumped the books in the trunk. "No, it's a book drive. It's my service project. I'm collecting books for a big sale. All the seniors have booths and we're donating the proceeds to the homeless."

"That's great, Ellen." My high school had been more about keggers and pot than helping the public. I wondered if Ellen knew those same people she was helping would likely kill her if they knew the truth about her. That was the world I'd grown up in. I kind of liked Ellen's more. "I think y'all are doing some good work."

"Well, I'm glad you think so because I expect to see you there buying stuff," the teen replied with a saucy smile. She hopped in her old sedan. "See you later!"

I walked back to the building, trying to ignore the lump in my throat. I waved at some of the teachers heading out. They were supernaturals, too. They accepted me and most of them knew my

background. They were just people trying to live their lives and do the best they could for their kids. I hated my father so much in that moment I had to shove the emotion down or I was sure the look on my face would scare the kids.

I opened the door and walked down the hall to Liv's room and decided to think about another emotion. I always felt it when I walked these halls and people called out cheery greetings. It was acceptance and sometimes it felt awfully close to redemption.

Nope, I was still gonna kill her. She was making me tear up and I couldn't accept that. I'm not the kind of girl who cries.

I threw open the door, and Liv was sitting at her desk grading papers. She looked up with a sunny smile that immediately turned wary.

"Okay," she said in her most patient voice. "Maybe I shouldn't have talked to Helen but…"

My eyes narrowed. "No buts, Liv. You sold me out."

She snorted and rolled her brown eyes. "You're such a drama queen. It's one little case. You know you need something of substance. You can't spend your whole life hiding from the world."

"No, I can't hide from anyone if you keep giving away my hiding spot," I pointed out. She was tapping her foot, the three-inch heeled shoes making a rhythm of judgment on the tiled floor. "Damn it, Liv, I'm not a missing persons expert."

Her eyes softened and she smiled. "Yes, you are. You're an everything expert when it comes to this. You have amazing instincts, Kels. You just don't trust them anymore. You have to stop punishing yourself."

Sitting against the edge of her desk, I crossed my arms defensively. "It seems like you're the one punishing me."

"Again with the overdrama. You're worse than my students." She sighed and rested her chin in the palm of her hand. "She needs you."

"And what if I can't find her daughter?" I gave up on the angry approach. I couldn't keep it up with her.

She leaned beside me, letting our shoulders touch. We sat like that when one of us needed comfort. "Then you'll at least have tried and Helen will know someone gave a damn. I'm not asking you to succeed, Kelsey. I'm asking you to try."

"Fine." How was I supposed to say no to that?

Liv gave me a hug. "Excellent. Now that we have that out of the way, I can move on to the freakier news." Her pretty face twisted into a rueful grimace. "I'm moving to public school as soon as possible."

"But you love this school." She was the one lying because I happened to know this was her dream job.

"Yeah, well, at public school you don't get memos like the one I got today." She handed an important looking piece of paper my way. It was meant to catch the eye, printed on bright yellow paper so no one could possibly miss it. "That memo informs all teachers that no matter your chosen method of birth control, you should also begin using a condom."

"And you're getting this advice from the principal, why?"

"Because we have a fertility god in third grade this year who came into his powers over the summer," she said with a playful frown. "Apparently being around the little sucker makes you ovulate. Mary, the third grade teacher, is already two months along."

I tried to place the name, but all I could see was a fifty-year-old with a sweet smile. That couldn't be her. "But school's only been in session for two months."

"Yup. That's the point. It gets worse. Mary swears she went through menopause five years ago. Does Costco sell condoms? I'm making Scott put two of those babies on if he wants to touch me."

"Be really safe, go for three." I sighed because the day was getting away from me. I'd already gone over all the information the super-organized Helen Taylor had left me. I had a list of all of Joanne's contacts and every bit of information her mom could think of. I had her driver's license number and her social security number. I had the names of her roommate, her RA in the dorm, and a schedule of her classes. The first thing I'd done was search some of the social networking sights for any sign of her.

You would be surprised how often kids hide things from their parents that it would be so simple for them to discover if they checked their kid's Facebook status. No luck with Joanne though. Her Instagram page hadn't been updated since the week before and then all the smiling pic told me was she'd been studying for a Biology quiz. I needed to go and talk to her roommate. I wished I could say that Liv was wrong and I didn't have any instincts, but something was telling me that the police were wrong.

Joanne Taylor was in trouble and waiting until tomorrow to get started wasn't in my nature. Now that I was on the case, I had to get going.

"All right," I said, pushing myself off the desk. "I need to get over to the SMU campus."

Liv smiled, seemingly excited at the prospect of my working something more interesting than a rear-end collision. "Do you want some company? I can play Watson to your Holmes."

I shook my head at the thought. "Sure. Come along and make sure I don't spook the co-eds. I'm gonna run to the bathroom and then I'll be good to go."

Liv pulled her shoulder-length auburn hair out of its sedate ponytail. "I have to call Scott and then I'll be ready."

"What are you gonna call him? A douchebag?" I was only half joking. He really was a douchebag.

"Ha ha," Liv replied, her hand already on the phone.

She dismissed me and I ran down to the nearest bathroom, carrying my version of a handbag. It was big. I'd heard someone call it a messenger bag once, but I'm not sure if there's a technical term for it. It was where I kept the files I was working on. I also had a notebook, my phone, a bunch of business cards, and my little .38, which I had a permit for. I hadn't needed to use it yet. So far all my clients had been polite and I was good enough to not get caught when I took pictures of cheaters. I opened the door to the bathroom and headed to the sink. If I was really honest with myself, I would admit I didn't carry the gun because I was scared a client would get pissed. Deep down, I knew one day my father would show up again and I wanted to be ready.

The cold water felt good on my hands, and I couldn't quite resist the urge to splash it on my face. I wasn't wearing much makeup anyway. I took a deep breath and prepared myself to go back into that world I'd never really left behind. My best friend was a witch and I spent a lot of time at this school surrounded by teen werewolves and shifters and even a pre-teen fertility god.

If my dad had any idea what went on at this school…I didn't even want to think about it. He'd left town ten years ago and I hadn't seen him since. I needed to stop hearing his footsteps behind me. Liv was right. I needed to come out of hiding. I needed to find a way to forgive myself for that day when I was sixteen.

Not going there. I stared at the face in the mirror, so familiar and yet such a stranger at times. My dark brown hair was in a utilitarian ponytail. When I took it down, it would reach halfway down my back. It wasn't practical, but I couldn't bring myself to cut it. It was thick and had a natural wave to it that the humidity wreaked havoc on. I should cut it short, but I liked the way it looked. I liked the way it felt when a man's hands ran through it. It made me feel feminine and pretty and sometimes it was the only thing that did.

I'm not unattractive. My features are perfectly symmetrical and I have big brown eyes. My mouth is a little on the smallish side. I have a fit body, but I think my boobs are on the small side. I'd had men describe them as a nice handful, but they aren't as round and lovely as Liv's.

That was what I needed. If I was going to get through this case, I needed a guy who thought I was hot. It had been a while since I got laid by an actual, real, doesn't require Double A batteries man. I needed some mind blowingly good sex to take my mind off things. I grimaced at myself in the mirror. I didn't exactly know anyone who could give me that. I'd tried a few one-night stands with guys I met at the local bar before I realized that drunken men are not the best lovers. I might need to settle for good sex. I needed something more than a one-night stand and less than an actual scary relationship.

"Oh, god," I heard Olivia say from the doorway. Her eyes were wide as she stared at me and she was shorter than before. She had changed into her beloved Converse. "You're thinking about getting laid. That's your 'I can't find a decent man' face."

I turned. "I didn't know I have a face for that."

She nodded seriously. "You do, indeed. You also have a 'stay out of my business, Liv' face."

It was my turn to nod. I was really sure I had that face. "I'm using that one right now."

She chewed on her bottom lip, a habit she'd had since I met her in tenth grade. "Yeah, that's probably not happening. I think it's a good sign that you're interested in sex again. Come on. Put on your 'serious PI' face and let's go back to college. It'll be fun. Maybe we can find a hot college boy for you to play with. You're a mysterious older woman. I bet they'll go crazy for you."

I groaned at the thought of Liv pointing out potential boy toys the rest of the afternoon.

But I put on a little lip-gloss before I left anyway.

* * * *

I turned off Mockingbird onto Ownby Drive while Liv shoved another CD into the player.

"When you get all big time with this gig, I think we should get you a better car," Liv said as she fiddled with the volume.

"I like this car." I'd had the blue Jeep since I was twenty. I'd gotten her after saving up for two years, and even then my mom had chipped in. Jamie had done the needed mechanical work to get her running at full speed and still did the upkeep on her. I had zero desire to drive anything nicer than the navy blue Jeep I'd lovingly kept running for the last six years.

Liv laughed as I started looking for parking. "Do you ever get rid of anything? Okay, how about this? How about you get a couple of big paychecks and we replace the sound system in here?"

"That's a deal." I had no idea where she thought those big paychecks would be coming from. Mrs. Taylor had given me a five hundred dollar retainer and I wasn't sure she could afford much more than that.

Liv liked her music loud and very rock and roll. Though she dressed like the high school teacher she was, her tastes tended toward hard rock and punk. I wondered if her students knew how much time we used to spend in clubs banging our heads and drinking beer. I always got wistful when I thought of those days. It seemed hard to believe they were gone. I was only twenty-six. I should still feel young, right?

"Will you just park, please? The building is right there." Liv pointed to the stately looking dormitory.

"I have to look for an open visitor space. The campus police are always on the lookout for a ticket writing possibility."

She pointed. "Take that one right there."

It was a prime spot and obviously reserved for staff. I pulled in anyway because Liv can be bossy at times and I didn't have the energy to argue with her over how far she had to walk. "I'm sending you the bill for the ticket."

She reached into her stylish bag. She pulled out a piece of plastic. It was shaped like one of those parking stickers that hang from your rearview mirror, but it was completely blank. "Oh, ye of little faith." she said as she placed it properly.

"New charm?"

Liv was a practical witch. She was always looking for new ways to use her talents to make our lives less expensive.

"They'll see exactly what they expect to see," she said with a proud grin on her face. "I already tested it out. I left my car at Love Field when Scott and I went to Vegas. I parked in the arrivals section for three days and presto…no ticket."

We got out of the car and started to walk up the lovely tree-lined sidewalks toward Joanne Taylor's campus home.

I reached in my bag and pulled out a business card. I hoped Helen Taylor had done her job as we approached the front desk. It was manned by an efficient-looking girl in her early twenties.

"Hello, how may I help you?" Her nametag identified her as Sharon.

I smiled my most professional smile as I handed her my business card. "Hi, Sharon. I'm Kelsey Atwood. Helen Taylor was supposed to call and inform…"

Sharon's eyes went big and tears started to form. "Yes, absolutely she did. The director told me you were coming. We all love Joanne. I can't believe this is happening. Do you think it's a serial killer? Do you think she's just the first? How should I protect myself?"

The questions were rapid fire and hit me with the blast of a machine gun. It was all I could do not to step back because she was leaning forward over her desk. I shot a look at Liv. We sometimes communicated silently.

"And you call me overdramatic?" my eyes said.

Liv shrugged because she had nothing for that.

"Sharon, we have no reason to believe Joanne has done anything but freaked out a little and took an impromptu vacation. Really, that's the likeliest possibility." I was lying through my teeth, but if I didn't then the rumors would run wild. "Her mom just wants me to look into it. How well do you know Joanne?"

I wanted to smack Liv because she was staring at me with a maternally proud look on her face. I might be out of practice, but I knew how to handle a freaked-out girl. It was my experience that the most innocent of people tend to be the ones who freak out first. If you never struggled while growing up, it was harder to deal with the realities of the world when you got older. Sharon was obviously a child of privilege, and from her open face, I suspected that Mom and Dad loved their baby girl. I wasn't about to begrudge the girl her happy childhood. The world needed Sharons to keep it a pleasant place.

"She's in my Spanish study group," the blonde said. "We've also lived in the same dorm for two years. She's a super-nice girl. She even gets along with that roomie of hers and let me tell you, that's a job."

Interesting. I leaned closer. "Bitchy?"

Sharon shook her head. "Try witchy."

Liv tensed beside me. "What do you mean?"

Sharon was a fount of gossip. "You know, Cassie's a Goth, but not like cutesy. She's all pretentious and stuff. She talks about the goddess and Wicca and cursing people who do her wrong. It's all weird, but I'm a Presbyterian and we're supposed to be tolerant so I just smile and let her talk. It kind of freaks me out, though. It didn't seem to bother Jo."

I bet it didn't. I wondered how much Joanne's roommate knew about her. It all depended on whether Cassandra Lydell was a real witch. I doubted it. Two things gave her away. Wicca is a religion and not one where the followers tend to curse people. They have their threefold laws and stuff. Wicca had nothing to do with actual witches. The real things tended to not run around talking about the goddess, but I was grateful Liv was with me. She could tell me in a minute flat if I was dealing with the real thing or not.

I thanked Sharon, who showed me to the elevators. We made our way to the third floor. Room 315 was halfway down the hall, and I knocked on it shortly as I read the many notes on the corkboard secured to the door. Though it stated plainly that this was Joanne and Cassie's room almost all the notes were for Jo. The notes started out asking her to call so and so or saying someone had dropped by, but the newer notes begged her to get in touch. They spoke of deep worry. This wasn't a girl who bugged out on her friends.

"Wannabe. I'm getting nada and if she was even a minor witch I should feel something." There was no judgment in Liv's pronouncement, merely truth.

The door opened and I was faced with a walking, talking Hot

Topic mannequin. Cassie Lydell had the Goth thing down. She wore black on black on...surprisingly enough, more black. Her combat boots were black, as were the artfully torn fishnets that covered her legs. Her miniskirt was a more faded black which spoke of much use, but the T-shirt looked new. It was some band's tour shirt, and apparently the band really liked demons and poorly drawn Hell symbols.

"What do you want?" she asked through her black-tinged lips.

I elbowed Liv because she was trying hard not to laugh. Apparently she'd forgotten what it was like to be young and hyper-pretentious. I would have to pull out the pictures of her in her surplus army coat. It was a phase that came right after her skater year.

"Hello, I'm Kelsey Atwood. I'm investigating the disappearance of your roommate." I would have handed her a business card, but she would just stare at me like I was an idiot.

She did it anyway. "Okay."

I held my temper. "We need to come in and ask you a few questions and maybe look around at Joanne's belongings. It can tell us a lot sometimes."

She shrugged, her black bob shaking. She was a tall, lanky girl, and she opened the door, not bothering to wait for us to walk in before she tossed herself on her bed and started thumbing through a magazine.

I wasn't buying it. I could see Liv getting pissed, but she was missing some important signs. The minute I mentioned Joanne's name, Cassie swallowed not once, but twice. Her jaw had firmed into a hard line. It was the kind of thing you did when you were trying to control yourself.

"When was the last time you saw, Joanne?" I kept my voice quiet and sympathetic. I didn't need to give her anything to rebel against.

She didn't look up from her magazine, but I noted that she wasn't reading. Her eyes stared straight forward. "I don't know. Couple of days ago."

"Do you even care that your roommate is missing?" Liv asked, outrage in her voice.

Cassie tensed, but didn't look up. I widened my eyes at my friend. It let her know she wasn't helping. She sighed and her hands went up in submission. I needed to give her something else to do.

"Why don't you look through her clothes?" Liv loved clothes. She knew they said a lot about a person. "Tell me what you see."

"All right," she said, apology blatant in her tone as she walked to the small closet and started to look through it.

I turned back to my problem. Cassie had gathered her armor tightly around her, and I was going to have to push through it. I sat down on the edge of Joanne's bed and regarded the girl, deciding on the best tactic. "Did Joanne ever have any trouble with the girl at the front desk?"

Cassie glanced over the magazine with startled eyes. "Sharon? She's annoying, but I don't think she had a problem with Jo. Did she say something bad about Jo?"

I managed to suppress the self-congratulatory grin that wanted to come out. Now I knew she liked her roommate. Her default position was to never show she cared about anyone. "Oh, she didn't say anything. I got a feeling that she was one of those chicks who gets weirded out by anyone even slightly different from what she considers normal." I wasn't lying. Sharon had said the words herself.

Cassie's black lips turned up a little. We were making progress. "She's not that bad, actually. There are way worse than Sharon, but Jo gets along with everyone."

"She doesn't seem like the kind of girl who ups and walks away." I took in the small room. The differences were well delineated. Cassie's side of the room was messy and cluttered with clothes and makeup and CDs. Joanne's side of the room was pin neat. Her bookshelf held her textbooks, a couple of notebooks, and a stack of paperbacks with cracked spines.

Cassie set the magazine down. "She's not. I tried to tell her mom that she'd been acting weird but…"

But Helen didn't think Cassie should be saying anyone acted weird, I could guess. I leaned forward. I wasn't going to make the mistake of not taking her seriously. "How was she acting weird?"

She bit her bottom lip as though wondering exactly how much to tell me. I had to put a stop to that.

"Cassie, I'm not here to judge her. The crap I've done in this lifetime makes me unfit to judge anyone. I'm here to find her. The only thing I care about is figuring out what happened to her. I ain't the cops. You can tell me whatever and trust me, I've probably been there and done that."

Cassie groaned in frustration. "I don't know exactly what's going on. I just know she's been acting weird for Jo. She's been going out late at night and staying out all night sometimes."

"Clubbing?" I heard Liv ask.

"Maybe," the girl said, still a little wary.

Liv walked out of the closet carrying a handful of dresses on hangers. "Look at the labels."

I obediently read the labels on the beautiful dresses. They were awfully sexy for a sophomore good girl. "I don't know who Versace is."

Liv groaned and I guessed I hadn't pronounced it even close to right.

"Holy shit, that's a Versace?" Cassie asked and it was obvious she didn't borrow the other girl's clothes.

"They were in the back." Liv went through the dresses one by one. "Gucci, Zac Posen and Monique Lhuillier. I found two pairs of to-die-for Jimmy Choos."

"I take it those are expensive." I'm not a fashionista. I wear jeans and T-shirts. I have exactly one little black dress and one pair of good heels. It's all I need. But the fact that Joanne had clothes she shouldn't have been able to afford made me curious. "Check her underwear."

Liv was game. She opened the top drawer of the dresser. "Plain white cotton. Panties and bras."

"She tends to sleep in a T-shirt," Cassie offered.

I wasn't buying it. "Check the back of the drawer."

Liv's hand disappeared and her eyes widened when she came back with a handful of silk. "Wow. La Perla. This is freaking gorgeous."

I wasn't an idiot. Not even close. This particular leap I was taking had nothing to do with my so-called instincts and everything to do with connecting the dots. "Do you know when Jo lost her scholarship?"

If she'd ever had it in the first place.

Cassie's mouth dropped open and she stared at me for a moment. "How did you know that?"

I wasn't about to tell her I knew because most nice girls didn't prostitute themselves if they weren't seriously hurting for cash. She wouldn't be doing it if she still had a free ride. She might not be hooking in a traditional sense. I doubted that given the designer clothes and fancy undies, but she was making cash off some man, somewhere. "It was an educated guess."

Cassie shook her head and sat up straight. "I transferred in last semester in the middle of the year. Jo's roomie had dropped out so she got paired up with me. We got along okay. She was always studying or doing things at home. I was surprised she requested to room with me again this year, but I was up for it. She's a nice girl and she doesn't freak about the weird stuff. But I knew something was different this semester. She was out a lot and her grades weren't that great. I know it's only October, but she missed a test because she slept in. It wasn't like her. I asked about it and she said the foundation that administered her scholarship went broke this summer. There was some sort of scandal. She lied to her mom so she wouldn't worry. She said she was working at some club, but I don't know where."

"Were there any particular men who would come by wanting to see her?"

"Well, there's Darren. Jo's known him since they were kids. Obviously he has a thing for her, but she doesn't see him as anything more than a friend." Cassie thought for a second or two. "She spent some time with a professor. She had him last year for freshman English, but she's taking a special class with him this year on mythology and folklore. I think his name is Hamilton. She called him Peter, which I thought was a little weird. The profs around here tend to be conservative. She was doing some sort of project for him."

I stood up and glanced around. If Joanne was on the game then it made since that she probably kept an appointment book. "Where is her laptop?"

"She took it with her the night she went missing. For the last month or so, she took it everywhere because she'd gotten so behind she had to work whenever she got a few minutes."

I made a mental note to get her e-mail address from her mother and check to see if there was any activity. Hopefully Helen knew her daughter's provider. "Do you know if she had an address book or a day planner?"

"Not that I've seen," Cassie said. "Wait. Now that I think about it…she'd been getting calls, but not on her usual cell. When she came back to school this year, she had two phones. She would get a call and then she would write stuff down in a spiral notebook. I thought it was school stuff and she was making notes about a class."

Liv was already pulling out spiral notebooks. There was a thick stack of them on the shelf above her dresser. On notebook five, we hit pay dirt. There were three different addresses. One was in the suburbs. One was downtown, and the last one was in North Dallas, not far from campus. There were a series of numbers that looked like times and dates after the addresses and a couple of names. The name Alexander came after the North Dallas address with the last date listed and a time of one a.m.

The notebook in my hand felt like hitting the mother lode. This was what I needed. I stood and faced Cassie. "Thank you. This is exactly what I need." There was a brisk knock on the door and Cassie got off her bed to answer it. I gave her my business card and this time she took it. "If you think of anything else that might help, please call me."

Cassie started to open the door, but whoever was on the other side wasn't waiting. A young man shoved the door open, obviously not caring that he pushed Cassie aside. I was at her back, quickly propping her up so she didn't fall on her ass.

"Fuck me, you've got some nerve. I couldn't believe it when Sharon told me who was here. I had to see it for myself." He stormed in to the room.

At first I assumed he was talking to Cassie and I thought I was going to have to defuse a situation with a bad ex. After his next words, I had no doubt as to whom his target was.

"How dare you come here asking questions about Jo? I know who you are, hunter."

I pushed Cassie away because I wasn't hiding behind some little college kid. The young man in front of me was stocky, but nowhere close to filled out the way he would be in a few years. His eyes were dark, probably brown, but filled with rage, they appeared black. He was dressed in a flannel shirt and worn jeans. His brown hair was overgrown and he could have used a shave. He was everything one would expect from a werewolf, and a young alpha at that, I would bet.

"Let's get out of here, Kels," Liv said, her tone reflecting the thick tension in the air.

"Darren, what are doing here?" Cassie looked around, her eyes wide because she obviously had no idea why everyone was on edge.

Darren ignored her, but then I was betting he usually did. "I tried to convince Mrs. Taylor that this was a mistake. You think I haven't searched for Jo? You think I haven't tried to track her? What are you going to do when you find her? Are you gonna shoot her down like you did her father?"

His eyes were rapidly flickering back and forth between his forms. He might be an alpha, but he wasn't a terribly strong one. He still didn't have good control of himself. I needed to keep the situation as calm as possible, though what I really wanted to do was throw up that turkey sandwich I'd eaten. It sat heavily in my gut.

"I didn't have anything to do with that and Mrs. Taylor knows it." My voice held a calm I didn't feel. I didn't even think about going after my gun. It was in my bag, right there in reaching distance. I could have had it in my hand and pointed at the angry wolf in a second, but I wasn't even tempted. If he'd attacked in that moment, I likely wouldn't have defended myself.

He got right up in my face and I tried not to flinch. "Maybe you didn't pull the trigger, but you were there in spirit. You're always there. I know you call each other and tally up your kills. You hang out in your bars and talk about the carcasses you bagged. Tell me something, do you stuff your prey like some hunters do? I hear you have to get the head to the taxidermist real quick or we're rude enough to disintegrate before you get your trophy."

"What the hell are you talking about, Darren?" Cassie stared at him like he was speaking a foreign language.

"Shut up, bitch," he growled. "This is between me and the hunter, here. You want to try to take me out? You want to test me, or do you just go after prey animals and children?"

I stayed on my feet, but inside I was swaying and telling myself that there was no way he could know. No one knew except me and Liv and Jamie. And my father, but I didn't count him. Darren couldn't know what had happened that night.

"Back off." Liv got between us. Her voice was low, but it was full of menace. "You stay away from her, wolf. Jo's roomie might be a dabbler, but I promise you, I'm the real thing and you won't like what I do to you if you so much as lay a hand on her."

"Traitor," he hissed at Liv. He glared at me and his eyes made a promise. "This is not the end. Maybe we should start turning the tables on you. See how you like being hunted."

He backed out the door, careful to not let me out of his sights.

"Holy crap." Liv let out a relieved breath. "Let's get out of here. I think you have everything you need."

I swallowed and was sure my face was perfectly composed. I should be upset that I'd been saved by Liv. Sweet, gentle Liv had to get between me and an angry werewolf. I wasn't pissed at myself. I was a little pissed at Liv because there was a big piece of me that wanted everything Darren's twitchy hands had been promising.

"Yes, we're done here," I heard myself saying. I turned to Cassie, whose eyes were wide. "If you think of anything else, please give me a call. You can also call me if he gives you any trouble."

I doubted he would. He'd barely noticed she was there, but I wanted her to feel like she had someone to call.

I felt numb as I followed Liv back to the car. I felt like I had missed something essential in the confrontation with Darren, but I couldn't wrap my head around it. I was using my every brain cell to block out the images his words brought back. I drove back to Liv's school on autopilot, responding to her questions, but not really hearing her at all.

"Are you sure you're all right?" Liv hesitated, getting out of the car. "You could come home with me. I'll make some dinner and we can crack open a bottle of wine."

I could listen to Scott bitch about the things Liv did wrong and hear him mutter under his breath about how pathetic I was. No. I had other plans.

"I'm fine." I decided a little truth was necessary to really sell this particular lie. "Well, I'm not fine exactly. He brought back some shitty memories, but I have to move on."

"You do," she encouraged. "You aren't that person. You never were. You can't blame yourself for something that happened when you were sixteen years old."

I nodded because it was what she wanted me to do. She didn't blame me for what happened ten years ago, but she was wrong if she thought I couldn't blame myself. I wasn't the only one. There were ghosts that damn sure blamed me, too. But I already had a plan for exorcising those demons, at least for a little while.

"I'm fine," I assured her. "I'll talk to you tomorrow."

She reached out and gave me a quick hug. "Okay, Kels. I'm

sorry if I got you into something you aren't ready for. I was trying to help Helen. I really thought it would be good for you to work a case that meant something."

I shrugged off the concern. The goal now was to get Liv out of the car. "Everything is fine. I need to get home and get some sleep. I'll be ready to go in the morning."

She stared at me, her hand on the door. "You're going straight home?"

"Yes, Liv," I said in my best "don't mother me" voice.

She got out with a sympathetic smile.

Idiot believed me.

Chapter Three

"Wow," I managed to slur once I pushed my head off the bar and downed my shot. "This is really good tequila. It's so sweet and smooth."

Gil looked at me over the bar and he frowned, but I didn't really process it as disapproval. I was way too far gone.

"That's because it's apple juice," he said with a shake of his bearded head. "I cut you off thirty minutes ago, sweetheart."

"Seriously? Are you sure because I think this stuff is awesome."

"I'm glad you like it, darling." Gil hadn't been thrilled when I walked in several hours before, but he'd done his job and gotten me nice and toasted.

I wasn't even thinking about that asshole Darren or how guilty he'd made me feel. I was happy and really horny. I looked around the bar to see if there was anyone worth going home with. The River Bottom Pub was an out-of-the-way tavern in the bottoms along the Trinity River. It was a ludicrously crappy prefab building with a "backyard" filled with plastic tables and a place for horseshoe games. There were several subdivisions that had developed in the area and all the locals came here to forget their troubles. Unfortunately, most of their troubles had to do with wives and kids. I didn't play around with wives and kids.

"I called your brother about ten minutes ago," Gil said.

"Damn it, Gil. Why would you go and do that? I'm perfectly fine. I don't need my brother to come and get me. I can find my own damn ride home."

"With whom?" Gil asked, looking around because it was a Thursday night and it was after midnight. All but the most hardcore of drunks had gone home. It was a testament to how fucked up I was that I was still here.

I glanced around the bar. At this hour there were exactly four men still in the bar, and none of them would be potential partners on a sober night. Then again, I tended to not get laid when I was sober so I figured sobriety was way overrated. I pointed to the least hygienically challenged of the four. "How about him?"

"Sweetie, he's gay," Gil said.

"Seriously?" The truth was my gaydar didn't work after fourteen tequila shots.

"No," Gil replied, shaking his long beard. "But the fact that you have to ask whether a fat ass guy with a tattoo of a naked chick on his forearm is gay or not is a testament to your inability to make proper choices."

I laughed long and hard because it struck me as funny. I liked this place. It was nice. Oh, sure, it was followed by vomiting and a horrible headache, but for now it was a little like heaven. I was only thinking of pleasant things. I texted Liv and told her how much I loved her. If I'd had anyone else to call, I totally would have called them to express my love and appreciation, but I didn't have phone numbers for my World of Warcraft guild. I would have called Crozier and told him to meet me at the tavern for a drink or two. Oh, he was a shaman in a MMORPG game, but he was the closest thing I had to a crush on an actual human being. He was a nice guy and not related to me, so I sort of fantasized about him. If he'd been there, I would have jumped all over that and I had zero idea what he looked like. My shot at getting a little something was low this evening.

"How about it, Gil?" The bartender was safe to flirt with. "I've been coming in here for almost a year. When are we going to stop fighting this attraction we have?"

Gil threw back his thickly bearded head and laughed. I was too drunk to be insulted so I joined him. "Darlin', if I was thirty years younger you would still be too much woman for me to handle. I would take one look at you, think about how amazing the sex would be, and run the other way."

"Is that your polite way of calling me a hot mess?" I played with the shot glass that apparently hadn't held anything vaguely resembling liquor for a while. I needed to give apple juice another try. It was good. There was a little drop at the bottom of the glass and I licked the glass not wanting it to go to waste.

Gil shook his head. "Hot doesn't begin to cover it."

A good song came on the radio and I let Gil's comment go, preferring to sway to the music. Then I decided swaying wasn't a good idea and staying on my barstool was.

"Wow, that was fast." Gil's eyes stared past me toward the door. "I thought you were in Dallas."

I started to try to turn, but then my head kind of hit my folded hands and it was really comfortable so I didn't feel like moving. I laid my head down and started to drift off to a blissful sleep.

"I had my friend bring me out. He's faster than a speeding bullet." Ah, my brother Nate was here.

"I like to think so," a deeply sexy voice said.

That got my head to move from its comfy place. I turned and saw a really gorgeous blond guy standing in the doorway, looking out over the bar. He was sexy as hell in a leather jacket, and my hopes of getting well laid shot up. He was roughly six foot two, with big broad shoulders and the kind of straight jaw you only saw on movie stars. So very nice. Unfortunately, he was standing there with my brother, who looked really disapproving.

"Jeez, Kelsey, what the fuck happened to you?" Nathan asked as he approached me.

"Life," I replied with a little smile because I was still looking at hot blond guy. Wow, he was a hunk of masculinity. He stood there in his Green Lantern T-shirt and tight jeans and I knew he could rock my world. Sure, he looked like he was all of twenty years old, but it was a confident twenty. Looking at him, I could tell he was a dangerous boy. "Hello," I said with a boozy grin. I tried to thrust my chest out appealingly. They're small, but well rounded.

I saw Nathan go bright red. "Stop it, Kelsey. Leave him alone. He's married with three kids."

I stared at hot, young blond guy again and wondered if I had lost count of my shots. "Seriously? He looks too young to have three kids."

"Two boys and a girl," Hottie said in that deep Texas drawl that made my insides clench. I sighed as he smiled, slightly embarrassed at my attempts to hit on him. "And my wife is going to be pissed that I left Evan with Justin and Blake. We have to get your sister home so we can head back to Dallas."

Nate frowned at me. He was only eleven months older than me, but he could seriously play the big-brother card from time to time. "Let's go, Kels. Give me your keys so I can get you home."

I was so not ready to go. Unless hottie with three kiddos wanted to drive me somewhere. "Don't worry about me, Nate. Gil shouldn't have called you. I'm perfectly fine. I didn't mean to disrupt your game night. Were you playing D&D?"

He sighed. "No, we were in the middle of a game of Shogun. We probably won't be able to finish."

"Dave." I snapped my fingers as I figured out that Hottie McHotterson must be Nate's friend Dave. My brother had played with the same group of guys for about ten years. They got together almost every week to run D&D campaigns or play board games. It was strictly guy time because at least two of the men were married and needed time away, although apparently Dave brought his son along.

Dave laughed out loud. "Yes, I'm Dave. And you're Kelsey Atwood. I've heard an awful lot about you over the years. It's nice to finally make your acquaintance since we've played online together for the last six months."

My eyes got wide. "Oh, tell me you're Crozier."

He nodded and his deep blue eyes sparkled. There was something about those eyes and I wondered if Dave was completely human. They caught the light in a way that made me question him. "At your service. You might recognize my voice if you ever put on your headset and talked to the rest of us."

I didn't do that for numerous reasons, but my mind was racing. There was something about Dave that had me sobering up mighty fast. Every instinct I had was on high alert. Dave wasn't simply hot. He was supernatural. "You aren't human. What are you?"

My question was curious. I wasn't really afraid of him, but something deep inside said I should be.

Dave's smile vanished and I could hear Gil chuckle.

"Damn, girl, you'll be seeing UFOs next," he muttered.

"Time to go." Nate hauled me off the barstool.

I felt bad. It was an unstated rule of our world that we kept quiet around humans who didn't know about the supernatural. I'd been horribly rude to Dave, but Nate didn't give me a chance to apologize. He tossed me over his shoulder. Gil slid my keys across the bar and I wondered when he'd taken them from me.

The world was dangerously upside down and my stomach revolted at the change of perspective.

"I'll try to make sure she doesn't do it again." I heard the sheepish embarrassment in Nate's voice. It did more to sober me up than anything else. I hated the fact that Nate was ashamed of me.

He hauled me out of the bar and the brisk night air hit me. Nate's sneakers crunched against the gravel as he stalked toward my Jeep. He set me down against the Jeep as he got the door open. The world sort of tilted, but I managed to keep it together. I looked at Dave, whose eyes glittered in the dark, and I knew exactly what he was now that he was in his natural element. The night suited him.

"I'm sorry," I said to the vampire.

He seemed more curious than angry at almost being outed. He regarded me seriously. "How did you know? I'm pretty good at blending in."

"She always knows." Nate opened the back door to my Jeep. He was less than gentle as he hustled me into the backseat. "If you decide to puke, do it out the window."

"Maybe you shouldn't be so hard on her," I heard Dave say.

"You don't know how many times I've had to cart her ass out of a damn bar because she's just got to find the bottom of a tequila bottle. I don't like to think about the times I didn't get a call." Nate opened the driver's side and angrily started the car. Dave got in on the other side and Nate took off.

I watched the dark trees pass by as Nate drove toward my house. This part of Hurst was undeveloped mostly because it tended to flood during heavy rains. The trees were thick on either side of the darkened road. I stared into those woods and knew there were creatures out there. I could see their eyes reflecting off the lights from the Jeep.

"Has she always had good instincts?" Dave asked, his voice

quiet.

"It was like growing up with Scooby-Doo," Nate replied. "She always solved the mystery. If I lost something, Kels could find it in no time flat. She used to be a big old bundle of potential and then my dad took her on one of his little trips and she started pulling this shit. She was sixteen."

"I'd like to meet your father someday," Dave muttered, his voice dark.

"Well, if he ever shows up in town, I'll be sure to make the introduction," Nate replied.

And then it hit me. What I had missed before. "Why would a wolf be following a doe?"

Nate turned down Highway 10 and then made a left into my quiet neighborhood. The houses were all older here and many had been converted to rentals. "Probably hungry I bet."

Dave turned and looked at me, but now I wasn't so sure his name was Dave. Dean? Dale? Something with a D. "You talking about a were?"

I probably shouldn't be talking at all, but my defenses were down. "Yeah. I'm working this missing person case. She's a shifter, turns into a doe. The only lead I have is this werewolf, but don't wolves date other wolves?"

"For the most part." Dave was serious as he thought about it. "Wolves tend to be almost exclusively attracted to other wolves, especially the males. It's why they make such damn good bodyguards for the rest of us. They don't tend to have any interest in our women."

"This guy was interested." I wished the world would stop spinning. It was kind of moving to and fro as the car kept speeding on. I concentrated on my line of thought. "I don't know if I would call it love, but he definitely feels something for her. And why couldn't he track her?"

"Maybe he's a weak wolf." Dave watched me carefully, and I got the feeling I was being sized up.

"Nah." I wished Nate would slow down. It was really getting to my gut. "He was a baby alpha. He didn't have great control, but he was strong. He should have been able to track her. She hid her scent from him."

She'd masked her scent so Darren wouldn't know what she'd

been doing. She was either afraid of him or worried he'd tell her family.

Nate pulled into the driveway. He stopped the Jeep with an angry jerk. "Well, that explains it. You said you were going to stay out of the underworld. You're supposed to be pulling police reports for insurance companies, not trying to track down missing shifters."

"I had to take the case." I was getting sleepy and my stomach was still really upset.

"No, you didn't," Nate complained. "You couldn't resist. You couldn't stay away."

"It sounds like she's trying to help someone." Dave was the voice of reason.

Unfortunately, my brother wasn't big on reason. "No. She's trying to self-destruct."

"You hang out with vampires," I complained because he was being a little hypocritical.

Nate's eyes were hard, his mouth a flat line when he turned on me. "Yeah, well, I never tried to off myself because I couldn't handle my father's chosen profession."

Tears sprang to my eyes because Nathan couldn't have humiliated me more if he'd tried. I opened the door to the car. "Fuck you, Nate. The next time you get a call about me, pretend it's a wrong number."

I slammed the door behind me and heard Nathan cursing. I would have to find another way to spend my free time because I sure wasn't going to hang out with Nate and his friends online anymore. That shouldn't hurt so much, but it did. I wasn't good at making my own friends. I kind of sucked at it. Olivia was the only friend I'd made and she didn't have time for me anymore. God, I was so pathetic. I stumbled to the front door and then remembered I didn't have my keys.

"Shit." I wiped my eyes, wishing I wasn't so emotional. I didn't leave a spare key with anyone because I didn't trust anyone enough to give them the key to my house.

"Here." Dave held my arm to help me steady myself. He had the key in his hand and opened the door for me.

"Thanks," I muttered, not wanting the confident man who probably never had a single self-doubt even once in his preternaturally long life to see me crying.

"Nate's taking a breather." The vampire followed me into the small living room.

I sank down on the couch and closed my eyes, hoping he would take the hint. "I'm fine. I promise not to touch another drop of tequila and to switch bars the next time I feel the need to drink. I'll leave my cell phone at home so there's no chance of ever disrupting Nathan's game night ever again."

"I don't think that's what he wants." Dave's voice was quiet, but it filled the room. "Okay, I'm going to get back home. It's getting late and my wife really will kick my ass for keeping baby girl out so long. We're going into the dungeons on Sunday night. See you there?"

"I think I'm going to take a break for a while."

He sighed. "Yeah, I thought you might say that. I wish you wouldn't, but I understand the instinct to push people away. I hope you find someone who won't let you. Good night."

I sat up and watched the vampire turn and start out the door. "Dave?"

He turned with a sweet grin on his face. He had adorable dimples when he smiled. "It's Dan, Kelsey."

Dan. Daniel, right. "Sorry. It'll bug me forever if you don't tell me." I was at least self-aware enough to know I had to ask. "How the hell does a vampire end up with three kids?"

Daniel's smile was radiant and I knew he loved someone very much. "He opens himself up to possibilities."

And then he was off. I let my head hit the soft cushion on the side of the couch and the world slipped away from me.

* * * *

I woke up to the horrible urge to get to a toilet as soon as I possibly could. I threw back the covers, not bothering to wonder how I'd made it to bed, and stumbled to the bathroom, slammed the door, and made it to my knees just as everything in my stomach decided to make a repeat appearance.

After I'd finished the business of getting rid of the toxins left in my gut, I sat on the cold tile of the tiny bathroom listening to the argument going on in the living room. It didn't help the shakes I had.

"Give her a fucking break, man," I heard Jamie say.

"How about you give me a break, Jamie," Nathan shot back. "You're not the one who has to scrape her off the floor and haul her ass home every time she pulls this crap. You don't have to see her like that."

My oldest brother's voice was serious, and I wondered how long they'd been at this fight. "She hasn't pulled anything like this in almost a year. What the hell happened?"

I could see Nathan's hazel eyes roll. "She took a missing person case. The person is a shifter."

"Damn it," Jamie cursed. "Who the hell thought that was a good idea?"

"Me," I whispered because they couldn't hear me and probably wouldn't listen even if they could.

"Probably Liv." Nathan sounded exasperated and I wondered if he'd slept on the couch last night. "I already left a message on her cell giving her my opinion."

"Maybe it's a good idea." Jamie sighed. "She can't hide forever."

"Why not?" Nate asked. "Ninety-five percent of the world is normal. Why can't she ignore the five percent that's weird? She can't handle it."

"What do you mean she can't handle it? Trust me, Kelsey can handle just about anything out there. I would take her in as backup any day of the week. She's a badass. The only reason I didn't offer her a job with me was you talked me out of it. You were the one who thought she should come out here and bury her head in the suburbs."

It was nice to know my brothers didn't think I could make a single decision on my own. I'd worked damn hard, well, somewhat hard, to build my business, but for Jamie it came down to letting me bury my head in the sand. I turned on the cold water in my shower and thought about crawling back into bed. I could pull the covers over my head and let the boys fight it out. Instead, I shucked last night's clothes and nearly screamed as the cold water hit my body. Crawling back into bed wasn't going to help Joanne Taylor. It was Friday and I had a full day planned. I needed to talk to Professor Peter Hamilton and then tonight I was going to check out those addresses in her book. It wasn't Joanne's or Helen's fault that I got my ass roasted last night and felt like shit.

After I was vaguely clean, I turned off the water and wrapped a towel around my body. I brushed my teeth and decided to let my hair dry on its own. I was thinking I could sneak out, stop by Sonic for breakfast, and be in Dallas before noon. Before I'd gone on my bender, I'd managed to check into Joanne's e-mail accounts, with her mother's help. I'd found nothing there. I'd also looked up her class schedule. There was only one that really interested me. Professor Peter Hamilton's office hours were from one to three on Fridays. I just needed to get past the arguing boys. They didn't need me to decide how my life should go. The truth was I was feeling a little better. No matter what Nathan said, I was trying to help someone and that felt good.

 I swung the door open and ran into the middle of a hunk of nicely made masculine flesh. I caught my breath because I hadn't sensed him there at all and that was definitely a different experience for me. Usually I could tell when someone or something was close to me. It was all a part of having great hunter instincts. I was aware of my surroundings. This guy had been completely off my radar. I looked up and into the most seriously blue eyes I'd ever seen. They were so dark they were almost purple.

 Again, not human, but I couldn't tell for the life of me what this man was besides gorgeous. He made my breath catch.

 "If you're done with the physical parts of your hangover, might I tempt you with some coffee?" His generous lips cracked into a lopsided smile. His Texas accent was slow, but there was nothing at all uneducated about it. If I had to place a bet on his voice and the way he carried himself, I would say he'd been raised by wealthy parents.

 I clutched the towel closer. "You're tempting me with my own coffee? And who the hell are you?"

 I should have been worried about a massive hunk of nonhuman male accosting me outside my bedroom door, but I was too busy staring at him.

 "Well, sweetheart, I didn't bring any of mine." His eyes roamed the expanse of skin not hidden by the white towel.

 I forced myself to back away. The man in front of me was dressed in jeans and a T-shirt. He had well-worn cowboy boots on his feet. I would have pegged him as late twenties, no more than thirty. He was a big, broad man who stood almost a foot taller than me, which made him roughly six foot four. And he spent a lot of time in a gym.

"I'm not your sweetheart." I didn't like the way he made my heart pound.

"You can't possibly know that," the man said with a smile in his voice. I looked up, and that smile was on his face as well. His hair was a dark brown and cut way too short. I would bet it was thick and wavy when he grew it out, but his cut was almost military. "We just met so there's absolutely no way for you to know if you're my sweetheart or not."

I snorted, not a pretty sound. "I bet you say that to all the girls you accost coming out of the bathroom."

"Would it help if I told you there weren't that many?" He backed off a little, giving me the tiniest bit of space. "Normally, I'm a right bastard with everyone I meet."

My hand was on the door to my bedroom. All I had to do was turn the knob and slip into the room. He wouldn't follow me. I stood there, unwilling to leave him just yet. "What makes me so special?"

"Well, you're my best friend's sister to start with," he said.

"You're Grayson Sloane." Well, that did it. Jamie's best friend and part-time partner.

His grin faltered for the first time. "You say that like it's a bad thing."

"Jamie talks about you all the time." I quickly relegated any fantasies I was already having to the scrap pile. I wasn't about to start playing around with my brother's bestie. I'd tried that with Dan last night and it had gotten me in hot water. "Nice to meet you, Sloane."

I slipped into the bedroom and shut the door behind me. And I quickly realized that I'd been wrong. He did follow me.

"Dude, privacy." My towel had been about to hit the floor. I clung to it.

"Do not dude me, Kelsey. Get dressed and I'll make you breakfast." Gray was cool as he stood in the doorway, like he often found himself in a strange half naked woman's bedroom.

"I can find my own breakfast, thank you." I could feel my face going stubborn.

"Ten minutes, okay?"

"Have you listened to anything I said? I'll pick up something to eat on my way out."

"All right, then. Ten minutes." He smiled like I had politely agreed with him. "See you then, Kelsey. Don't try sneaking out. I'll catch you. Do you like your eggs scrambled or fried?"

"I like my eggs in between a biscuit and wrapped in foil so I can eat it while I drive." No matter how hot he was, he was rapidly getting on my last nerve.

"Scrambled sounds good to me, too," he said as he closed the door behind him.

I stared for a minute and wondered if the dude had been damaged. In his line of work, it could totally happen. I dressed quickly and used the towel to dry my hair as much as possible. Unfortunately I caught sight of myself in the mirror and then I was a little nauseous again. There was no doubt the girl in the mirror had a rough night. My eyes were bloodshot and there were dark circles under them. I was insane to think that whatever Grayson Sloane was up to had anything to do with wanting my glorious body. Because I looked rough. He was probably here to…oh, god. A really horrible thought hit me. I prayed he wasn't here to do that. I wouldn't be able to handle the mortification. I shoved my feet into my sneakers and stalked to the kitchen to confront the big guy.

"Are you here to haul me into rehab?"

Sloane stopped turning over the bacon he was frying and laughed. "No. I'm not here to drag you kicking and screaming into some twelve-step program. Jamie and I were practicing at the gun range when Nathan called. I asked Jamie if he minded if I came along. It was easier than dropping me back at my house."

"Are they planning an intervention?" The thought made me a little sick. I couldn't imagine a whole bunch of people sitting around begging me not to drink myself to death and sending me to a place where a psychiatrist would ask me why I drink. I would say hey, doc, have you ever seen a werewolf cut down in the prime of life? Ever been responsible for multiple homicides?

And then I would be placed on a 72-hour hold.

No. I wasn't heading to rehab.

Sloane pulled two pieces of bacon out of the skillet and laid them on the plate that already had eggs and a couple of slices of toast. The smell should have sent me reeling, but my stomach was pretty strong and it grumbled at the thought of my stubbornness costing me the bacon. Healthy appetite doesn't begin to cover what I have. Luckily, I've always had the metabolism to go with it.

"Are they planning an intervention?" Sloane's deep voice washed over me like a calm, warm rain. That voice was soothing. "Maybe. Nate seems a little freaked out. Jamie seems…encouraged, maybe. He thinks it's a good thing you're working again. According to him, you're talented and you're wasting your gifts working for insurance companies and angry divorcees." He handed me the plate and I gave up the fight.

I sat down at the kitchen table and dug in with gusto. "It's not like I've been sitting on my ass."

Sloane set a cup of coffee in front of me and then settled his big body onto my dining table chair. The morning light was kind to him, softening the hard planes of his face and making what was almost certainly a tough man look a little gentle. "Jamie thinks you should start working with us."

I laughed. Sloane was the only person Jamie worked with on a regular basis and even then, it was only when Sloane brought him in. Grayson Sloane was a certified badass. That's the only way to describe a real Texas Ranger. "Yeah, I bet I could pass whatever test your captain gives to contractors."

He shook his head, setting down his coffee. "Probably not, but then I'm given an enormous amount of latitude when it comes to who I work with. I answer to the *B* company captain, but that's technical. He doesn't want to know what I do. He wishes he didn't have to deal with me at all. It's why he doesn't question the reqs I put in for Jamie's services."

I took a long drink, the caffeine starting to work in my system. I supposed it was hard to be the Mulder of the Ranger world. Sloane handled all the "weird stuff," meaning anything even vaguely supernatural. He was probably an outcast among his own peers. It made sense that he and Jamie were friends. They understood the same world.

"Hey little sister," Jamie said, walking into the kitchen. "I like the new paint in the living room. How are you feeling?"

"Like shit," I replied before polishing off the toast. Yeah, food had done wonders for me. "But I still have a job to do so I'll suck it up. I'm sorry Nate felt like he had to call you. Last night was…a slipup. I ended up in a tense situation with a wolf and he apparently knew Dad."

Jamie let out a deep breath and slumped into the chair across from me. My thirty-two-year-old brother seemed so much older as he thought about our father. "I'm so sorry, Kels."

I sat back in my chair. "Do you run into many people who knew him?"

"I do," Jamie acknowledged. "The bastard cut a wide swath. There's no getting around it. He hurt a lot of people, and they don't forget that he's still out there. But they get used to me and if they don't, I kick their ass. I won't lie to you. If you want to work in this world, you're going to have to make them accept you. Believe it or not, Nate can help you more with that than even I can. Nate has some powerful friends."

I laughed at the thought. "Yeah, well, I probably won't be meeting them. I met one of his gamer geek friends last night and I'm sure he'll run the next time he sees me. I kind of hit on him."

Jamie laughed but Sloane didn't. He got up and poured himself another cup of coffee.

"Tell me about this case of yours," Jamie said.

I shrugged, looking at the clock. I needed to get out of here soon if I was going to make it all the way to Dallas. "It's a missing person case. She's a shifter, lost her college scholarship and went on the game. Unfortunately, I'm pretty sure she's in trouble. I've got an appointment with one of her professors in two hours. It's probably a dead end, but she'd been spending a lot of time with him according to her roommate."

"Hey, aren't you working some missing person cases?" Jamie asked Sloane as he settled back down.

"Yeah," the Ranger replied. "We have some missing supes. It's not a bunch, four cases, all young women, but considering how small the community is, I was asked to look into it."

"Were they hookers?" I asked, getting that tingle in the back of my skull that told me I was on to something.

"Not exactly," Sloane prevaricated. "Look it's an open case. I really shouldn't talk about it."

Something about the way he spoke had me sitting up tall again. He was hiding something. It was there in the way his eyes tightened. If not hiding something, he was definitely blowing me off when he shouldn't be. If he was working missing persons, he should want to trade notes. "But if I could get a look at your files I could maybe see a pattern. Were the girls all in college? Were they all from Dallas?

What do you mean not exactly? How do you not exactly prostitute yourself?"

"Whoa, slow down, sweetheart." Sloane turned to Jamie, his eyes wide.

My brother chuckled. "I told you. She's a bulldog when she's on a case. She really might be able to see something you missed."

Sloane seemed to consider it for a moment and a little thrum of excitement rode through me at the thought of looking through Sloane's files. The puzzle would be there, laid out for me to solve. Just for a second I thought I could do something, something important.

He turned his blue eyes on me. "How about we make a deal? You promise to not get trashed again like you did last night and I'll let you have a peek."

Humiliation swept over my body like a wave, and I watched Jamie tense. He was waiting for me to explode, but I was done wasting energy like that. Sloane wanted to be an asshole? Who was I to stop him? I certainly didn't have to take it though. I stood up. "Keep your files, Sloane. I don't need 'em. Lock up when you're done, Jamie. I take it Nate's looking for drugs?"

I ignored Sloane's stare and focused on Jamie, who relaxed a bit when he realized I wasn't going to make a scene. "You know how he is. Someday promise me you'll throw him a bone and leave a little bag of parsley or something hidden in your underwear drawer for him to find."

I leaned over and kissed my big brother's cheek. Sloane didn't matter. He didn't mean a thing to me. He was one more hot guy who thought he was better than everyone else. "I promise. Now, I'm going. I can't stand all the brotherly concern. Call you later."

I walked out without another glance at the gorgeous man I wasn't going to be seeing again for various reasons. I heard Nathan going through the drawers in my bathroom. I should have yelled and screamed and told him to keep his hands out of my business, but I didn't. Nathan had been the one to find me bleeding that day so long ago. If it hadn't been for Liv, he would have been the one to hold me while I died. He deserved some leeway.

"I hide my hardcore stuff in with the tampons, Nate," I yelled and giggled a little at the thought of him pawing through feminine necessaries.

Nathan's head poked out from the bathroom door. "Don't think I won't look, Kels."

"I know you will." Despite our fight the night before, I felt a great rush of love for him. He didn't understand me the way Jamie did and I annoyed him greatly, but he never backed away. Dan was wrong. I already had a couple of people who wouldn't let me push them away. "Your vigilance has kept me from becoming a heroin addict."

Nate's face softened and he gave me a little smile. "That's the plan."

I decided to needle him a little. He's my brother. It's my job. "Hey, and when you get to the little drawer in my nightstand, why don't you go ahead and change out the batteries on the vibrator? They were low a couple of nights ago."

I heard his strangled scream. "Disgusting, Kels."

I was smiling as I turned and ran into the brick wall that seemed to be shadowing me that morning. I tried hard not to blush because it would have been nice to have not mentioned a vibrator around Sloane. "Excuse me."

"I'm sorry." Sloane didn't move an inch. "I didn't have any right to make a dumbass statement like that. I was rude, but you threw me off a little when you mentioned meeting Nate's friends. It's a bad idea to be vulnerable around them. I don't like the thought of some of them taking advantage of you, but I don't have any right to judge. I wasn't really doing that. I was thinking more along the lines of protecting you, and I get that I sounded like a judgmental douchebag. I'm sorry."

I shrugged, unwilling to think about why I got a warm, gooshy feeling when I thought about Sloane protecting me. He was so stinking gorgeous, from his perfectly square jaw to his broad shoulders. He was so not for me. "Not a problem, Lieutenant Sloane. I'll keep my drunken affections away from my brother's friends. Have a nice afternoon."

A big hand settled on my arm and pulled me around. Before I knew what was happening, I was really close to Grayson Sloane. He was taking up all the space, making me feel small. It takes a whole lot to make me feel small. "Let me make something plain to you, Kelsey. I'm not your brother, so don't lump me in with them. I wanted to come here today because I'm interested in you and I have been for a long time. I've asked Jamie to set us up for a while now, but he thinks you're too fragile to date. I think if you're strong enough for meaningless one-night stands, then you can handle an honest to goodness date. Dinner tonight?"

I was sure my eyes were wide as saucers and I realized Jamie was right. I wasn't ready for this. No way. No how. Luckily, I had an excuse and it found its way out of my mouth. "I have to work tonight."

"You can take a couple of hours off," Sloane said smoothly. "You have to eat, right? I'll bring my files and we can talk about any similarities in our cases. We can call it a working dinner if date is too much for you."

But it wasn't work. I stood there with big, gorgeous Sloane looming over me and knew this wouldn't be professional. It would be personal and it wouldn't end there. If I thought for a second I could take what I wanted from Grayson Sloane and happily send him on his way, I would have thrown down with him at the first given opportunity. But something told me he wouldn't take his walking papers with aplomb.

I smiled with a jauntiness I didn't feel and pulled my arm out of his hand. "I think I'll skip working with you, Sloane. I'm kind of a loner. How about I promise when I solve my case, I'll let you know so you can close yours, too?"

I winked at him and walked out the door, got in my Jeep and took off. I drove to Dallas like the devil was following me.

Chapter Four

I walked across the tree-lined, stately campus of Southern Methodist University. I had unhappily parked about a flipping mile off campus because, unlike Liv, I didn't have a magical parking pass and I really needed to avoid tickets. I couldn't afford them. I hated to think about what my drinking binge had cost me last night. My local bar might be a shit hole, but they still charged for drinks.

I stopped and studied the map I'd picked up at the student center then took a quick left as my cell rang. I was prepared to ignore it as I had ignored all of the increasingly pissed-off texts from Liv. If she was escalating to actual calls, I might have to turn off the phone. I glanced down at the number and a cold chill went through me. I ran my thumb across the screen because this person would never accept that I didn't answer. She would call and call and leave message after message.

"Hi, Mom."

"Kelsey, this is your mother," she said in a too-loud voice.

"I know, Mom. You don't have to yell."

"I need you to call me, Kelsey" She carefully enunciated each word. "I talked to your brother and I'm worried."

"Mom, why should I call you? I'm talking to you now." I was the one screaming because she always thought she was talking to a machine and this could seriously go on forever.

"Oh, it is you, dear." My mom sounded delighted. "It's so refreshing for you to answer. You know how bad I am with these new tech things."

Yes, like cell phones, although my mother might have been talking about regular old telephones. It wasn't that she was old. Her upbringing had been unusual, to say the least.

"I'm fine, Mom. Nathan didn't need to call you." I read the name of the building I was standing in front of. Not the one I was looking for, so I kept walking.

"Well, I'm glad he did, Kelsey Jean," she said, her voice firming.

I sighed. I was in trouble. "It was no big deal. I'm even up and working. I'm on a case, a paying case, so I should really…"

Mom ignored me entirely. "Nathan believes that drugs might be involved."

I groaned and rolled my eyes as far back as they could go. "Nathan always thinks drugs are involved. Nathan is clinically insane. Talk to Jamie. He'll tell you I'm fine."

"I already talked to Jamie and you're obviously not fine since you turned down a date with that nice Grayson Sloane. Jamie said Gray was devastated."

I bet that's what Jamie said. I was betting Jamie had said it while laughing his ass off at the thought of his sister turning down his superhot friend. "I think he'll recover, Mom."

I stopped in the middle of the sidewalk as the hair on the back of my neck started to tingle. Eyes were on me. I wasn't anonymous anymore. Someone, something was watching me.

"Well, you're not getting any younger, Kelsey. That man is quite the catch. He's attractive and respectful and he has a good job. You already know he gets along with your brother so he would fit in well," my mother continued as I turned slowly, searching the crowds to find who was watching me.

The students rushed around as the hour changed and classes were being released, only to start again in the next ten minutes. It was Friday and everyone wanted to get where they were going. I studied the campus for signs of someone not terribly interested in getting somewhere.

My mother continued to expound on the many blessings of

Grayson Sloane. "He's so polite. He's come to dinner a couple of times with your brother and he always comments on your pictures."

I wasn't sure how I felt about Sloane studying my high school graduation photos. What was his real interest in me? I wasn't in his league looks-wise. It was hard for me to believe he'd seen my picture and known instantly he wanted me. I shook my head because I needed to concentrate on figuring out who was following me.

My mother's voice went low, like she didn't want anyone overhearing her next words. "And, dear, I think he would be a considerate lover."

"Then really, Mom, you should give him a try." Ah, my eyes lit on a familiar face. There was my little stalker. He watched me from a tree across the quad. The wolf from yesterday stood there. Darren's brown eyes narrowed as he caught me staring. "Look, Mom, I gotta go."

I bore down on the werewolf, and there must have been something in my eyes as I closed in because he looked startled at what he saw there.

"Well, I won't keep you then," she said breezily. "Don't forget to come by for dinner and we'll talk some more about Grayson."

"Good-bye, Mom," I said between clenched teeth and I dropped the call. "Don't you say a word."

"The hunter was talking to her mommy. Sorry to interrupt," Darren bit out sarcastically.

I was just about done with Darren. I felt like shit, my head was still pounding despite the caffeine, and I really wanted to be back in bed. I didn't want be here dealing with Darren's obvious mental problems. "Look here, wolf, I'm trying to help the Taylors. I haven't done anything personally to you. I'm not my father. I realized what a horrible human he was a long time ago, and if he were here I would shoot him myself. So back the fuck off and let me do my job."

I turned and began to stalk away.

The baby wolf was hard on my heels. "Are you really trying to find her?"

I sighed and stopped. I'd finally found the right building, but I didn't want to go into the professor's office with a werewolf in tow. "I'm looking for her. I think she's in trouble. You dogging my every footstep isn't helping."

Darren, who was in another flannel shirt and jeans, seemed to deflate. "I think she's in trouble, too. She told me she was working, but I followed her one night and she went to this club downtown. It was a school night. She never used to do stuff like that."

"Did you follow her into the club?" So Joanne had a reason to mask her scent. Darren was obviously nosy.

Darren nodded. "I followed her to the club, but I couldn't get in. It was real busy. They have this line waiting to get in and the bouncer has to let you go. That night the bouncer was this asshole from the pack who's jealous that my dad is the alpha. Dad put him in his place a couple of months ago and he was getting back at us by not letting me in. Jerk."

So it was a supernatural club. That made things harder. "But Joanne got in?"

Darren nodded. "They let her walk right in. I waited for her, but when she came out she was with some guy. I'm pretty sure he was a vamp."

"Blond guy?" I'd only met one vamp, but in a city the size of Dallas there wouldn't be many. I hoped it wasn't Dan. He seemed like a nice guy. It would be a shame to have to kill him.

"Nah, this one was dark haired and really creepy looking," the wolf said. "I mean the dude gave me the creeps and that's not easy. I started to yell at him to leave her alone, but then there were bouncers and threats and they kinda hauled me out and told me not to come back. It got me in trouble with…well, everyone. Jo was pissed the next day. She wouldn't take my calls. She wouldn't see me. I was worried about her."

I believed him. At least, he believed himself. Sometimes denial could be a powerful thing. "Why are you willing to talk to me?"

A flush stole across his skin. "My dad came by last night and told me to leave you alone. He said some bigwig came by and ordered all the wolves to either help you out or get the hell out of your way. His name's Trent. He works for the big guy."

"I don't know anybody named Trent. Why would he care who gets in my way?" I glanced at my watch. This was one mystery that would have to wait. I was going to miss the professor if I didn't hustle. I pulled out my card and handed it to Darren. "If you think of anything else, give me a call."

"Okay." He clutched that card, looking at me like he'd been hoping for more. I regretted leaving him there like that, but false hope wasn't going to help.

I walked up the steps to the building where Professor Hamilton had his office, feeling Darren's eyes on me all the while. Who the hell was this Trent guy and why would he think to look out for me? It was possible he knew one of my brothers. I would have to ask them if they had mentioned my problems with the wolf to anyone. It pointed out a major issue I had. I'd been out of this game for a long time. The truth was I'd never really been in it. I didn't know anyone.

I started climbing the steep stairs to the third floor as my mind whirled.

My father only knew who the alphas of the local packs were in order to hunt them. He certainly didn't try to work with them the way Jamie did or have supernatural friends like Nathan. Dad might have known the local players names and habits, but I needed to get them to cooperate with me. Jamie had told me Nathan had powerful contacts in this world. It was hard for me to believe. Nate managed a software store. He was slowly working his way through college a class or two a year, but he certainly didn't scream power player. I would have to talk to Nate and see if he knew who this Trent person was. If he had an inclination to help me, then I would call him and introduce myself.

Peter Hamilton's office was halfway down a quiet, dim hallway. It was so quiet I wondered if he'd skipped out on his office hours. It was a Friday afternoon and from the lack of students roaming around, I would say most of the building had called it a week. Who kept hours on Friday when the fall air was crisp and the sunshine was practically perfect? I knocked briefly on the professor's door and was surprised when he called out.

"Come in."

I pushed the door open and Peter Hamilton was sitting at his neatly appointed desk. It seemed incongruous for a college professor to be so neat and organized. The books on the shelves that lined three of the walls were neatly placed and I was certain he could find any single one of them in a second. There were efficient-looking file cabinets behind his desk and a small refrigerator. His desk was clean, only a sleek laptop marring the perfect lines.

"I don't believe I know you." Hamilton was as neat as his office. He wore the uniform of a stately college professor, trousers, white dress shirt and a snazzy sport coat. He was maybe pushing forty and he wasn't an unattractive man. He was kind of bland.

"My name is Kelsey Atwood." I introduced myself and he briefly shook my hand. I was surprised by the softness of his skin. It wasn't that there wasn't strength in his hands, but they were soft, much softer than mine. He took special care with his hands. "I'm working for Helen Taylor."

"Ah, yes, Joanne's mother. I spoke with her briefly. She hasn't been to class this week, I'm afraid." His voice was cultured, with a hint of a British accent though I knew he'd been born in Tallahassee. It was a pretentious affectation.

I nodded and he indicated it was all right for me to sit down in the chair across from his desk. "I'm aware of that. I was told she spent a lot of time on your class."

"We meet twice a week, on Tuesdays and Thursdays, for an hour and a half per class, but it's a late afternoon class," the professor explained. "I'm afraid some of our discussions run long. We get involved in the work. We often move from class to the pub across the street where we argue long into the evening."

"Sounds like you have some dedicated students."

A smirk crossed his face as he sat back. "I'm grateful I've instilled such loyalty and passion in my students."

If he were female, I'd have started counting up the cats. I wondered briefly what male spinsters filled their houses with. I was betting a whole lot of well-organized books. His shelves here were full of them. There was the requisite literature by luminaries like Joyce, Forster, and Dickens, but there were other less obvious choices. There was a large volume titled "The Encyclopedia of Vampire." I was unaware that vamps had started writing reference books, but I was willing to go with it. There was a field guide to identifying demons. I could have saved him the hours reading that one. Demons are the ones who try to eat you. I turned my attention back to the professor. "This is the second class Joanne has taken with you?"

He nodded shortly. "Yes, Joanne is an excellent student. She did her final essay last year on the relevance of Bram Stoker's *Dracula* to today's genre fiction. It was a good paper. I invited her to join us for this class. It's mostly made up of sophomores and juniors, but there are a few seniors."

"Her roommate said she spent more time than usual on this

class."

He shrugged. "It's a rigorous class. I know some people think there isn't a lot of value in what I teach, but I think we can all learn from history."

"History? I thought you taught English."

"I do, but you can't study literature and the minds of the great authors without understanding history. My class is contextual. I teach freshman English and any number of literature courses, but over the last ten years I've become interested in lore and mythology. It was my Classical Mythology and Urban Legends that Joanne was in."

"So she was studying Greek gods and stuff?"

He shot me a dismissive smile and I knew my intellect was coming into question. "So much more than that. The religions of the past are the 'mythology' of today. Zeus and Hades perform the same functions as the gods of today's religions do. They were a way for people to explain the unexplainable. They were a conduit between humans and the divine. But our lore, our stories are even more important. They seek to unveil that which is hidden."

"And what is hidden, Professor?" I asked, interested in his answer to my question. He had the look of a man who truly believed.

And then it was gone. He smiled and it was a smooth expression. He was back to lecturing. "Our hidden desires, of course. That which we desire is what mythological creatures represent. And our fears. Do you know that to this day, true Romany gypsies still bury their dead standing up?"

I returned his smile with one of my own. He was speaking my language. "Yes, they do it so when their dead relatives become revenants, they will only be able to walk forward through the dirt rather than clawing their way to the surface and giving in to the insatiable desire to consume living flesh."

He clasped those super soft hands together. "Very good, Ms. Atwood. I'm rather surprised. It's a small folk legend, but still practiced in some areas. The dead consume living flesh to become immortal."

"Like vampires?" I tried to lead the discussion to my place of interest. Joanne was obviously involved with a vampire. At least, according to Darren, she was. It would be interesting to see if she was studying them as well.

He shook his head and frowned. "Not at all. A revenant is

nothing more than a zombie with reasonable intelligence. It insults the vampire to put the two in the same sentence. A zombie mindlessly seeks flesh. The flesh is temporary—useful but dumb. Blood is the basis of life. It holds the soul. This is the nourishment the vampire seeks."

I wanted to roll my eyes, but I was turning over a new leaf. I nodded like he was telling me something important. "I understand. Vampires are important in this class of yours?"

Professor Hamilton's eyes lit up, and I knew I'd hit on something. "Vampires are the pinnacles of our desires, Ms. Atwood. They are death and life immortal. They are the gods of this age."

I couldn't argue with him on that. Pop culture wise they were experiencing a renaissance. You couldn't turn around without another brooding vampire trying to sink his fangs in to someone. I wondered if Daniel had seen *Twilight*. I doubted seriously that he had ever once sparkled.

"I really liked 'Buffy,'" I admitted with fondness.

He huffed, showing his utter disdain. "I'm talking about the real thing, Ms. Atwood. Vampires have been taken over by simpering romance novelists and their ridiculous female fans. The true vampire is a creature of great darkness. They don't spend their time whining over human females. They are the bringers of death to the unworthy and life immortal to the blessed few."

Which proved that the good professor didn't know crap about vampires. My father had, for the most part, avoided vampires like the plague. He told me he avoided them because they were dying out on their own anyway, but I thought it was because they were too badass to risk a confrontation with. What the professor had wrong was how a person is made a vampire. They aren't. You're either born one or not, and no one can tell who's a vampire until they die and rise again. I heard a rumor a few years back that a king could actually sense latent vampires and turn them while they're vital, but as far as I knew it was just a rumor. A vampire king is so rare as to be legendary. It's a story vampires tell fledglings to scare the crap out of them.

"So you sat around and talked about vampires?" I didn't need to set him straight. He wouldn't believe me anyway.

He sat forward, his eyes narrowing. "You don't believe in the supernatural?"

"You would be surprised what I believe in."

"Imagine if they were real. Lonely gods walking the earth. What if you could talk to one? What would you ask it? Would you worship the vampire? Leave it gifts and pray for the hand of those who defy death to seek you out in kindness?" He gave me a moment to ponder his completely pretentious words. Then he sat back and let out a deep breath. "These are the questions we ask."

It was time that I asked one of my own. "Professor Hamilton, were you having a sexual affair with Joanne Taylor?"

His swift reaction told me a lot, which was precisely why I blindsided him. His face went blank as though the question caught him completely off guard, and I knew in an instant that he hadn't even considered it. "No, I don't sleep with my students. That might be what other professors do, but I consider it beneath me."

I believed him. "I apologize. I had to ask. You're an attractive man and she was a lovely girl."

He preened under the compliment. "Well, I will admit Joanne had a little crush on me. It's inevitable. Young girls look for powerful, intelligent men to protect them, but I have my work to think of. I could be dismissed if I was caught with a student. I owe them my work, you know."

"Was Joanne involved with anyone in class?"

He thought about that for a moment. "Not that I could tell. She actually held herself apart a bit. She certainly participated, but she had odd ideas about things. Once she posited that vampires were almost exclusively male, which makes no sense. She got laughed at and she was quiet for a while after that. I don't know."

Wow. Joanne had seriously skirted trouble with the Council. If she'd been giving away secrets, she could have been hauled to the Vampire Council and tried for treason. It wouldn't matter that she wasn't a vampire. Those men—because she was right they were almost all men—took their privacy seriously. It was another line of questions I should ask, but I needed a vampire to interrogate. I might have to go back on my vow to stay off the computer for a while. Dan was the only vampire I knew. He seemed like an odd sort of vampire since he had three kids, but maybe he could point me in the right direction. Possibly he could introduce me to some of the power players, if I asked nicely.

"I thank you for the time, Professor." I sent him a grateful smile. He was a weirdo and he gave me the creeps, but it was hard for me to see him as a hardened killer. I would check a little more into his background, but I wasn't going to get anything more from talking to him than a lecture on his intensely wrong views on vampires. I had a sudden thought. "Can I get a class roster from you?"

He stared at me, seemingly befuddled by the query. "I don't know that I have a copy. Why would you need that?"

"It's standard procedure," I lied. I didn't have any standard procedures. "I need to know who Joanne's classmates are. I might need to question some of them."

He frowned. "I don't know if I like the thought of you harassing my students."

"Do you like the thought of one of your students going missing, Professor? If your precious students have any information on where Joanne is, I would think you would want them to step up."

He backed off immediately. "Of course, of course. I'll talk to the office staff about putting that together for you. I really must ask you to leave. I need to work. You've taken up enough of my time."

I saluted the professor and quietly exited his office. I made my way to the stairs, all the while plotting. I didn't believe for an instant that a man as organized as Peter Hamilton didn't have his class rosters at his fingertips. He probably could produce every roster for every class he'd ever taught, but he'd lied to me. He didn't want me to know who was in that class. Well, I was going to find out. I wasn't sure how yet, but I could ponder it all night while I staked out the first address in Joanne's notebook.

* * * *

I stopped at a convenience store and stocked up. There's a reason most PIs are overweight with a tendency to have coronaries. Salads simply don't work as stakeout food. I bought a six-pack of Dr. Pepper, some M&Ms, a bag of Doritos, and a single beer. Okay, I bought a single Dr. Pepper and a six-pack of beer. I was still freaking hung over. I stand by the beer choice. I stopped by a street vendor on Good Latimer and bought a couple of tacos and a churro before heading north into a much nicer section of town.

I located the building indicated by the address in Joanne's little spiral. It was one in a long line of Victorian townhouses. I took stock of my surroundings and was pleased to find a small office building across from the residential street. It came complete with a parking garage that would nicely serve as my nest for the night. It was a little ways away from the actual house, but I had my camera with a high-powered telephoto lens, so I didn't need to be super close. I tried to turn into the parking garage, but it was private and required a security code. Luckily, there was no actual guard on duty so I parked the Jeep down the street, shoved all my gear into a backpack, and hiked.

It was after six by the time I found the perfect perch. Everyone seemed to have gone home for the weekend and there wasn't a car in the garage. I walked up to the fifth floor, which afforded me an excellent view of the townhouse.

Like all the houses on the small block, it was well maintained and obviously expensive. This was North Dallas, the nicest part of town. The small complex of townhomes was surrounded by superior stores, restaurants, and small, exclusive companies. I noted, as I polished off a really excellent beef taco, that while all the other streets in the area had pedestrians walking on them, this street was completely empty. It was kind of odd. I studied the small block of townhomes. There were six in all and they looked like they had serious square footage. Probably three bedrooms or more. So where were the cars in the driveways? Where were the silly signs on the doors that announced the house was established in such and such year? Where were the bikes, dumped in the yards by kids running in the house to dinner? Where was anyone at all?

The lights in the middle townhouse came on at precisely six forty-three. Sundown. The hairs on my forearms stood straight up. Now I knew why there weren't bikes on the lawns. I would bet my life that all six townhomes were connected on the inside and I was staring at a vampire club.

I took a deep breath because a couple of things were becoming clear to me. One, Joanne Taylor had been playing a dangerous game. She was a hooker, but it went beyond that. Vampires wanted more than sex. Oh, from what I understood, they wanted the sex. Vampires could feed off sexual energy, but their primary source of energy was always blood. Sometimes the vamp got a little overeager and took too much. Joanne might be stronger than a regular human, but she needed the proper blood volume to survive. The second fact I realized while staring at that club really scared me. The freaking

Vampire Council had to be involved. If she was working at a vampire club, then the Council knew about it.

I didn't want to get involved with the Council.

Everything I knew about vampires I knew from my father and from the stories my mother has told me. Mom's dad was a hunter, but not exactly one like my dad. He'd hunted at the request of the Council or a pack where, for political reasons, the alpha chose not to dispense justice himself. Every so often my grandfather would get a call and he would leave his backwoods home in East Texas and hunt down some supernatural creature that had gone crazy or caused too much trouble. Granddad was particularly good at hunting werewolves. He always had an order of execution and he only killed wolves who met the criteria for a "righteous" kill.

My dad was pretty much the opposite. While Granddad had many friends in the local packs and was respected, my father was a revenge hunter. I twisted the top off a beer and let it coat my throat as I thought about my father. His mom and sister had been torn apart by a wolf who went crazy. My granddad had been the one to hunt the wolf and he'd found my seventeen-year-old father in the process. He felt bad for the kid and brought him home where he taught him everything he knew about hunting. I would like to have known my granddad better, but he died before my father left us and we weren't permitted to have anything to do with a traitor. Mom had only managed to sneak away to visit her dad a few times. While my father had been more than happy to take my grandfather's training and his daughter, once Dad had everything he needed he decided to have nothing more to do with the old man. Having a friend or two in the nonhuman world was the same thing as treason in my father's mind. I suppose my brothers' and my lifestyle were a big old "fuck you" to Dad.

I shook my head and took another swallow. My mind was wandering. Dad had known the basics about vampires. Rule number one—don't fuck around with vampires. Rule number two—see rule number one. Vampires are a genetic anomaly. There's something in their DNA that clicks on when death occurs. The vampire rises and takes blood and then, as long as he continues to take blood, his body functions. The vampire is stronger than a human. Most are stronger than wolves and shifters. They develop different powers over the years and this forms their class system. Warriors tend to be the strongest of the strong. They're fast and kill with ease. Most vampires can be described as warriors, but there are others as well. Some have exceptional mental powers and others can make you see things that aren't there. I've heard that some can even fly, but until I see it, I ain't believing that one.

They also have the most organized, powerful central system of government in the supernatural world. The Vampire Council rules the supernaturals with an iron fist. I'd heard vague rumors that there had been a change at the top of the Council, but trust me, they're still the same assholes, different faces. If Joanne Taylor was killed by a vampire it would be hard for me to prove it and even harder to bring him to justice. The Council protects their own.

I sighed and settled in because I wasn't going to let some group of old, and I mean old, politicians stop me from finding out the truth. I pulled out my camera and concentrated on the front of the building. I took a bunch of pictures, getting the lay of the land, so to speak. The first limo arrived shortly after full dark and contained a group of females. It surprised me because I had understood that the women who worked in the vampire clubs tended to live there. They were slaves. These women didn't look like slaves, but they were dressed in heels and short dresses and ready to party. Their clothes reminded me of the dresses Liv found in the back of Joanne's closet. I made sure I got close-ups of the girls as they headed into the building. A big guy opened the door and I caught the briefest glimpse of a blonde-haired woman greeting the girls.

I twisted the cap off beer number two and my body was finally relaxing after a day of tormenting me. I shifted on my knees and decided that I would put a pillow in the back of the Jeep for times like this. My knees were hurting from kneeling on the hard concrete, but I didn't want to stand up. Even though I was a long way from the club, vampires have damn fine senses, and I didn't want to get caught.

A Mercedes pulled up and the big guy was moving quickly to get to that car. He hauled ass to open the door for the dark-haired man who tossed his keys at him. I snapped off a few quick photos before really studying the vampire through the lens. I engaged the zoom and got my first good look at a vampire who didn't play games with my brother.

He wasn't the tallest man I'd seen, but he was powerfully built.

His eyes were gray and seemed extremely cold to me. His hair was brown and slicked back. He wore a tailored suit and black tie. The male radiated superiority to everyone around him. He breathed in the night air and I felt the air of anticipation from him even across the block and five floors up. He was hungry and he wanted blood.

The vampire took the steps two at a time in his eagerness to get to the door. The thin, blonde woman was waiting to greet him. She nodded formally as he entered the house and she closed the door behind him.

I sat back on my heels. He'd given me the serious creeps and I hadn't even seen the dude's fangs. I made a mental note to buy a crossbow at the earliest given opportunity. I was taking another swig of my rapidly warming beer when every single one of my instincts went on full alert.

I can't properly describe it, but it's never steered me wrong. I know when I'm no longer alone. I slowly put the beer down and reached into my bag, carefully palming my .38. I closed my eyes and opened my ears. Whoever was coming for me was making their way up the ramp from the lower levels. The sound was somewhat slow. There was something impatient about the brisk thuds. Whoever it was, they weren't really trying to hide their progress, but that didn't mean they weren't dangerous. I pulled myself up onto the cement column, making sure my sneakers were hidden from view. I had to let one foot dangle off the ledge to make sure no one could see where I was hiding. I pulled the .38 close to my chest and made sure the safety was off. I closed my eyes and listened. The sound was getting closer and closer, the *click clack* getting more and more pissed off as it made its way up the ramps. I was beginning to suspect who was after me, but I couldn't be sure until I had visual recognition. Even with my suspicion, I intended to give whoever was coming up that ramp a reason to reconsider.

"Damn it," I heard a feminine voice say. The female sighed and started up the ramp to go to the top floor of the parking garage when she stopped and turned. I smiled. She'd seen my stuff on the floor of the garage, but she still hadn't seen me.

"Kelsey?" Liv asked hesitantly. "Are you here?"

I leapt from my hiding place and had her perfectly in my sights before she had a chance to breathe.

"Holy shit!" Liv screamed and jumped back at least two feet

before landing on her ass.

I grinned down at her. "You were looking for me?"

"Bitch!" she breathed, her eyes wide. "I hate it when you do that."

I have to admit I enjoyed the way she had to catch her breath and clutched her chest, like she could stop her heart from racing. "Then don't try to sneak up on me."

Her eyes narrowed and I knew she was no longer thinking about her fear. "Sneak up on you? I've sent you twenty texts. I left ten voice mails. I told you in the last one that I was working on a locator spell and that I would be here, in this very place, in twenty minutes. I don't know how else you want me to announce my damn presence."

I shrugged and clicked the safety back on the gun. "I guess I missed that."

Liv scrambled up, her heels clacking against the cement. "Yeah, right. I believe that. You've ignored me all day."

"I'm working," I said because I knew that tone. I was about to get a massive lecture on the evils of alcohol. I smiled bitterly as I twisted open beer number three.

"I can tell." She shook her head at the empty beer bottles and food wrappers. "Nathan called me last night. Between that and your drunk texting, I figured out you fell off the wagon last night."

"I wasn't aware I'd been on the wagon." I got back on my knees because Liv might want to throw an intervention, but my night was far from over. Another limo was pulling up.

I was clicking pictures of three vampires and two women. These were kind of strange looking vamps, I thought as Liv's tirade continued. She was saying something about me throwing my life away. I was thinking that vamps didn't normally wear jeans and hockey jerseys. The tall, lanky vampire was wearing just that and he had his arm wrapped securely around the shoulder of a dark-haired Hispanic girl who, if I had to guess, was a werewolf.

Curious. I wondered if the wolf was a hooker. Liv continued on, telling me how dangerous it was to get drunk when I had no backup, but I was thinking no on the hooker bit. The vamp's smile was a happy one. There wasn't anything salacious about it, just a sweet joy. I doubted the woman in his arms was anything but a girlfriend. He was careful with her. The other vampire with a female seemed a little European to me. They had a certain style that American men didn't have and confidence in their own sexuality that few American men possessed. This vampire was wearing a dusky rose silk shirt over dark brown slacks and he looked wholly masculine in them. He held hands with a blonde in a short skirt and a wide smile. The last vamp seemed young and I meant that in a vampire fashion. If I was a betting girl, I would lay money that he'd recently started walking the night and the two older vamps were showing him the ropes.

"Have you listened to a word I said?" Liv asked, her hands on her hips.

I turned and tried a conciliatory smile. "Alcohol bad. Sobriety good."

She rolled her eyes. "Give me a damn beer."

I tossed her the coldest one I had left. She sank down and regarded me with serious brown eyes.

"What are we doing here, Kels?"

The limo drove off and I wondered if that was it. "I'm working a case you sent me on. You're bitching at me. That's what we're doing here."

"You know what I mean."

I looked down at my best friend and gave up the fight. "It's a vampire club. It's one of the addresses in Joanne's book. I think she worked here."

"Sheee-it!" Liv took a long swig. "A real vamp club?" She knelt beside me, looking over the concrete barrier.

"Four vamps have already gone in and it's early," I commented.

"I've heard they like to get the whole dinner thing out of the way."

"Four vampires." From what I understood, they were rare and tended to spread out. "Do you think that's the whole population of North Texas?"

Liv snorted. "Not lately."

I pursed my lips as I thought about the implications of diving in. I knew that Liv, Nate, and Jamie had been careful to keep any news of the supernatural world out of my hearing for the last ten years or so. I was about to open the door. "What do you mean?"

Liv's shoulder-length golden brown hair was in her right hand as she twisted it around. It was an unconscious mannerism she used when she was contemplating a problem. "You know Nathan doesn't think it's a good idea for us to keep you in the loop. He really thinks it is best for you to stay out of this world entirely."

"He worked you over good, didn't he?"

Liv sighed. "He showed up after school and yelled at me for a while. He told me I was driving you to drink."

"It wasn't you, Livie," I said with a sarcastic grin. "I totally drove myself. That's what got my ass in trouble in the first place. Next time I'll walk."

She punched me in the arm. "Don't joke. I think Nate's wrong. I think you need this. I don't think you'll be able to live in the normal world. You'll have to keep too many secrets and deny too much of yourself. So, do you want the lowdown on the vamps?"

I hesitated, but only for a moment. Liv was right. It wasn't like ignoring the supernatural world had made me blissfully happy. "Hit me."

"The Council moved to Dallas almost ten years ago," she said.

Now my eyes were wide. "Seriously? I thought they were based in Paris and had been since…forever. What the hell are they doing in Dallas?"

"The king lives here."

"There's an actual vampire king and he lives in Dallas?"

"Yeah," Liv replied. "He's the real deal. He took out the old Council ten years ago when they started to threaten the wolves and shifters. Only one member of the old Council survived the war. Now the Council formally governs the supernatural world and the seats are held by the various species. The king is the head of the Council. There's a seat for vampires, werewolves, shifters, witches, humans, and the Fae. The king only votes in the event of a tie."

"Wow." I finally understood what it meant to be flabbergasted. "That's amazing. And everyone's getting along?"

"Not as well as the king apparently expected," Liv admitted. "He's already had to put down two attempts to overthrow him. I think after all those centuries of iron-fisted control, some groups are going a little too far with their newfound freedom. My coven leader says the king's looking for a solution. He wants to create a kind of law enforcement for the supes."

I laughed because whoever took that job was a fucking idiot. "Nice, he wants a sheriff. Well, good luck to him."

I got back to watching the house. They were careful. I couldn't see a damn thing through those windows, and I started to wonder how good an idea it would be to try to sneak in. Or maybe I could get a date. They seemed to be letting dates in. From what I understood, only vampires, companions, and slaves ever got into one of those clubs...Then my mind made another mental leap.

"He got rid of the slaves," I whispered.

Liv shook her head enthusiastically. "It was one of the first things he did. He freed all the slaves, though a lot of them stayed with their vampire masters, but the vamps have to prove they're paying their staffs."

"Then who's feeding all these visiting vamps? If the king is here then I assume he has a court. If the slaves are gone, who's going to feed the vampires?" I asked, already knowing the answer.

Liv's mouth formed a perfect little *O*. "Hookers. Holy crap, Kels, you're right. Someone's bringing in hookers to fill up the clubs."

"But other supes would be better than grabbing a bunch of human girls off the street," I commented. "Some asshole is recruiting supernatural college girls to prostitute themselves to vampires."

Liv thought about that for a second. "I get your point, but what else are they supposed to do? The vampires have to eat. The king won't let them enslave humans anymore."

"Look, Liv, I don't have some moral problem with it. If some chick wants to work her way through college on her back then good for her. But Joanne is missing and I don't think she's in Mexico with a john. I think she's dead and I think it had to with her job."

"Really?" Liv teared up.

"Sorry," I said, taking a deep breath. "If I had to bet on it, I would say I'm hunting for a corpse."

"Helen's going to be devastated," Liv whispered.

I hated that I couldn't be more positive, but I knew that girl was gone. I also knew the possibility of finding a corpse was small. Supernatural creatures deteriorate quickly after death. It was one of the ways they hid from humans. Vampires turned to ash and wolves and shifters decomposed at an accelerated rate. After a few days, there wouldn't be much left.

"I need to talk to someone about getting into that club."

Liv went a pasty white. "Oh, no, Kelsey. They don't let humans in that club. You have to have a vampire escort to get past the front door and I wouldn't try sneaking into the back if I were you. The club would be trapped. It should have weird charms and wards all over it."

"Then get me a meeting with the king," I said simply. "He can get me in."

"Yeah, I'll get right on that," Liv said. "Kelsey, I think going into that club is a bad idea."

"Oh, nice car," I commented as a black Bentley purred up the street and stopped in front of the club. I got behind the lens and took a good look at the vampire who gracefully got out of the beautiful beast he'd been driving. He was immaculately dressed in a three-piece suit that had to have been made for him. The pinstriped suit hugged his body perfectly and he moved with a predatory grace. I pegged his height at right around five ten. Not the tallest man, but he had presence. He was old.

I pushed the button on the front of the camera to get a close-up of him. His face was slightly hawk-like. His dark eyes were fringed by some really spectacular lashes any girl would have been proud of, but there was no question about his masculinity. He screamed male and I responded to it. His sensual mouth was turned down and he was controlled, emotionless. He smoothed back the black silk of his hair and made sure his jacket was perfect, but I knew it was just a habit. I almost felt as if an odd connection formed between us in that moment. I could practically sense what he was feeling. He wasn't meeting anyone. This whole thing was routine for him, and he was bored with it all. He needed something. He needed someone to shake him up a bit.

Lonely. He was lonely.

The vampire handed his keys to the valet politely and I saw him sigh as he walked up the steps. It was like he was forcing himself to do something that had become dull for him. His ennui was evident in the slump of his shoulders once the valet was gone and he thought he was alone.

Something in him called to me. I knew him. Not in any real sense, but I understood the man standing there, wondering if it was even worth it. I probably looked that way a hundred times a day. The inanities of life were an anathema to me and yet they were, at times, the only things that kept me going. I wondered what it would be like to touch him. Would he view sex as something boring, as well? Would it be a mere physical function that needed to be attended to, or was what he needed a lover? Did he long for a woman in his bed he could share more than an orgasm with?

I prayed Liv hadn't caught my bald interest in the vampire. I didn't want to have to explain why I was imagining all manner of dirty play with the handsome nightwalker.

I didn't take my eye off him, enjoying the view of his nice backside as he made it to the top of the steps. I was about to get a picture of that hot ass when he turned. It took everything I had to stay as still as possible because he was looking my way, his eyes taking in the building I was in. He smiled suddenly and I caught my breath. That smile was honest and revealed white, even teeth. He stared directly at me and put his right hand over his heart. The vampire bowed, a courtly gesture, as though he was a knight and I a lady he wished to greet. He cocked a single eyebrow.

He was inviting me to join him.

I let the camera drop from my face. I was both scared shitless and completely fascinated at the idea of running down the ramp, taking his hand, and walking into that club with him. I could ask my questions about Joanne. I could find out who she'd been seeing and how long she'd been on the game.

I could find out how good a vampire's bite felt.

"Kelsey, I think that vampire can see you," Liv said quietly. "Maybe we should go."

I stood up, not taking my eyes off him. I let him see me. He wouldn't hurt me. Somehow I knew it. His lips curled up in the sexiest smile. He would be my escort, my guide. "You go. I'm going in that club. I think I just got a date."

"Nice," a low voice growled behind me and I was something I almost never am—startled. "If I'd known I needed fangs to get you to go out with me I would have shown you mine."

I actually squealed a little bit as Grayson Sloane closed in on me. Where the hell had he come from? He bore down on me and I saw Liv take a step back. Sloane put a big arm around my shoulder and faced the street. He shot the vampire the finger.

"Try again, Vorenus," he shouted.

Even without the telephoto lens, I could see the vampire's face fall briefly and then that mask he'd been wearing slipped back into place. Whatever odd connection we'd had shut down entirely, and I felt its loss. He turned without a backward glance and walked into the club.

I slapped at Sloane's big chest. "That was rude. That might have been my only chance to get in that club."

Sloane's blue eyes were hard as flint. "You aren't going anywhere. Consider yourself in protective custody, sweetheart."

"What?" I practically screeched the question.

Sloane held up an eight by ten black and white photo. It was a picture of me walking across the SMU campus earlier today. It was lovingly captioned in red ink with the words "Keep that bitch out of our game, Sloane."

I sighed. It wasn't ink, I guessed. It was more than likely blood.

"So you mentioned something about dinner?" I asked because if I was about to get my ass hauled into protective custody, I was at least going to get dinner out of it.

Chapter Five

I stared across the elegant table at my captor. I thought of Grayson Sloane that way since I'd been told in no uncertain terms that I was off my case and I wouldn't be going home. Liv had been told to take a hike. Sloane used kinder words than that, but it was basically the same thing. After he informed me of my sad state, I'd been hauled to an expensive steakhouse on Lemmon Avenue. I felt underdressed, but it was the kind of place where if you walked in they expected you had money. Texans with money didn't take kindly to being told how to dress. The hostess at the front acted like Sloane had planned the evening out. Despite the full waiting area and bar, she greeted him by name, immediately showing us to a private dining room.

"How did you find me?" I asked the question calmly because I wasn't one to turn down a meal. If I'd gone home, I likely would have stopped at some fast food place and gotten the el cheapo special of the day. "I didn't tell anyone where I was going. Liv used a locator spell. Do they train the Rangers in the dark arts?"

The light in the room was low and there was a candle on the table between us. It was a romantic setting complete with elegant glasses and china. This place didn't scream "working dinner" to me. It kinda whispered "get your lover in bed." My eyes got big as I checked out the price tags on the menu.

"Nothing so exotic." The hulking Texas Ranger who had, only an hour ago, verbally shot down a vampire and taken me into custody, radiated uncertainty as he watched me. "I turned on the GPS locator in your phone."

"You can do that?" Maybe I should check into doing that to Joanne Taylor's cell phone. It would make missing person cases so much easier to deal with.

He shrugged. "Yes, when the occasion warrants it, law enforcement is allowed to work with the phone company to track down missing people."

I nodded and decided on the petite filet. It was reasonable. The price wasn't. The price was ridiculous, but considering the rest of the menu it was reasonable. Besides, petite sounded dainty and feminine. It probably wouldn't fill me up. I set the menu down. "You could have called. It might have been simpler."

His eyes gleamed in the low light, and I was struck again by how hot the man was. "You wouldn't have answered. You would have taken one look at the number and ignored the call. I would have gotten your voice mail all night long. You're scared of me."

I snorted. I couldn't have him thinking he had the upper hand like that. "Yeah, I'm real scared of you." Except, I kind of was scared of him, though not in a physical sense. Being around him made me antsy in a boy/girl, he'll never like me the way I'll like him way, and I really hated that. I really hate feeling vulnerable. "I'm annoyed by you, but you're not exactly terrifying."

"Look, Kelsey, we got off on the wrong foot." His eyes were coaxing and his hand started to reach for mine before he realized what he was doing and pulled back.

"Which foot is that, Sloane?" I will admit that I enjoyed having him on the ropes for a change. He was being so careful with me that it was easy to needle him. "Is that the foot you put in your mouth when you tried to tempt me away from my alcoholic lifestyle, or the one you shoved up my ass when you threatened to toss me in jail if I didn't come with you?"

He stared blankly at me for a moment and I think I had shocked him. Then he threw back his head and laughter filled the small private dining room. He laughed for a good long time and even the waitress was smiling as she brought the wine Sloane had ordered.

"Lieutenant Sloane, your wine." She poured a small amount into a glass and he was grinning as he took a deep whiff and then tasted it.

"Excellent," he pronounced and she proceeded to pour each of us a glass. "Try this, sweetheart. I'm finding this pinot pairs well with the taste of my foot in my mouth."

He ordered the center cut filet, a loaded potato, and a glazed carrot. I gave the waitress my order. It was the ladies filet with broccoli and I hoped it filled me up. Despite my tacos from earlier, I was already hungry again. I've always had a ridiculously high metabolism. Liv keeps telling me it's going to catch up to me, but twenty-six years in I can still eat whatever I want and maintain my size six. I was kind of worried about looking like a total pig in front of the hot guy across from me. It tends to weird the guy out when I eat twice what they eat, and I won't even go into how much I can drink. Guys really get intimidated on my fifth beer. Any dates I had usually ended up being spectacular failures. Not that this was a date because it totally wasn't. It was more like a kidnapping, but I still didn't want to look bad in front of him. I smoothed down my T-shirt and wished it was at least new. It was an old concert T-shirt from my college days with the name of a punk band splashed across it.

He shook his head when I finished my order and had the waitress stop. "Why don't you bring us a couple of lobsters, too?"

She nodded and walked off.

He stared at me seriously. "What was that about?"

"Dinner. I thought." Had I burped and not noticed it? That could happen.

"Kelsey, I've been friends with your brother for a couple of years. Do you seriously believe I haven't heard stories of your legendary appetite?"

"I don't eat that much." I was going to kick Jamie's ass the next time I saw him. What did he do? Did he go around advertising that his sister was a complete freak? Did he have a stand-up routine focused on how weird I was?

"Hey," Gray said softly and this time he let his hand find mine. He covered it with his big one and squeezed a little. I should have pulled away, but I enjoyed his warmth too much. "I wasn't insulting you. You're different. It's nothing to be ashamed of. It's one of the reasons I'm interested in you."

"Did you really ask Jamie to set us up?" Not that I was going to go out with him on a date that didn't involve some form of kidnapping. I was simply curious. In our last year of high school and the first two of college, I tended to date friends of guys who wanted to date Liv. Since then the pickings had been slim.

He smiled and it lit up his face. It took him from brooding to gorgeous with one little tug of his lips. "I've been bugging your brother to give me your number for about a year and a half."

I whistled because that was a long time to wait. "And it never occurred to you to look me up in the phone book? I'm pretty sure if you can turn on the GPS in my phone you can find my number."

"I respect your brother, Kelsey. He said you weren't ready so I backed off. You should know, though, that I had planned to require your investigative services in a couple of weeks if I couldn't get Jamie to come around. I was tired of waiting."

"What was I going to help you with?"

His smile turned rueful and he looked younger than his thirty years. It softened the hard lines of his face and made my heart melt a little. "I don't know. I was going to come up with something. I was going to show up on your doorstep sooner or later, Kelsey Atwood."

He took a drink of his wine and sat back. I tried the ruby-red liquid. I was really more a beer girl, but I wasn't going to let it go to waste. It tasted rich on my tongue and I vowed to expand my horizons. "Well, now you can really use my services. Tell me about the missing girls."

And just like that he clammed up.

"Kelsey, it's an ongoing case," he tried smoothly. "I'm not at liberty to talk about it."

I huffed a little and sat back. I wondered briefly if Jamie was forever going to be the only man who believed I could get a damn thing right. I should have taken my chances with the vampire. At least he would have been honest about what he wanted. Sloane tried to tell me he was interested in me, but then didn't want to talk about my work or his work. We were single people in our late twenties/early thirties. We *were* our work. I took another long drink of the wine and focused on something other than the man across from me.

I needed to find a vampire, possibly one named Alexander. I wondered if I showed up at the club at sundown tomorrow night, if this Vorenus person would be there. He'd seemed willing enough to talk with me. At least he'd seemed flattered by my attention. I wondered if it proved once and for all that I had a death wish that I was a little excited at the thought of meeting a strange vampire.

"I don't like that look," Gray said quietly.

I drummed my fingers on the table. "It really doesn't matter, Sloane. You won't have to put up with it for long. So, are you going to call Jamie or do you want me to?"

His handsome face was a mask of confusion. "Why would we call Jamie?"

"To come get me. Did you expect me to walk home? You made me leave my car." I had been willing to come with him because I thought we were going to discuss the case and that photograph of me. I was not willing to buy whatever he was selling without some sort of explanation.

His jaw tensed, forming a stubborn line. "I told you you're not going home. He knows who you are."

"Then I'll stay with Jamie. You can't expect me to sleep in some fleabag motel until you solve this case. That's completely unrealistic." Jamie could protect me when I couldn't protect myself. I wasn't planning on mentioning anything at all to Nate. He would have me in a jail cell with a phalanx of armed guards, and then he might sleep well for the first time in over a decade.

He swallowed once and then decided to plow through. "You're staying with me. My house is secure."

"Yeah, I bet it is." Now I knew his game and I wondered briefly if he'd set this whole thing up himself. He must be really hard up if he had to go through all of this just to get laid. He should do what I did. He should prowl a skanky bar, get really plastered, and lower his expectations. It worked every time.

"I have a room for you." Gray frowned my way. "I'm not going to jump you the minute I get you home. If it would make you feel better, you can ask your mother to join us, or your friend Olivia."

Both of whom would be shoving me into the Ranger's arms as fast as they could. No, thank you. "I'm not staying with you. You can't force me to. If you insist, then I'll take the motel."

"Why?" He was looking down at his hands. They were big hands. His voice was grave and when his eyes finally found mine, I saw a wealth of pain in his deep blue eyes. It made me stop my sarcastic inner commentary. "I wouldn't hurt you, Kelsey. I would try hard to never change around you. I have excellent control over my form. You wouldn't have to see that…side of me."

Now I was confused. "I didn't think you would hurt me physically, Sloane."

"My name is Gray," he insisted.

"What do you change into, Gray? Why would you be afraid of hurting me?" I was really interested and on more than a personal level. I have excellent instincts and, while I knew that Gray wasn't entirely human, I couldn't tell what he was. It bugged me.

Gray's eyes went stubborn as though he knew he'd made the wrong move and wasn't sure how to take it back. "I thought Jamie told you and that was why you didn't want to be alone with me."

I gazed deeply into his eyes. He wasn't a vampire, obviously, but he also wasn't a werewolf or shifter. He didn't have the right energy. I couldn't put my finger on it. If he was a witch then he wouldn't have talked about changing. Hags could change, but they were exclusively female. Fae creatures didn't shift form, either. They used magic to affect glamours, but they didn't change their essential forms. I could only think of one other species with the power to change forms and the very real potential to hurt someone they liked. The room turned cold around me as I realized the truth.

"Please tell me you're only half demon."

He seemed to retreat, everything about him becoming smaller somehow. His shoulders hunched, his head drooping a bit and his eyes slid away from mine. "My father was a demon. My mother was an ambitious human. I'm a halfling. I seem to be more human than demon, though. I have the physical strength of a demon and I can change my form, but I don't want to kill everyone I see or cause chaos for no reason. No one ever believes me on that so don't even try to pretend. I know the spiel. A demon's a demon. We're evil."

A full demon was. I agreed with him whole-heartedly on that count, but I had grown up in the supernatural world. My mother had talked to me about a halfling friend of my grandfather's all the time. They'd worked for the Council together on several jobs. He'd had a wife and kids and he'd always been a loyal friend. The way my mother told it, halflings came in two kinds—the kind that took after the demon part and the kind that stayed true to their human souls. Though she'd said even that kind could be assholes, too. Assholiness, according to my mother, was not limited to demon DNA.

Sloane pushed his chair back. "I'll call your brother. He'll watch out for you. As long as you stay away from this particular case, I think this perp will leave you alone. He seems to want to keep this between me and him. Don't worry about the check. I'll get it. I'll catch this guy, Kelsey. I promise you that."

He turned to go and the easiest thing in the world would have been to let him. Let him think I didn't want to have anything to do with a half-demon and I wouldn't have to ache at the thought of his pain. I didn't like caring about someone I'd just met. I didn't like…anything I felt when I thought about Grayson Sloane.

"Why me?" I couldn't let him walk out like that. "Why this sudden pursuit of me?"

He turned back around and I could see he really didn't want to walk out either. "It wasn't sudden. At least, it wasn't for me. I've wanted you since I went to your mom's for dinner with Jamie and I saw a picture of you and I knew I'd finally found you."

"Found me?"

He laughed a little and weariness overcame his handsome face. I had the most insane urge to force him to sit down, to massage the back of his neck and kiss his forehead until his troubles went away. "I was never going to tell you this. I was going to pretend we just met through Jamie. Well, it doesn't matter. My father…one of his powers is prophecy. He can see certain futures and determine outcomes and often change it. I don't do any of that, but every now and then I get a flash of the future. It's a little movie in my head. I'll touch something or I'll walk into someplace and it triggers the power in me."

The room seemed quiet and I was aware that we were alone. It was intimate and not at all scary. "Where did you see me?"

"I spent the night in a hotel in Dallas." His voice was rich and I got the feeling he enjoyed the story he told. He might be thinking twice about telling it, but it was close to his heart. "I'm from Houston originally, but the job I was interviewing for was here in Dallas. My family had money and I inherited it when I was sixteen, so I kind of waste it as much as I can. I took the bridal suite because it was the only suite left. I always spring for the best. It's a game in a way. Let's see how much of my mother's money I can waste. Anyway, I interviewed and it went great. I spent some time in the bar, but something compelled me to go back to my room alone. The minute I laid down on the bed, I saw you."

"What was I doing?"

He smiled and it was sweet and carnal. "Me, honey. You were doing me. It was our wedding night and I was so happy. I remember feeling happier and more…complete than I've ever felt my whole life. I was with my wife. She was beautiful and difficult and mine. I thought about how hard you were on the outside and what a stunningly giving woman you were on the inside. I saw your entire fucked up, gorgeous soul, and it melded with mine. I tried that whole weekend to see it again, but it was gone after that first night. I didn't see you again until two years later when I walked into your mother's house. I told myself I had to wait until the time was right. I told myself not to fuck this up. Of course, I still managed it."

I felt my whole face go red with emotion and I tried hard to force the tears that threatened back, but he said it with such great longing that I couldn't argue with him. He believed in this and that made me want to believe, too. Who didn't want to believe there was one person out there who could complete them? Who didn't feel lonely enough to want that?

He stood there and looked down at me with such deep desire. It went past anything sexual and I wished I could have seen what he saw that day. His eyes were filled with regret. "Look, I know I screwed everything up so I can be honest with you. I love you. I know that sounds ridiculous and it's too soon to say anything like that, but you're the other half of me. You always have been. You always will be. If you need anything, I'll get it for you. All you have to do is call me."

He stared at me for another second. In that weird time, I felt like I saw myself through his eyes and it was a revelation. I was fucked up and yet I was still beautiful to him. For one stupid moment, I felt radiant and I couldn't let it go. I jumped out of my chair and my hand was on his arm. He turned and the minute he saw my face I was in his arms. They caged me and I felt safe and small and feminine in a way I hadn't up to that point.

I lifted my face and he kissed me.

It was gentle at first, a meshing of lips as he lowered his mouth almost reverently to mine. He had to bend over to press our lips together. The moment our mouths met, something seemed to open up inside me. He gently ate at my lips, his tongue barely a whisper, but I felt it there almost begging entry, and I softened against him. I'd had sex before. My experience wasn't vast. It wasn't nonexistent either. My sexual history up to Grayson Sloane consisted of seeking a way out. I indulged in sex for the same reason I drank that last tequila shot I didn't need. I wanted to get out of myself for a while and not think about anything.

Gray's kiss didn't simply take me away. It was so much more than a meeting of lips that led to something else. I was more myself than I had ever been in my life. I didn't want to be anywhere but right where I was—in his arms.

I let my hands trail up his body, feeling the strength of him. He was all muscle, from his lean waist to a chest that felt like a well-made statue against my hands. Pressing my body against his, I sighed and opened my mouth. His hands tangled in my hair and I had no idea how much time passed as his tongue danced with mine. When he groaned, I felt it deep in my own body, and everything that was female inside me answered him. He pulled me close, his hands dangerously near my ass, and I felt how much I affected him. His erection rocked firmly against me, not trying to hide what he wanted. His cock was hard against my stomach and I went up on my toes, trying to get it where it belonged. It belonged at the center of me. He belonged inside me.

The door to the private room opened and I was pulled roughly from my little slice of nirvana as the waitstaff entered carrying trays of food. Gray let me go, his hands shaking as he steadied me against his chest. He laughed, a nervous sound, and I couldn't help but lean against him and laugh, too. The waitstaff was professional and pretended like they hadn't interrupted a serious make-out session. I felt like I was sixteen and my mom had caught me with my boyfriend. It was silly and innocent and I felt younger than I had in years.

"Kelsey," Gray said achingly, and when I looked into his eyes I saw such devotion in them. It scared me, but I decided to try a little bravery.

"Gray, I don't know about the whole love thing," I said honestly because it was all too fast for me. "But how about we start with dinner?"

He smiled. "All right, sweetheart."

* * * *

"So who was the vampire you appeared to have a distinct dislike for?" I polished off the last of my excellent lobster. I'd drowned it in butter.

We'd spent the majority of dinner on safe topics. He talked about being a Texas Ranger and how obnoxious it was when people called him Walker. I talked about the weird parts of growing up with two ridiculously overprotective brothers. We stayed far away from anything too emotional. We'd had that portion of the evening and it was nice to laugh. Now I was ready to push him on the professional level.

He smiled as he finished his steak. "His name is Marcus Vorenus. Until tonight, I really didn't have a problem with him. He's fairly easy to deal with and almost always reasonable. I didn't like him looking at you though. He seemed interested."

"He felt old." I ignored his possessiveness. I wasn't used to anyone feeling that way about me, but I couldn't forget that odd connection I'd had with Vorenus. I played with his name in my mind, rolling it around and letting it run through my brain.

"He is old, sweetheart," Gray said and I was getting used to the endearment. "He's roughly two thousand years old. He was born in ancient Rome. As far as anyone can tell, since the coup Donovan led, Vorenus is the world's oldest walking vampire."

"He seemed sad." I could still see his face when he realized Gray was there. He'd been smiling before, and then I'd watched it all go a polite blank. I wondered what it must be like to be so unique in the world, to remember a time no one else could recall, to have seen so many people he undoubtedly cared about grow old and leave him.

Gray made a choking sound. "Uhm, I don't know what the guy has to be sad about. According to my research, he's worth about a billion dollars, has an important seat on the Council and the king's ear. He backed Donovan in the fight and Donovan won. He's one of the most influential individuals in the supernatural world."

"He was sad," I reiterated. Money didn't fix all your troubles and power sometimes caused more. I'd felt his weariness. Even with the distance between us, I'd felt as though I'd bumped against his soul.

Gray considered me for a moment. "What did you get off him? If you had to guess, what class of vampire would you say he was?"

He was testing me. I didn't mind. I was actually kind of happy he wasn't treating me like a china doll the way he had before. I had no desire to be anyone's sweet little princess. I wouldn't be good in the role. "If you forced me to guess, I would say he's an academic. He's not physically strong, but he has mental powers. The other vampires walked right into the club, but not him. He knew I was there. He felt me."

And I'd felt him.

Gray's lips turned up in an approving smile. "If I'd had you, I wouldn't have needed six months worth of research to tell me that. Vorenus is an academic. He's also an intensely powerful persuasive, which is why it's a damn good thing I was there tonight. He was trying to pull you to him."

I sat back. I didn't think so. He'd asked, and politely at that. He'd felt my interest in him and replied with an invitation. I hadn't felt like he was taking my will. The push to go to him had come from inside me and not some outside force. As attracted as I was to Gray, I'd felt something for the vampire, too. He'd felt a little like a kindred spirit.

I let that image go as Gray continued talking. "There are some people who believe Vorenus was the one behind the coup. It makes sense in some ways. Donovan was a king, but it seems hard to believe a kid a couple of years out of college could pull off something like taking down the Vampire Council. He had to put together a powerful group to back him."

"This Donovan guy is the king?" I tried to wrap my brain around the fact that the entire supernatural world had changed while I'd been hiding.

Gray poured himself another glass of wine. "Yes, he is, and he's dangerous. Do you understand what the term king means in reference to a vampire?"

"It's a technical term. A vampire king would be stronger, faster than other vampires," I responded. He would be able to kill other vampires with ease. "Genetically they're extremely rare. He's a super predator."

"Yes, I think that's a good way to describe Donovan." Gray's hand toyed idly with mine as he spoke. "You should know that one of the first things he did when he took the throne was to break off all contact with demonkind. The only reason he allows me an audience is my status with the Rangers."

That was news. Vampires and demons had a decent relationship for as long as anyone could remember. Their alliance was tightly bound by contracts, and law ruled their actions. From what I understood, they met once a decade or so and renewed their treaties. "Did the king break their contracts?"

"Not exactly. He follows the letter of them, but he refused demons a seat on the Council," Gray explained. "The rumors are that he'd promised them one and then turned his back on them when the time came. He also refuses demonkind when they request an audience. The current contracts had a ten-year term, with an extra four years built in to cover anything that would come up. Like if the demons found themselves involved in a war or the vampires couldn't make it to the negotiating table. They have four years from the end of the contract before it's void. We're on year two of that extension."

"Donovan refuses to negotiate? What happens if he never comes back to the table?" Demons could be controlled with contracts. Without one, I didn't like to think about what they would do.

"We'll find out in two years. Some say Donovan's simply playing hardball, but I think there's something personal behind it. There are some of us who fear Donovan is going to let his distaste for demonkind push this plane into war. He hates them."

"You keep saying they," I pointed out, wanting to understand Gray. "You don't refer to demons as we."

He leaned forward, his mouth a flat line. "I'm a halfling, Kelsey. I'm actually stronger than most full-blooded demons, but it doesn't matter when it comes to this. Contracts are written in very specific language. The agreements between vampires and demonkind are only for full bloods. Donovan doesn't have to follow any law but his own when it comes to me."

The waitress walked into the room after hesitantly opening the door. I hid a grin because I thought she was trying to make sure she didn't walk in on us throwing down on the table. Since that kiss, Gray had been sweet and not at all handsy. The waitress set down the check and thanked us. Whether she was thanking us for coming in or for keeping our clothes on throughout the entire meal, I wasn't sure. Gray pulled out a credit card and shoved it in the bill. The waitress strode off to run the card and I thought about what Gray had told me about the new vampire order.

"Liv said the king was looking for a sheriff."

Gray laughed, the sound bitter. "Donovan has no respect for any law he didn't make himself. Don't think for a minute he's trying to do something noble, sweetheart. He was a criminal before he was a king and that partner of his...I won't even go into him. If there were any way to pin something on him, I would arrest him in a heartbeat. The king is playing with words when he says he wants a sheriff. He's trying to pretend he isn't as bad as the last Council."

I'd heard the last Council wanted to enslave the supernatural world, so this dude must be a real winner. "If he doesn't want a sheriff, what does he want?"

"The technical term is *Nex Apparatus*. It means death machine. He wants someone to do his dirty work so his hands stay marginally clean."

I'd heard the term before. It gave me an icky feeling. "He wants an assassin? Why doesn't he appoint a vampire? A *Nex Apparatus* is always a vampire."

The waitress brought the check back and Gray signed it with a flourish. "That's the thing about Donovan. He's a tricky one. If he thinks it will help him politically to have a non-vampire death machine then he'll find that man and when he does, he'll use his talents to his own betterment. Come on, sweetheart. I want to get you home."

I stubbornly sat back and ignored the hand he offered to help me up. I cocked an eyebrow and waited. We had settled the fact that I was willing to explore this attraction I had for him. I was willing to look past his demon half. Actually, he didn't know it yet, but I kind of wanted to see those fangs of his. What we hadn't settled was his refusal to talk about our case, and there was no question it was *our* case.

He sighed and I saw the weariness in his eyes. "Can we talk about this at home, Kelsey? Please?"

I didn't like the idea of giving in, but I let him help me up and lead me out of the restaurant, his big hand on the small of my back. I was going to have to deal with my newfound weakness when it came to Gray. As we waited for the valet to bring the truck around, I was already thinking about, maybe, playing around with him when we got to his house. Would it be a really bad move? The man already claimed he loved me. In his weird brain, we were already married, so why shouldn't I? I didn't have to promise him anything beyond a night together. I was thinking about making a move on him in the car when he tensed beside me.

"What's taking him so long?" Gray asked, annoyed.

Then I felt it. It was an instinct, like a bug creeping up my spine. We weren't alone, not even close. I surveyed the buildings around us, trying to find the eyes that watched us.

"What is it Kelsey?" Gray asked, his voice quiet and dead serious.

"There are eyes on us." I knew they were there. Two, maybe three people were watching from a distance, their attentions focused on us. The street itself was empty, far too empty for the time of night. This wasn't some residential part of Dallas. There were always cars here, always people walking about, and yet there was a hush over the place.

Wards, most likely. A good witch—and I'm talking about skill, not intent—can ward a building or even a piece of land. The wards would make humans attempt to avoid the space. They wouldn't even realize why they changed direction. They simply took a turn they hadn't been planning because that ward whispered to them.

I peered down the street and sure enough, every car coming our way turned.

"You carrying?" Gray's Colt automatic was in his hand and he flicked off the safety.

I eased my hand into my bag and felt for my little .38. I pulled it out and nodded at Gray.

He frowned down with a shake of his head. "What the hell is that? That won't hurt a puppy much less a supe. Are you planning on giving them a splinter with that thing? Does that even have silver ordnance in it?"

I narrowed my eyes in irritation. "No, I wasn't planning on getting into a firefight with a bunch of supes. I was planning to spend the night quietly staking out that club. And why would I carry silver bullets? I only own a gun in case one of my divorce cases goes bad. Trust me, my .38 gives Johnny Cheatsalot something to think about."

He growled at me and I smiled because it was kind of sexy. "Come on. Stay behind me. I don't know what the hell is going on, but I'm going to get you out of here. We're going to the truck. I have a 12 gauge in there you can use and I can call for backup if this gets too hot. Usually a bunch of police sirens scares these things away."

Gray stayed close to the wall and started to move toward the side of the building. There was a small parking lot between the restaurant and the building next to it. His free hand reached out for mine, and he tugged me close to his big body. I had the distinct feeling he intended to place himself between me and anything that might be coming our way. I'd never had real backup before. I'd been in a few tight spots, but I was always alone, and this felt different. It made me squeeze his hand tightly and vow not to let him get hurt for me.

"Do you think this is about the case?" I asked.

"I have to assume he's after you. He's been playing games with me for almost a month. I don't think he likes you poking around. I promise I'll tell you all about it if you'll get in the truck and let me handle this." He brought my hand to his mouth and kissed it sweetly. "It would be even better if you would get in the truck and drive as fast and far as you could. Drive until you get to Jamie's house and tell him what's going on, okay?"

"Yeah, that's not gonna happen." I might never have had a partner before but I was fairly certain one of the rules of backup was not driving off and leaving them behind.

He sighed. "Well, I can try. Stay close."

Gray turned the corner and I heard his shocked gasp. I ran into the back of him, but I managed to take a peek around his shoulder. Pure terror gripped me as I got a look at what was waiting for us. I took in the sight of the dismembered corpse that used to be our valet. Twenty wolves growled and twitched around it, their heads coming up in unison as they realized they weren't alone. They moved forward almost as if they were one entity. They were out for blood.

Ours.

Chapter Six

"Run, Kelsey," Gray commanded as he started firing into the nearest wolf. The wolf's body bucked with the impact of the large caliber bullet. He slammed into the brick wall across from us and his body slumped down with a whine.

Ignoring Gray's orders, I selected a smaller brown wolf, or rather he selected me because he roared toward me at a breakneck speed. I aimed and fired and managed to hit the wolf right between the eyes. I was proud of myself for staying cool and accurate under pressure, and as the wolf's head whipped back, I opened my mouth to make a crack to Gray about splinters working pretty well when you lodge them in someone's brain. Yes, I was about to point out Gray's mistake in underestimating my little no-silver-bullets .38 Special when the brown wolf got back up and growled my way. He seemed more annoyed than dead, so maybe the time had come to follow orders. Gray wanted me to get help. He was a Texas Ranger after all. He probably knew what he was doing.

"Kelsey, I am fucking serious," Gray growled as he fired his pistol into the throng of wolves coming for him. They were starting to surround him. "Get your ass out of here. Get back in the restaurant and call the Dallas PD for some backup or we're going to die out here. Move it!"

He kicked out at the black wolf running for him. His booted foot connected with the wolf's jaw, and the sound cracked through the air as it broke. Gray moved with a fluid grace that spoke of long training sessions and an innate ability to fight. I started to back up because I didn't have any real training in this type of confrontation at all. I avoided it and I would only end up being someone Gray had to save. As he was twisting to get another shot off, I saw that his eyes were changing. They were a deep purple, but hints of red were starting to form.

"Please, Kelsey," he practically begged and I realized that he really needed to change in order to properly fight, and he didn't want me to see him that way. He would rather lose than allow me to see that part of him. I backed up, hating the fact that I was going to leave him, but I didn't see what else I could do. I couldn't physically fight off twenty wolves. I glanced around and wondered if I had miscalculated. There were so many.

"I'll make the call," I shouted over the howls, growls, and moans of pain. "You hold on."

I turned, sick at my stomach because they were so ferocious. Even as I rushed out of the alley, I still saw the image of Gray in the middle of all those teeth and claws and I started to run. The sooner I heard those sirens coming, the faster I could get back to Gray. He said he had all the strength of a demon. I had to hope he healed like one, too. I had to hope that without me around, he would give in and change and get some fangs and claws of his own. My mind was racing with all those thoughts so it took me a moment to register the fact that my path was blocked.

I stopped on a dime and just avoided falling on my ass as I backed away from the men walking toward me. I dropped my gun, but then it had proven fairly useless, so I left it as I tried to back away from the men coming at me. They weren't tourists out for a late-night stroll. The two men walking with purpose toward me were werewolves. They hadn't fully changed yet, but then they needed opposable thumbs to drag me back to the fight. There were two of them, one dark haired and the other a blond with icy eyes. He strode forward, fully confident in his ability to handle me.

"You're not going anywhere, honey," the blond said with a little smile. He had almost platinum hair and it curled, making him look a bit angelic in the face. His hands were already sharp claws, those icy eyes predatory. He might have been good-looking if he didn't seem like he was going to kill me at any moment.

My heart pounded. They pressed in, herding me back toward the alley. There was nowhere else to go. If I ran they would catch me and then I wouldn't be any good for Gray. I turned and called out for Gray, and then I didn't care about who was behind me. Big, strong Gray was being held down by four wolves who had taken their human forms again. They pinned him, each with one of his limbs in their claws. Blood welled up from where those vicious claws sank in. He struggled, trying to buck them off, but a fifth wolf walked up, changing in mid stride from a big gray wolf on four feet to a bulky man on two powerful legs in the blink of an eye.

He looked straight at me as though he wanted to communicate something. He dropped to one knee and took Gray's neck in his powerful hands. The threat was right there, unmistakable. He would twist Gray's neck until the spinal column snapped, and there was no coming back from that no matter how good his healing powers were. It was a neat, bloodless form of decapitation.

"Kelsey!" Gray fought harder as he realized I wasn't where he'd hoped I would be. He shouted at the men holding him down. "You leave her out of this."

I got my glimpse of his fangs as he snarled at his captors. Stark white and curved slightly inward, those fangs were substantial. They weren't meant for a feeding. They were meant to tear and destroy. I could see he desperately wanted to use those fangs on his captors, but there were too many of them. He couldn't get a decent position to fight. He was completely helpless and my heart ached to see him that way.

"Please," he said when he realized he couldn't win. I could tell he was used to the fangs in his mouth because they didn't change the way he spoke at all. His voice was still deep and solid. "She's a human. She can't hurt you. Let her go and I'll do whatever you want me to do."

"Calm down, demon." The blond seemed to be the only one talking. He never glanced down at Gray. He only seemed to have eyes for me. "This isn't about you. It's always been about her, and we seriously doubt she's just a human."

I didn't have time to ponder the wolf's statement because I found myself in the center of the alley and the wolves were prowling.

Their big tails twitched around me and harsh growls filled the space. Those guttural growls reverberated off the walls until they filled my whole world.

I turned and then twisted again, my panicked movements forming a circle because I didn't want to lose track of them, didn't want them attacking my back. The task became impossible. I couldn't keep them all in my sights. They were everywhere and I saw no way out.

Before that moment when the wolves started to circle me, I would have told anyone who asked that I would welcome a chance like this. Death wish. My brothers always said the words with a shake of their heads. I'd been looking for it for a long time and now that it was here, all I could think about was Gray. I'd just met him and I wouldn't be able to see if it could work. I knew deep down that it probably wouldn't, but I wanted that shot to see if I could be happy with him even for a little while. I was so pissed off that chance was being taken away from me, but I didn't see a way out. Maybe this was all for the best since I knew why they were here. My past had finally caught up to me.

I couldn't fight them all off.

"You can fight them," a voice whispered in my head. It was oddly familiar and it came from deep in my brain. It wasn't my subconscious. My subconscious voice was definitely more feminine and sarcastic than the deeply masculine authority speaking in my brain. This was an outside influence. It had to be whoever was watching. The wolves prowled around, but I stopped and looked at the building behind me. It was the only one with a view to where I stood, the only place from which to watch this complete clusterfuck of a scene play out.

I saw nothing. Not even a shadow.

"Calm down and open your senses," the voice commanded. So familiar. Through the haze of my fear, I tried to place it. It was like trying to remember some character actor you see in movies all the time but never know the name.

"Kelsey, you can do this," the voice said calmly. "They're just wolves. They're not even alphas. You can handle them. You simply have to stop fighting your instincts."

"I don't have any fucking instincts!" I shouted to the faceless idiot in my head. Who gave a damn that they weren't alphas? They outweighed me each by seventy pounds at minimum, and I didn't even have my crappy firearm any more.

But you do, something said and this little voice was all me. *You have those instincts. Don't you remember that day? Your father didn't run away because he was tired of his family. He ran because he was afraid, Kelsey. He was afraid of you. After what you did, can you blame him?*

My hands shook as the wolves moved closer. This was why I hid. This was why I had stayed away from this world for ten years. This was why I ruthlessly controlled my temper with alcohol and sarcasm and pushing away anyone who might challenge me. I avoided confrontation and remained calm at all times to avoid that beast that always seemed so close to the surface. There was nowhere to run. I felt something build in me. It started in my gut and radiated until it filled me.

"Yes, Kelsey," the voice in my head said. I could practically feel his satisfaction. "Don't fight your instincts. Let it flow."

Abruptly I realized I didn't want that son of a bitch in my head and I shoved him out. I felt his surprise as I threw down a wall between us and he couldn't talk to me anymore. I didn't need the peanut gallery telling me how to fight.

I knew how to fight.

I crouched down and let that instinct flow over me like a warm, angry blanket. I'd denied it so long that it was a drug invading my veins. It burned through me and I felt a little high. It felt good to not deny it any longer. I closed my eyes and knew where every wolf was and exactly how he would try to strike me. I knew how I would react. I saw the moves in my head and knew I could and would win. This wasn't the instinct that told me when I wasn't alone or the one that let me know when someone was lying.

This instinct was base and primal. It told me to kill.

The first wolf struck, seeming to know that I was ready to play. I kicked out, using my position to shove up and catch him under his snout. Though I'd never fought a wolf like this, I knew where to hit him and how much pressure to apply. When he went down, I crushed his jaw with a strong, downward kick, feeling it break against my foot. He might be able to heal that, but it would take a while. He wouldn't be any good for the rest of this fight. He was down and that was good enough. I could finish him off later, when it was quiet and I had the time to do it right.

I dodged the two wolves who attacked next. I rolled to the left and hit the side of the brick wall. Something cold hit my hand and I found a nice long piece of rebar someone had conveniently left behind for me. It was slender but strong and would work beautifully if enough pressure was applied. I bounced up and landed on my feet, twirling my newfound weapon as the wolves tried to surround me again. I let them. A neat little circle would make them easier to kill, that dark voice that was all mine said.

When the circle tightened, I swung the metal staff around and brought it down on the wolf in front of me as I kicked out and caught the one behind me. They both went down and I continued the successful move as I turned and took them down two by two, my blood pumping in a satisfying way it never had before. I didn't think. I acted and reacted, my body a tool of the instincts riding me. I brought the rebar down on the last wolf and for good measure, I stood over that big black canine and shoved the rebar through his torso. I did it with a vicious sort of glee, enjoying the sounds and the way the blood spurted out of the wound I caused.

Maybe Gray should be more afraid of me than I was of him. Gray wasn't the only one with pieces of himself he wanted to hide.

That was when I knew something was distinctly wrong with this whole scenario. The four men holding Gray were the problem. They held him down, but their faces were expressionless. It didn't make sense. There should have been something in their eyes; rage, blood lust, anything. Packs are close-knit. I'd killed most of their pack, but they did their jobs with blank looks and bland eyes.

Definitely wrong. I looked down at the wolf at my feet with rebar sticking out of his chest. He lay there and while everything seemed right on the surface, something was off. I pulled the rebar out and it felt weird. It came out too easily. It slid out like a hot knife cutting through butter, but this was flesh. I should have had to use force to get that weapon back out.

There was another roar from the far side of the alley. A second wave had gathered. Another ten wolves moved toward me, but I wasn't buying it.

I held the bloody rebar at my side and relaxed, letting the night air rush across my senses. It told me everything I needed to know. No smell. I couldn't smell blood or wolves or anything but the faintest whiff of whatever aftershave Gray used.

The wolves were big, their claws enormous, and yet they didn't scratch along the concrete. I could only hear Gray breathing and then yelling.

"Kelsey! Look out!"

I opened my eyes and there was a huge brown wolf leaping through the air to attack me. His mouth was open and it was full of snapping, snarling teeth, waiting to rip me apart. His claws were long and they would sink into my flesh as he started to eat me. Or they would if he was real.

The wolf attacked and I walked straight through the illusion.

"Shit." I heard a new voice curse from the back of the alley. Now we were getting somewhere. Whoever was pulling the strings knew I wasn't going to play anymore.

Gray still struggled hard against his illusionary captors. Whoever was pulling this magic was damn good. Gray really believed they were stronger than him. He held his own body in a very awkward position, with all four limbs off the ground because he truly believed there were men restraining him.

"It's an illusion, babe," I said matter of factly. "You can get up."

He fought his captors, still captured by the magic. He stared at the men holding him, pulling his own limbs in a desperate attempt to get away. "What are you talking about? Kelsey, they're going to get you. Please!"

Another two wolves were attacking, but I could see how insubstantial they were. As they bore down, I swiped a hand through them and they disappeared like a wisp of a cloud.

"They're not real, Gray," I said calmly as I sensed something that was. I smiled as I pointed my little staff down to the end of the alley where a man stood. I hadn't seen him before and maybe I wasn't supposed to see him, but he was there all the same. He was a Goth god in leather and denim. His long black hair hung around his face. He really was a lovely man. A bit pale, but he had potential. Note, I said *had* potential because I was about to kill the son of a bitch, though not until he answered a few questions. I raised my voice so Gray could hear me, but I didn't take my eyes off the man behind the curtain. "Nothing has been real since we stepped into this alley. Nothing except him."

The Goth god's mouth turned down and his hands were on his

hips. "How the hell can you see me?"

I shrugged. "Dude, you're just standing there. I'm not sure how you expect me not to see you."

I noted he had black polish on his nails as he pointed back at Gray. "He can't see me."

"Then he needs glasses," I shot back. "Now, whatever the hell you are, we're going to have a talk."

"Not on your life, sister. I think we have what we need." He winked and took off running.

Not happening. Gray continued to plead with me, but I was confident he would be all right. I took off after the witch, or whatever could pull that kind of magic. I wasn't really thinking too much about his species as I chased him up the street. He was fast, really fast, but I turned it on. I didn't question the fact that I'd never run so fast or that I wasn't even breathing hard as I continued my chase. I sidestepped pedestrians without even thinking. If they even realized I was there, I didn't notice. All I saw was that black leather jacket trying to get away from me, and I thrilled at the fact that it was getting closer. I was going to catch him.

He crossed a street and I registered in my peripheral vision that a car was coming. I jumped, landed on the hood and sprang forward, not missing a beat. The Goth boy had caught that move and he stopped, his mouth hanging open. He'd finally realized he could run, but I would catch him in the end.

"What are you?" He stood there in the middle of the sidewalk. He didn't seem to care that people were walking all around him. They didn't see him there. They altered their paths to avoid him, not one meeting his eyes.

"I was about to ask you the same question." I steeled myself. I was going to get answers out of him one way or another. "Who are you and why are you testing me? What do you want from me?"

He shook his head, black hair moving around his pale face. He kept his hands at his sides, but I saw a glint of metal. "Damn it. My master's gonna kill me."

Then he lifted a gun and shot me. I registered the bullet hitting my chest, but it was weird. It didn't go completely in and there was a strange hissing sound. I pulled it out and threw it to the ground as a fog started to develop in my head. Even with the fuzziness, I moved forward. I needed to get my hands around him. He was my prey and he was right there. All I had to do was reach out and grab him.

Another shot and another hiss.

I staggered forward, unwilling to give up.

The Goth guy shook his head as I inched ever closer to him. He shot again and this time I was going down. My knees hit the pavement with a painful thud and then I fell forward, not even able to move my arms to brace the fall. I caught a glimpse of the man who'd tricked me and then shot me as he loomed over me.

"God, I hope I didn't kill you," he muttered and then he was gone.

Somewhere, as the world was getting darker, I registered the pounding of feet racing toward me and Gray's desperate voice. He was calling 911, barking orders for assistance.

A warm hand enfolded mine. It was so nice to feel someone, I thought as I started to float. I tried to squeeze his hand so he could maybe keep me tethered to the ground, but I was already flying.

"Hold on, sweetheart," he said. "Please hold on."

I was already gone.

* * * *

"Three hours, Gray," I heard as I started to come out of the fog. I squeezed my hands into fists to get the circulation back in them. I registered that I was lying on a bed. The world seemed way too bright as I opened my eyes. I had to stop myself from shivering and there was an awful antiseptic smell coating my nose. There was the steady hum of several machines and the sound of Jamie's voice. "She was with you, in your care, for roughly three hours and she's in the hospital."

Yep. I was in hell and hell was a hospital.

"Well, I didn't plan it that way, Jamie." Gray's voice sounded ragged, like he'd been yelling for hours and it was going to give out soon. "Do you think I wanted her hurt? I fought like hell."

"You were supposed to take her to a nice dinner." Even without seeing Jamie, I could tell his teeth were grinding together as he spoke and his fists were at his sides. "You were supposed to treat her like a lady and be gentle with her. Damn it, you promised me you would be good to her. You were not supposed to get her involved in your little war with dear old Dad."

"I don't think it had anything to do with demons," Gray tried to explain.

"I don't give a shit who was involved. My sister is in a coma. What are you going to do about it? If you don't have anyone who can help then I'll call Nathan and have him bring some of his friends in. We'll see what they can do."

"Don't you dare," Gray growled.

It was time to force myself up before my potential boy toy and my eldest brother tried to kill each other. I wasn't going to be allowed to languish in the so not comfy bed. I pulled out the IV in my arm and sat up. I don't like IVs.

"Tell me I'm not in a hospital. Tell me this is some back-alley clinic that will take payment in sexual favors." I couldn't afford a hospital. The world still seemed a little gauzy as Gray was at my side before I could form another sentence. "Why am I in a coma?"

"Call the doctor," Gray ordered as he framed my cheeks with his hands. His handsome face gave me something to focus on and I wondered briefly if I'd finally managed to get to a state of alcohol poisoning. My mouth was so dry, and I couldn't remember a damn thing. How had I gotten to a hospital?

"Where am I?" I forced the words out of my mouth.

Gray ran a hand soothingly across my forehead and then his fingers massaged my scalp. I sighed because it felt so nice. "You're in Parkland, sweetheart. We're in the ER, but they're moving you up to a private room soon. God, Kelsey, I thought you were going to die. The doctor said you might never wake up. You took three doses of Ketamine, one almost in your freaking heart. If I ever find that fucking piece of shit witch, I'm gonna take him apart limb from limb."

"Why would someone shoot me with horse tranquilizer?" I asked after searching my addled brain for what Ketamine was. "Get my neck." It was so sore. My whole body ached and it felt like I'd been hit by a truck.

Gray's hands moved obediently down to my neck and started rubbing the muscles there. I sighed and felt him relax as well as his strong fingers worked from my neck to my bunched up shoulders. "I don't know exactly what was going on. You don't remember? You don't remember the wolves and the man in black with the gun? You chased him and he shot you so he could get away. I would have followed him, but I couldn't leave you. God, I couldn't leave you there."

I was so tired, but I could feel my strength starting to come back. I had the feeling back in my extremities and my mind was starting to get sharp again. "Tell me what happened. Maybe it'll jog my memory."

"What's the last thing you remember clearly, Kels?" Jamie asked, looking at me over Gray's shoulder.

"I remember the restaurant." I let my mind wander over the evening. Thankfully it was coming back into focus. "I ordered too small a steak because I didn't want Gray to think I was a big old pig, but then he told me that you had already told him I was one so I went ahead and I ate a lobster."

"Two lobsters, honey," Gray said, chuckling. "You ate mine, too."

Jamie was not amused with our banter. "After the restaurant. What do you remember after that?"

I sat up and Gray moved in behind me. I should have been annoyed. The man was invading my space, but it was nice to lean against him. It was nice to feel his strong chest against my back and I wondered how I'd gone so damn long without the feeling of warmth surrounding me. It made it easier to concentrate.

Wolves. I'd been surrounded by wolves and there had been a voice in my head that wasn't my own.

"I killed a bunch of werewolves." I could feel the staff in my hand, the weight welcome. I could kill them all with that little piece of metal, I remembered thinking. They'd been stupid to send in these wolves. These wolves weren't even alphas. I shivered at the thoughts running through my head. Someone had been there watching me. He'd talked to me, his voice deep inside my brain. He wanted me to kill the wolves, but the wolves weren't real.

"I remember the magician." The word seemed to fit him. I could see him, though not clearly. He'd had dark eyes and long black hair. He'd worn leather and jeans and black motorcycle boots. He'd been standing at the back of the alley and everything I fought had come straight from his brain. "The magician ran and I chased him. He talked about his master."

"Well, that's the Ketamine talking, all right," a middle-aged, briskly efficient-looking doctor said. Her hair was pulled back in a neat bun. I was reprimanded harshly for pulling out my IV, but then told it wasn't completely unexpected as Ketamine could have hallucinatory effects. It often made people act irrationally. I didn't mention I made it a habit to act irrationally all on my own. The doctor checked my eyes and frowned at Gray, who was on the bed with me, but he ignored her.

The doctor surveyed my chart like she needed to read it twice to believe it. "The surprise is that you're awake at all. You should still be in a coma. If you had asked me, I would have bet against you. I would have said you wouldn't wake up. You're a lucky girl. According to the latest blood tests, you've metabolized the drugs completely. I can't find a reason to keep you. I'd rather you stayed overnight for observation, but all your vitals are perfectly normal. Your eyes are clear. You're breathing fine. I'm not sure, at this point, that we didn't misdiagnose you. Perhaps our toxicology results were wrong. Otherwise, this is a flat out miracle. If you want to go home, I'll let you, but you need someone with you tonight in case there's a delayed reaction."

"I'll take care of her," Gray said.

The doctor shook her head and gave me a sisterly smile. "I thought he'd say that. The lieutenant has been throwing some serious weight around tonight. The whole hospital has been jumping trying to handle your case. There's something about a Texas Ranger flashing his badge and barking orders that commands respect. It didn't hurt that he threatened to call the governor."

The Ranger in question shrugged as though it wasn't a big deal. "I did some work at the governor's mansion a few months back. He owes me. Big time."

The doctor promised to get a nurse started on my discharge paperwork. The minute the doctor left the room, my brother rounded on Gray.

"I'll take her home with me." Jamie stared down at Gray. It was the only time he could look down on the taller man. While Gray was big and had a powerful build, Jamie was lanky with a much smaller but deceptively strong frame. "You're obviously more involved in your father's business than I thought you were. Kelsey, get dressed. I'll have Nathan pick up your car."

"They weren't coming after Gray," I insisted, rolling my eyes at Jamie's father act. He didn't do it often, but there were times he used the six years between us as a blunt object with which to beat me about the head and shoulders.

Jamie crossed his arms over his chest as Gray chose to smartly withdraw. The Ranger moved from behind me and started gathering everything I would need to get out of here.

"And how would you know that, Kelsey Jean Atwood?" Jamie asked. "You were hit by some asshole with three, count them, three veterinary doses of Ketamine. Did you note I said veterinary doses? There was so much of that shit in your system you should be dead. There was no mistake in the tox reports. He shot you with enough of that stuff to kill a horse, much less a hundred and twenty pound woman. What the hell have you done that would constitute someone wanting revenge like that?"

"I'm annoying." A thought occurred to me. "Maybe I ran out on a bar tab."

Jamie wasn't in the mood. "Damn it, Kelsey. Don't you joke about this."

"Fine," I said with a sigh. "But it wasn't about Gray. It was about me. Someone was testing me. There was this voice in my head. He was telling me to relax and let my instincts take over. He seemed to think I could do all these fighting things. I'm not explaining this well."

"I don't know about the voice in your head, sweetheart." Gray brought over my jeans, T-shirt, and bra. God, I wondered who had taken off my bra. Gray set the clothes down on the bed. "But you could fight. She was amazing, Jamie. She moved like I've never seen a human move before. You said she was a badass, but I didn't believe you until I saw her fight."

"Maybe you got hit with that shit, too, Gray," Jamie said, disbelief evident in his posture. "My sister doesn't fight."

"She sure as hell does," Gray replied with admiration. "If tonight was any indication, she's had a lot of training. You said it yourself. She has excellent instincts. They were on full display."

Jamie's green eyes lit with frustration. "I meant she's a badass investigator. She has great instincts when it comes to sizing people up and finding things. My sister isn't some street fighter. She has absolutely no training. Our father didn't train Kelsey the way he did me and Nate. He mostly ignored her except when he needed bait." Jamie's face was savage and I heard Gray's startled hiss behind me.

His hand came up on my shoulders as Jamie continued his tirade. "I swear to god, if I find out you're using my sister that way I'll send you to the Hell plane myself, do you understand?"

I sat up straight and was surprised to find I was very steady. Any weakness was gone. "Back off, Jamie. He isn't using me. He tried to protect me. He tried to get me to run and leave him alone with a pack of hungry wolves. He was ready to do whatever it took so I got out of there. I don't know exactly what happened in that alley, but I know it was about me and I trust Gray to watch my back. I'm going home with him and you have to deal with it."

Gray's satisfaction was practically tactile as he put a protective arm around my shoulders. "I'll take care of her, Jamie. I promised you that. I mean to keep that promise."

"You know what he is?" Jamie asked shortly. He obviously didn't want to go into it. I could tell it was a hard subject for him but he needed to make sure I was up to date.

"He told me," I replied.

Jamie shook his head and smoothed back his fashionably shaggy hair. "All right. You're an adult. If you know what you're getting into, I'll back off." He walked over and kissed me on the forehead. "I love you, little sister. You call me if he steps out of line." He strode to the door. "And Kels, I'm neglecting to mention this incident to Nate since it involved actual drugs. I don't want to know where his paranoid brain would go. See that you keep your mouth shut."

I nodded because I didn't want to think about Nathan riding herd on me. That would be embarrassing. The door closed and I was alone with Gray and wearing nothing but a thin hospital nightgown and a pair of zebra striped cotton underwear.

Gray sat down on the bed beside me. "Are you really feeling all right? You can stay here tonight if you feel the slightest bit weak. I'll stay with you."

"No way." I got to my feet. I wanted to be ready when the nurse had the paperwork done. "I'm sure this place charges by the hour and I don't have insurance. I need to run before they figure that out."

I had my clothes in my hands when Gray pulled me back. "I already took care of the bill, Kelsey. You don't have to worry about it."

His eyes registered surprise so I was pretty sure my face was a decent reflection of the rage I felt at that statement. "I can handle my own bills."

"Okay," he allowed, calmly proving he wanted to live. "I know you can but…" His brain was working a mile a minute and I watched as he selected and discarded several scenarios in which I would reasonably accept his financial assistance. I waited patiently and a pleased smile finally came over his face. "It's a work related expense. You've been on the clock since I picked you up earlier tonight. Don't you normally bill your clients for stuff like this?"

Smooth bastard. I had to give it to him. He was smart. "Fine. But if we're partners, I need to know everything." My smile was sweet since it felt a little like victory.

Gray was intelligent enough to know when he'd lost. "I'll go over everything with you in the morning. Now, let me help you get dressed."

I laughed as I opened the bathroom door. "Not on your life, mister."

His blue eyes were hot as he looked at me and he had the confidence of a man who was sure of the woman he was with. "I'll just see it later, sweetheart. I mean to have you naked soon."

"Good luck with that." Even after everything that had happened, I could feel the heat building between us. It scared me more than the magician.

He invaded my space, his big hands on my waist, and he hauled me close. His lips hovered above mine. "Luck has nothing to do with it."

He lowered his head and there was nothing of the previous gentleness in his kiss. He plundered. His tongue mated with mine, showing me exactly what he wanted our private parts to be doing later on tonight. He was rapacious. He was sultry. He was very persuasive.

When he finally let me go, I was ready to do him on the hospital bed and damn any nurse who walked in for the show. No man I'd ever met could get me as hot as fast as Grayson Sloane could. My knees were weak and it had nothing to do with my previous tangle with horse sedatives.

"Go get dressed, sweetheart," Gray said, amused at the look on my face. "I've decide to wait until I can do something about your nudity. Otherwise, it's too damn tempting."

I let out a deep breath and cleared my head. I walked into the bathroom and started to untie the gown. I needed to get this relationship back to somewhere safe.

"So, Sloane," I said through the door. I hooked my bra and went to work on the jeans. "Why have you been so scared to bring me into this case? Are you afraid I'll screw it up?"

"I'm not afraid of you. I believe Jamie when he says you're good."

"I'm damn good." I smoothed the T-shirt down. I wished I'd brought in my bag so I could gloss up. I settled for finger combing my hair. "So what's the trouble?"

"It isn't you." His face was grim as I opened the door between us, and I knew I was finally getting somewhere with him. "I don't know many men who would want the woman they love involved in a case with Jack the Ripper."

Chapter Seven

I woke up alone in the middle of Gray's enormous four-poster bed, the light of day forcing its way through cracks in the curtains and sending filmy light through the room.

The night before came back to me in a totally embarrassing flash.

I'd fallen asleep in the cab of Gray's big black pickup. The hum of the road had sort of lulled me to sleep after all the stress of the night. I vaguely remembered Gray lifting me from the cab and carrying me inside his house. I snuggled against his warm body and hadn't bothered to try to hold on. I'd been so tired I'd woken, saw it was Gray carrying me, and went back to sleep.

I sat up in bed and shook my head at the thought of it. I was a loner. I liked being alone. Except that now I had to accept the fact that it wasn't preference that kept me alone. It was fear and habit. I'd pulled back so harshly after that night when I was sixteen that I'd convinced myself I didn't need anything from a man but a quick, occasional lay. I trusted Gray on a fundamental level and I didn't really know him.

I had to consider something I never had before. Maybe this was what they meant by finding "the one." Maybe there actually was a "one." I liked Gray. I really liked Gray—like super liked, maybe-one-day-would-think-about-the-other-four-letter-L-word like.

I grinned goofily and then forced the dippy smile off my face. Liv would be beside herself at the thought of me even thinking the words true and love in the same sentence. Which I wasn't, but even thinking I liked a guy was kind of a big freaking deal.

Of course my potential soul mate wasn't here now. I touched the indentation in the bed where his body had lain against mine. I didn't remember it, but I instinctively knew it was true. Gray would have cuddled me, pulling me into his arms. He might have been somewhat happy I was unconscious and unable to fight him, but I was going to prove less stubborn than he imagined. The night before had been enough to make me rethink the whole playing hard to get thing. Life was really freaking short and you never know when some weird magician/witch is going to try to kill you by running some crazy test that ends with horse tranqs.

Oh, I wasn't saying anything yet about love or commitment. I was still too wary to put myself out there like that, but I hadn't felt this way about anyone before and it felt good. If Gray really wanted a partner, I was willing to give it all a try. Liv was right. It was far past time to move forward. What had Dan said to me? He told me he'd embraced possibilities and he'd seemed ridiculously happy to have done so. Was I really so less deserving? Stretched out in the warmth of Gray's bed, smelling the glorious evidence of bacon frying, I had to wonder if I didn't deserve a little happiness.

I didn't bother with my clothes from the night before. At some point in time, Gray had undressed me and slipped one of his T-shirts over my head. It hung to my knees and covered everything I needed it to. More than that, it was comfy and I liked being comfy. I got out of bed and let my bare feet find the hardwood floors. I wandered into the bathroom. Gray hadn't been kidding about his family's money. Most of my house could fit in his bathroom, and I was pretty sure he hadn't been forced to buy his sinks and faucets when Lowe's had a sale. And that tub…I was already thinking about what we could do in that tub. It was built for two or more.

I cleaned up and then went looking for Gray. I crept almost silently through the house that seemed far too big for one person. It was elegantly decorated, but it didn't seem much like Gray. It had been done in tasteful neutrals and I figured a designer had furnished this place.

Except for the den. I walked through the small room that was obviously used for entertainment and I smiled. Everything else about the house was designed with a nod to exquisite taste, but this room was all about comfort. There was a large screen TV that dominated the room and a big leather couch with a La-Z-Boy. I could see Gray there yelling at a Cowboys game on a Sunday afternoon, beer in one hand.

"I'm in the kitchen, sweetheart," I heard him yell across the house.

"Okay," I said more to myself than him because he shouldn't have been able to hear me. Demonic hearing is pretty sharp. I shrugged and followed the sound of his voice.

The kitchen was as well designed as the rest of the house. The cabinets were a deep rich cherry and the countertops were marble. Gray worked efficiently over a top-of-the-line stove. Pancakes were already stacked neatly on the small breakfast table. There was a carafe of orange juice and two place settings. It was intimate and I realized I had zero experience with relationships. I had never in my twenty-six years had breakfast with a man. I hadn't really slept with one either, not in the sleeping close, arms wrapped around each other sense. *What the hell was I doing here?* I asked myself with a sense of panic.

"Drink some coffee," Gray ordered with a knowing frown. "It's only breakfast. It's not an engagement ring."

But that would come if Gray had his way. He thought we would get married and fulfill his little psychic flash. I couldn't see myself in a fluffy white dress walking down the aisle of a church.

Gray laughed and I saw the utter ridiculousness of my panic. I didn't care what his vision said. I had control of whether or not I got married. This was just breakfast and I was freaking hungry. I took a drink of coffee and forced myself to relax. "Sorry. I've never done the whole breakfast thing with a man before."

"Of course you have," Gray pointed out in his calm Texas drawl. "We had breakfast yesterday."

I shook my head and took a seat on one of the barstools so I could talk to him as he cracked open a couple of eggs. "That was different. My brothers were there and I was recovering."

"Not so different. Your brothers are blissfully absent today, but you're still recovering. How do you feel this morning?"

"Surprisingly good." I didn't seem to have any ill effects from the drugs that Goth asshole had pumped into me. "How are you?"

"Beyond my heinous sexual frustration, I'm fine," he said with a wink.

"Yeah, sorry about that." It probably didn't bode well for the relationship that I fell asleep on our first night together.

Gray reached across the bar to tenderly brush the hair out of my face. "You needed rest more than me last night. I'm glad you could sleep. I was happy you were willing to come home with me. After I failed you with the wolves, I thought you might want to go home with your brother."

"He doesn't cook like you do." Jamie microwaved everything.

"Well, breakfast is about the limit of my talents," Gray admitted. "Get used to bacon and eggs."

"And you didn't fail me. You couldn't see through the illusion. I couldn't for a while. Whoever that witch was he was damn good."

Gray didn't seem to agree with me, but he moved on. "I already put out some feelers. I'll figure out who the fucker is. I didn't get a great look at him. He was running away when I made it to the scene. Do you remember what he looked like? I could bring in a sketch artist."

I tried. I really did, but all I could get was black hair and a pale face. I could remember a lot about that night. I remembered the wolves and the men who chased me back into the alley, but when I tried to picture his face, my mind went a little fuzzy. It was likely one of his powers. "I think his eyes were dark. Can we ask some of your underworld contacts? A guy with talent like that wouldn't go unnoticed."

Gray sighed as he plated the rest of the food and I followed him to the table. He held the chair out for me and I sat. "We should talk about that, actually. I don't have a lot of contacts. I'm not…well liked."

I frowned as I stabbed one pancake and then another, dragging them onto my plate. "Why? Because you're half demon? That seems a little hypocritical. You can't help who your father is."

He laughed, but it was hollow. "No, I think my father is the least of my worries in this case. I'm law enforcement."

I dug into the excellent pancakes. "So? The king is supposedly looking for his own law enforcement. Shouldn't you all work together?"

Gray laughed at my naiveté. "It can be hard for supes to function in the real world. An awful lot of them are criminals. Don't get me wrong. There are supes in the police department, of course. I'm just different. I don't discriminate. If a supe steps out of line, I don't send him to the Council for a slap on the wrist. I bring them to trial if I can and I put them down if I have to."

That sounded reasonable to me. "And the king doesn't think that supes should have to follow the laws of the regular world?"

"No, he doesn't. He believes supes should rule themselves and the only real law is to stay hidden. Donovan and I have had a few run-ins. The last was when I lawfully arrested a group of wolves for running an illegal gambling den. He used his influence to get them out on bail and then, of course, they disappeared. I had linked that group to drug running, but they were gone before I could prove anything."

I was a little outraged at the thought. "Maybe this Donovan person was involved."

"I doubt that," Gray said evenly. "He was a thief at one time, but he's been careful to stay away from drugs. More than likely he handled the situation himself, but I don't have any proof. So you can see it can be hard for me to function sometimes. They don't exactly want to talk to me. I've been getting stonewalled on this case."

I perked up because it was morning and he had to talk to me. "I would expect that they would want to help you figure out who's killing their daughters. Maybe they'd also like to know who's prostituting their daughters out."

"Figured that out, did you?" Gray sat back in his chair. "I can tell you who's doing that, sweetheart, but I doubt he's involved in the deaths. He's an asshole of epic proportions, but he's hardly a killer. Well, not the serial kind. I've heard stories of what happens when you cross him, but then women never cross him."

"Why?"

"He's a fertility god, so believe me when I say he has a way with women. He runs a club downtown. Everyone in the supernatural world goes there."

"If you don't think he's involved in the murders, why bother with him?" I reached for another pancake. Luckily Gray seemed to have made enough for a small army.

"I think that club of his gets us access to information. It's kind of the hub of that particular world," the Ranger said seriously. "There's only one problem. I can't get in."

"Because you're law enforcement?"

"That and I might have tried raiding the club about a year ago," Gray explained with a sigh. "I also might have actually arrested the asshole before I had concrete evidence on him. He pushed me to it. Dev Quinn is such a prick. He has a mouth on him that would make a saint crazy. I have no idea how he's still alive. Someone should have shot him for mouthing off a long time ago."

I kept my amusement to myself since this seemed to be a serious subject for Gray. I was kind of interested in meeting anyone who made Gray that crazy. "So he's banned you from the club."

"Yes, he has." Gray's expression turned ruthless. He obviously had a plan. "But there's a party there tonight. If you have an invite you don't have to stand in line."

It was a good plan and I could only think of one small flaw. "And we're getting invited how?"

Gray's kissable lips turned up in a smile worthy of the Cheshire cat. "Well, this is where you come in."

* * * *

Gray walked out of the shower and I admired the work that must have gone into that chest. I had something to tell him, but I just sort of stared and maybe drooled a little. The cell phone in my hand hung limply at my side as I ogled him. He was one rock-hard slab of man.

He wore a towel wrapped low on his hips. The stark white contrasted the tan of his skin and nothing else. His shoulders seemed even broader without the trappings of clothes and it got better from there. Gray had a six-pack and he was cut all over. The water clung to his skin, defining the muscles of his body. A large tattoo covered the left side of his chest. At the center lay an elaborate dragon surrounded by what appeared to be flames and odd-looking symbols. It was strangely beautiful and I had to force my eyes away from it. He had a smaller towel over his head as he strode out of the bathroom and he was rubbing his hair dry when he finally noticed me enjoying the show.

A slow smile curled over his sensual mouth. "I guess I can't complain. Turnabout is fair play, darlin'."

He'd seen me in nothing but a towel, though I seriously doubted I was as impressive a specimen as he was. I was aware of how alone we were and how close we were to that big bed we'd slept in last night. It wouldn't take much to let my hands find his tapered waist and pull the towel off. I could push him down on the bed and do what I'd wanted to do from the moment I'd seen his blue eyes. I could strip down and it wouldn't take long before I was ready to ride him. So why wasn't I doing that? Why was I standing there, breathless and the tiniest bit afraid? When did I get to be so damn shy?

"Liv says okay." I blurted out what I'd come in here to tell him in the first place.

Gray gave his head one last rub and then tossed the smaller towel back into the bathroom. "She's got the invite?"

I nodded, wishing it were that easy for me to do my hair. Two minutes of rubbing and Gray's hair was dry. I had to dry my hair for an hour or it frizzed, which was why I usually walked around with frizzy hair. The only reason I didn't cut it was because I worried it was the only thing about me that was pretty and feminine. It was really lovely when I paid it proper attention. Now it was in its normal ponytail. I felt plain next to Gray's god-like attractiveness.

"Yeah. She was invited. Apparently this person is in her coven. It's her birthday so they have some sort of VIP room reserved. Liv said it would be easy to get you in because the invite is for her and Scott, but it's ninety-nine cent wing night at Kirby's Hot Wings so he can't go."

That caught Gray off guard. "Seriously? His girlfriend's got a big party to go to and he's going to sit in a bar and eat hot wings?"

I nodded. "It's his way. I'm sure Alan will be sitting beside him, drinking cheap beer and commenting on the waitress's ass. Alan's a shifter and his best friend. I think secretly they're in love, but afraid of deciding who gets to pitch and who gets to catch."

Gray's hands were on his lean hips as he radiated outrage. "You should know that won't be happening with us. I'm sure as hell not about to let my woman waltz off to some fancy party looking hot as hell while I stare at some eighteen-year-old's ass. If you're going to a party where a bunch of men are going to be drooling all over you, I'll be beside you ready to kick the ass of the first one who does more than look."

I laughed, but there wasn't a whole lot of humor behind it. "You'll have a long time waiting for a fight then, Gray. I'm afraid I'm not a fancy-party kind of girl. I don't know what line of bullshit Jamie's been feeding you, but I don't date much and the truth is I haven't had to turn many men down. I don't get asked out. Any sex I've had in the last couple of years, and there hasn't been much of it, has been men I picked up in bars and trust me, they weren't choosy. I'm not the girl who guys fight over."

Gray moved in close, and I could smell the soap on his skin. His hands cupped my shoulders, warming me. "You would be surprised how many men want you. They're just intimidated. You're a little prickly, but I see through it. And god, Kelsey, don't you dare even think I don't want you."

He pulled me close and I could feel how much he wanted me. His erection pressed against my belly. It seemed to be built along the same lines as the rest of him—extra large. Heat flashed through my system, sizzling along my skin. My hands went around his back, feeling the softness of his skin in contrast to the thick-corded muscles there.

I breathed in his scent, letting it fill my little world. He smelled like soap and aftershave and some unique spice that was Gray. I'd never let myself revel in the closeness of another human body. Even with my brothers, our affection was more along the lines of punching each other in the arm than hugs. I was pierced by the sweetness of another warm body against mine, a strong hand running along the curve of my spine. I wanted him so much in that moment, but not for just sex. I wanted to lose myself in his care. I wanted to put my head against his chest and hear his heartbeat, let my own beat in time with his. I longed for him to tell me again that he loved me.

I wanted to believe it so much that it scared me.

I pulled away and Gray sighed.

He let me go, though I could tell he wanted to push the issue. "Go on, Kelsey. I need to get dressed and make a few calls. Why don't you wait for me in the den? I won't be long and then we can go over what we're looking for tonight."

I was out of the room before he'd finished the last sentence. I hated my cowardice and wondered what it would cost me this time, but Gray seemed like a big old fire I was close to getting really burned by. I forced my heart to stop racing as I made my way to the den. I had to relax around the man and decide what the hell I wanted. He was going to start thinking my name was synonymous with cold shower if I didn't stop running away or falling asleep every time he got a hard-on.

My mouth was still dry, the only lingering effects from the night before, so I walked through the den and into the kitchen. I opened the door to the stainless steel fridge and pulled out a bottle of water. Gray's fridge was well stocked. It was totally different than mine, which usually only held days-old take-out containers and beer. Gray was acquainted with grocery stores.

"Is there anything I can help you with, ma'am?" a soft voice asked, and I nearly dropped the water as I turned. I needed to get my head out of my ass because I was tired of getting snuck up on.

The small man who stood before me was at least an inch shorter than me and probably weighed ten pounds less. He was dressed smartly in a severe black suit and dark silk tie and appeared to be a courtly gentleman of around sixty years.

But there was something wrong with him. Something about him that made me look twice and then again.

He continued speaking as I tried to put my finger on it. "I must say I am surprised to see a female here. The master usually stays with his female…dates rather than bringing them back to his home. I should warn you, my master rarely stays more than one night with any female. If you'll leave your address on the bar, I will send you the requisite bouquet to thank you for your sexual services."

I laughed outright at that because it was so awkward. I knew I was supposed to be horribly embarrassed and outraged at the thought, but it struck me as funny. What can I say? I have an awfully dark sense of humor. It was obvious that the servant didn't approve of Gray's sexual conquests, so I had to needle him a little. It was all a part of my perverse personality.

"Don't worry about the flowers. I already got the cash, buddy. Your boss was generous with the tip." I gave the shocked servant a saucy little wink.

"My master has brought a prostitute back to his home? This is the home where he is supposed to one day bring my mistress. How dare he?" The little man drew himself to his full height, and as he turned I caught the slightest glimpse of red eyes before they flashed back to dull brown. "I shall speak to Master Grayson immediately.

You should prepare to leave. Your services will no longer be needed."

"You're a demon." Now that I really looked at him, I could see the faintest outline of haze around his body, like the lines were softer where his flesh met his clothes. "Are you wearing a glamour?"

He turned back to me, his eyes flaring and a little look of wonder coming onto his face. "You're the Hunter."

I think I was happier when he thought I was a hooker. Hookers make people happy. "I'm not a hunter. I don't do that."

The older man's smile was sly. "That isn't what I meant, miss. Hunter is what you are not what you do. I apologize sincerely for mistaking you for less. I am Syl. It is my honor to welcome you into my master's home. If you do not mind, I will dispense with the glamour. I prefer my own skin, though if it offends you I will, of course, suffer through."

His face was sour, as though he expected me to choose whichever option caused him the most discomfort. I shrugged and opened the bottle of water. I was glad we weren't going to talk about my father's profession. "Do what you like. It won't bother me."

"And a kind mistress at that," the demon purred and the old man was gone, replaced by a red-skinned demon with tiny horns. The dimensions of the demon didn't change. He was still shorter than me and his clothes were exactly the same except for the shoes. Goat-like feet poked out from his trousers.

"See that's freaky." I took a long drink.

A single shoulder came up in a gesture that told me he'd heard it all before. "It is normal where I come from. Your pale skin seems a little…freaky to me."

"I can live with that," I said, slowly digesting the fact that my almost lover had a demonic housekeeper. "So you work for Gray?"

"I do, indeed." He went about putting the kitchen to rights, gathering dishes and wiping down countertops. He poured a glass of orange juice and set it in front of me. "I have been Master Gray's familiar since his birth. I was a gift from his father. Here, drink this. It's freshly squeezed. It has to be better than bland water. Or would you prefer coffee? I can make anything you like."

I took the drink because I wanted to get back to the topic at hand.

"His familiar? Like a witch's familiar?" I asked, confused by the terminology. I ignored the fact that he'd been given a person...bipedal humanoid as a gift for his birthday. My father had been concerned with werewolves. I knew next to nothing about demons.

The orange juice was sweet, though it had the slightest hint of peppermint. Interesting. I took another drink, the juice cool on my tongue.

"In a sense." Syl took off his suit coat and rolled up his sleeves with practiced grace, further exposing inches of red skin. "I could be the focal point for his talents if only he could be persuaded to use them. He prefers to pretend they do not exist, so they flash on him at the oddest times."

I slid onto the barstool and watched the little demon toil. He seemed perfectly comfortable talking to me now that he had ascertained I wasn't a working girl. He was efficient and quick, and within minutes I couldn't tell that Gray had cooked breakfast at all. "Are you talking about his prophecy powers?"

His red eyes widened and a big grin came across his face, showing off his small, curved fangs. "He has already told you of his gifts? I thought he would play it more coyly. This is exciting. And you accept his parentage? Many would not."

I didn't like it. It was creepy to think that Gray had a father working his mojo on the Hell plane, but then I wasn't exactly blessed in the fatherhood department. I couldn't expect Gray to overlook a crappy dad on my side if I wasn't willing to do the same for him. "We don't get to pick our parents."

"No, we do not," Syl agreed. "I suspect my master would have selected a different sire had he been given the choice. He rarely speaks with his father. The master really only acknowledges the Hell Lord when he...forces the issue."

"I probably don't want to know how a Hell Lord forces the issue." Jamie had said something about Gray being at war with his father.

Syl shook his head sharply. "No, miss, you do not. It would be easier on my master if he simply took the call in the first place. He is a stubborn boy. Perhaps he is coming around though. We all learn in the end."

"What are you doing here, Syl?" Gray's harsh question broke the quiet little repartee Syl and I had established. Gray walked in from the den and he'd changed into jeans and a black T-shirt. His eyes were on Syl, his whole face tense. "I told you to stay away today. I called you last night."

The demon dropped his head and submissively bowed. "I apologize, my lord. I did not check my voice mail. I was merely attempting to clean the kitchen and to see if there was any way possible I could help the lovely female you brought home to mate with last night."

I choked on my drink as the laughter bubbled up, but Gray didn't see the comedy.

"You will keep your mouth shut about her, Syl," Gray ordered, his face hard as granite as he bore down on the servant. "Now go. You can stay in the guesthouse or...wherever. I don't care, but I don't want you around her, do you understand? You tell the rest of them to stay away from her, too."

The demon refused to look Gray in the eyes as he slid by and slunk toward the door leading to the patio. There was a pool in the backyard and a small structure that must be the guesthouse Gray was talking about.

Syl stopped at the door, though he didn't turn around. "I apologize if I offended you with my presence, miss."

"I wasn't upset at all." I felt sorry for the little guy. He slunk away quietly and I turned to Gray.

"Don't, Kelsey," Gray said immediately. "Don't you let him in an inch. That's what they do. He's a demon, a full blood."

"He seemed perfectly nice." I finished off my juice. He made a mean fresh-squeezed juice, but Gray didn't seem to want to hear praise for his staff.

"That's how they trap you. Do you think they'd ever get anyone to sign a contract if they came at you with fangs bared? They come off as charming and quirky and then, when you think they couldn't possibly be so bad, that's when they get you."

I was a little offended that he seemed to think I couldn't handle one small demon. He'd been the one who couldn't see through an illusion. I'd known right away there was something wrong with Syl. He hadn't fooled me. "I'll try not to let him get me, then. He wasn't trying to get me to sign a contract, Gray. He was offended at the thought that you brought a hooker back to the place where you should only enjoy marital bliss."

I was rewarded with Gray's mouth hanging open in complete shock. He stared at me for a moment before giving in to the urge and laughing until the force of it shook his whole body.

"He thought you were a hooker?" Gray managed to wheeze. "Why the hell would he think you were a hooker? I've never been to a hooker in my life."

"He did seem surprised." I had to fess up. "I might have mentioned you were a great tipper." Gray shook his head and I felt compelled to explain. "He told me you never spent more than one night with any female."

"That's bullshit, Kelsey," Gray said, sitting on the barstool beside me. "I've had girlfriends before. They were never serious, but then I'm only thirty and I've been looking for you for the last several years, so I think I can be forgiven for not settling down." He reached out and grabbed my hand. "I'm sorry, sweetheart. Syl…he's a constant reminder of a life I've tried to leave behind. I've tried to get rid of him on many occasions. When I fire him and refuse to let him work he causes trouble. Lots of trouble. It's better that I let him do a little work and ignore him for the most part."

"You said something about the rest of them?" I asked, remembering that he'd told Syl to tell the rest of them to stay away from me. I wondered if there was an army of neat-freak demons waiting to dust Gray's bookshelves.

His thumb rubbed across my palm as though he deeply enjoyed the contact. "My father is insistent. He sends messengers and servants. They're really spies. He tries to keep tabs on me. He'll know about you. Syl tells him everything. I would have preferred to keep you off his radar."

I laced my fingers with his. "Gray, I don't think that's going to be possible unless you plan on a short or very private relationship. Were you planning on keeping me hidden?"

"No, I'm not. I've already announced my intentions to your brother. I don't intend to hide them. We'll deal with my father." He sighed and smiled. "Now, how about I turn your attention away from my truly awful family with something even more awful?"

"If you're ready to explain the case to me, then I'm beyond ready to listen," I said, steeling myself to get down to work.

Gray gracefully stepped down from the barstool and helped me down as well. "All right, but don't forget I warned you. I would rather keep you out of this, but...damn it, I need your help. I'm at a loss. I've never dealt with anything like this."

I let him lead me to a small room behind the kitchen just before the door to the garage. He opened it and I walked into his nightmare. The room was an elegant, masculine office with a big desk, computer, printer, all the things one would expect from a well-organized investigator. There was a large white board covered with notes and photos. My eyes went straight there, past the carefully written notations and the neatly drawn lines and right to the photos.

"Oh my god." I took a deep breath and thanked the universe for my formidably strong stomach. I'd expected to see postmortem photographs, but this was something completely different. There's something distant about the pictures crime scene investigators take, as though the person taking the photo can step back and make the scene emotionless, logical.

If that was true, then the person taking these photos wanted to show the true horror of death.

"These weren't taken by the police."

"No. He's been sending them to me for a month." Gray stood behind me and it was hard for me not to reach back for his hand.

The pictures were black and white and I was grateful for it. I don't think I could have stood it if they were in color. Even without the color, I could almost feel the rage from the photos. Rage and useless, meaningless death.

I forced myself to stare at the first one. It took a moment to truly understand that what I was looking at used to be a female. The body was torn and cut, but it wasn't an animal attack. This was a focused form of torture. I noticed that her hands were over her head, wrists shackled together.

"He uses silver," I said, trying to banish the tears that threatened. I needed to be cold and professional. I didn't need to think about the indignity these women had been put through. I didn't need to feel the pain and torture someone had inflicted on them. I needed to see what was there. I needed to look at it without emotion.

"Yes," Gray replied quietly. "He uses silver, either cuffs or chains or rope, to hold them down. His victims, so far, have been either wolves or shifters. He has to hold them down in some fashion. These aren't women who would go down without a fight."

"How many?" I moved to the next, forcing myself to see, really see each photograph.

"Five victims so far. I've only managed to ID the second one." He pointed to a series of photos on the far right side of the office. "Her name is Laura Nesson. She's a wolf from the Fort Worth pack. It's smaller than Dallas, but not insubstantial. The only reason I managed to ID her is from an arrest record. She was arrested for DUI two years ago and has a juvenile rap sheet a mile long."

I moved down the line, taking in what I could of the women's faces. And then my heart fell. I'd seen the last face. She'd been smiling, her whole life ahead of her in the photo I'd seen. I was going to have to tell Helen Taylor that her precious daughter was gone. She would have to survive another unthinkable loss. Tears blurred the picture before me, but I forced myself to point. "I can ID that one. Her name is Joanne Taylor. She's my missing person."

Her pretty blonde hair was matted with blood and she was completely naked. She'd been made as vulnerable as a female could be, all of her intelligence and hard work, all of her love meaningless against one man's hatred. Her torso had been sliced open with surgical precision and it was obvious she'd had organs removed.

I couldn't help it. I sank down to the floor and I cried. All I could see when I looked at that wall was Joanne Taylor's smiling face. She was young and ripe and ready for the world and the world had eaten her up. She was her mother's darling and I was the one who had to tell her mother she was gone forever because she'd lost her fucking scholarship. Such a simple thing. Twenty thousand dollars shouldn't be the price of a life, but I knew deep down many were cheaper even than Joanne's.

Gray knelt beside me, his arms enveloping me. I was surrounded by his warmth and sank into the comfort of it. "I'm so sorry, sweetheart," he whispered as he rocked me gently. "I wasn't sure it was her, but I thought it might be. Is this your first murder case?"

I let him hold me. If he'd apologized for showing me this, I would have pushed him away. I would have stood up and been the professional I knew I should be, but Gray was smarter than that. He let me cry and he didn't make me feel stupid for doing it. After a long while, I nodded as an answer to his question.

"It's hard," he said. I looked into his face and saw a wealth of compassion there. "Your first murder is always hard, especially when it didn't start as a murder case. You thought you could find her and be the hero and put a family back together, and now you have to tell a mother that her baby is dead. It's horrible. I won't lie to you. I'll come with you, love. I'll help you talk to her, but I'm going to ask you to give me until tomorrow. This is the worst of the worst, honey. This is a serial case and it sucks, but you can help me. You figured out in twenty-four hours what it took me weeks to get. I took forever to piece together that the girls were working at that vampire club. I need you. I need you to look at all the evidence and tell me what I'm missing. I need you to go into Ether with me tonight and get people talking. They don't want to talk to me, but I think they'll talk to you."

I nodded, unsure why he thought people would talk to me, but I was willing to try. I was willing to do anything to figure out who this asswipe was. I sniffled and let Gray help me up. He handed me a tissue as I forced myself to look at the pictures again. Gray had grouped them by victim and timeline. I noticed that beside the photos there were a few letters taped to the board. I read the first one, noting the bad handwriting.

Dear Boss, allow me to introduce myself again. I am an artist who has not worked in years. I give you this, my work. I don't like whores, as I've stated before, and the town is full of them. I'll rip 'em 'til they're gone. Catch me if you can. No one has yet.

JTR

"He's pretending to be Jack the Ripper." I'd read enough and seen enough movies to recognize the drama.

"Oh, yes, he seems obsessed with the Ripper," Gray replied seriously. "He has good intell though. I'm the only one who received the letters. The press hasn't been informed of anything. I have to believe this guy's a supe or he wouldn't know to send his 'art' to me."

"Have you found any bodies?"

"I figured out that the first three were killed in a warehouse in south Dallas." He pointed to one of the pictures. "See, he got part of a logo in the shot. It took me a couple of days, but I tracked down the warehouse. It was abandoned but I found some silver chains and some blankets. He was using it as his workshop. I staked it out, but he didn't come back, and I got that letter a day later."

> *Boss, clever, clever but I see you. You can't catch me cuz my work is powerful good for the world. I'll move my studio but I won't stop 'til you nab me. I enjoyed this last one very much. She went down nice and just cried a lot. I like it when they know it's time to go. I've moved all the bodies to a proper location, though they'll be soup by the time you find them...if you find them.*
>
> *JTR*

"You think he's a hunter," I said quietly because I was thinking the same thing.

Gray didn't take his eyes off the wall. I knew he'd memorized the pictures. He would carry them around with him and the vision might never go away. "The thought has crossed my mind. I also wondered if it wasn't a vampire."

"Why waste the blood?" It was obvious the women hadn't been drained before he sliced them up. Vampires tended to be practical creatures. Of course, if he was looking for attention then it would have been a lot easier to get it by killing human prostitutes. He could dump the bodies and get all the press he wanted. If a hunter was trying to expose the underworld, he would dump the bodies where they would be found before they disintegrated. "It's a supe, not a hunter. This person respects the rules in one fashion. He's making sure humans aren't involved. He hides the bodies somewhere they will be allowed to disintegrate and he's only pulled you in. You're the legal authority. Are we sure he hasn't contacted anyone in the Council?"

"No," Gray replied. "That's one of the things I'd like to ascertain tonight. I can't get into the vampire club itself. There's no way to sneak in. I tried. It didn't go well. These girls tend to start their night at Ether and then move on to the vampire club. We get in with Liv's help and try to figure out who our other three victims are." Gray went to a large file cabinet. He pulled out a handful of pictures. They were close-ups of the faces in the killer's "art." Gray had tried to make them as normal as possible, but I'd seen the complete picture and I was still disturbed.

"And we look for a vampire named Alexander," I said. "He was one of Joanne's regulars."

Gray nodded and pulled me against his chest. I was getting used to his spontaneous affection. I think that was the point of it. Instead of being shy, I let my arms go around his waist to enjoy the feel of him. Instead of holding myself back, I let my head rest against his chest. I was being drugged into trusting him and I seemed helpless against it. His hand rubbed up and down my back.

"I'll look through my files and see what I have," he said. "You need to get ready for the party. I called Liv myself and she'll be over here in an hour. She's says it will take all day to get you ready."

Now my head shot up in surprise because I didn't like the sound of that. "Why? I thought it was going to be easy with the engraved invitation."

"That invitation is for Liv and her boyfriend," Gray explained. "I'll be playing the role of Scott this evening, at least until we get through the door. You can't get in on the invite so we have to go a different route. I know Dev Quinn and if there's one thing he likes in his clubs, it's beautiful women in beautiful clothes. He might be married, but he's not blind. A gorgeous girl can walk into Ether with absolutely no wait time. Liv's working up a charm that will make the bouncers believe you're a witch."

I would go along with the charm, but there was one thing I wasn't sure about. I cringed at the thought. "Am I going to have to wear heels?"

Chapter Eight

"Stop being such a baby," Liv whispered in my ear as she smiled at a handsome werewolf who walked by. She gave me a little nudge as if to say "smile."

Though there was a party going on all around me, I didn't feel like smiling. Ether was stunning, but my mind was preoccupied with my feet. "They hurt."

"They're gorgeous and they're only three-inch heels," Liv shot back. "They're practically flats. I'm wearing four-and-a-half-inch heels and you don't hear me complaining. What did you expect me to do? Those Converse of yours don't go with a little black dress."

I shifted, trying to get used to my size seven-and-a-half red torture devices and got my first look around Ether. I stood at the bar, waiting for Gray to get back from dropping off our coats. Liv had worked some serious magic on me, and I wasn't only talking about the charm I wore like an anklet. I looked damn good in a tight black dress with a plunging neckline. Liv had insisted I didn't need a bra and my breasts were firm and the skin creamy against the black fabric. She'd forced my hair into curlers, and the dark brown locks flowed down my back in waves. I'd complained bitterly at the half hour she played around with makeup, but I couldn't argue with the results. The hair and makeup gave me the illusion of being feminine and soft. It had been worth it to watch Gray's mouth drop when I walked into the room. I would never do it on a regular basis, but it might be fun to dress up every now and then.

And it had totally gotten me into the club. I hadn't even waited in line.

"What do you know about the guy who owns this place?" I asked, curious about Gray's nemesis.

Liv sighed. "I haven't actually met him, but I saw him at Open House. He's the dad of the little fertility god. He's a big fertility god."

"So I take it he's hot?" An unattractive fertility god would likely be ineffective.

"Oh, Kels." She stopped and sighed, a blush making her cheeks pink. "He is the definition of hot. If you google the word 'hot' you get summer temperatures in Texas and a big picture of Devinshea Quinn. He's sex on two legs. I couldn't take my eyes off the man."

It was good to know she could still act like a teen at a boy band concert. "Gray thinks he's a criminal."

Liv *humphed* and frowned. "I don't think so. I can't imagine that. He certainly doesn't need the money. The man bought us a new gym—not gave a donation—just wrote us a check. He owns a bunch of clubs and has some corporation in the human world. He's an actual faery prince. His mother is the Seelie queen."

I wasn't convinced. Gray seemed adamant about the "faery prince" being a bad guy. Liv's crush wasn't exactly a good reason to overlook a Texas Ranger's experience and instincts. The club was something, though. It was hopping. It seemed like everyone in the supernatural world was spending their Saturday night here. The dance floor was full of life and the whole club was filled with a pulsating beat. It was unlike any place I'd ever been in. I spent my time in rundown bars where the goal was to get drunk as fast as possible. This was a place to meet friends and have fun.

"Hey, don't look, but that guy is checking you out," Liv said with a little grin.

She is stunning so I was sure she was the one being checked out. I looked across the trendy bar area and over at the edge of the dance floor where a brown-haired man stood. He was dressed in slacks and a dark silk shirt, and he was definitely looking at me, though I didn't get a sexual vibe off him. He seemed more curious than anything else. His head cocked to the side and his eyes narrowed, but the dude was checking out my face and not my boobs.

He took a deep whiff of the air around him. He was a wolf, no doubt about it. His eyes closed and stopped for a moment, as though he needed all his faculties to assess that smell. They snapped back open and even across the distance, I could see they had darkened, taking on a more wolf-like characteristic. He stared directly my way and then made a beeline for me.

"Oh, Gray is gonna be pissed," Liv said. "It looks like you have more than one suitor tonight."

I kind of thought about running because that was one determined man. He pushed his way through the crowd.

Liv didn't seem to sense the predatory nature of the man. "He's cute and all, but I think Gray's hotter. He looks too much like you. You would look like brother and sister. But it'll do Gray good to know he isn't the only interested party."

"Do I know you?" The man stopped in front of me. He was a little taller than me, but the heels did give me a few inches. He was built on lean lines for a wolf, but I wouldn't underestimate his strength. "What pack are you from? Are you from Nevada?"

I shook my head. No extra suitors here, just a big case of mistaken identity. "I've never been to Nevada. Sorry. I'm not from any pack. I'm not a wolf. I'm a witch."

I kept to my cover story, but he didn't look like he was buying it. What was keeping Gray? He was going to be pissed all right. He was going to be pissed I was drawing attention to myself. I noticed several people watched us. The bar seemed abuzz with people talking behind their hands as they took in our little scene.

"No, you're not a witch." His hand came out quickly, grasping my wrist, and then his nose ran along my bare arm up to my shoulder. I tried to pull away, but he held me tight. "You're not a wolf, but you smell like someone I knew. Are you sure you've never been to Vegas? What was your father's name? Was he a drifter?"

I pulled back firmly, unwilling to answer his questions. I had been in the place for exactly ten minutes and I was already confronted with my father. The bastard never let me be. "Let me go."

"Hey, she's from Texas." Liv tried to get between us and I bet she was ready to give that wolf a taste of an actual witch. "Her dad was from Arkansas and he was a mechanic. Let her go or I'll call security."

The werewolf let go, but he didn't back away. "I'm sorry to be so pushy, but this is important. My nose doesn't lie."

"Hey, Zack, I need your help. Have you seen the munchkins? I'm supposed to be watching them, but the little suckers got away from me. Z will kill me if they burn down the club," a new voice said, and I found myself staring at another werewolf.

The place was thick with them tonight.

"Good, I can use your help, too. Smell her," the guy named Zack demanded.

"I don't want to be smelled." I tried to back up. The bar stopped me. I ran flat up against it.

"Leave her alone." Liv pushed at the wolf with brown hair. The new wolf was taking a whiff.

"Hey, Zack, she smells like…"

"You!" I shouted, not caring who was looking because the new wolf was startlingly familiar. Much of the night before might still be foggy, but I recognized that platinum blond hair. Familiar light-blue eyes looked at me. I'd stared at them as he'd stalked me and thought about how icy cold they were. Tonight they weren't as arctic, but I knew them all the same.

The blond wolf gave me a huge smile and a wink. "Yes? Do you recognize me from my career as a male model? Or did I break your heart in a past life because you loved me and I love boys?"

I wasn't about to joke with the little fucker. I poked him right on his hard chest. "I remember you from the time you tried to kill me."

The wolf went completely pale and Zack stepped in, trying to protect his friend. "You must be mistaken. Neil wouldn't try to kill a girl."

Neil frowned. "I wouldn't put anything past me, but I don't remember trying to kill this one. I've never seen you before, honey."

I growled because when surrounded by wolves, it seemed like the right thing to do. "It wasn't really you. It was an illusion. Obviously that damn witch knows you because he has you down. You look exactly like he projected."

"I'm sorry. There's some mistake. We don't hang out with witches," Zack said patiently. "We're wolves. We don't do the whole magic thing so I'm afraid we wouldn't know anyone who could do that."

"Umm, hello, what about Chad?" Neil said, looking at Zack like he was a dumbass.

Now Zack was the one growling and Neil took that pretty damn seriously. Those baby-blue eyes got wide and they appeared to have a silent argument. It was obvious who won. Neil looked like he wanted to tuck his tail between his legs and run.

"Who's Chad?" I asked in my most threatening voice. It didn't help that I kind of tottered on my heels.

"No idea." Zack had all the smooth confidence of a born liar. He used his thumb to indicate his cohort. "And I wouldn't listen to him. He's slow, if you know what I mean."

I focused every bit of my intimidation powers on the weak link. "I'll ask again; who's Chad?"

"Uhm, I really…I don't know what you're talking about," the blond wolf said and there was something a little desperate in his eyes.

"He's lying," Liv said as though it was a hard fought and won revelation.

"You think?" I shot back because blondie was starting to sweat. I decided to test a theory. Goth boy had known this wolf and given the fact that his illusion had been the brightest, most real of the bunch, I had drawn a conclusion. "You're telling me you don't know a man, probably twenty-five or so, stringy black hair, Goth black nail polish. He was kind of fat."

"There isn't an ounce of fat on his body," Neil said righteously. "And his hair isn't stringy. It's perfect."

Zack sighed and shook his head. "You're such a dumbass, Neil."

I pounced quickly. "You tell me where I can find him. We have a few things to work out. Tell him he sure as hell better bring more than tranquilizer darts if he wants to take my ass down. I fully intend to beat the shit out of him once I figure out what he wanted from me."

"Well, I would tell him all that, if I had any idea what gorgeous, sweet, loving guy with a ridiculously low body fat percentage you're talking about," Neil said with a toss of his blond head. He turned to Zack. "No one ever tells me anything."

"I can't think why not," Zack deadpanned.

"Now I have to figure out a way to tell everyone I screwed up some weird plan concerning some strange chick who smells like a wolf but isn't that I didn't even know about. Well, I can think about it while I'm tracking down the destructo twins. Maybe they'll have mercy on me and make the club explode. I doubt anyone will be able to yell at all my blown up bits."

I'd had enough out of that drama queen. "Look here, I'll take you apart if you don't…"

"Oh, shit, Kels." Liv pulled on my arm. She pointed up and I saw Gray being dragged along by two big bouncers. He was yelling at them as they started to lead him up the stairs.

I was torn. I really wanted to force that damn wolf to talk. I could do it, too. Oh, I wasn't sure about the brown-haired wolf. He seemed like a pretty solid liar to me, but that blond wolf would wilt like an orchid under a heat lamp once I started in on him. I glanced back up at my kind-of, sort-of boyfriend. He was so pissed I knew he was going to get into big-time trouble and then we wouldn't learn a thing.

"Damn it," I swore under my breath, glaring back at Neil. "We're not done. Count yourself lucky that my escort is an idiot, but don't think this is through."

"Not by a long shot," I heard Zack swear as I walked away.

I cut across the bar area to the small set of stairs on the far side of the club. It probably led to some damn security office and Gray had been made as a cop. It was the haircut. I was sure of it. No one in the supernatural world had a military cut. It screamed authority figure.

"Ma'am," a deep voice at the bottom of the stairs said. "That floor is employees only. Please step away."

I couldn't get around him. He was really freaking big. I had to settle for yelling from the bottom of the stairs. "Gray!"

Liv ran to catch up. "That's her boyfriend. Where exactly are they taking him? What did he do?"

The big wolf snorted. "He pissed off the boss, that's what he did. If you don't want to piss off the boss, I suggest you head your pretty little selves back to the bar and enjoy the rest of your night. If the boss kills your ride, let me know and I'll arrange a limo to take you back. It's all part of the service."

I'd just about decided to see if my heels could be used as some form of weapon when Zack's voice cut through the thick tension.

"I'll vouch for her, Len," Zack said and Len immediately backed off. Zack's eyes were guarded as he studied me. He nodded toward the top of the stairs where Gray disappeared into the open door. "You know the asshole cop?"

I could feel my mouth tighten. "I know the lieutenant."

He gently grabbed my elbow and started up the stairs. "Keep your eyes on the witch, Len. It's obvious we're gonna have trouble with the whole group."

I followed the werewolf, climbing the stairs as fast as my three-inch heels would allow me.

"Where are you taking me?" I was grateful I'd been paranoid enough to strap one of Gray's .45s around my thigh. Weapons were not allowed in the club, but while the bouncers had searched Gray, they hadn't bothered with me or Liv. I felt the comforting weight of it on my leg and knew it would be loaded with silver ordnance. Gray had prepped it for me. I wasn't going for it yet, but if I had to shoot our way out of this, I would.

"We're going up to the office so we can figure a few things out." Zack pivoted when we reached the top step. "I won't hurt you. Don't be afraid. I just have a few questions."

"Doesn't seem fair for you to expect me to answer your questions when you won't answer mine," I grumbled as he slid a key card through the door and it opened.

"I've answered every one of your questions," he replied with an enigmatic smile.

"You lied." I was escorted into a small, intimate room.

"Prove it." The wolf laughed and I got the feeling he was enjoying this. He kept breathing deeply, as though he liked the smells around him and wanted to fully appreciate them.

Gray sat sullenly in a chair that was placed in front of a big desk. "I'm sorry, Kelsey. They nabbed me the minute I walked past the bar. Apparently the staff was given a lecture on how important it is to keep me out."

"There's a picture of him in the security office. They throw darts at it." Zack waved to the two bouncers. "Thanks, guys. Let payroll know I'll sign to pay out the bounty."

"Bounty?" I looked from Zack to Gray.

The bouncers left, closing the door behind them, and I was struck that someone thought this Zack person could handle both Gray and me. I was confused because he didn't seem like an alpha to me, but he had a lot of wolves following his orders.

"What did you expect, Sloane? Dev doesn't like being arrested. You hauled him out of here last time in front of the entire club," Zack pointed out. "He's gonna like you even less in a few minutes. I believe you'll find you've interrupted some alone time with his wife. They had the whole condo to themselves tonight. You'll be lucky if he doesn't shoot you. Now, tell me what her name is and where you found her. Is this some kind of game you're playing, Sloane?"

"I'm here on an investigation." Gray shook his head. "I'm not playing any games. Kelsey is a contractor. She's a PI who's working with me. You should let her go. She doesn't have anything to do with Quinn's arrest."

"Your name is Kelsey?" Zack said my name slowly, as though tasting it.

"Yes." I wondered who the hell I resembled that the werewolf would be so concerned with who I was. "I'm Kelsey Atwood."

I pulled a card out of the purse I'd fought Liv on carrying. The tiny clutch she'd sworn went with the dress couldn't hold anything more than a cell, some gloss, and my cards.

Zack studied the card. "Atwood? Any relation to Nathan?"

"He's my brother." I hoped I wasn't about to get Nate in serious trouble.

Zack started to say something when twin doors slid open revealing an elevator that led directly into the cozy office. The lights in the office were dim, giving the entire place an intimate glow, but the elevator lights rushed in and I got my first glimpse of the notorious Devinshea Quinn. He radiated anger as he strode out of the elevator, still buttoning his white dress shirt. Black slacks hung low on his ridiculously muscled hips. Gray had definitely interrupted something.

I swallowed once and then twice. Dark hair. Emerald eyes. The most perfectly masculine body I've ever seen in my life. The man practically had a fucking halo around his hips, and by hips I meant his goddamn cock. It had a halo. He was…stunning and it wasn't simply the gorgeous body or the next-to-perfect face. It was something about him. You looked at that man and you just knew he could take care of you, and I meant that in the dirtiest way possible. Liv had described him as a fertility god, but he was a SEX god. There was no other way to describe him.

"You can close your mouth, Kelsey," Gray said harshly.

A deep flush crashed through me. I was going to apologize for staring, but the sex god had a few things to say to my date.

"You motherfucker," that glorious bit of masculinity spewed as he faced off with the bigger, way more demonic man. It didn't seem to faze him. "How dare you show your face in my club? I told you what would happen if I ever caught you on one of my properties again."

"Bring it on, Quinn," Gray snarled back. "You have any idea how long I've waited for you to give me a reason to take you down?"

Gray stood and faced the club owner over his desk. The men were inches from each other and I worried Gray was going to kill the man. It didn't seem like it would be anywhere close to a fair fight. Gray had all the power and strength of a demon and the faery was…well, he was a faery…with an awfully dirty mouth.

"Oh, you sad sack, piece of shit demon, you couldn't take me down if you tried." His green eyes lit with a vicious sort of glee. "Oh, wait, you did try. Didn't fucking work out for you, did it? How was your suspension, Lieutenant? Hope you had a good vacation."

"You cost me a month," Gray admitted.

"Did you visit Daddy?" Quinn asked, sarcasm dripping. "How was the Hell plane? Did it feel like home? Clock's ticking for you, isn't it?"

Gray's eyes narrowed. "I spent the whole time investigating you. I don't care who you sleep with. I'm going to prove all of it. I'm going to prove the illegal gambling, the gun running, the mob connections. You're dirty as hell and I'm going to bring your whole house down."

The sex god practically vibrated with rage. "You come anywhere near my family and I will make the Hell plane seem like a good hiding place. I swear you lay one fucking hand on my wife or my children and I'll take you apart piece by piece."

Gray's face was tight, his eyes faintly cruel as he got in the other man's space. "I note you don't try to protect your other lover."

Quinn rolled his eyes, his disdain plain. "Daniel can handle himself. Maybe it's time I let him handle you, Sloane. You've become a nuisance. Zack, show the lieutenant to the door. Make sure he doesn't come back. I don't want to see this fucker again."

"Fine, boss, but I want to know about her first," Zack said and I could hear the willpower in his voice.

"You leave her out of this." Gray strode over to take my hand.

It appeared we were going to make a hasty retreat. My heart dropped at the thought of not being able to use this opportunity. Tomorrow I had to inform Helen Taylor her daughter had been murdered and I couldn't even tell her I'd made any headway on who had done it. I knew beyond a shadow of a doubt if I could convince Devinshea Quinn to take me seriously that he could get other people to talk to me. I was certain deep down that our perp was a supe, so this was his world. If Gray wasn't effective here, then I had to step up to the plate.

"Mr. Quinn, my name is Kelsey Atwood." I used my most polite and even voice as I pulled away from Gray. Gray was pissed, but I had to salvage this. Just because he was getting his ass kicked out didn't mean I had to get mine tossed, too. He'd asked for my help. I hoped he wasn't too angry at how he got it. "I'm investigating a series of murders, and I could really use your help."

The faery turned his attention to me as though he was surprised to see someone else was in the room. All of his anger and attention had been focused on Gray. He stared for a moment and I thought he was going to tell Zack to chuck me out. He sighed as though resolving himself to something. "You have ten minutes, Ms. Atwood."

Gray reached for my hand again, this time yanking me toward him. "No, Kelsey. If you think I'm leaving you alone with him you're crazy. He hates me. You have no idea what he's capable of."

"He's capable of answering my questions." I needed him to understand. He held my hand in a firm grip and when I tried to pull away, he tightened around me.

"No," Gray said implacably.

"Hey." Zack tried to get between us. His eyes changed colors and I saw the beginnings of claws flash from his hands. "You're hurting her. Let her go."

"She's mine," Gray insisted with intent in his eyes. He would fight this Zack guy if he stepped between us. It looked like my lawman had a little caveman thrown in for good measure. "She comes with me."

Quinn sank back into his chair and there was a deep weariness in his eyes as he regarded the scene playing out in front of him.

"Shouldn't that be up to Ms. Atwood? Do you intend to force a female against her will, Sloane? It would be in your character, I suppose."

Gray dropped my hand immediately. "I'm asking you to come with me, Kelsey."

My stomach knotted because I was about to make a huge mistake, but I couldn't help myself. I wasn't going to side with Quinn. I wasn't betraying Gray. I was being true to our case. He was a Ranger. He would understand when he gave it a little thought.

I backed up just enough to let him know I was staying. "I'm sorry. I only want to ask him a couple of questions. We need those IDs. I'll come downstairs when I'm done and we can go back to your place."

His face hardened, his eyes turning to stone. "Don't bother." His gaze slid across me and I saw the rage there. "You made your choice. I'll show myself out, Quinn."

Gray turned and strode out the door. It was all I could do not to rush after him and beg him to forgive me. I felt his physical absence keenly. It was like all the warmth had left the room. I banished the tears that threatened and turned to Dev Quinn because Gray was right. The choice had been made and I had to live with it. I'd chosen my job over Gray, though at the time I'd really thought I was saving the situation. "Do you mind if I sit?"

He indicated the chair in front of his desk and turned to the wall behind him. He pushed the panel and revealed a small refrigerator. He pulled out a frosty bottle, snagged two glasses, and sat down behind his desk.

"Dev?" Zack asked.

The faery shook his head. "Talk to your master, Zack."

"Come on," Zack said, exasperated.

Green eyes gave away nothing. "You have to talk to him. I can't give you anything. Please, go make sure the lieutenant doesn't cause any more trouble tonight. She's perfectly safe here. Your nose knows the truth so you know damn well I won't harm her."

The werewolf turned and he seemed as irritated as Gray had been as he walked out of the room.

Quinn poured the cold liquid into the shot glasses with practiced skill. "Please, join me, Ms. Atwood. I'll be perfectly pleasant, I promise. I'm afraid the lieutenant brings out the worst in me. I have issues with authority. My wife thinks I should go into therapy to deal with the problem, but I'm perfectly comfortable with it."

I sank down into the chair and tried to banish the horrible feeling that I'd lost something important. Had I been wrong to not blindly follow him? "Sure."

"It's for the best," Quinn said, holding out a glass to me. "I can see plainly you have feelings for him, but...he is what he is. He can't change his fate and he'll drag you down with him."

"He's only half demon." I took the glass in my hand and shot it back. It was vodka and it was so smooth, it was practically water. Maybe if I had another ten shots or so I could forget that look in Gray's eyes.

Quinn poured two more shots. He seemed familiar with the process. "Do you know what I am?"

"You're a fertility god."

His eyes bled to a startlingly deep green. It filled his entire eye and left no white. It was...beautiful. A person could get seriously lost in those eyes. His voice was deeper and held a hint of an Irish accent when he spoke again. "I am, indeed, Ms. Atwood. It's one of my talents to be able to see what a person needs and wants sexually. It's something of a portal into a person's soul. You seek comfort, love, caring. You haven't found them yet. I can see that you and the lieutenant are well matched on that front. Sex with him will be exciting and it will feel like heaven, but he needs more than you can give him, more than any woman can give him. You will love him and he will break your heart. What would you say if I told you I could offer you a viable alternative? I know a man who could give you the things you crave while taking only what you are willing to give. The relationship won't be as intense as the one with Grayson Sloane, but neither will it be as painful. It would be a loving friendship between kindred spirits."

"Mr. Quinn, I didn't come here for your advice on my love life." I didn't want to hear what he had to say. As far as I could tell, it didn't matter anymore. Gray seemed to be done with me the moment I caused him trouble. I was a whole shit ton of trouble so it was better to know at the beginning. "If I only have ten minutes of your time, I would prefer to use it on work."

His eyes were back to normal and so was his voice as he took another shot. The boy could drink. "Again, I apologize. I certainly have no intentions to kick you out when the ten minutes are up. Trust me, this is the most interesting thing I'll be doing for the rest of the evening."

I matched him drink for drink. It was starting to loosen me up. "I got the distinct impression we'd interrupted something interesting when Gray got hauled up here."

He smiled and it lit up the room. It might be easy to see where Gray could dislike this man when he was shouting obscenities, but when he poured on the charm, it was impossible to not smile with him.

"It was getting somewhere," he said with an intimate laugh. "Unfortunately, I'm certain that's over. My goddess was yawning even as I walked out the door. She's asleep by now and I won't wake her up. Our daughter is teething and getting over an ear infection. The last few days have been rough. While Evangeline might be feeling better today, my wife is still recovering. Daniel took the baby with him. How he manages to play games with her, I don't know. I hope she doesn't chew up the boards. Those games are surprisingly expensive."

"Evangeline? Are you talking about Evan?" Dan had mentioned he brought his kid with him to game nights. I guessed I was looking at the possibility Dan had embraced.

Quinn shuddered. "Only Daniel calls her that. Well, and all the wolves. It's a terrible nickname for my beautiful little girl."

"And Dan is your…?" I asked and then realized what a rude question it was. "Never mind. That's none of my business."

Quinn took his time with the vodka, savoring it. "I'm not offended, Kelsey. Daniel is my partner. We're best friends, business partners, closer than brothers. We share a wife and our children. It is a common relationship where I come from, but it's looked down on in this plane. The good lieutenant certainly looks down on it. My wife is hurt most by the prejudice. Daniel and I don't care what people think of us."

"Well, I've seen you both and I'd just high-five her," I said without thinking about it. "Crap, did I say that out loud?"

Quinn threw back his head and laughed. "Yes, you did, but don't worry about it. I find you quite charming, Kelsey. Much more charming than your…well, than I would have expected Sloane to score. Now, what is this case you're investigating?"

I pulled out my phone. I'd scanned the files and pictures into it when I realized Liv wasn't going to let me bring my bag. "I need to know if you recognize any of these girls."

I passed him my phone with the pictures cued up, wanting to see if he could ID them all.

He ran a finger along the screen and his face sobered up quickly. "These girls are dead."

"Yes, they are." I watched his face, but all I saw there was sympathy.

He closed his eyes and took a deep breath. "I know this one's name. She's Joanne Taylor. Damn it. I recognize the rest of them, but I cannot place their names. I'm sorry. I can find out for you."

"Are you the one who got them their…work?" It was a delicate question and I tried to keep it professional.

He sat back. "Obviously you know they were prostitutes, though I doubt they would have considered themselves such. They were mostly college girls who needed a little money and didn't mind spending some time with vampires. Some of them had sex with their dates and others simply fed them. I didn't directly get them work in the club, though I set up the system."

"Because the king freed the slaves?"

"That was certainly part of the problem," Quinn admitted. "The world changed quickly and we're all scrambling to keep up with it. It seemed a smarter idea to use willing females than to tell the unattached vampires to fend for themselves."

Put like that it made a whole lot of sense.

Quinn's fist came down on the desk. "Damn it. When this gets out the wolves and the shifters will blame the vampires. Is there any way to keep this quiet while we find out who's committing these crimes? Our alliances are still fragile. There are many in the werewolf community especially who think it was wrong to join with the vampires. Something like this could…it could start a civil war."

I gnawed on my lip while I thought about that. I hadn't considered the ramifications outside the obvious one. "I don't intend to give any interviews or anything, but people are going to notice their daughters are missing. I have to tell my client that her daughter is dead. I can't lie to her."

"I understand," the fertility god said. "I wouldn't wish for her to not know, however if there is any way to keep the investigation quiet, it would help keep the peace. How can I help you? If Helen is your client, she can't be paying you much."

"It's fine. She paid me to find out what happened to her daughter. I'm not going to stop because she doesn't have the money for me long term. I need to catch this guy, Mr. Quinn. Even if Gray refuses to help me after this, I'll stay on."

Quinn opened the top drawer of his desk and pulled out a checkbook. He quickly wrote out a check and passed it to me. "Will that help your efforts?"

As it was more money than I'd made in the last several months combined, I had to nod. I was thinking of all the things I could buy with that money. I could upgrade my laptop. I could walk through the gadget stores and buy all the cool little things that would make my job so much easier because I knew beyond a shadow of a doubt that I wanted to take on more interesting cases. Images of night vision gear played around in my head.

"Excellent. Then consider me your client. That's your retainer. Please let me know if you need more. You'll need to get into the vampire club."

I tore my eyes away from the ridiculously large check. "Yes, I need access to the club. Can you tell them to expect me?"

"You'll need an escort. I can't send you in alone and whether or not the lieutenant is reasonable, I can't have him in the club." He looked thoughtful for a moment. "I'll have a vampire take you through the club. I know just the man. People will talk to you around him. You'll find him helpful. Also, if you find yourself in need of a tracker, feel free to contact me and I'll let you use Zack. He has an excellent nose, as his master is bound to discover tonight."

The door to the office opened and I turned to see a small boy cautiously entering the room. He had a mop of dark hair that fell almost in his eyes. He had on sweat pants that were nearly worn through at the knees, a Spider-Man T-shirt, and sneakers that needed to be tied. He looked like he was maybe eight or nine, and there was no question who his father was.

"Lee," Quinn said and it was obvious he had gone into father mode. "You were supposed to spend the evening with your Uncle Neil."

The boy let the door close behind him and approached his father with big brown eyes that seemed to seriously consider the question.

"He got lost, Papa."

"Did he?" Quinn asked suspiciously. "And your brother? Did Rhys get lost as well?"

The tops of Lee's shoes suddenly seemed very interesting to the boy. "I need to talk to Daddy."

"Daddy is out," Quinn said firmly. "He had a meeting to go to. You'll have to deal with me."

"Maybe I can wait for Daddy to get home."

"Or we could call your mother." That came out more as a threat than an alternative.

"I'll tell you." Apparently Daddy was the first choice, but Mama was the last. "You don't have to bother Mama."

There was a long pause. "Lee, I'm waiting."

"We were just playing," Lee started.

I watched as the fertility god swallowed in fear. I could have sworn the man went pale. "What were you playing, Lee?"

"Hide and seek," the boy answered. "Me and Rhys were hiding and Uncle Neil was seeking."

"Did Uncle Neil know he was seeking?"

The boy shrugged. "I think so. I heard him yelling a lot. He's not real good at it."

"And where did you decide to hide, you little hoodlum?"

"The armory," Lee said.

Quinn's mouth fell open and I could practically see his heart begin to pound. "How did you get into the armory? It's locked down. You have to have a key card."

"Well," Lee started to explain. "Granddad told me I should practice so I stole Uncle Zack's key and he didn't even notice, but then I got hungry so I left it with Rhys and the door closed and I can't get him to come out."

Quinn was quickly on his feet. "Oh, goddess, he'll think the C-4 is Play-doh." He scooped up his son. "We are never telling your mother about this."

"That's what Daddy always says," Lee replied.

Quinn started to carry his son to the door. "I apologize, Ms. Atwood. If you don't mind waiting, I can send your escort up in a moment. He can show you around Ether and you can ask your questions. I'll arrange for you to meet with the management at the vampire club tomorrow night."

"Thank you," I said, trying not to look too amused. I was far less intimidated by the harried father than I had been by the ruthless club owner.

"As for you," Quinn was saying as he hurried out, "you may never be left alone with your grandfather again." He turned to me. "If you hear a loud boom…well, it'll be too late then. Never mind."

The door slammed on his way out and I was surprised at how quiet the room was. Right outside the door a huge party was going on but up here it was peaceful. Too peaceful. I wondered where Gray was. Had he already stormed off? Was he home yet? Was he still cursing my name? I had been an idiot to think it could work.

A man like Grayson Sloane needed a sweet, pretty wife. He needed one of those women who would support him and help his career. I would drag him down. I would go to a social function and be a complete moron. I wouldn't know which spoon to use or when to stop drinking. I shook my head to banish the self-pitying thoughts. It had been a pipedream, nothing more. It should teach me a lesson. I should have slept with him before he knew me well enough to dump me.

I reached over and poured myself another shot of vodka. Quinn had left it behind and he'd kind of been the one to cost me the possibilities Gray had represented, so I figured he owed me. I slammed the vodka and poured another. I sipped this one as I checked out what a fertility god viewed as a good workspace. It wasn't what I would have guessed. There was a corner with a comfy chair and a bookshelf.

A big portrait adorned the wall opposite the desk. It was what Dev Quinn wanted to see when he glanced up from whatever he was doing. I moved to it, studying it carefully. It was a family portrait, though one unlike any I'd seen before. A bright smiling redhead sat in a field of green grass. She sat between two men, smiling at the camera. I recognized the vampire, Daniel, and the man I'd just met. They were all dressed in white, making a stunning contrast to the deep green of the grass. Each man had a boy in his lap. They were twins and I recognized Lee, though Rhys seemed to have his father's green eyes. Lee's eyes were unique. A small, toothless baby girl was in the woman's arm, her baby hands outstretched toward Daniel. She had a cap of red hair and was her mother's mini me. Happiness. It was the only word to describe that picture. I felt my eyes prick with tears at the thought that I would never have anything as good as that picture.

I turned quickly as the door opened and took a deep breath. My vampire escort was here.

Chapter Nine

"They make a beautiful family," a soft, accented voice said from the doorway. He was backlit from the blue light coming from the club and I only saw his silhouette.

I turned quickly, hoping he wouldn't catch me crying. "Yes, they are lovely."

One minute he was behind me and the next, he was right in front of me, his hand cupping my jaw. His thumb gently rubbed across my cheek, sweeping away the tear caught there. I should have backed away, but I was too surprised to move. Vampires are fast.

"Did Devinshea make you cry?" the vampire asked with a melodic accent. Italian, I realized as I recognized the man from last night. "He can be rude, though not usually with a woman. Should I talk to him?"

"Marcus Vorenus." His name came out as a breathy revelation.

In the dim light of the office, I saw a smile break over the vampire's face. It tugged his lips up and caused his dark eyes to crinkle appealingly. It took him from a gorgeous work of art to something far more dangerous. He was simply a handsome, approachable man when he smiled.

"You're the girl from the club." He looked me over with appreciative eyes.

"I am. Sorry about the other night."

He stepped back and dropped his hand, wariness taking over. "You came to look for me?"

"No." I wished I could lie to him. "I'm a private investigator. I'm here on a murder case. Mr. Quinn kind of became my new client. He said I needed an escort, so I suppose he picked you. I wasn't stalking you or anything. I was staking the place out and you happened to be there."

He leaned back against the desk. "An investigator? Very interesting. You must be a good investigator since you already know my name. Why don't you tell me yours?"

"Kelsey Atwood." I wondered if the universe was having fun kicking the shit out of me. I'd just gotten dumped by one guy out of my league. Now I stood alone in a room with another too-beautiful-for-me man and I was determined not make an idiot of myself over this one.

"Kelsey. An interesting name for an interesting girl," the vampire said. "It used to be a surname. Old English, I believe."

"I have no idea," I admitted. "My mom liked the sound of it. Are you really two thousand years old?"

I would guess he wasn't older than thirty-five. His head moved ever so slightly, an aristocratic gesture in the negative. "Not quite. If you include the twenty-two years I walked the plane as a human, I have one thousand nine hundred and fifty-nine years."

The enormity of that number really hit me.

"Tell me, Kelsey." His mouth turned down as he stared back at me. "Give me the first thought you had when I told you how old I am."

"I thought that was a lot of time for regrets."

He was in my space again, though he didn't actually touch me. "Almost all humans have a different reaction. They say how much I must have seen and how amazing it must be to never have to die."

"I guess it says something about me." I wished I'd given him a less than honest answer. "I think about what you must have lost along the way. How many people you would have cared for only to have them die on you. I wondered if you shut down after a while and you don't care anymore or if it was important enough to keep some edge of humanity so you let yourself ache. I don't think I'd want to be immortal."

"I do a bit of both. I choose who I ache for carefully, but I never want to be so distant that I can't feel passion and love. It's the only reason to walk the earth." He didn't touch me, but I could feel his presence. "Do you belong to the demon, little Kelsey?"

"No," I said quietly. "He doesn't want me now."

"But you want him."

All I had to do was say no and the vampire would offer himself to me. We had a strange connection, Marcus Vorenus and I, and if I hadn't met Gray when I did I would have been all over him. But I had met Gray and, even though he'd walked out on me, it seemed too soon to consider anyone else. "Yes."

"He is a fool." The vampire backed up again. His face was once more pleasant, but without the emotion that lit him previously. This was Marcus Vorenus as he wanted the world to see him—cool and regal, distant. "But then aren't we all? I thought, for a moment, that Devinshea was doing me a favor. I thought, perhaps, I was reading too much into our situation. I see he is still playing a game with me."

The vampire sounded bitter and I hated the fact that I'd made him feel that way. "I'm sorry. I wasn't trying…"

"It isn't your fault, dear girl. You must be careful around the fertility god. He always knows what he's doing when he puts two people in an intimate situation. He knew I would be attracted to you. He knew you're precisely the type of female to pique my interest. He also knew that you are involved with another man. This is his way of telling me it's time to go home, that there is nothing here for me."

A second wave of loss hit me and I'd only just met this male. I'd been looking forward to his company, but I didn't want to hurt him further. He seemed sad enough as it was, as though the world had turned on him. I didn't want to add to his trouble. "I'll ask Mr. Quinn for another escort. I'm sorry to have taken up your time. I'll wait here for him. I'm sure he'll be back."

I sat down again in the chair where I'd talked to Quinn and tried to hold myself with as much dignity as I could muster. I prayed the next vampire he sent me was obnoxious and unattractive.

Marcus kneeled at my side. "I'm sorry, Kelsey. I should not have tried to drag you into my troubles with Devinshea and Daniel. My only excuse is that I've been thinking of you ever since I saw you last night. I'm a bit tired of wanting women I cannot have."

Now I was the bitter one. "Then you should stick by my side,

Vorenus. I can assure you after you spend a little time with me, you'll change your mind. They all do after I pull a gun on them or yell too much. And this ain't me." I gestured to the dress and shoes. "This is someone else's magic. I'm a jeans and T-shirts kind of girl and I don't do relationships well, obviously. I drink too much, cuss too much, and can be unpleasant to be around. I think you'll discover your heart is perfectly safe around me if you give me the chance to annoy you."

Marcus's eyes closed with a shake of his head. "He knows me so well." When he opened them again, he was perfectly smooth and polite. He stood and moved to sit across from me. "Let's forget this portion of the evening and begin again. I'm Marcus Vorenus, your escort. Consider me your knight and your guide. So, tell me, how may I aid you? I am entirely at your service."

A deep gratitude swept over me. Vorenus gave me exactly what I needed to get on solid ground again. I pulled out my phone and spent the next twenty minutes going over what I knew with the vampire. As he was an academic, he was quick and gave me several tips. He pointed out the small streak of sunlight in one of the photos that I had missed. Laura Nesson had been killed during the day. Or at least photographed.

"There are only a few vampires I know who can daywalk," Vorenus explained. "Myself and the king among them. This particular killing occurred when?"

I enlarged the picture, pointing to the bottom of the photo where the date was visible. The photos were taken with a digital camera that recorded the date. "Last week. I believe that was a Thursday."

He nodded his regal head. "I thought so. The king and I were attending a meeting in London that day. I can show you the ticket from my flight and give you any number of witnesses to my whereabouts. The king, well, he prefers to fly on his own. I assure you he was with me that day."

I was already making progress. I thought it couldn't be a vampire and this was proof. Vampires don't hide during daylight hours. They sleep and they don't have a choice about it. Unless they can daywalk, as Marcus and the king can, they were stuck. My first instinct was right. This was a human or another type of supe.

Marcus stared at the photos, flipping through them. He studied them with a clinical detachment Quinn hadn't been able to produce.

"These girls all look vaguely alike. I would say they're all within three years of each other in age."

"Serial killers tend to have a type. Do you recognize any of them?"

"Oh yes, Kelsey." He ran a long finger across the screen. "I've fed from all of them at one time or another. I've had sex with some of them as well."

I stared openly at him.

"Don't judge me, little one." He cocked a dark eyebrow and let his cheek rest against his right hand. "I'm a vampire. I feed off blood and sexual energy. It's my nature. Have you ever been bitten?"

"No." I hoped I wasn't blushing. The intimate atmosphere of the room did nothing to take away from his attractiveness. The soft light seemed to cocoon us and his accent was so melodic I wondered if there wasn't some magic behind it.

I really wondered what it would feel like to feed Marcus Vorenus.

"Well, it's difficult to feed one appetite and not the other." Vorenus explained even the most salacious acts with a simplicity that made it seem normal. He was practical and forgiving of even his own foibles. It made him easy to talk to. "In order to not harm our partners, it's necessary to use a bit of magic to pull them in. This makes the bite intense and pleasurable. It's only natural to follow the taking of blood with the taking of the body. The orgasm is much sharper after a feed. When the connection is right, I've found a bond can be formed. Only a vampire with a disciplined mind is capable of feeding without sexual intercourse. It's an instinct."

"You said you fed from all of them, but you only had sex with a few," I pointed out.

"Let me correct myself then. Only a disciplined vampire or one who is terribly bored with it all can walk away," Marcus said. "I have no mistress currently. I haven't had one for a long time. When I have no feelings for the woman beneath me I prefer that she have no feelings for me, either. For me, especially, the bond can be intense. I do not wish to form such an intimate connection with a woman I might not like on a fundamental level. For me, there must be an intellectual liking as much as a physical draw. I use the prostitutes because there is nothing there but an exchange. At times, the instinct is too much and I must take a woman, but I make sure she gets something out of it as well."

"Cash."

"Yes," he replied. "It's what they need."

The door to the office opened and Quinn walked in preceded by two subdued boys. The boys stopped and stared at us, but Quinn was having none of it.

"You two, march, both of you," Quinn barked at his sons, pointing at the elevator at the back of the office. "You get in that elevator and be glad that I'm more terrified of what your mother would say than I am angry with you. You're grounded. I'll come up with some less dangerous reason why to explain the grounding to your mother."

The one with the brown eyes looked sullen and like he wasn't going to take being grounded well. There was rebellion in that one's eyes. The green-eyed boy, who must be Rhys, seemed untouched by his father's anger. His T-shirt was covered in black stuff and I wondered if he'd been rolling around in gun oil. He simply smiled and waved at me as his father punched the button for the elevator.

"Hello," he said. "You're pretty. I'm Rhys."

"Hi," I said, unable to not smile back.

"Are you going to kiss my Uncle Marcus?" Rhys asked. I heard Marcus sigh beside me and knew this wasn't the first time Rhys had embarrassed his "uncle" in front of a woman.

"I…"

Lee rolled his eyes. "No, dummy, Uncle Marcus wants to kiss mommy, but he's too late."

Rhys nodded wisely, and he shoved his thick black hair out of his eyes. "Yes, it's sad. Girls are only allowed two husbands and they should only kiss their husbands. Do you already have two husbands?"

"I don't have any." I wondered what surreal world I'd fallen into.

"Then you can kiss Uncle Marcus. I would say you should wait for me and Lee because you're really pretty, but Lee's gonna marry Mia and he says he doesn't want for Mia to kiss anyone but him." Rhys leaned over and whispered loudly. "He's weird."

I bit my lip to keep from laughing.

"Hey, you could kiss my Uncle Declan." Rhys's small face was completely open and he smiled like that was the best idea in the whole world. "He's from Faery and he's gonna be king, so he can have two wives. He says he wants his next wife to be the kind of girl who doesn't shove a hot poker up his ass every time he opens his mouth."

"Rhys!" Quinn shouted.

Rhys looked around, wondering what he'd said to offend his father. "Well, she doesn't look like she has a hot poker."

"Rhys said a bad word," Lee pointed out. "I get in trouble when I say bad words."

"No, I didn't. Uncle Dec said a bad word. He said ass." Rhys realized what had come out of his mouth and his small hands quickly covered his mouth like he could push the words back in.

Quinn frowned down at Rhys, his head shaking. "What is wrong with you? Haven't I taught you any manners? What am I saying? Hasn't Daddy taught you any manners?" The elevator door opened and Quinn hustled his sons into it. "You go upstairs where Albert is waiting to put you to bed."

The doors were almost closed when Lee poked his little head out. "Rhys was right. You are pretty." He ducked back in as the doors closed and they were gone.

Quinn stood staring at the elevator doors. After a second, he looked back at me. "You'll have to forgive them. They're…precocious, to say the very least."

I smiled because the boys were really fun. "They seem sweet."

"They seem that way, yes. That's usually when something falls on my head." Quinn's eyes narrowed cautiously as he took in the scene. "You're happy with Marcus as an escort?"

Marcus frowned, but I nodded. I was happy with him. Talking to Marcus was easy and I felt comfortable with him. He wasn't at all what I had expected a vampire to be like. He was funny and polite. He put me at ease because I sensed he would accept me as I was.

"Yes. Thank you. He's been very helpful."

Quinn's face turned faintly cruel as he looked from me to the vampire. "And you, Marcus? Are you willing to show Ms. Atwood around or do you prefer to sit about and sulk over things you can never have?"

The way he said it pissed me off. Before thinking about the fact that I didn't really know these people, I got up in Quinn's face. I didn't care how hot he was or how much cash he could offer me. He

142

had a bad habit of insulting men I liked. I got up and faced the fertility god, making damn sure my shoes were planted firmly. I didn't want to wobble.

"Look, Mr. Quinn, if you're using me in some way to hurt him, then you can take your cash and go to hell. I'll find another way into the club. Maybe you think I'm some fluffy idiot you can point in whatever direction you choose, but I assure you I'll figure out what your little plot is and I'll turn it around on you. You gave me Marcus and I consider him my partner. Back off."

Quinn watched me quietly. Every word I said forced his lips into a wider smile. I was beginning to think I just kept falling further into whatever trap the fertility god had planted. "I'm sorry, Ms. Atwood. Marcus and I have some issues, but I won't bring you into them and I certainly believe he's the best partner you could have in this endeavor. I hope we can have a good relationship. I could use an investigator on call. Things seem to go awry around here a lot."

Marcus stood and offered me his arm. It was an old-world gesture. Gathering my things quickly, I slipped my hand through his arm.

"Come, Kelsey, I will show you around the club," the vampire said shortly.

"You'll take care of her, Marcus?" Quinn asked as the vampire opened the door and the sounds of Ether assaulted me.

The vampire turned, his eyes narrowed on the faery. "You knew I would."

As the door closed behind us, I noted the look of satisfaction on Devinshea Quinn's face.

Marcus's face was tight and I could feel the rage pouring off him. I turned to him before we started down the first step. I had no idea what was between the fertility god and the vampire, but I had a feeling I'd made things more difficult for Marcus.

"Did I do something wrong?" I asked over the noise of the dance floor.

Marcus took a deep breath, and when he glanced back at me there was a calm look on his face. Marcus Vorenus did not wear his emotions on the surface. He kept them deeply hidden and I wondered how close you had to be before he shed the polite mask he wore. "Not at all, Kelsey. The prince and I are at odds. It's nothing to concern yourself with. I promise it won't affect my ability to aid you in your investigation. Allow me to show you around."

I thought about the gorgeous redhead in the picture. She was obviously Devinshea Quinn's wife. The boys had mentioned that Marcus wanted to kiss her. He had a thing for the faery's wife and it didn't look like the faery wanted to share more than he already did. Marcus mentioned problems with Daniel as well. I wondered if he'd had an affair with the woman in the picture. She was everything I wasn't—polished and beautiful and sunny. She had a centerfold body and a stunning face. She probably wore beautiful clothes and didn't complain because they were made for her. It occurred to me she was precisely the type of woman Gray needed.

"Kelsey!" Liv was practically on top of me the minute I hit the bottom of the stairs. She threw her arms around me and pulled me away from Marcus. "What's going on? First you disappear, then Gray storms off and he wouldn't tell me anything except to talk to Quinn because you chose him."

"I didn't choose Quinn." Gray had lost his damn mind. You would think I'd tossed off my clothes and begged the fertility god to take me. "I stayed behind to ask him some questions. I did what we came here to do. He stormed off because he hates Quinn, but we need him."

"Kelsey, we need to go," Liv said. "I don't think it's safe for you here. Gray said that guy might be after you. Without Gray, I think we should leave."

"Your friend is perfectly safe." Marcus stepped up to stand beside me. "I will escort her around and allow her to ask her questions. No one will bother her."

Liv put one hand on her hip and eyed the Italian. "And who will protect her from you?"

"Liv," I said, rolling my eyes.

Marcus bowed formally. "I give you my word as a gentleman that she will come to no harm. Allow me to introduce myself. I am Marcus Vorenus."

Liv's eyes got big. "Councilman Vorenus?"

"At your service," he offered with a courtly nod. "You must be Olivia Carey. Devinshea explained you were here with Kelsey. He promised he would speak with you about Kelsey so you wouldn't be worried."

A delicate blush stained Liv's face. "He talked to me, all right, but I kind of watched him. His mouth was moving…I was thinking about other things."

"Nice, Liv," I laughed. "Your hormones kick in at the worst times."

"Well, he's just so…you know," Liv said, willing me to agree with her.

"Oh, he's hot, but I kind of agree with Gray on this one. He's a dick. Not that I let that fact get in the way of taking his money." I sighed. Gray wouldn't like me taking the faery's money, but at least I didn't have to fight him on it. "Why don't you go back to your party, Liv? The councilman will show me around and then we can call a cab."

Marcus waved off the suggestion. "I'll take you home, Kelsey. I promised to escort you tonight and a ride home is all part of the service. I would be happy to take Ms. Carey wherever she needs to go."

"About that," Liv said with a frown. "I need to go. Scott and Alan are too drunk to drive home. Mr. Hot Faery has a driver waiting. I got that much from our conversation. Are you sure you'll be okay?"

I said all the right things to make Liv believe I was going to survive the night and she was off. Marcus began to politely show me around Ether. He explained the procedures and protocols for how the club worked. We walked the perimeter of the club with him showing me some of the security features. Ether, he explained to me, was considered a "place of peace."

I enjoyed my time with him. I sat and had a glass of wine as he told me stories about his time here. We fell into an easy friendship and I had to wonder if he was the man the fertility god had spoken of, the alternative to Gray. There was no question of our chemistry, but it was an almost familiar thing. Like I'd known Marcus for a long time.

Eventually, I forced myself to get back to work.

"The girls would begin their evening here," Marcus explained as he pointed out the bar and the VIP room.

Finally, I was making some progress. "Why here and not the vampire club?"

Marcus shrugged. "This is an excellent place to meet for many. I prefer to see it as purely a business transaction, but some would

145

rather have a different experience."

"The girlfriend experience?" I'd heard the term before. Rather than simple sex some johns wanted to "date" their prostitutes.

"For many, this is the way they find female companionship," Marcus explained. "In the past, slaves would be taken or human lovers would be found."

I stared at the throng on the dance floor. They were carefree and young and it was Saturday night. I didn't think I'd had many Saturday nights like this. "So why don't the vampires take human lovers anymore? It would make things easier."

"And when the humans decide to leave? In the past when a vampire took a human lover, the woman or man in question became the property of all Vampire. It's one of the ways a slave was made. The slave was never allowed to leave. Another place for the human would be found if the relationship became tenuous, but once you entered our world you did not leave."

No wonder the king was having trouble. He'd upset the entire foundation of the vampire world when he freed the slaves. "So a vampire can't take a human?"

"It must be approved by the Council," Marcus replied. "The vampire cannot reveal his secret to the human until he or she has been approved and that approval is hard to come by. There are, of course, some who know the truth. It's easier to get those approved. If a woman is in this club, then she is considered fair game. She knows our world and is a part of it. This is why it's dangerous for you to go about unescorted. You're beautiful and vibrant, and any number of vampires would love to drag you away and make you theirs."

I laughed at the thought of some vamp dragging me off by my hair. "So they're going to think I've already been claimed since I'm with you."

"Yes, they will assume I have taken you as my lover. Since I'm on the Council, they will believe the relationship has been approved. You're under my protection."

"And who was supposed to protect the girls who work the club?"

We walked around the dance floor and into a smaller room. People here were playing cards and talking quietly. It was a lounge and it was much easier to have a discussion here. The vampire quickly found an empty couch and indicated a place for me to sit.

"A woman, a former slave, runs the vampire club you saw me at last night," Marcus explained. "Her name is Stacy Sears. I'll introduce you tomorrow. She and Devinshea set up this system and she'll be able to give you the names of the women in the photos. I'll make sure she answers all of your questions."

He said it like he was going to have to use force. Tomorrow was going to be very interesting.

"Vorenus." A low growl came from the doorway to the lounge.

Marcus and I turned to see a huge, hulking man inhabiting the doorway. He quickly stalked over to meet his prey. He moved with a fluid grace that had only one word to describe it—werewolf.

Marcus didn't seem to be at all intimidated by the wolf, but he moved closer to me. He put his arm around the back of the couch above my shoulders. It told the wolf that Marcus had already laid his claim. I doubted it was necessary. Wolves didn't tend to have relationships with non-wolves for anything more than an occasional one-night stand.

"Joseph." Marcus acknowledged the wolf with a slight nod.

"We have a problem and you're the only one who can solve it." The wolf didn't sit, preferring to stare down at the vampire.

"Well, I'll do whatever I can to help," Marcus offered graciously. "Kelsey, this is Joseph Castle. He's the local alpha for the werewolves."

The alpha looked me over. "Kelsey Atwood? You the girl Trent told me about? You the one he warned my son to stay away from?"

"I suppose so, though I have no idea who Trent is." I could see the similarities between Joseph and his son Darren. They were both tall, dark, and completely annoying.

"Trent is the head of the queen's security. My boy can be an idiot sometimes," Joseph said with a sigh. "He was telling everyone who would listen how he scared the hell out of you and sent you running. I told him it wasn't something to brag about, scaring a woman."

"I think I held my ground well enough, Mr. Castle," I said with a smile. Darren had been telling tales.

Joseph's eyes went from me to Marcus, taking in how close we were. I could easily see he was making the deductions Marcus wanted him to make. "I don't think my boy knows you have powerful…friends. You should be careful around vampires, miss. Lots of girls seem to be missing lately."

Marcus's arm came down around my shoulder and curled softly. It was a request. I kept my mouth shut because sometimes I can get my questions answered without ever saying a word.

"Which girls?" Marcus asked without a hint of deception. He was good.

"Patty Kincaid and Britney Miles," Joseph said. "Neither one has been seen or heard from in a couple of weeks. Both of those girls were pretty wild. It isn't the first time Patty's up and left and Britney was having trouble with her mom. Darren tells me this doe he's been friends with is missing, too. She's the girl you're looking for, right?"

He was looking directly at me and I answered him. "Yes, she is. I was hired to find her by her mother."

"You got anything yet?"

I had to prevaricate. "I'm meeting with my client tomorrow to go over the investigation."

"Yeah, well, they probably don't have anything to do with each other," the alpha said. "I don't know why Darren wasted his time on some prey animal when he should be finding a mate. Those deer always end up in trouble when they leave their own. Look, Vorenus, here's the real problem. Some of my pack is talking about the fact that those two girls were known to…well, to hang out around vampires."

"You mean they accepted money to feed the vampires." I was beginning to realize Marcus didn't hesitate to say things plainly when he needed to.

Joseph frowned and I could see he didn't approve of the practice. "Yeah, that's what I mean. Some of my people are saying that this whole thing is a subtle way of forcing us into serving the vampires. The Council is just a front."

Marcus sat up and stared at the wolf. "That is ridiculous and you know it. Those women are not forced into anything. They choose to work. And the king has done everything he can to ensure the wolves are heard on the Council. Your leader holds a seat and a vote, and he doesn't hesitate to bully everyone he can into making laws preferable to your kind."

I heard the wolf growl low in his chest and Marcus stood up. It was clear the vampire didn't intend to show the wolf any signs of submission.

"Our women whoring themselves to your kind ain't preferable to me, Vorenus." Joseph's eyes turned distinctly predatory.

Marcus was smaller than the werewolf, but he held his ground even as the larger man crowded him. The lounge got quiet as though everyone was waiting and watching the two men to see if they would come to blows. Castle's hands were twitching like Darren's had. A need for anger management ran in the family.

"You need to back away from me, Castle." Marcus's accent deepened as the air became charged with the potential for violence.

"I know all about what goes on in that vampire club." Castle didn't follow the vampire's advice. If anything he got closer, towering over Vorenus. "I know how you use our women. How many of our potential mates have you fucked?"

"Several, I'm sure," Marcus replied simply.

His fangs were out and I needed to take control of this situation. I let my hand drift up my thigh and carefully unsnapped the holster that held the .45. I palmed the gun and clicked off the safety. Gray had taught me how to use this particular gun and I hoped I remembered everything he'd said.

"Damn. Maybe my son is right. Maybe we've given up our pride and our souls for a bigger slice of the pie. Maybe we have sold ourselves out to the vampires." Castle turned and gestured to me. "You like to fuck our women so much Vorenus, maybe we should return the favor and screw some of your bitches. How would you like that, Councilman? You want to share?"

I felt the charge off Marcus and knew he was about to do something really awful. I stood quickly, quicker than the werewolf could respond to, and I shoved the barrel of the .45 against his chest.

"How about I share my toys with you, Castle?" I asked with a smile on my face. Someone had seen my illegal weapon and was running for security. Damn it, I was going to get tossed out on my ass after all, but not until the wolf and I had come to an understanding. "Tell you what, I'll give you one of these sweet little silver bullets and we can call ourselves even. I'll even do you the favor of lodging it firmly in your heart. Back off the vampire and I swear if you refer to me as a bitch again, nothing and no one is going to stop me from hurting you, do you understand?"

"Is there a problem, Castle?"

I looked to the doorway and saw Zack was standing there with four security guards.

"Yeah, there's a problem, Owens," Castle all but snarled. "Your security is lax. Marcus's girl here's got a gun on me. Thought this was a place of peace, but apparently any old girl can waltz in with a gun."

Zack crossed his arms and walked into the room. He didn't seem to be rushing to the alpha's aid. It didn't make sense to me. Zack wasn't an alpha so he should have been submissive to the obvious alpha. Yet Zack stared him down. "I think you'll find Ms. Atwood is in Quinn's employ. It's perfectly legal for her to have her firearm and apparently she needs it. Kelsey, you can let the wolf go. He won't try anything."

Marcus nodded my way and I let the gun come down to my side. Marcus quickly gripped my hand and pulled me to his side.

Castle looked me over with a grudging kind of respect. "You're fast, girl. You sure you're human?" I didn't answer and the wolf turned his vitriol on the vampire again. "You tell all those vamps to watch themselves. We find out they're hurting our daughters and the king will have a real problem on his hands."

Castle turned and left the room.

Marcus seemed in control once more and I wondered if it bothered him I'd stepped up. Some men didn't like a woman defending them. It struck at their pride and since Marcus was the epitome of old world, I had probably made a huge mistake trying to save him. I tried to step back, but Marcus held my hand firmly in his. I wondered if I was about to get a stern lecture on letting him handle his business when he pulled my hand to his mouth and placed a fervent kiss there.

"*Dove sei stato per tutta la mia vita?*" he asked, his dark eyes warm and his lips curling into a smile meant strictly for me.

I had no idea what he was saying, but I liked the way he said it.

"What the hell was that about, Marcus?" Zack asked, though he was still looking at me.

Marcus curled my arm around his. He shrugged negligently. "The wolf and I had a small difference of opinion. You should tell your master that the wolves are getting restless. He will have problems with them."

"And you? Were you intending to let that wolf tear you apart?" Zack asked.

"He would not have been allowed to do so," Marcus said in a

low, seductive voice. "Kelsey would never have allowed the big bad wolf to harm me. I was perfectly safe."

Zack's eyes narrowed as he looked at us. "Yes, I think she can hold her own. You're lucky you took that check from Dev or I'd be forced to kick your butt for carrying in here. As long as you're working for the boss, you'll be allowed a gun in the club. Now, I think it's late. I've been informed to call Stacy at the club and make arrangements for you to meet with her tomorrow night." Zack held out his hand. "Let me have your cell. I'll program my number in and you can call me if you need anything."

I reached in my bag and pulled the phone out.

The wolf quickly entered his numbers and handed it back. "I need to get home. My wife is going to have my head staying out so late. My daughter won't go to sleep until I kiss her good night, so Lisa is dealing with one cranky baby girl. Why don't you escort Ms. Atwood home? She has a big day ahead of her tomorrow."

"It would be my pleasure," Marcus said. "Come along, Kelsey."

I was tired and I'd gotten everything I was going to get out of tonight. I had four of five girls ID'd and an invitation to get into the club. It was probably time to call it a night.

"Do I get to ride in the Bentley?" That was one sweet car.

"If that is your preference, then certainly." He led me out of the lounge.

It was getting late and the crowd was starting to thin out. I wondered if Gray had already gone to bed, if he'd already forgotten about me. Maybe he'd called up an old girlfriend.

"You are thinking of the demon?" Marcus's face was a polite mask once more.

"No," I lied. "I was thinking about the case. Maybe Quinn is wrong and I should talk openly about it. Maybe if the wolves knew it couldn't be a vampire they would back off."

"I doubt it," the vampire replied, patting my arm. "That small faction of wolves wouldn't be swayed by your evidence. If they discovered there had been murders and they had been conducted during daylight hours they would simply accuse me or the king himself."

I thought about what I hadn't told the vampire. Maybe it was time for full disclosure. "What if they knew the murders were being committed by a copycat?"

Marcus stopped. "Who is the murderer copying?"

"This is so cliché," I said with a sigh. "He could try being a little more original. He seems to like his murders old school, this guy. He's gone back to the original, if you know what I mean. He's pretending to be Jack the Ripper."

Any color Marcus had drained quickly.

"That's bad?"

"Oh, Kelsey," Marcus said with a shake of his head. "That's bad for all of us. I doubt he is performing the killings himself since some have been in daylight, but if he isn't involved it will be a miracle."

"Who are you talking about?"

"His name is Alexander Sharpe."

"Joanne met with an Alexander on a couple of occasions." I got that thrill that came with knowing I was on the right track.

"I'm sure she did."

"Why are you so sure he's involved?"

"Because Alexander Sharpe was Jack the Ripper," Marcus replied simply. "Now, he is a vampire. He might also be the one who brings down the king."

Chapter Ten

"Seriously?" I stopped almost in the middle of the dance floor. "Jack the Ripper is a vampire?"

Marcus gave me a stern look and pulled me along. "Keep your voice down, Kelsey. There are always ears listening here. We can talk about this in the car. Wait for me at the bar. I must go and retrieve my keys. Try not to cause trouble."

"I didn't try to cause trouble before," I said, aware of the grumpiness in my attitude.

The vampire ran his index finger along the curve of my cheek. "You don't have to try, *bella*. I'm certain that trouble simply follows you."

"Well, I hid from it for about ten years, so maybe it's making up for lost time," I replied with a sad smile.

Marcus ordered the bartender to attend me with an imperious wave of his hand. "Give my *bella ragazza* anything she would like. I will return shortly."

I managed to hop up on the barstool with minimum effort. I'd practiced the move a lot. "How about a cup of coffee?"

What can I say? I was trying to do what the vampire wanted of me. I was trying to be good. Something about Marcus Vorenus calmed me. I wanted my head perfectly clear for our ride home and not because I worried he would try something. I enjoyed talking to him. He seemed to accept that I was a hot mess and perversely it made me less of one.

The bartender poured a cup and I let the smell wash over me as I tugged off my heels. I let my poor toes breathe for the first time in hours.

"Hello." A deep voice caught my attention. I looked up as a man slid onto the stool beside me.

I took a quick sip of coffee. The new guy sent a smile my way. The bartender didn't even try to offer him anything. I wondered if we were getting close to last call. "Hi."

"I'm Michael."

"Good for you." I pulled out my phone. It was almost 3:00 a.m. No wonder I was tired.

"I haven't seen you around here before." His voice was all kinds of dark chocolate deep, and I sensed his infinite patience. "A pretty girl like you, I would have noticed. Are you from out of town?"

"I'm from suburbia." I was a little shocked by the growing revelation that I was getting hit on. When it rained it poured. I turned to the newcomer and took him in. He appeared to be roughly twenty-five, with naturally wholesome good looks. His hair was a medium brown and his eyes green. He was pretty and if I hadn't been surrounded by manly men like Gray and Marcus, I likely would have been totally taken in. "Vampire?"

"Only if you like vampires, honey," came his sure reply. "Why don't you let me buy you a drink and we can discuss the situation."

Yep, he was a vampire all right. I was all about the vamp tonight. "I'm pretty sure my escort would have a problem with that."

"Escort, huh? You're definitely new here," Michael said with a satisfied smile. "As I happen to know no one's managed to get through the approval process lately, you're fair game." I felt a warm rush across my skin. "Let's go back to my place. I'll take good care of you. You'll like me, honey."

I could hear his voice inside my head. It whispered to me and told me all the ways he would care for me. Surprisingly, sex was only a part of it. He wanted to take care of me, to see to my needs and ensure my happiness. I wouldn't have to do anything but allow him to make me happy. His magic was warm and soothing and I wasn't having it. Remembering how I'd shoved the guy out of my head before, I mentally threw a wall up and the whispering stopped.

Michael jerked back. "How did you do that?"

Before I could answer, Michael was out of his barstool and being tossed across two sets of tables. Luckily the place was close to empty and Michael hit the ground yards from where he'd started. Marcus bore down on him like a hawk after a bunny.

"You think to take what I've claimed? *Figlio di puttana!*"

Michael had the good sense to try to placate the enraged vampire. His hands were out defensively as he got to his feet. "I'm so sorry, Marcus. I didn't know you had taken a lover."

"And my Kelsey did not mention this fact to you?" His tightly controlled body turned to me and I was really glad I could answer him with complete honesty.

"I told him my escort would be mad." I didn't bother getting out of my chair. Marcus had this one handled.

The vampire shook his head like I'd explained something. "You'll have to excuse my mistress. She's new and has not had time to fully understand our ways. I will, of course, tutor her."

"What did I do wrong?" I asked, curious because Marcus's rage was deflating.

"An escort is merely a date." Marcus smoothed out the lines of suit. He walked over to me and helped me down. Without my heels, I was significantly shorter than the vampire. With the shoes we'd been almost evenly matched, but now he looked down on me and I got the feeling he liked being taller. "The proper word to explain my relationship to you is master."

I couldn't help it. I snorted. It was not an attractive sound. "As if."

Marcus's lips curled up in what I took for a sign of his amusement. "It's a euphemism, of course. Everyone knows who the true master in the relationship is."

Michael had picked himself up and looked like a kicked puppy. "Sorry. I thought…"

"You thought she was alone," Marcus allowed. "You thought she was soft and beautiful and if she was here and alone then she was looking."

"I thought I'd hit the jackpot," Michael said with a sad shrug. "Guess I'll go to the club for dinner. I hate that damn club. What do I have to do, Marcus? I've tried three times to get women approved and I get turned down. I'm sick of being alone."

Marcus looked at the younger vampire, compassion in his dark eyes. "I understand. I'll talk to the king tomorrow. I have several females in my employ back home in Venice. They would love to have a vampire for a lover. Their families served me for centuries. Would you like to meet one of them?"

Michael perked up fast. "Seriously, you would do that for me?"

"I would, if only to keep your eyes off my lovely Kelsey," Marcus said with a slight bow.

Michael grinned and nodded my way. "Well, I can look at her all I like, but I promise I won't try persuasion on her anymore. She kicked me out of her head faster than I could start my proposal. What is she? Is she a witch? She's damn powerful."

"Yes, she is," Marcus murmured and he quickly assured Michael he would get back to him about the woman and led me off.

He strode toward the door of the club, sweeping me along in my bare feet. The doorman nodded as Marcus hurried through. I jogged to keep up with him.

"Are you upset with me?" He was suddenly in a big hurry to end our evening. I pulled back. Maybe he'd figured out how bad traffic could be and he didn't want to drive thirty to forty-five minutes to take me home. "Look, Vorenus, I'll call a cab if it's too much trouble."

He continued on, not looking back at me and I'd had enough. I planted both feet and ceased moving. The vampire turned, his eyes flaring with anger. I pulled my hand out of his.

"What did I do?" Where had I gone wrong this time? At least I'd understood how I pissed Gray off. Was Marcus that upset that I'd gotten some words wrong? It didn't seem like that would make him mad, but I didn't understand protocol.

"I'm not an idiot, Ms. Atwood." The vampire's eyes seemed to rake over me, and there was no admiration in them. "Perhaps I am since I spent the evening mooning over a *piccola puttana*. Tell Devinshea his plan did not work."

"What does that mean?" I pulled away from the man I'd been becoming friends with. I should have walked away, but I wanted to know what he'd called me. I had a sneaking suspicion and it made my heart hurt. Stupid that I'd gotten so close to him in the course of a few hours. "If you want to insult me at least do it in a language I understand. Be a man. What did you call me?"

"Little whore."

I'd wanted to see what he was like when his guard was down and I was getting it in full measure now.

I reached out and slapped him full on across the face, enjoying the satisfying crack of flesh against flesh. I pulled myself up to my full height and really wished I'd worn something other than a stupid dress. I'd have felt less vulnerable if I'd worn jeans and a T-shirt. I would have been myself and I would have remembered to not trust people. I'd stared at myself in the mirror at Gray's place and thought that looking pretty made me pretty, but it didn't. I was still my father's daughter and I still couldn't find someone to accept me as I was.

"Fuck you, vampire," I said with all the anger I could manage through the hurt. When the hell was I going to learn? I tried to stalk past him. I would get to the garage with as much dignity as I had left and I would call a cab. I hoped I had enough cash. I doubted they would take my IOU until I could cash the faery's check.

"Tell me you're not working for the prince." Marcus grabbed my arm.

"I'm not telling you anything except good-bye."

"You seriously expect me to believe that you are innocent? That you aren't working with him?"

"I don't give a shit what you believe. Let me go." I managed to get my arm out of his hold.

"You're a witch with the power to avoid persuasion," the vampire accused. "Persuasion is my talent, but you know that. You're the perfect person to send to me. You can tell your boss that until I hear the words from the king, I won't leave. If the king wants me gone then I'll go, but Devinshea can't trick me into doing something to get me banished. He'll have to try something else."

"I'm not a witch, asshole." I pulled off the little anklet charm Liv had made for me. I held it up, pointing it Marcus's way. "I'm a piddling human who has no idea what you mean by avoiding persuasion. If you mean I won't let some fucker in my head tell me what to do, then I guess I'm guilty. If you don't mind, I'll get the fuck out of your line of fire."

I started toward the elevator.

"*Merda*," I heard the vampire curse. I might not know what it meant, but I knew a dirty word when I heard it.

I didn't turn around. I kept walking. I made it to the elevator and pushed the button. The doors opened and I got inside. I stared blankly at the keypad and remembered Liv had pushed a bunch of numbers in like a code. I didn't remember the damn code. I'd been looking up at Gray, thinking how handsome he was in his suit. I hated men so much in that moment. I was going to have to go through the indignity of getting back off the elevator, walking past the pretended-to-be-a-nice-guy vampire and back into the club. I so wasn't doing that. I pushed a single number, thinking I'd get out of here and call Liv and maybe she could talk me through it. I pushed the buttons randomly, but the doors wouldn't close.

"You have to know the code," Marcus said quietly, standing in the doorway.

"I'll figure it out." I let the chill I felt climb into my voice. Cold. Cold was better than hot. Hot brought tears. Cold was much more dignified.

"Tell me you are what you say you are." There was a slight pleading in his voice. "I...no longer know what to believe. *Per favore.* Please."

There was no mask left on Marcus's face. He looked tired and sad and I couldn't help but respond. I felt as tired as he looked. "I'm just a girl, Vorenus. I met Devinshea Quinn a couple of hours ago. I kind of thought he was an asshole, but not nearly as big an asshole as I think you are. Please let me go home. I want to go home."

The vampire said nothing as he stepped into the elevator and pressed the series of numbers that started it moving. I held myself as far from him as possible.

"Take the car, Kelsey." He held his keys out.

"I'll call a cab."

"Please," he begged. "I've made a complete ass of myself. Just take the car. I'll send someone to retrieve it tomorrow. I would prefer if you would allow me to drive you, but I understand if you do not wish to be with me."

"I just want to do my job, Vorenus." I felt stupid holding my shoes, but I couldn't force myself back into them.

"Of course," he said evenly. "I'll make certain everything is ready for you tomorrow. It would be best if you allowed me to go with you. By now everyone believes you're my mistress. If I make arrangements for another vampire to escort you, it would be...confusing. I swear to you that I'll be on my best behavior. I will not hurt you again."

I smiled as casually as I could. Everything that came out of my mouth was a total lie. "You can't hurt me. It's fine. You and the faery have some sort of war going. Leave me out of it. I want to close my case and then you never have to deal with me again. I'll be professional if you will."

"I will be whatever you want me to be, Kelsey. I would do anything to take back the last ten minutes. We were becoming friends."

"Yeah, well, I'm sure a councilman has enough friends. He doesn't need a two-bit PI hanging around." The elevator stopped.

"You would be so wrong, *cara mia*," Marcus said so achingly I turned to him.

I was about to ask him what he meant when I saw Gray's truck sitting right in front of the elevator and it seemed like all the air in the world fled. My breath caught almost painfully in my chest at the sight of him. I wondered if I would ever get used to how beautiful he was.

"Kelsey?" Gray said as his head came up. He was sitting in the cab with the door open.

"You came back for me?" I got out of the elevator.

His previously pristine suit coat was tossed aside and his tie was gone. His shoulders were slumped as he got out of the truck. "I never left, baby. I just waited. I'm so sorry. I was wrong. I was a bastard. Please, please forgive me." He came to stand right in front of me and lowered his forehead to mine. "Please, baby. Please forgive me."

My shoes fell to the concrete floor as my arms wound around his waist and I leaned into his warmth. I knew I should tell both men to go to hell and sink back into the shell I'd spent years perfecting, but I wanted what Gray had to offer so much. He'd lost his temper. It wasn't like I hadn't done that before. I got pissed off and said things I didn't mean all the time. I let my head rest against his chest and felt the strong beat of his heart as his arms tightened around me.

"Thank you for taking care of her," I heard Gray saying. At least he was trying to be polite.

"It was an honor, Mr. Sloane. Her work is important. I will help her and you in any way I can. Feel free to call upon me." When I looked around to say good-bye to the vampire he was already gone.

"Let's go home, sweetheart," Gray said, weariness plain in his tone. "Did he behave himself?"

"He was fine." He had been for the most part and there was a part of me that mourned the fact that he wasn't still here. "The two of you have a lot in common. You both can't stand Dev Quinn."

His handsome face fell and he sighed. "I'm sorry, Kelsey. I let him get the best of me again. I should have called him and explained the situation and asked to be allowed in to investigate. I shouldn't have tried to sneak in." He noticed my bare feet and swung me up into his arms. I felt so small and delicate when he carried me. I suppose I was small and delicate compared to Gray. It was nice to feel feminine.

Gray carried me around the truck and settled me into the cab before going back for my shoes. He handed them to me and then got into the driver's seat. As he drove I filled him in on everything I discovered. I told him about the trouble the Council was having with the wolves and the fact that one of the murders occurred during the day. I discussed the fact that apparently the actual Jack the Ripper was alive and well and living in Dallas. I didn't mention that Marcus had been sweet and kind and up until he thought I was working with his nemesis, we'd had a real, undeniable chemistry. That was done and probably had been more a figment of my imagination than anything else.

"Are you sure Vorenus didn't try anything on you, sweetheart?" Gray asked and I could tell he was being careful not to show his temper. He hadn't liked the fact that I'd shown up with the vampire, but he was smart enough to know that a big display of masculine jealousy wasn't going to help his cause. "It's hard for me to believe he could spend time with you and not try something. He's a powerful persuasive. He can make you do things you don't want to do."

"I know." I didn't really want to talk about that portion of the evening. For some reason, I wanted to keep my time with Marcus private. "He explained it to me. I told you, Gray, he didn't try anything and he got angry with the one vampire who did try."

"What?" The question was a curt slap of the tongue.

I sighed and leaned my head against the window of the truck. I must be tired or I would have known better than to mention that incident.

"Kelsey?" He wasn't going to let me off the hook.

"Some vamp was looking for a date and he tried to persuade me to go with him. Marcus took exception, but he didn't have to since I'd already handled it."

Gray got on the freeway, which was blissfully clear at this time of night. "How did you handle it?"

"I don't know." I wondered if we were going to get into another fight over this. If we were, I'd rather go to my place. I was antsy. I'd been through the emotional wringer and all I wanted to do was sleep. I didn't think I could take another big scene. I had to hope Gray's patience wasn't wearing thin on the sexual front. "I tossed him out of my head and that was that."

Gray was thoughtful as he exited the freeway and started down the road to his house. I enjoyed the silence for a moment and let the evening's events wash over me. All in all it had been pretty crappy when I really thought about it. I'd been used by men all night. Gray tried to force me to choose between him and work. Quinn tried to use me as a pawn in his war with Marcus. The local alpha treated me like a piece of ass. Marcus…that had almost hurt even more than Gray. I expected that Gray would realize I wasn't the girl for him. I just hoped for a little more time before he figured it out. Marcus wasn't a lover. He was a friend who I thought I might not have to pretend around.

"Kelsey, we're home," Gray said softly and I realized the truck had stopped. His hand came out to run the length of my arm. "Let's go to bed, sweetheart. We'll go over everything in the morning and figure out what to do."

He got out of the truck and was around to my side before I could open the door myself. He helped me down and hustled me into the house, locking doors and setting alarms. He nodded toward the rear of the house where his bedroom was. "Go on, sweetheart, I'll be with you in a minute. I want to check on a few things first."

When I got to the kitchen, I noticed a small tray had been left for us. Syl, no doubt. I passed on the wine, preferring a bottle of water, but I took two of the cookies. And yes, I then turned and took another two. I munched on the pepperminty chocolate chip cookies as I made my way to the back of the house.

I turned on the shower in the bathroom and let my clothes fall to the floor. A steaming hot shower sometimes helped. I was still alone when I got out. I noticed the clothes I'd worn yesterday were clean and neatly folded on the long marble counter. Syl must have been busy while we'd been gone. When we'd left earlier in the evening, the bathroom looked like a girl bomb had gone off. There had been makeup, curling irons, and clothes everywhere. Though it had hurt Liv's heart to leave behind a mess, Gray had insisted we be on time. Now the bathroom was pristine.

I dried off and quickly got into my panties and one of Gray's T-shirts. It was comfortable. I could lie in bed staring at the ceiling for hours in it.

I heard Gray before I saw him. He was standing in the doorway, his shirt gone, his feet bare and a look in his eyes that told me what he wanted. I caught my breath at the sight of him. He was so freaking gorgeous, with perfectly tanned skin that bespoke of hours spent working in the sun and that thick dark hair I wanted to run my fingers through. If I had the chance, I would convince him to grow it out so it waved and curled and went wild in the mornings. His eyes were rich and hot as he looked over me, but he didn't make a move yet and I just knew I couldn't do it. I couldn't sleep with him when I knew it wouldn't work between us. It would hurt too fucking much when he was gone.

There must have been something in my eyes because his whole body seemed to deflate. "I'm gonna take a shower, Kelsey. Go to bed, okay?"

I hated that I'd disappointed him, but it was better this way. "Where's my bedroom?"

He checked the flare of anger that I watched wash over him. His reply was even and controlled. "I didn't attack you last night and I won't tonight. Get in bed. If you can't trust me enough to even sleep beside you then I'll take the couch, but I'm not leaving you alone. Now let me take the coldest shower in the history of time so we can get some sleep."

I fled the bathroom and crawled into the big bed where we'd slept the night before. The sheets were smooth and cool against my skin and I stared up at the darkened ceiling. I listened to the sounds of the shower and wondered why I couldn't take what little happiness I was offered. Why was I so afraid of the pain that would come? Didn't I want to feel even the tiniest bit alive?

I fought back tears and eventually the sounds of the water

Ripper

running and the fan overhead lulled me to sleep.

    I hurry to keep up with my dad, but the boots he's given me to wear are Nate's and they're too big.
    "Keep up, girl," my father says gruffly.
    The leaves beneath my feet crunch and the air is cool all around me. It's winter in the Ozarks. We drove all night from Dallas to get here and then camped during the day. Dad grew up here. I want him to take me to his old house. He took Nate and Jamie to meet his cousins, but he told me we don't have the time. He never lets me meet the people he knows. When his friends come by the house he tells me to stay in my room, that there will be hell to pay if I come out. I don't think my dad wishes he'd ever had a girl because, as far as I know, none of his friends are even aware of my existence.
    He is ashamed of me.
    I wish he'd given me Nate's gloves. My hands are cold, but I don't complain. He almost never takes me anywhere with him so I don't mention my discomforts. If I do a good job, maybe he won't hate me so much. Maybe I can prove I can hunt like the boys. Dad hunts werewolves who eat people and make humans miserable. He's a hero so it makes sense he doesn't have time for me. I have to prove my worth and then he'll train me like he did Jamie and Nathan. I know that my brothers don't want Dad to train me, but I can do it. I know I can.
    My heart races as my father looks around the woods and decides this is the spot. I can see the Little Red River from here. It's low in this part of the woods but cold, so cold. The woods here are isolated and filled with game. I let the cold air wash over me and I know that my father is right. Wolves are in the woods.
    "They're here, Dad," I say with a glimmer of excitement. I can tell they were here. That has to mean I'm a hunter.
    My father frowns down at me. "Don't talk too much, girl."
    "But I can sense them."
    Now my father looks downright mad and I wonder what I said to make him that way. I try to be so good around my dad. He's only hit me once or twice, but it really hurt when he did it, so I try to avoid making him mad. When he hit me in the face, it left bruises and then I had to skip school so I didn't have to explain.

"Little freak." My father turns away from me. He sets his pack down and starts to pull out the things he will need.

Despite the cold Arkansas mountain air, I flush. I should never, never talk about those weird flashes I get. I thought it would make him see that I was a hunter like him, but anytime I mention how I can sense things or feel them he gets mad and calls me a freak.

"I'm sixteen," I want to yell at him. I'm not a little girl anymore.

I stand there in the chill as the moon starts to rise and realize I can never, never tell him about the dreams I have. At night, mostly on the nights when the moon is full, I dream of running. I am alone in the woods and the solitude is perfection. I run, starting on two legs, but ending on four. When I change, the world is different. It's better. I can see everything with my new eyes. Smells and sounds are sharper. There is nothing in these dreams except the hunt. Well, and the brown wolf who hunts with me. But I try not to think of him. My father would not like to know that I dream sometimes that he's a wolf.

"We'll put you on that tree there," Dad says, his voice harsh. Mom says it's because he smokes too much and there's disdain in her voice when she says it. Sometimes I think she hates my father. She always seems happy when he goes on his trips. That's when she takes my brothers and me places. When Dad is gone we go out to eat, and when I was younger, we went to the zoo and parks. Sometimes we went to East Texas to see my granddad. I wish I'd been able to spend more time with him before he died.

"Do I get a gun?" I ask quietly because I have to keep my voice down.

My father laughs like I said something hysterical. "No, idiot. I'm not giving you a gun." His green eyes seem cold. They always seem that way. His gaze slides past mine. He never looks me in the eyes. I think he doesn't like brown eyes. I'm the only one in the family with dull brown eyes. He calls them muddy.

I want to question him, but that's when he usually uses his fists.

He picks up a length of rope. "Go stand by the tree. Take your coat off first."

I do what he tells me to do. I start to shiver and not entirely from the freezing air. I can hear the wolves howl in the distance. He starts to wind the rope around me. My arms are free, but he wraps the rope around my waist. I am utterly helpless to run.

"What are you doing?" I begin to panic. I stay still though because he's my dad. I want him to love me. Maybe if I do this for him, he'll see that I can help him.

He tightens the rope and secures it. It burns against my skin it's so tight. He's good with knots. I watched as he spent hours teaching Jamie and Nate how to tie knots. I watched from the stairs of our little duplex because he didn't teach girls. Sometimes Nate would come up after bedtime and he'd show me what he'd learned.

"There." He finishes up, tightening it further, and I can tell he's happy with his work.

"I'm cold," I say before realizing I shouldn't complain.

"Suck it up, girl." He looks me over and then pulls out his wicked large bowie knife. "This'll bring 'em."

I try to beg him not to cut me, but it doesn't work. He simply turns my forearms over and cuts a long gash in both. I start to bleed. There's a lot of blood. How much can I lose?

"I'll stitch you up when it's over," he says, but I'm not sure if I believe him. He walks off and I know he's hiding. He'll pick a spot where he can shoot quickly and efficiently.

I get woozy from the cold and all the blood. My arms feel strange, like they should be numb, but they're tingling. My arms are covered in blood and I wonder if he means to let the wolves get me. It would be easy to pick them off while they're feasting. My father says wolves go crazy when they eat humans. They love it, love the kill so much they don't think about protecting themselves. They're vicious animals.

I think about my mom. Dad picked me up from school. He'd been standing in the courtyard where I waited every day for Nate. Nate was a year ahead of me at Bell High School, and he always drove me home in that piece of crap Ford Mom had saved to buy. Yesterday had been Thursday and Nate had chess club. Dad thought it was for pussies, but Nate liked games, so I waited for him in the courtyard. Dad told me we were going hunting. I wonder if he even told Mom. I wonder if she thinks I ran away. Did Nate spend time looking for me?

I sense them before I see them. I look up and in the moonlight I can see them. My heart speeds up. There are four of them. They approach me cautiously. I wonder why. Why aren't they growling? I am a helpless human. I am food. They should attack immediately because they hate us. They eat our flesh. The small group comes from across the river and I see for the first time this creature my father taught me to hate.

The wolves are brown, two larger than the others, though they seem small compared to the way I envisioned them. They crouch down and sniff the air, but I know my dad always masks his scent. The largest of the four looks at the rest and then comes in close. I know instinctively that she is female. I never expected her to be so beautiful. She's graceful as she approaches me and she whines a little in the back of her throat and then snorts like she's done something foolish. She sits back and I watch as she changes. One minute she's a brown wolf and the next she's a girl, maybe a year or two older than me.

"I bet you don't speak wolf," she says with a soothing smile. She keeps her words calm. "Don't be afraid. I won't hurt you. Who did this to you?"

Why is she talking to me? She's supposed to attack. Wolves don't help. Wolves don't have warm brown eyes. The others are changing. Two boys and another teenaged girl.

"It's all right," she says. "It's just my obnoxious kid brother and our cousins. Is the person who did this to you gone?"

They're kids. They're just kids like me.

"I can go get my dad," the girl offers. "He'll track this jerk down and make sure he doesn't hurt you again."

The boys are young. One is maybe ten and the other can't be more than six or seven. He sniffles and wipes his nose on his forearm.

"I think we should go, Tina," the other girl says. "We can send the pack back for her. We should never have come this far out."

But it's too late. The first shot rings out and I watch in horror as the girl who offered to help me looks down at the circle of red opening on her chest like a blooming rose. The bullets are silver and her eyes are blank before she hits the forest floor.

I see the next few moments in slow motion. The ten-year-old boy is next and then the girl. The little boy stands there, looking down at the girl named Tina. He cries and I think he asks her to get up. He doesn't leave her. He doesn't run. He loves his sister and it costs him his young life. I watch as my father shoots him between the eyes.

My father is an awfully good shot.

The forest is quiet again and I hear the crunch of his boots as he crushes leaves beneath him. He is a large, dark figure in the moonlight, gun still in his hand. He looks over his kills.

"They were kids," I manage to say through my tears. They wanted to help me and now they were dead.

"Yeah," my father says with a wealth of satisfaction in his voice.

"Daddy?"

His eyes are vicious as they look at me. "Don't you call me that, girl. You call me sir."

It was what he insisted on. I held my tongue. He was going to realize his mistake and he was going to feel bad.

He kicks the body of the ten-year-old boy over like it's a piece of meat. "I always like to get 'em before they have a chance to breed."

Something snaps inside me. I feel like I am a bottle of champagne and the cork is coming out. Rage bubbles up and flows from deep within. I have been lied to. The wolves aren't animals. They're different. Perhaps the wolves who killed my grandmother and my aunt were bad, but these wolves weren't evil. The girl had been like me. I realize, too, that he intends to leave me here, staked out and bleeding. He will never tell my mother. He'll pretend he doesn't know what happened to me. Maybe he'll shoot me and bury my body out here, then he won't have to deal with a muddy-eyed freak anymore.

I don't know how I do it, but the rope tears around me. I am strong all of the sudden and the cold is gone, replaced with a hot, satisfying anger.

"What the hell?" I hear my father whisper as I shrug off the bonds.

Something dark and deep takes over. I can feel it. It's as though a door has opened in my soul and a piece of me I never knew before has been unleashed. I'm a bundle of instincts now. Two are foremost in my mind—survival and revenge. My father lifts the rifle, but I am faster. It is in my hand as he pulls the trigger, the shot flying wildly, impotently through the air. I hold the weapon in my hands and it feels good when I twist the metal. The gun will never work again. I toss it aside as my father backs away from me. I can smell his fear.

He is prey and no longer my father. He is meat that has done wrong to me and he will pay. He attempts to hit me, but I no longer allow such liberties. As his fist shoots out to connect with my jaw, it is so simple to block him. He moves like a man in slow motion. I simply raise my hand to catch him. His fist is large but I manage to crush it anyway. He cries out as his fingers break beneath the pressure I apply.

I have legs, too. I use them. I kick out neatly like I have done this a thousand times before. I catch him in the gut, knowing exactly where to place my heel so all the breath is pushed from his body. He would fall back and away from me, but I hold his broken hand like a tether between us. He falls to his knees and I crush his nose with my free hand.

"Kelsey," he cries, but he's too late.

He tries to pull his knife, but I smile down. I took it from him when he wasn't looking…

"Kelsey," a sharp voice startled me awake.

I fought him blindly, only knowing the nightmare still had me in its clutches. Gray pinned me, his big body covering mine and holding me down.

"Kelsey, wake up," he commanded.

The fog began to lift as I realized I'm not in those woods any longer. I was with Gray. I could feel the heat of his body, the satisfying weight of him on top of me. The ceiling fan turned overhead and I took a deep breath. "Gray?"

His face gentled, his hands coming down to smooth back my hair. "It's all right, baby. You're here with me. It's okay."

He got off me and sat down on the edge of the bed. He turned on the small light on the nightstand. "Is that better?"

I nodded, still shaking from the dream. This was why I rarely went to bed sober. When I passed out, I didn't dream about that night.

"Was it about your dad?"

"How do you know about that?" I asked, my voice as sharp as broken glass.

Gray looked down at me unflinchingly. "Jamie told me. You're not the only one who has nightmares. We were on a stakeout a couple of years back and he fell asleep. He blew our cover when he woke up screaming. He told me about the things your father forced him to do. He told me about how it was nothing compared to what he did to you. I intend to kill your father if I ever find him."

"Are you looking?" I wondered who my father would be more afraid of, me or Gray?

"I've been looking for him for almost a year," Gray admitted. "I had a solid lead that he was in Canada, but a man can get really lost in the Yukon. I don't have the time to track him like I should. If it would make you feel better, I'll take some leave and I promise you, I will find him."

He was serious. If I told him to, he would put in for a sabbatical and go to Canada to try to kill a man he didn't even know so I would sleep better at night. No one before ever cared about me so much. It wasn't that I didn't have friends or brothers who loved me, but Gray was different. I shook my head. He could kill my father, but it wouldn't stop the dreams. I couldn't bring myself to tell Gray that the monster in my dreams wasn't my father.

It was me.

I felt a gentle hand brush against my cheek. I wanted to tell him to stop. I didn't want to be touched, but I allowed it. Gray seemed to need to do it. It got easier to handle until I leaned into his hands, wanting it. Until the need overcame everything else. His fingers brushed against my skin and I felt the electricity between us.

"Tell me," he whispered against my hair.

I hesitated. I hadn't told anyone but Jamie and Liv. I should blow him off. Tell him something about being scared of wolves.

Instead, I opened my mouth and told him everything.

He ended up moving behind me while I told him about my childhood and that night in the woods. He didn't interrupt me, merely let me lay back against the comfort of his chest. He rubbed my shoulders and my arms, willing warmth and relaxation into my bones. It was easy in the soft light to believe he would protect me. It was easy to believe I could tell him anything.

I wanted to not be alone anymore.

"I walked away from him," I finished tonelessly. "I think he was alive."

There was no judgment in Gray's voice as he replied. "And you never saw him again?"

I shook my head.

"I'm sure he was alive," Gray said. "I did find a John Atwood matching your father's description. I tracked his movements from Atlanta up to the Yukon. He was still hunting. Honey, what you did to him was in self-defense."

I kept my mouth closed. I didn't tell him that my father had been down and defenseless and I kept right on beating him until I heard wolves coming. The pack had been looking for their children and that was when I ran. I hadn't been able to face them.

"How did you get to a town?"

"I walked." I hadn't. I'd run, faster than I could have imagined because those wolves had been looking for me and I doubted they would have been in the mood for explanations. I'd run and when I could, I'd tracked back to the river. I swam a few miles in the freezing water to mask my scent. I'd made it to Heber Springs ten miles away, walking in twenty-degree temperatures, wet and without a coat. I evaded the police and managed to steal warm clothes. When I was properly dressed, I found a truck stop and a waitress let me use the phone. My brother picked me up eight hours later.

I didn't even catch a cold.

Gray ran a hand down my left arm, seeking the scars that should have been there. "Are you sure he cut you? You don't have any scars."

"I guess it just seemed deep." I remembered the feeling of that knife cutting deeply into my forearms. I remembered the way the blood welled and how weak I felt.

I didn't mention to Gray that six months later, I'd slit my own arms from wrist to elbow. I'd heard that was the best way to commit suicide. I'd cut hard and deep, sure that it would end my guilt, my suffering. That was when Nate and Liv had found me.

I like to say they saved me, but sometimes I wonder because the truth of the matter is I don't have those scars either.

The dream was gone, but the feelings were still riding me hard. I wanted to stop talking, to stop the unwanted emotions from swamping me. I wanted…Gray.

I sat up and turned around to face him. I reached out and traced the hard line of his jaw. His face was all angles and planes. If you studied his features separately he was too hard to be handsome, but something about Gray softened the ultra masculine lines and made him beautiful. I leaned in and pressed my lips against his. His callused hands found my hips and stroked up to my waist. We kissed for a moment, our tongues tangling, and though I wished I could stay there for hours, I knew that wasn't what men wanted.

Men liked it fast and hard and they wanted a woman who did, too. I reached over and turned off the light.

"Hey," Gray protested.

"I want you." I pulled the T-shirt over my head. I felt much bolder in the dark. I was determined to have him and to be the kind of lover he wanted. I couldn't be the kind of woman he needed, but maybe I could give him what he required in bed. The last thing he would want is to waste a bunch of time kissing.

I stood up and slid out of my panties. I let my hands find the band of his briefs and tugged them until his cock came free. I felt the full length of him. He gasped as I squeezed his erection. He was big. He was much bigger than I'd ever had before and I didn't have the addition of alcohol as a lubricant, but I was determined. I straddled him and, before I could convince myself it was a bad idea, I reached down and forced myself onto his incredibly hard dick.

"Kelsey," I heard him say and it didn't sound sexy. It sounded a little like a protest.

I wasn't moving fast enough. It hurt, but I tried to work my way onto him. I had him about halfway in when he flipped me over forcefully and he pulled out. The light came on. I felt my body flush when I realized he was furious.

"What the hell was that?"

Embarrassment flooded my system, so much worse than anything I'd felt before. I knew I wasn't great in bed, but I'd never had a man shove me away and ask what I was doing. It was usually obvious. I managed to sit up and reached down to grab the sheet. I pulled it calmly up to cover my body. Calm. That was the key to getting through this debacle. I didn't do what I wanted. I wanted to cry. I wanted to run and lock myself in the bathroom because I'd made a complete fool of myself. I wasn't sure what I had done to offend him because he'd been hard as hell, but he obviously didn't want to have sex with me.

I shrugged as casually as I could. "Sorry, I misread the signals. Oh, well, can't be sexually compatible with everyone, I guess."

His jaw dropped open at the comment and he spent way too long a moment looking at me. I wished the light could have stayed off because I felt completely naked under his scrutiny. I had to look away and I wished he would leave. I thought about getting up and walking out. It was almost morning as it was. I could call Liv to come get me. I stayed where I was because I didn't want him to see me naked again. It was obvious I wasn't his type.

His voice came out on a low growl. "What the hell have you done to yourself, baby?"

"What does that mean?" I asked irritably. I had to find the one guy in the world who wanted to talk about his freaking feelings.

Gray sat down on the bed again and he reached out to take my hand. I wouldn't give it to him, so he settled his palm on my knee. He seemed calmer, but I thought getting the pity lecture might be worse than actually having him angry with me. "Have you ever made love, sweetheart?"

I laughed. "Don't be ridiculous, Gray. I'm not a virgin. I've had sex before."

"With anyone who gave a shit about you?"

Now I was pissed because he'd hit the nail on the head and I didn't want to face that fact. I no longer cared if he saw my tits. I pushed his hand off me.

"Fuck you, Gray," I said with every intention of getting out of the house.

Any softness in his face was replaced with iron-hard will. As I started to get up, his hand shot out and grabbed my ankle. Before I knew what was happening, his full weight pinned me to the bed and he used his hands to twist something around my wrists. It happened so quickly. Before I could take a breath, I was on my back with Gray pressing me into the mattress. My hands were bound tightly together with what looked like black lace.

I stared up at the sight of my hands, too shocked at the moment to be truly pissed off. "Are those my panties?"

Gray didn't move, continuing to use his two hundred twenty pounds of pure muscle to hold my one twenty down. He leaned to the side and I heard the nightstand drawer open.

"They are, indeed, sweetheart." His erection was even harder than it was before and I hadn't thought that was possible. He twisted his hips to grind it against my pelvis. "Those are your pretty little panties and these are my handcuffs. Regulation Ranger issue." He snapped one around the material between my wrists and the other he clipped to the wrought iron in the headboard. My arms were completely useless, held over my head and locked to the bed. He felt safe enough to get up and look down at his handiwork.

I was completely naked to his roaming eyes. I'd never felt quite that naked before though I certainly had been. Sex had been quick. Get the clothes off. Get the deed done. Gray hadn't gotten that memo. He left the light on and sat back, his eyes on my body.

"I think I'll take charge now." He leaned over and covered my mouth with his. I had nowhere to go and no way to protest so I got to do what I wanted to do in the first place—enjoy the feel of his mouth on mine.

The man knew how to kiss. Slow at first, like he was softening me up and he was. The longer he brushed his lips against mine, the more I relaxed. I let go of what had happened before when his tongue dragged over my lower lip and he started whispering to me.

"You're too beautiful, Kelsey. I can't go fast. I want it to last. I want it to last forever." His hands framed my face, like I was something precious and had to be handled with delicacy. "I could kiss you forever."

His tongue plunged in, twisting around mine, like muscular velvet stroking into me. He held my head in both his hands, keeping me still for his plundering. Over and over again he kissed me. Until I caught his rhythm and we were in tune. I breathed when he did. My heart seemed to time to his. Intimacy. I didn't understand the word before Grayson Sloane kissed me.

He finally sat up with a satisfied smile and one hand reached out to tweak my nipple.

I hissed at the sensation. It was part pain, but after the first little flare, the sensation seemed to go straight to my pussy.

"Now let's talk about how this is going to go, my love."

"Do you often tie women up, Gray?" Of all the things I'd expected him to do, this hadn't even been on the list.

His smile was sensual and his accent deepened when he was aroused. "As often as they'll let me, darlin'. I like it. You look so fucking gorgeous like that. Later, I'll tie your legs down, but this first time I want them around my waist, squeezing me when you come. And you will come. I'll make sure of it."

Wow. That did all sorts of things to my insides. I felt a warm rush of arousal as my pussy came alive at the thought of him inside me. I lusted for this man. Before I simply wanted the physical release of sex and the nearest available guy would do, but now there was only Gray.

He was so beautiful and I wasn't.

I worried no one else would ever do it for me after him. I also worried that I had no idea how to give him what he wanted. Arousal fled a little as doubt came roaring back. I hadn't made love before. He was right about that. I'd degraded myself because somewhere deep down I thought I deserved it. Gray was offering me something completely different and it was terrifying.

"All right, you had your fun, lawman. Untie me."

"Is my tough girl scared?" He reached out and let his fingertips brush across my chest, making my skin tingle all over. "Do you want out so you can run away and pretend you're not vulnerable to me? That's not happening. It's obvious to me you have no idea what you're doing and I aim to teach you."

"Go to hell, Gray." I pulled at the bindings on my wrists. If I was really honest with myself, I didn't try hard.

His eyes went dark and serious. "I'll get there, baby, but I'm not going until you understand a few things." He knelt on the bed and placed his big hand on my belly. I practically quivered at his touch. "Listen to me and listen well. I love you, Kelsey Atwood. I love you and I'm going to fuck you."

"That doesn't sound so loving to me." Fuck wasn't a word I associated with love.

He leaned over and kissed my shoulder, moving to my neck. "Only because you don't know the difference between getting laid and spending hours fucking someone you can't live without. I'm going to love you until you don't remember what your pussy felt like without my cock in it." He trailed his hand down and gently slid his middle finger across my clitoris, parting my labia and delving inside. He sighed. "That's better. When you jumped on me you weren't even wet. It's not supposed to hurt. Don't you look at me like that. I'm not judging you. I'm telling you that I'm different from some guy in a bar. I love you. I'll take care of you."

I took a deep breath and decided to play things differently. My instinct was to run, to push him away because I already felt too much for him. But I couldn't walk away from Gray and not only because he was really good with bondage. If he broke my heart at least I'll have loved someone, just once.

I nodded.

"Thank you, sweetheart," he said almost reverently. He stood and moved to the end of the bed. His hands ran up my legs and I sighed because it felt good and warm everywhere he touched me.

I let my head fall back. "You can let me out, Gray. I won't fight you."

He raised my foot up in his hand. "Hell no, Kelsey. I got you where I want you. Like I said, I'd tie your legs to the post, too, but I have plans for them. I'll go easy on you tonight, but eventually I intend to introduce you to some…exotic play."

"Just how kinky are you, Grayson Sloane?"

His lips tugged up in a dirty little grin. "I have a kink or two, but I promise you'll like them."

"Are you one of those dominant people who'll expect me to kiss your feet and call you master?" We needed to get that straight right off the bat. I wouldn't be doing any of that. I was willing to discuss other things, but the master bit was not negotiable.

"If you're asking if I want to be in charge, then yes. I want to be in firm control of our sex life. I get the feeling I won't be in control of anything else. I'll want to tie you up and eventually I want to spank that pretty ass of yours. I know what I'm doing. I will never ask you to kiss my feet, Kelsey," he promised as he held mine. "But I will always kiss yours."

He sucked my toe into his mouth and I gasped. I had never thought of my toe being even vaguely erotic, but I had been wrong. He flipped me over on my belly, the restraint he'd improvised twisting smoothly and allowing the action.

"What are you doing?"

"I'm kissing you. Are you going to ask me a question every two minutes?" He licked and kissed his way up my calf. When he got to the back of my knees, he pressed his tongue there and I nearly came off the bed. "Because if you are, then I'm thinking about getting you a gag."

"That's rude," I said even as I squirmed under his assault. One hand firmly caressed my ass. I tried to breathe, to get enough oxygen into my lungs that they would start to function again.

He kissed up the length of my spine, running his tongue along my curves as though he was prepared to taste every inch of me.

There was nothing for me to do but lie there and let him worship me. That's what it felt like. It felt like adoration, like I was worthy. Yes, what was happening was sexual, but Gray was right. There was so much more to it.

He flipped me over again and when I glanced down, his face hovered on my pussy. He breathed in deeply and closed his eyes but not before I saw a rush of satisfaction.

"Spread your legs for me, Kelsey." He was up on his knees and I could barely take my eyes off the sight of that big cock jutting out proudly from between his legs. It curved about halfway up his flat stomach. His hand came out and stroked it up and down while he waited for me to comply.

I knew what he wanted. I wasn't sure it was something I wanted to do. I hadn't liked it at all the one time a guy had tried it on me. It was awkward and he'd bitten me a little too hard.

"I don't like that." I pressed my legs firmly together.

"I didn't ask you what you liked," Gray said and I could feel he was being patient with me and that his patience was rapidly coming to an end. "I told you to spread your legs. You promised to trust me. Give me two minutes. If you don't like it, I'll stop. Now, obey me and spread your legs or that exotic play might come sooner than you think."

His voice had reached a dark, deep place and I was fairly certain he'd threatened to spank me. Though I certainly wouldn't have admitted it to him at the time, the idea kind of got me hot, too.

Two minutes. I could last two minutes. It would be embarrassing, but Gray wanted it and maybe part of pleasing Gray was taking risks. With conscious will, I forced my legs apart and allowed Gray to slide his body between them.

"You're so pretty." I could feel the warmth of his breath on my sensitive flesh. He kissed me lightly and I tried to not shake. Again, I should have listened to him. This felt one hundred percent different than some drunk guy. He didn't dive right in and I started to think that Gray didn't do anything fast. He took his time, enjoyed himself fully.

"I'm going to shave you," he promised, rubbing his fingers across the curls on my pussy. "You'll be gorgeous bare and I'll be able lick every inch of you. I want you to think about that for a minute. I want you to think about how good it will feel when my tongue dives deep inside. I can fuck you with my tongue. I can worship you, licking every sweet inch of this pussy."

His tongue flicked out and barely touched my clit. He stopped and then gave it a single long lick.

"Oh, god." I was on the verge of something. Something good.

He hovered there, letting the heat of his breath wash over me, teasing and tantalizing me until I was taut and strung, like a harp waiting to be plucked. "Oh, I think I spent my whole two minutes talking about eating your pussy instead of actually doing it. Does that make you happy, baby?"

He was such a bastard. He was going to make me say it. He wasn't going to let me take the easy way out. He gave me a choice. Keep my mouth shut and he would stop and then I might save face, but I wouldn't know where all this led to. Or I could give him what he wanted.

"Don't stop, Gray."

"What do you want, sweetheart?" Gray asked with a satisfied look in his eyes. "Would you like me to do that again?"

"Yes." I wasn't going to hold out on him. God, if he would do that again I might come, really come, like the books described or they talked about in the movies but people like me thought was all bullshit. If he sucked me there I thought I would be able to fly.

His head came up, a curious and mischievous look in those gorgeous eyes. "I'm surprised because I thought you didn't like it."

I kicked at him as much as I could with him between my legs. "Jerk, you started this."

The lines of his face tightened, his eyes darkening to that deep violet I'd come to know meant he was emotional. "Give me what I want."

Somehow I knew. He didn't want me to beg. He wanted the truth—our truth. "It's better because it's you. I want it because it's you."

"And it only works this way because it's you, baby." He settled between my legs again. "And I didn't start this, but I do promise I will finish it. I will never leave you unsatisfied."

Two fingers began to move inside me, filling up my pussy. I was wet, wetter than I'd imagined I could be, and Gray reveled in it. He seemed to love it, groaning as I pushed onto his tongue, practically begging him for more. He set a staccato rhythm with his fingers and when he sucked my clit between his teeth, I cried out and shook as everything below my waist came apart. It was strong and powerful and I sobbed, unable to stop the emotion that flowed as righteously as the pleasure.

Tears flowed freely down my face when Gray covered my body with his and he used the little key to release my hands.

"I think I want your arms around me, too," he whispered as he tossed the cuffs and panties aside.

His eyes met mine, holding them as if he knew this was an important moment and not time to play games. I felt the broad head of his cock at the juncture of my body, but he hesitated.

Finally I could touch him and I let my hands find the silk of his hair. "What's wrong?"

"Nothing," he said. "Everything's perfect. You're mine, Kelsey. I won't let anything come between us. Not ever again. Trust me. Trust me to take care of you."

At the time I thought he was talking about sex. I thought he was talking about love and opening my heart to him. I couldn't have known how much darkness was ahead for us. I couldn't have known how quickly that promise would be broken. By him. By me. I only knew that lying there with my first real orgasm strumming through my body, I would give him anything.

When that big cock thrust inside me, I realized what I'd been missing. I'd been missing my other half. He filled me. My whole world seemed to focus, to become smaller and larger in the same moment.

Smaller because there was absolutely nothing outside the circle of his arms. He surrounded me utterly. He was all around and inside me. He filled my every sense and I didn't need anything but him.

Larger because I'd been alone and now I wasn't. I wasn't just Kelsey. I was a part of Kelsey and Gray.

I sighed and put my arms around his broad shoulders. He started to thrust, not trying to keep his weight off me. I loved the feel of his weight pressing me into the mattress.

His cheek rubbed against mine. "You feel so good, baby. It feels so right."

I wrapped my legs around him as he finally managed to work himself in to the base of his cock. I sighed as I felt his balls gently rub against my ass as he pulled out again and thrust home.

"I can't wait, Kelsey," he said almost apologetically as he pushed up to his elbows.

He shoved hard into me, slamming his full length in, and I looked up in wonder at the expression on his face. His eyes were closed as he concentrated on hitting my clitoris with his pelvis. I gasped as it started to build all over again. My hands found his tight backside and I squeezed to hold him there, not wanting him to come out of me even an inch.

Gray groaned and picked up the pace, and with a little twist of his hips sent me careening over the edge for the second time that night. As I bucked against him, wanting to prolong that amazing feeling, Gray stiffened above me and I felt him jerk as he came. He said my name over and over as he flooded me with his orgasm. He fell forward, his head next to mine, my body pinned deliciously under his.

"I love you, Kelsey mine," he said.

I wrapped my arms tightly around him and held on even as I started to fall asleep. As my heartbeat slowed and a pleasant languor invaded my entire body, I wasn't afraid of dreams. I wouldn't dream about that again because I was in Gray's arms and they would keep me safe.

Chapter Eleven

I stared at the pictures on the wall, my fingers idly playing with the coffee mug on the desk. It was easier to view the pictures as pieces of a puzzle rather than actual acts against human beings. In the end, to solve a murder you have to shove your emotions aside and look at the evidence dispassionately. There was time enough for righteous anger later when I knew who to direct it toward.

The Sunday morning light streamed in through the open window and I knew it was a glorious fall day outside. By afternoon it would be warm enough to not need a jacket, but I grew chilled knowing what I had to do.

I had to tell Helen Taylor that her daughter was dead.

"Mistress," a soft voice said and I turned to see Syl standing in the doorway. His voice hissed around his fangs. "Is the coffee not to your liking? I could make some tea."

I gave the red-skinned demon a slight smile. I found a night of really exhaustingly awesome sex made me awfully polite. "It's fine, thank you, Syl."

I took a long drink of the coffee. It was hot and had that little bit of peppermint in it. It was delicious, even better than the coffee I'd had when Gray had brought me breakfast in bed.

I have a boyfriend. The thought kept going through my head and

I found it warmed me on a day when I should have been cold.

But Syl still made the better coffee.

"I am glad my mistress enjoys it," the demon said, looking inordinately pleased with himself. "How else may I serve you?"

I turned to look at him. He hadn't bothered with his usual glamour. "I have a small problem." I'd woken up with a real issue, but the solution was right in front of my face. I knew Gray didn't want me to have a lot to do with the demon, so sending him out of the house for most of the day would solve two problems. "I only have the clothes I wore on Friday and the dress Liv loaned me. Gray won't let me go home. Is there…"

The demon's eyes lit up. "I would be honored to acquire new garments for you. I enjoy shopping very much and have a decent eye. I will ensure that my mistress has the loveliest clothing."

"Let me get you some cash." I would have to go to an ATM, but I knew there was a convenience store a block away. Surely Gray wouldn't mind me popping down the road. It wasn't far.

The demon waved off the thought with a shake of his horned head. "The master would never hear of it. I have a card with which to purchase household items. I will use it. The master has more money than he could possibly use and he would definitely want his intended to be taken care of. After last night, I consider myself your servant as well as his, my mistress."

"Why? What'd I do last night?" I'd seen Syl the night before, but we hadn't spoken. He'd left a bottle of wine, a pot of tea, and a tray of cookies on the bar before he'd slipped out. It was kind of nice to have someone who always supplied me with food.

"You mated properly with my master," Syl said with great satisfaction. "I know you humans have formalities, but the master knows you are his true mate, so I consider myself at your service."

I tried really hard not to flush. "Okay. Good to know." I thought briefly about refusing and arguing, but I was close to figuring out what was bugging me about the pictures on the wall. I could always pay Gray back later, after I had Dev Quinn's insanely large check tucked away in my bank account. "Go, then. I'm a size six. I need something professional for this afternoon and something dressy for tonight. I like black."

The demon bowed deeply and was off in his pursuit of "garments."

Gray was still running somewhere in the neighborhood. He'd kissed me good-bye thirty minutes before and I'd wondered why he felt the need to run after all the energy we'd burned off in bed. He'd awakened me three times to have sex.

Make love. I had to mentally correct myself. Gray and I made love. It was raucous and dirty and Gray was seriously kinky, but it was love. It was also tiring and I could use a nap. Not so the inexhaustible Grayson Sloane. He'd put on a pair of sweats and a T-shirt and taken off at a brisk pace. He'd had energy to burn, like his body couldn't shut down.

My brain was doing the same thing. There was something off about the pictures. It had been bugging me ever since I first saw the horrible "works of art" the Ripper had sent to Gray. One of the photos poked at me—the one of Joanne. I couldn't put my finger on it, but I kept coming back to it again and again.

I studied it carefully that morning. There were three photos of her, just like all the others, but one in particular kept my interest. At first I thought it was because I felt as though I'd known the girl. I'd become emotionally invested and it was messing with my head. But as I continued to look at it, I had a feeling deep in my gut that it was important. I knew there was something there.

I stared for a long moment, the heat from the coffee blowing up through the air. What was it about this one picture that bugged me? On the surface it was no different than the others. Joanne lay on her back, unseeing eyes staring at the camera. Her body was wrapped in silver chains, her hands over her head. I shivered at the thought that I'd probably looked that way last night when Gray had tied me up.

I wasn't going to even think about that. It was completely different. I concentrated on the photo. Her torso was sliced open with a neat, surgical precision, but it seemed to me like Joanne had less blood in her pictures than the rest of them. Joanne was the only shifter in the group. The unknown girl was a wolf. There was something about her that screamed wolf to me. I bet she came from a different pack than the Dallas wolves or they would be looking for her.

Did shifters bleed less than wolves? I seriously doubted it.

Time ticked by. I finished my coffee and I stared.

Gray returned. He yelled hello to me and that he was taking a shower if I thought I needed one, too. I heard that, but only vaguely in the back of my mind. I waved him off and he seemed to sense I needed space.

Why Joanne? If this person was going after wolves, it seemed to me he loved the thrill of the hunt and wresting life from a strong, proud creature. Joanne was a doe. While she might be a little stronger than a human, she had nothing on a wolf.

Which one of these is not like the others? Which one of these doesn't belong?

I groaned in frustration because it didn't make sense. I turned to the computer on Gray's desk and decided to change tactics. I googled Jack the Ripper. Thirty minutes later I knew more about the asshole than I ever wanted to. As I would be interviewing him tonight, I should have done it first thing. He'd killed at least five prostitutes in the White Chapel section of London. He'd mysteriously stopped and some people posited that he'd been caught and either killed or placed in a mental ward. I knew for a fact he was happily walking the Earth plane.

White Chapel.

Something stuck in my head about the name. It was a low-rent district in London during Victorian times, so why did the name ring a bell? I quickly typed in the words White Chapel and Dallas into the browser and got absolutely nothing. I sat back and then decided to try again. He'd killed wolves from both Dallas and Fort Worth packs. I tried Fort Worth. Nothing. If the computer had a neck, my hands would have been around it. Frustration welled. I knew something was there, but I couldn't find it…

White Chapel + DFW

"Whites Chapel Cemetery." The website came right up. I breathed with an expectant air of triumph. It was in Southlake, not far from my own little house in Hurst. The entire Metroplex was dotted with small suburban cities, each with their own histories. Whites Chapel Cemetery was old enough to have a historical marker.

I jumped up and dashed for the bedroom.

Twenty minutes later, Gray slid me a frustrated look from the driver's side of his truck. "I don't see why it had to be this second. I didn't even get to dry my hair."

I was watching the GPS. It said we had another five minutes until we got there. Gray had been cranky ever since I forced him into the truck. "I thought you wanted to solve this case."

"Kelsey, I do," he said with only the slightest bit of condescension. I forgave him because he was a big bad Texas Ranger and I was a twenty-six-year-old PI who'd had her license for less than eight months. "But I don't see how going to a cemetery is going to help. I seriously doubt he's burying these girls. He probably puts the bodies somewhere and waits for them to decay."

"Joanne's only been dead for a week," I pointed out. "It's entirely possible she isn't gone yet."

He sighed and turned where the bossy GPS voice told him to. "Possible, but not likely. I think you're trying to put off the inevitable. I told you I would handle Helen Taylor."

Now I wasn't so forgiving. "She's my client. I'll handle her. If you think this is such a wild goose chase then take me a few miles back and I'll get my car and do it on my own."

I needed to pick it up anyway, but I'd put it off since I was going to the vampire club that night.

His hands tightened around the steering wheel. "That's not going to happen, Kelsey. Look, your part of the case is over, sweetheart. You were hired to find out what happened to Joanne Taylor and you did. Case closed. There's absolutely no reason for you to do this."

My heart clenched a little. Why was he pushing me aside?

Last night and the night before, he'd been all about us solving the case together. He'd told me how much he needed me. He'd said he couldn't solve the case without me.

Today, I was supposed to go my merry way? I thought briefly about how casual he'd been at breakfast, like a man completely satisfied with the outcome of the night before. I'd thought he'd been happy because he had me right where he wanted me, madly in love with him.

Maybe, I allowed for the first time, he'd just been satisfied he'd seduced me and could move on. It wouldn't be the first time a man had lied to a woman to get into her pants. It might be the most elaborate lie, but not the first.

"I thought you needed my help." My voice sounded even. That was good because I kind of wanted to go straight to screaming harpy.

He sighed. "You did a good job. You got me new info. Now I need to handle the case on my own. I'm trained to do this, Kelsey. I have all the resources I need to get the job done."

"You can't get into the vampire club."

"I'll deal with that problem when I have to."

What kind of plan was that? "And I'm supposed to do what? Go back home and forget this ever happened? Go back to pulling police reports for lazy liability adjusters?"

He turned his deep blue eyes to me. His mouth firmed and he was ready for a fight. "Yes, that's what you get paid to do. If you don't get back to it, you're going to lose your business and then what will you do? You worked hard for it."

Then what would I do? This was coming from a man who told me he was marrying me and would treat me like a princess. He had more money than god, but I needed to worry about my business?

And he was wrong. I hadn't worked hard. I'd spent most of the time playing solitaire or napping or chatting in the weird little café across the parking lot. Now that I was on a case that meant something, I realized how hollow my job had been before. I'd been drifting like I always had. Now I saw something I could be really good at. I could make a difference. Marcus had said last night that my work was important. I liked the sound of that.

"Look, sweetheart. There's no reason for us to fight." Gray's voice went all kinds of smooth. He reached out to play with my knee as he took the last turn. "I have a lot of work to do on this case and you need to get back to your work. I talked to Jamie this morning. He's going to stay with you for a while so you can get back to your office. I'll see you on the weekends, okay? Once this case is finished, we can sit down and really talk about the future."

He was dumping me on my brother. My entire body went cold. I hadn't seen it coming. All my instincts went haywire around this man. It shouldn't be so shocking that he was the one who ripped me apart.

"Sure, Gray. That'll be fine. Why don't you turn around and drop me off at home." I had to turn off my emotions or I would lose it in front of him, and my dignity was all I had left. I could call Liv and she would help me get my car. Once I was mobile, I could continue on my own. I had that Zack guy's number. I would call him ASAP and he'd put me in touch with Marcus Vorenus so he'd know where to pick me up tonight. I had my little black dress and it would have to do. Maybe Liv could talk me through the whole hair thing over the phone.

I thought about anything other than the fact that Gray was

dumping me after one night.

"Sweetheart?"

I turned to him, perfectly clear eyed. "Yes, Gray?"

I wouldn't take the sweetheart thing personally anymore. He probably called all of his conquests sweetheart. He probably forgot their names.

He pulled into the cemetery parking lot. He calmly put the car in park and twisted his big body around to look at me. "I don't like the look in your eyes."

"Well, you don't have to put up with my looks if you take me home."

He tried to pull my hand into his, but I tugged it away. "Baby, I'm trying to protect you. Your part of the case is over. You can get out."

"You're trying to get rid of me," I stated plainly. He needed to know I wasn't going to fight him on it. He didn't want me. That was cool. It wasn't. It was a gaping wound in my chest that was never going to heal, but I wouldn't cry around him. "Not a problem, Sloane. I know the drill. Take me home and I won't sit around and wait for your call. I have to say, the whole 'I love you' bit took it a little far. I would have fucked you without it and probably sooner. Go easier on the next girl."

"Hey," he said, his voice an angry huff, "I don't deserve that."

I wasn't willing to argue with him. He'd tell me he didn't mean it that way and that he really would call me. He probably would the next time he needed someone willing to play dirty games with him. He was pretty hardcore, and I bet it scared some women off. When he got hard up, he'd remember my name. He'd lie because that's what men did and he'd get pissed off when I didn't believe him. It was better to argue about something substantial.

"I won't be some clinging vine and I won't be the vengeful ex, but I expect something from you, Sloane. If you see me around I expect some professionalism from you. I am still on this case."

"Your case with Helen Taylor is over."

I pulled out my ace in the hole. "Yes, the case with Helen is over, but I have a new boss. My case with Dev Quinn is just getting started. He gave me a large retainer last night and told me to solve this thing. I'm his new in-house PI." I threw open the door as his eyes were widening. I hopped out. I would call someone to come get me so I didn't have to spend another minute with him. "Why don't you be on your way, Sloane? I'll continue my wild goose chase and you can start looking for your next lay. Don't worry about me. I'm sure Quinn can send a car to pick me up."

I slammed the door behind me and willed the tears to shrivel up before they started down my cheeks. I settled the strap of my bag across my chest and walked up to the cemetery gates. They were old and made from wrought iron. At this time of the day they stood open, welcoming visitors.

"Kelsey!"

I ignored the bark from Gray and hoped he would take the hint and leave. I strode into the cemetery, letting the sights, sounds, and smells wash over me. It was peaceful and heavily wooded. The headstones marked the passage of the town's pioneers. The newest stone I could find was from the thirties. This place was more about history than real world use. It would be a place for classes to come and learn about history or art students to do those grave stone rubbings they sometimes did. At night, it would be for teens making out or trying to scare the crap out of each other. It was perfect for what our Ripper would want to use it for.

"Don't think you're walking away from me like that," Gray said, hauling me around by the elbow.

"Stop," I ordered and there must have been something about my voice because he did.

The grass. It had been disturbed. There was a faint line, like something had recently driven over it. I knelt down and looked. There were two lines and they were too small and close together to be tires. I shivered as I realized what they were. Feet, splayed out as someone dragged them along.

"He killed again last night."

"Yeah, I know," Gray admitted.

I rolled my eyes. He really did want me out of the loop. So much for our grand partnership. He was out of luck. I stood up and followed the line. Here and there I got the faint impression of a footprint in the ground where the grass was thinner. It wasn't a sneaker because the print was flat, but I would bet it was a man's foot. I walked along and Gray followed me silently. I followed the trail up a small hill and into a secluded part of the cemetery. No one could see us from the road.

"Kelsey, I can smell something," Gray said, stopping me.

"What is it?"

"Decomp," he replied. "My senses are better than yours. At least my nose is."

"There's a fresh body here?"

"More than one," he replied grimly. "Though only one is really fresh."

Despite his protests, I headed up the hill. When I got to the top, I searched around and there it was. In the far back, I could see where the ground had been disturbed. He'd tried to pat it down, but nothing could fully cover it up.

"Here," I said, standing over it. "We dig here."

Gray already had his cell phone in hand. "This is Lieutenant Sloane for Nicole Ward. Hey, I got a weird one for you." He gave this Nicole person our present address. "Bring along whatever you have for soup. Yeah, one partial and several decomposed wolves. Thanks." He shoved his phone in his back pocket. "The forensic specialist will be here in fifteen minutes. Don't touch anything. She's an expert with supernatural cases."

"I'll try not to damage your evidence with my fumbling, Sloane," I said acerbically as I forced myself to be content with looking around. There was another place that looked like it had been recently disturbed.

"I don't deserve that, either," he said in a gruff voice. "Where the hell is this coming from, Kelsey? You're acting like a scorned woman, but I haven't scorned you, quite the opposite. I love you. I've already told you I fully intend to marry you, so what's up with the hell hath no fury act?"

"You have a funny way of showing your affection, Sloane."

"My name is Gray," he insisted. "You can't go back to last names just because you've decided you're pissed with me and you can't lie about working for Quinn because you want to set me off."

"I can do whatever I want, Sloane. You want to shove me off at my brother, fine, but don't expect me to walk away like some obedient little woman. It ain't happening. And I'm not lying about Quinn. I have a lovely check for twenty-five grand that I intend to cash at my earliest convenience." I walked a couple of yards to the other pile of earth. It was well trampled down and little shoots of grass were starting to come up.

"What the hell did you do for twenty-five thousand dollars?" The question was ground out of Gray's mouth, and I could see his eyes getting dark. He clenched his fists at his sides.

"Nothing, yet." I have to admit I enjoyed the fact that I could have some sort of effect on him. I was mad. Shouldn't he be, too? "Tonight, I'm going to the vampire club with Marcus to talk to the original gangsta himself. Quinn is letting me into the club so I can interview the vamp who claims to be Jack the Ripper. Then I'm supposed to check in with my new boss tomorrow."

"You aren't going anywhere, Kelsey." His hands shook. Strangely, it didn't make me any less reckless. I knew he wouldn't hurt me. Well, he wouldn't physically hurt me. "If you don't want to stay at home with Jamie then you can hole up at my place, but you are off this case. You will not be going into that club. I forbid it."

I rolled my eyes. "It's not dangerous, Sloane. No one's going to bother me. Marcus explained it all and he set up our cover. After last night, everyone thinks I'm his mistress so they'll back off."

The tree next me sort of exploded as Gray shoved his fist through it. I managed to hold my ground and when he looked at me with red-tinged eyes, I shook my head. "I thought we weren't contaminating the scene."

"Fuck the scene," he snarled and got into my space. "What did you do with that vampire?"

"I walked around with him and I talked to him," I explained. I didn't let the halfling back me up a single inch. "He introduced me to some people and they drew incorrect conclusions. He treated me like I had a brain in my head. I liked him."

"Yeah, you like him? Get to know him fast because I swear I'm gonna kill him," Gray said. "I'll rip his heart out and then we'll see how he feels about sniffing around another man's woman."

"Nice, Sloane," I shot back. "Very caveman-like. I don't get the righteous indignation. You're shoving me to the side. Am I not allowed to have a life after Grayson Sloane is done with me?"

He enunciated his words carefully. I got the feeling he was rapidly reaching the end of his patience with me. "I am not done with you. You are the most frustrating woman I have ever met. You're going to make me pull out every piece of hair I have and damn it, woman, I won't look good bald. Let me make this plain to you. You're mine. I'm trying to protect what's mine. He killed again last night and this morning I got a letter saying you're next."

My mind flooded with the possibilities. "That's perfect. I can be bait. We set me up and let him come after me."

He stared at me for a long moment with his mouth hanging open. It wasn't the first time I had gotten that reaction from him. I wondered if a lot of things knocked the words out of him. Somehow I doubted it. I thought it was probably a reaction he only had to me.

"Are you going to kill another tree?" I asked after he was quiet for the longest time.

"No, Kelsey," he said, a little breathless. "I think I'm gonna give you my gun and let you shoot me. It'll be for the best. It'll be a hell of a lot quicker than the heart attack I'll have someday." He took a deep breath. "That is the stupidest thing you've ever said."

I shrugged. "Only because you haven't been around me for very long."

He shook his head and before I could move away, he grabbed me and kissed me senseless. "Okay, baby, I love you. Why is this so important? Why can't you give it up? I would feel so much better if I knew you were safe."

I leaned into him. I couldn't resist this man when he touched me. I melted like butter when he said he loved me. If he really thought I was in danger, he would have come up with some stupid plan to protect me. "It's important to me because I can do this, Gray. I can find this guy. I'm tired of hiding. You want me to come out of my shell, well, this is it. You can't have it both ways. I can go to ground and hide and be the person I've always been afraid I really am or I can stop hiding and become who I want to be."

I didn't tell him that he was a big part of why I needed to do this. I needed to feel worthy of him.

I felt him nod against me. "All right, sweetheart. But I am not using you as bait."

"I still need to get into the club." I pressed my luck. "You can't kill Marcus."

"I find out he's laid a hand on you and I promise I will," Gray said.

It was time for me to live up to my previous words. It was time to be really brave. "I like Marcus, but I don't love him. I love you, Gray."

He drank the words down like a man dying of thirst. His mouth was on mine, tongue sweeping in with none of his former polish. He kissed me, pressing me against his body. "You won't regret it, Kelsey. I'll take care of you."

"And I'll take care of you," I promised.

"Wow," a surprised feminine voice said. "Big old manly love 'em and leave 'em Sloane has an honest to god girlfriend. Will wonders never cease?"

The faintest hint of a blush stained Gray's cheeks as he smiled ruefully at the woman standing on the hill with a large case in her hand. "Hello, Nicole. Allow me to introduce my fiancée, Kelsey Atwood."

He hadn't actually asked me, but I didn't mention that to the perky looking blonde with round glasses. Her eyebrows practically reached the sky. "Seriously? Chambers is going to win a bunch of money. The office pool had you never getting married. Wait. Atwood? As in superhot stud Jamie Atwood?"

"He's my brother, but, wow, you have an entirely different notion of hot than I do," I admitted.

The blonde grinned as she set down her enormously cumbersome pack. She looked almost too small to be able to carry it, but she did with an ease that spoke of long use. "We can't all get someone as gloriously perfect as Sloane there. Besides, I like Jamie. He's the right size for me, not too big, not too small. Sloane would crush me."

Sloane did kind of crush me, but I liked the feeling.

"So where's the site?" Nicole asked, looking eager to start working.

Gray pointed down and Nicole grimaced.

"This is about that serial case you've been working, isn't it? Wolves, right?"

"This is where he's dumping the bodies," Gray confirmed.

Nicole surveyed the site and got to work. Gray started to explain what she was doing and how she was doing it. Forensics for supernatural cases tended to be a lot harder than a regular case. For the most part the evidence collected was meant to be a case for the Council rather than a court of law. While the general public believed that supernaturals were myths, the government had known about them for a long time. I knew the Army made use of them. Most law enforcement had carefully selected people who would liaise with the supernatural world. Gray had the hard job of having to deal with the full Council. Gray would produce his evidence against the accused to the full Council or a single member who would then take it to the Council and an order would be written. Sometimes it was for incarceration, but often it was an order of execution. If Gray took matters into his own hands, he was forced to stand before the Council and have his kill be declared "righteous."

"How many times have you had to go before the Council?" I asked, never taking my eyes off Nicole's incredibly thorough examination of the site. She had an entire chemistry set on a small folding table.

"Three times," Gray replied. "Luckily, I had excellent evidence and Quinn isn't on the Council. That brother of his is, but he doesn't seem to give a crap about righteous kills. He's a kill 'em all kind of guy."

"So when you take your evidence to the Council, do you have to go through the whole ceremonial thing every time? How long do you have to wait for the full Council to sit?"

Gray smiled and it was that lopsided grin that told me he was embarrassed by whatever he was about to say. "I have a councilman I regularly meet with. He always takes my calls and has been easy to deal with up until now."

"Marcus," I guessed.

"Yeah. He's an incredibly smart man and very interested in justice. He's consulted with me on a case or two. I wouldn't call him a friend, but I certainly got along better with him than anyone else on the Council. He's quite tolerant, if you know what I mean."

Except when he thinks you're working with Quinn against him, then Marcus could be quite emotional. I chose to not bring up the subject. "So you're willing to kill the only man on the Council you actually get along with? Won't that make your job hard?"

"He touches my wife and I won't give a damn about my job, darlin'," Gray promised.

"I have five bodies here, Lieutenant." Nicole was staring at her laptop screen. It was all incredibly high tech. The laptop was connected to some strange medical looking equipment. "All five of these are female and werewolves. Four are in an advanced state of decomposition and the fifth was placed here sometime in the last twenty-four hours. I'll bag that one and take it back to my lab, but from what I can tell she died from blood loss. Someone really sliced her up. I think she might be missing a kidney, ewwww."

"And the other site?" Gray asked.

"Strange." Nicole surveyed the second, smaller grave over her glasses. "Only one female and she wasn't a wolf. It's definitely a shifter of some kind, but I'm not sure what. I've collected a sample and I'll be able to run it better at the office. My field machines aren't as accurate."

Something gold glinted in the grass a few feet from me. "What's that?"

Nicole made sure the latex gloves she was wearing were snug before she reached down and picked up a small gold necklace that was lying in the grass. She held it up and in the light I could see it was engraved with a J.

"Joanne Taylor," Gray said with a sad shake of his head. His cell phone rang and he looked down. "Speak of the devil. I have to take this, Kelsey. I'll be right back."

"I think you'll find she was a doe," I told Nicole.

Nicole bagged the necklace in an evidence bag. "I'll start there then. The latest victim shows evidence of being tied up. Her wrists are burned pretty badly, so it was probably silver."

Gray grabbed my hand. "We have go, Kelsey. Nicole, can you handle the rest?"

"Of course," the efficient tech said. "I'll have my report on your desk Monday morning."

"Good," Gray said and started to haul me out of the cemetery.

"Where are we going?"

"That was Vorenus." Gray guided me along, his long legs eating up the distance. I ran to keep up. "He's on his way to Helen Taylor's. She got a package this morning."

"Oh, no," I breathed, picking up the pace. "Tell me she didn't get those pictures."

"She did, sweetheart," Gray affirmed. "The entire doe community is in an uproar. We have some damage control to do."

We hopped into the truck and as we pulled away, something about the necklace played around in the back of my mind.

* * * *

When we turned down the narrow road to Joanne Taylor's home, I knew we were in trouble. The street was lined with cars. We had to park a block away and walk. Gray held my hand, but I disentangled us as we approached the house.

"I'd like to look somewhat professional, please," I said at the annoyed look he gave me.

We were moving up the sidewalk toward the Taylor's small two-bedroom home when a limo stopped and Marcus Vorenus stepped out. He said something to the driver and then the limo slid down the road. His dark eyes turned to us but if he had an emotion in his body it didn't show. He was polite and a little cool. "I've been waiting for you, Lieutenant. I thought it proper that we enter together. We must show that the Council and law enforcement are working together. Good afternoon, Ms. Atwood."

I knew Vorenus was an academic and that meant he could walk in the daylight. That particular class of vampire wasn't the strongest. They didn't begin to compare to warriors, but academics had their own abilities. They were the smarty-pants of the vampire world. Their powers were almost entirely mental. Persuasion. Instinct. Intelligence. I'd heard they tended to get obsessed with subjects and became super experts.

Even though I know all the facts, I supposed I still thought it would be odd to see any vampire walking in the daylight, but Vorenus practically shimmered in light. As Daniel had been at home in the velvety darkness of night, Marcus belonged in the sun. It clung to him, lighting his skin and nearly giving the man a halo.

"Hello, Councilman." It was awkward because it came out a little breathy, a little flirty. I hadn't meant it to, but the minute I was close to him, I felt more at ease than I'd been before.

Gray was all business. "When did Helen call the Council?"

"I received her call about an hour ago," the vampire explained with his calm authority. "She told me what had happened and I promised I would come. I also promised to inform the king this evening. I was lucky she called me at all. She's been told that vampires killed her daughter."

"Well, that's only to be expected," Gray said, not a trace of compassion in his voice.

"Some of the killings took place during the day," Marcus

pointed out.

"So, he had an accomplice or he has special talents." Gray wasn't willing to let up.

Marcus sighed as though weary of all the games. "Are you playing devil's advocate, Lieutenant? Or are you accusing me of something?"

Gray stared at the vampire with cold blue eyes. "All of the girls went into that club. None of them came out alive. The way I figure, a vampire has to be involved."

"Why would a vampire waste the blood?" I hated the tension between the two of them.

"Who knows why a vampire does anything, darlin'." Gray emphasized the endearment. "They enjoy games."

"Ah, but Lieutenant, vampires are not the only ones who enjoy games, are they?" Marcus posed his question with the hint of a questioning smile. The vampire looked dapper in a perfectly tailored pinstriped suit and a snowy dress shirt. His red silk tie was a splash of elegant color. "The rumors are that you very much enjoy games. This killer likes bondage and I believe has a problem with vampires. Perhaps I don't have to look far to find a suspect of my own."

I put myself in between the two men who seemed like they were ready to throw down. "If the two of you are finished acting like two bulls about to lock horns, you might remember that Marcus was in London with the king when one of the murders took place and Gray was with me last night. There are security cameras in the parking garage. They can verify his whereabouts until we left. I can verify them the rest of the night. The only person he managed to tie up last night was me."

"Kelsey!" Gray radiated disapproval. I guess demons weren't big on sharing.

"Well, apparently everyone knows your kinks, babe," I said with a shrug. "Stop beating the crap out of each other. I'm going in. If you two want to take potshots, stay out here."

Marcus nodded my way. "Of course. I apologize."

"I'm sorry, sweetheart. I'll behave," Gray promised.

We started to walk up toward the house, the men following my lead.

I knocked briefly on the door and was admitted into the house. The air was quiet and thick with grief. The windows were all open, letting in the sunlight and the afternoon warmth. But I felt a chill as I saw Joseph Castle sitting next to Helen Taylor, his meaty hand patting her lightly on the back.

The whole herd seemed to have come out. I could tell the deer from the other shifters in the room. They all had wide, dark, gentle eyes. They stood close to each other, as though they could physically share their grief and in doing so lessen it. I wondered what it felt like to have a whole group of people to depend on, who huddled together in times of trouble, held each other when tragedy struck. It seemed like a beautiful thing to me.

And a wolf was among them.

Yeah, somehow I didn't think he'd come here to protect them.

Marcus stepped up, holding out a hand. "Helen, the Council offers you condolences in your time of grief."

Helen took his hand, her head held high. "Thank you, Marcus. I appreciate you coming out."

"You're late, Councilman," Castle said, a sneer in his voice. "Do all the vampires have their stories straight?"

"Mr. Castle, the vampires are sleeping," Marcus replied, his tone revealing nothing of the contempt he must feel for the alpha. "I come to offer condolences and to introduce Mrs. Taylor to Lieutenant Grayson Sloane of the Texas Rangers. He's handling the case for the human authorities and recently discovered your daughter was involved."

Gray tipped his head forward. "Ma'am. I apologize for presenting myself in such a casual fashion. I was actually working on your daughter's case when I got the call."

Helen's eyes seemed dazed. She looked around like she wasn't really hearing anything until she focused on me. "Kelsey Atwood?"

"Hello, Mrs. Taylor." I was quieter than usual. I felt the heavy weight of guilt. She'd likely been dead before I even got the case, but I couldn't silence that voice that told me I should have found her. I should have been there. I should have known.

It's funny how illogical an instinct can be.

"Is it true? Did you find her?"

I took a deep breath. "I did. I'm so sorry. There's no mistake. I found her body not an hour ago."

She stood up and held herself with such dignity I wanted to weep for her. Castle tried to stand next to her. She regally shrugged him off. "I would like to speak with Miss Atwood alone."

She didn't wait, merely walked off expecting me to follow. I trailed after her silently, gesturing to Gray and Marcus not to follow me. She walked through the kitchen and into the backyard. It was small and neatly kept, with old shade trees and rose bushes along the chain link fence. She turned to me, her eyes so much older than the first time we met.

"You found my daughter. I thank you for that." Her voice was hoarse. I wondered if she'd screamed when she'd seen the evidence of her daughter's fate. How long would that image stay with her, obliterating all the good memories. She'd been forced to exchange visions of her daughter smiling and alive for horrors untold.

"I don't know that you should thank me. I didn't save her."

"Likely no one could save her. We're much like the animals we turn into. Always prey. It isn't in our natures to fight, to protect ourselves. We try to run, but everyone else is faster. I don't blame you, dear. I would prefer to know than to be left waiting forever in vain for her to come home."

How close had my mother come to that fate? It struck me that the world really was filled with predators and prey. Most people didn't have to face that fact—or learn which side they belong to. Helen Taylor had known from birth. "Is there anything else I can do for you?"

She nodded slowly. "You can be honest with me. You're the only one I trust."

"Yes, ma'am." I knew what she was going to ask me and I knew that I would tell her the truth no matter what councilmen and faery princes and even Gray wanted. This was a contract between me and Helen Taylor, and I would not break it.

"Was my daughter involved with vampires?"

"Yes."

She took the news with stoic pride. "Do you believe they killed her?"

I let out a breath of relief. If she'd left it there, I would have stopped. I was glad to be able to tell her my thoughts. I was sure Castle had been filling her head with his. "My instinct tells me no. One of the victims was killed during the day and the only two daywalkers in Dallas have ironclad alibis."

She brushed that off with a wave of her hand. "Only Academics can daywalk. It's not in their natures to kill in such a manner. A warrior, yes, but not an academic. Castle expects me to believe the king has something to do with this. The king is a good boy."

Though I hadn't met the king, simply by his nature he was the baddest ass among badasses, but I liked that docile Helen called him a good boy like he was just another kid on the block begging for cookies.

"I can't rule out that some vampire might have an assistant, but it doesn't add up for me. I'm going to the club tonight and the Council promises me an all-access pass."

She sighed and her body sagged down into a worn chair. The vinyl used to have a pattern, but the Texas sun had faded it. Grief had faded Helen Taylor's natural sunniness. "It's good for you to keep looking. Castle doesn't want to look past his own theories. Having a vampire slaughtering werecreatures plays to his political ambitions."

I sank into the seat next to her. It didn't surprise me that the alpha was making trouble. He'd seemed to be looking for it last night. "What's he saying?"

"That the vampires have made us their slaves. It's the same thing he's been saying since the king forced him to shut down his gambling businesses. It cost him a lot of money," Helen said wearily. "I think the werewolf alpha is trying to start a rebellion and he's using my daughter. I don't care about any of it. I want to know who killed my daughter. I know I didn't pay you much…"

"It was enough." I didn't mention Quinn's money. I wouldn't have stopped even if he hadn't stepped up. I would still be here. "I'm going to get to the bottom of this, Mrs. Taylor. I promise."

Her hand came out to slowly pat mine. It was a motherly gesture, soothing and second nature to her. "You're a good girl, Kelsey. Find out who killed my daughter. I trust you. You won't allow politics to sway you."

"Ma'am, I don't know enough about politics to let it sway me," I admitted.

"Why don't you go back inside?" She let her face find the sun. "I like the peace out here. I think I'll sit for a while."

I started to get up and had made it to the door when her soft voice made me turn once more.

"Kelsey?"

"Yes, ma'am?"

"When you find him, what do you intend to do?"

"I intend to kill him, ma'am," I said because it was the truth.

"Like I said, you're a good girl. No one fights for us. It would be nice for once to have someone on our side."

Now it wasn't guilt, but responsibility that ate at me. If this really was a vampire—the mysterious Alexander—then the Council would likely want it hushed up.

I couldn't allow that to happen.

The screen door closed behind me and I could see easily why Helen Taylor wanted to stay outside. The minute I walked into the house, I was struck by the oppressiveness of the grief. I thought it odd that when Helen needed solitude to think and let it all sink in that she was bombarded with people. I walked through the small kitchen crowded with relatives and friends. The table was laden with food. I noted the requisite Jell-O mold hadn't been touched yet, but then it didn't seem like many people were eating. Even my appetite seemed to have fled.

I could hear Marcus quietly arguing with Castle in the laundry room. He was trying to keep it down, but Castle had no such qualms. Gray was off to the side, sifting through some papers. It was probably the letter and the photos Helen had received. He would take them into evidence, but she would never forget.

Then I sensed someone watching me. I stopped, not turning. Most people would avert their eyes at that point, but I still felt them on me. I didn't want a fight, but I also couldn't walk away. When I turned, I realized a fight might have been better.

"Do you think it hurt?"

My heart sure as hell hurt looking down at Nancy Taylor, aged fifteen, who had seen far more death in her young life than any kid should. She was painfully thin in a pair of jeans and a T-shirt emblazoned with the name of some rock band I'd never heard of. I was sure when she'd gotten dressed this morning she hadn't been thinking she'd attend a wake.

"I don't know," I answered, knowing I was probably lying. In this, I couldn't give her the truth. It helped no one and offered so much pain. "I hope not."

"You're the PI my mom hired, right?"

"Yeah."

"I need to talk to you about something."

I cast a short look back at Gray and Marcus. "Okay."

I followed Nancy down the hall and into her room. It was an explosion of teenaged girl. There were posters of rock stars and actors and cutout photos of the "hot guys" from magazines alongside pictures of girls and their shining, smiling faces. There were several photos of Nancy and her sister. She was neat for a teen, meaning I could kind of see the floor. I wasn't exactly OCD so I couldn't complain.

"My mom says you're a hunter," Nancy started, her brown eyes wary.

"I don't hunt like that." Oddly, I didn't feel the same rush of shame today. I simply explained to her. I was able to meet her eyes as though the night before had purged the shame I'd always felt. I was able to breathe.

"So you don't hunt people like me. You hunt bad guys."

That pretty neatly summed up my new chosen profession. I hunted bad guys. The only way to make up for what my father did was to stop other people from doing it. "I try to."

"That's cool," the teenager said. "My dad was killed by a hunter, but not one like you."

Again, no rush of guilt, only a deep sympathy for what had happened. "I know. Your mom told me. I'm sorry about that."

"Mom thinks Jo was doing bad things."

Wow, how had I gotten into this conversation? It was a veritable field full of land mines. "Your sister was trying to get by like the rest of us. She wasn't bad."

The girl shook her blonde hair. The ponytail was like an exclamation point. "That's not what I mean. I mean Jo wasn't doing it for the reason you think she was."

I sat down on the frilly pink comforter and gave her my absolute undivided attention. "I thought she needed the money."

"It's true that she lost her scholarship and Mom didn't know," Nancy explained. "Jo didn't want to worry her, especially since she applied to the Council for a loan. With her grades she would have easily qualified. It's a program the queen set up a few years ago. Anyone under Council protection can apply for a loan to go to school or get training to get a job. You have to pay it back, but not for a while, and Jo said the interest rate was good, whatever that means."

Every reason I could think of for Jo to be in that club flew straight out the window. "Then why would she work at the vampire club?"

Nancy played with her hair, twisting it around and around her right index finger. "Jo was really good friends with this girl named Britney Miles," Nancy said and I kept my face perfectly blank. I recognized her as the first victim, but no one else knew she'd been found. "She was a werewolf, but Jo got along with everyone at school. Jo got worried about her when she didn't make it to their weekly movie date. Everyone thinks she's bad news and probably ran away with some guy, but Jo didn't think so."

The room went cold around me as I knew what Nancy Taylor was going to say next, and everything fell into place. I had underestimated Jo Taylor. I had looked at her and seen a sweet little doe. I'd seen prey. But sometimes even the sweetest of prey can turn hunter when something they care about is in harm's way.

"Jo went to the club undercover," Nancy said. "She went there to find out what happened to Britney."

She'd played the hunter and she'd been killed. I wondered for a moment if the same thing wasn't going to happen to me.

Chapter Twelve

Marcus followed us back to Gray's house after we left Helen Taylor's. There was no more talk of me going back to Hurst, no more pushing me aside. Gray was quiet the whole ride home as though he knew he'd lost the fight.

I couldn't stop thinking about the Taylors. No matter what happened, I had to push on. Even if it meant going against the Council and the king. No one else wanted justice. No one really wanted the truth. Not even Gray. He wanted me safe more than he wanted the truth, but the need burned inside me.

The guilt I'd felt before had somehow morphed, becoming a need. I needed to find this killer, needed to bring him into the light.

Marcus and Gray headed to his office, but I couldn't sit there and listen to them go over the case again. I still hadn't figured out what bugged me about the photos and it gnawed at my gut. I was restless. I headed to the kitchen where Syl had again been busy.

If there's one thing I loved about Gray's, it was the open-all-day buffet. I didn't have to rummage around to find a snack. I didn't have to settle for day-old bread or hustle to a vending machine. Syl always provided. There was a tray of fruit and cheese on the bar along with wine, water, and juice. I poured myself some juice and downed a ton of crackers and cheese.

I sat in the kitchen for the longest time eating and drinking. It was peaceful after the stresses of the day, but I knew I had the night to come.

After a while I heard Marcus leave, promising to return for me in two hours. I sighed because I didn't want to leave my happy little nest of quiet and food and minty juice. I got up though. I forced my limbs to move because I had a job to do.

Syl had left me two very nice outfits laid out on the bed. The shopping bags said Niemen Marcus, so I probably didn't want to look at the tags to figure out how much I owed Gray. I could totally leave the tags on the elegant business suit. I didn't need it at this point. I was going to have to wear the wine-colored sheath dress with an almost Asian looking neckline. I was surprised at the conservative nature of the dress. The neckline was quite high and the skirt would hit me a little past the knee. All in all, I'd expected a bit more trashy chic from a demon, but then I supposed Syl wouldn't want me to look like a hooker. I was his master's intended after all. He seemed to take that seriously.

I turned on the shower and pulled off my clothes. Gray's shower was one of those walk-in masterpieces of plumbing technology. It didn't have anything so pedestrian as a shower curtain, like my tiny shower-tub combo. Nope this was a little room in itself. I stepped inside and sighed as the hot water hit my skin. I needed to feel clean again.

Heat suffused my skin, finally seeming to penetrate, but I couldn't relax. I worried that I might not until I solved this case.

"Hey."

Gray was standing in the doorway to the shower. He'd gotten rid of his shirt and his jeans hung low on his hips. My eyes caught on the tattoo on his chest. Torso really. It covered his left pec and wound around his body. My demon with the dragon tattoo.

"What made you pick the dragon?" Somehow it fit him. I couldn't imagine him getting drunk one night and stumbling into a tattoo parlor and picking something random. It wasn't random at all. That dragon seemed to be a piece of him.

His eyes were on my breasts, heat pouring off him, but he was still as he replied. "I didn't. I had no choice in the matter. I turned thirteen and when I went to sleep that night, I was taken by my father to the Hell plane. It was the first time I met him, the first time I had to go there. When I went home, I had this tat. Well, I had the beginnings of it."

He really went to the Hell plane. His father was really a Hell Lord. I knew it on an intellectual level, but seeing that tat reminded me that even Hell had its beauty.

His jaw had tightened, his body stiffening the minute he told me the truth. I'd shed my shame the night before in telling him my story, but Gray still had his. If it was anything like mine, he hadn't really earned it.

I walked up to him, feeling awfully proprietary. We'd had a crappy morning and my first instinct was to pull away. Or it should have been. I always pulled away, but I didn't want to be anything but close to Gray. I ran my fingers along the dragon. There was something visceral about the tat and I gasped a little when I could have sworn the thing moved.

Gray caught my hand and held it there. "Don't. He likes it. He likes it as much as I do."

"He?" Now that my hand was still, I could feel something. The dragon was warmer than Gray's skin and there was a restlessness to it, as though the skin was vibrating under my touch. Was it alive?

Gray's eyes had that slight tinge of red to them that let me know his demonic half was being stimulated. "It feels good, baby, but I know it shouldn't. You have to move your hand. I like it too much."

"Why is it wrong?" It might feel good to him, but I kind of liked the sensation, too. Odd at first, but then it almost seemed to hum against my palm in a pleasant way.

"It's part of my demonic life. Kelsey, when I was thirteen it was small. It grew with me and it wasn't like I sat in some chair and had it added to. It's my family mark. My father touched me and then I had this thing on me. I never changed before that day, never had the strength or power."

Likely hadn't been immortal. His father had somehow turned on his demonic genes. It might account for his human nature. If his father hadn't shown an interest, he might never have been more than a slightly stronger than normal human.

His father cared for him. Normally, that would be a good thing, but a Hell Lord's love was probably fairly obsessive.

"So it's alive?" I didn't move my hand.

"I don't know. I try not to think about it, but since I met you, I feel it more and more." His eyes closed. "It feels so fucking good to have you touch me."

Not just him. He meant he liked it when I touched it. "Let go of my hand."

His eyes came open and I saw the pain there. He lifted his hand. "Of course."

He didn't understand anything at all. I ran my fingers along the tat, tracing the lines of the dragon as it hummed against my skin. There was something ferocious about it, but I wasn't scared. It was a part of Gray and that meant it somehow belonged to me. I petted it.

The damn thing practically purred for me.

When I looked up, Gray's eyes were flashing red and I saw the beginnings of his fangs.

"I don't want you to go tonight. Do you know what I do want?"

Oh, I know what he wanted. He wanted me safe, but there was more to it. Deep down, he wanted me to stay home and wait for him, to be the sweet woman who gave up all the danger because she trusted her man to save the world. The caveman inside wanted me tending his elegant cave, serving him dinner, waiting for him in bed.

I wasn't that girl. I would never be that girl, but if I could fight my instincts, maybe he could do the same.

And maybe there were two sides to the man. Maybe I was talking to the wrong side. I'd seen the human side of Gray. He kept the other side hidden so well it was easy to forget it existed, but could he ever be happy never feeding that part of his soul? Could he be at peace with a woman who didn't accept all of him?

I dropped to my knees in front of him.

"What are you doing?" Gray's voice had gone guttural.

When I glanced up, his eyes flashed red and his hands were trembling. "I'm taking care of you. All of you."

I kissed his tat, feeling it spark off my lips in a way I can only describe as electric. Gray groaned and he seemed to struggle to stay on his feet. His skin heated under my fingers as I licked the outline of that magnificent dragon. My dragon.

Gray's hand sank into my hair and he pulled me off with a jerk. That brief pain seemed to sensitize my skin, making my nipples hard, my pink parts soft.

"It's never fucking done that." He was panting, his hands on the fly of his jeans. That was when I noticed the way his nails, usually perfectly manicured, had become neat talons. "It grows with me, but I never fucking felt it move on my body. I never felt it…want. It wants you."

"You want me. It's a part of you so it gets to have me, too." The temperature seemed to have spiked in the room. Hot water splashed across my skin, but it was the sight of Gray peeling his jeans off and tossing them aside, his cock already hard and wanting.

His cock. That dragon that seemed restless on his skin. They both wanted me. And they belonged to me.

My own personal demon lover was savage, riding the edge of our morning fight and what was still coming this evening.

"I want to kill Vorenus. I want to rip his throat out. I want to kill every vampire who thinks he's fucking what belongs to me. Mine, Kelsey. You're mine. Come here."

I let go of all those old instincts. New ones flared inside me. They were both alien and comforting at the same time. My old instincts were born of pain and suffering. These came from a place deep inside me, my primal self. They were untouched by years of neglect. They were simply me and touching that dragon, feeling it bend to me had sparked them back to life.

My lover needed. He needed this, needed me submissive to his sexual whims so he could handle what I had to do. He would shove down his hate, his jealousy, his possessiveness if I would give him these hours of respite.

I could do that. I wanted to more than anything.

I was his supplicant for the moment. I suppose there are some women who would never bow in front of a man, but I've discovered that often a true partnership is never equal all the time. It's a trade, a fluid bending from partner to partner when the need arises. One on their knees, worshipping the other and then the positions flip as easily as day turning to night. I never want to be so strong that I can't love enough to bend.

Not even after what happened.

But this night, oh this night, I was happy on my knees in front of my lover.

"Link your hands behind your back," Gray ordered as he moved toward me. "Hold them there until I give you permission to move. If you need it, I'll tie them together."

"I can handle it," I said breathlessly. This was a good place to be. I wasn't thinking about inconsequential things like how pretty I was compared to him or how it all could fall apart. I was only thinking about the warm water on my back and how gorgeous he was standing there looking down at me with his deeply blue eyes, big hands stroking his dick. He had to be careful because those claws were out. I should have been worried about those claws, about the red sheen to his eyes, but somehow I knew he wouldn't hurt me. The claws, the fangs, the fury I knew sat beneath Gray's calm exterior—they were there to protect me, never to hurt me.

"Suck me, Kelsey." His big body crowded mine. Strong legs spread as he brought that clawed hand to my hair. The edges sizzled along my scalp as he got a good hold. One hand stayed on his cock, guiding it into my mouth.

He pressed his dick to my lips and I got my first real taste of him. I licked at the head of his cock, getting a feel for every groove and curve of him. It was a mix of soft skin and hard muscle.

"Take it." That dark voice of his seemed to have a straight line to my pussy.

I kept my hands behind my back and it forced me to focus on my mouth. I couldn't touch him any other way, so I put all of my love and affection into kissing and licking and sucking him. I dragged my tongue around his cockhead before sucking him inside. He was so big, but I was determined to take him. He was mine and I would take him all.

I looked up and he was staring down at me, opening himself more than he ever had. He let me see the red of his eyes, licked his tongue over his fangs. Alien and so beautiful to me. He stared down at the place where his cock invaded, took territory, claimed me.

I sucked him deeper, needing all of him. Our connection was electric, a visceral thing I could feel that went beyond the physical. I could drown in him and I would be happy to go.

His hips flexed and he hit the back of my throat and it was all I could do not to gag. I concentrated on breathing through my nose and after a moment I could focus on the cock in my mouth. I let my tongue whirl around it as I sucked hard when he tried to retreat.

He hissed and moaned as he shoved back in. He advanced and retreated, every inch a delicious struggle. I ran my tongue around the head, loving the way the ridge felt in my mouth. When he hit the back of my throat, I swallowed and Gray nearly cried with the pleasure.

"Enough." He tugged on my hair, pulling his cock from between my lips. His face was savage as he dropped down.

His mouth covered mine, threatening to devour me. My tongue played along those fangs of his. So much destructive power and yet they only brought pleasure to me. His claws tickled across my skin before he palmed my breasts. Every inch of my flesh felt alive and simmering. I was a good girl and kept my hands locked behind my back, offering my body and soul to him. He roamed the plains and valleys of my flesh with his fingers and his tongue. He sucked a nipple into his mouth and I nearly came then and there.

"Spread your knees further," he ordered urgently. He groaned as he forced his claws to recede. He touched me, his fingers soft on my skin. "I'll keep them sheathed from here on, baby. I want to touch you."

I did as he asked and he shoved two fingers high into me. It was easy since I was dripping wet. He used his thumb to rub my clit and I moaned my approval.

"Good, you're ready," he said and I protested when he pulled his hand out. "Now, hands and knees."

I let my hands go and knelt on the wet tile. My knees were spread and I was about as submissive as a female can be. I was presenting to him, offering for him to take whatever he wanted from me.

Gray immediately moved in behind me, roughly making a place for himself at my back. Before I knew what was happening, he had thrust his cock in to the hilt. He wrapped his hands around my hips for leverage and started to pound into me.

"You don't forget this when you're with that vampire tonight," he groaned as he pushed in with his dick and pulled me back with his hands.

I was caught, penetrated and helpless and god help me, I loved every second of it. I felt alive as I gave over to Gray, his cock claiming me in the most primal fashion. Over and over he slammed into me.

"You don't forget who you belong to. You say my name."

"Gray," I managed to cry out as I shoved back against him. He felt so good. I don't know how I survived without this feeling. I was completely addicted to him. He was better than any drunk or high I'd ever experienced. None of that made me feel like I was precious, beloved. When Gray was inside me, I was all the things I feared I wasn't—lovely and graceful and worthy. I didn't question the feeling. I welcomed it as I welcomed him. I wanted my body to be his home, his safe place as he was becoming mine.

"You're mine," he growled as he found that magic spot deep inside my body. "You belong to me."

I came apart in that wild rush of pleasure I would always and forever associate with Grayson Sloane. It was a flash fire inside my body, a bomb that detonated deep within and sparked through, bringing life and heat where I needed it the most. The orgasm made my toes curl, my eyes roll back. "I belong to you."

I was Gray's and he was mine. I kind of floated down. It was all I could do to stay upright, but then Gray tensed and I felt him pulse inside me as he came with a low shout. His hands squeezed my hips almost painfully as he ground out his pleasure, filling me up.

When he let go, he fell against my back and both of us lay there on the floor, our bodies satisfied and my heart so full of him.

"I love you so fucking much." He growled the words against the nape of my neck.

I found a deep pleasure in lying with him, our bodies in synch, breathing and beating in time as the warmth of the shower rained down on us. There was peace in this place.

"Shit. Oh, baby." He scrambled off me.

"What?" I was starting to come out of my lovely languor and I didn't want that. I turned over and sent him a frown.

All of the demon was gone. His eyes were back to deep violet and his hands were simply big and strong. I was a little startled at the fact that the dragon's eye had closed. It had been open before, looking ferocious and hungry, and now there was a sated sleepiness to the sexy bastard. I'd satisfied that part of Gray.

Gray looked younger than before. It was subtle, but I would have sworn the lines around his eyes were lighter, as though some of his worries had fled. His lips curled up and a soft expression lit his face as he stood up, water dripping off his body. "You are the sexiest, grumpiest kitten ever."

My hair was plastered to my skin and I was probably a mess, but I felt like I was glowing. "I think that's a compliment."

He got to his feet and gently hauled me up with him. "I nicked you, baby. I would say I'm sorry, but that was the best sex I've ever had so I'll get you a bandage and treat you like a queen for the rest of my life. My queen."

He lowered his head and kissed me, long and slow this time.

I could feel where he'd nicked me. It was a little sting on my right hip. It would bleed briefly and then fade away.

Bleed. It would bleed because I was alive and that was what living things did. We bled. When we're wounded, when we're flayed open and laid out, we bleed.

I pushed at Gray and he was the grumpy one then.

"What?"

"I know how Joanne is different. I figured it out."

* * * *

"So all the other girls had burn marks on their wrists and some even across their arms," I explained to Marcus as he drove the Bentley through the streets of Dallas.

Night had fallen and we were on our way to the vampire club. My body still hummed with excitement. It was partially the aftereffects of sex with my superhot demon lover, but there was also the thrill of the hunt. I could feel it. I was getting closer, and those pictures had given me another clue. I knew how Joanne was different and it was far more than her species.

"They struggled," Marcus pointed out. His melodic accent seemed even more intimate in the close confines of the car. "It's only to be expected."

"But Joanne Taylor's arms aren't burned at all," I finished triumphantly.

The vampire slid me a curious stare. He seemed very interested in my thoughts on the case, and I got the feeling he was endlessly fascinated with what I was going to say next. He seemed to genuinely enjoy arguing points of logic with me. "Joanne was a doe. Perhaps she simply didn't struggle at all."

"Not buying it, Vorenus." I enjoyed arguing with him, too. Since that moment I figured out what I'd been missing, I'd been filled with the most delicious energy. It practically burst out of me and Marcus had been so amused by my pacing and talking to myself and the wild hand gestures I make when talking things through that he hadn't noticed we were running late until Gray had pointed it out with a sour look on his face. Despite Gray's wariness, Marcus and I had been arguing back and forth in a thoroughly pleasant manner ever since. "First, even a simple little doe will fight for her life. Second, Jo Taylor had a backbone. No question about it, girlfriend had a pair, if you know what I mean."

Marcus laughed as his hands expertly steered the big beast of a car. "I have no idea what you mean, but I like the way you say it."

"Hey, that's enough of that," Gray growled from the backseat.

I turned around and rolled my eyes at my grumpy boyfriend. He was completely against me having anything whatsoever to do with Marcus. I needed him to understand that besides friendship, I had zero designs on the vampire. Hell, I could barely handle the man I had. I wasn't looking to take on another.

"So why do you think Joanne is different?" Marcus asked blandly.

"There are many reasons she doesn't fit the pattern, Councilman. For one thing, she's the only non-wolf."

"Wolves are much more common than any other wereanimal," Marcus pointed out.

"Secondly, she's the only one of the victims who was buried separately."

"All the wolves were buried in a single grave," Gray affirmed.

"Jo was buried separately. He took care with her. She was the only one who was buried with her jewelry. All the other girls were completely stripped down with nothing left to help identify them." Now for my grand finale. "And I believe she was dead before he cut her open."

"Why do you believe this, Kelsey?" Marcus didn't argue with me. He merely wanted to know how I had drawn my conclusions.

"Because of the lack of blood," I explained. "If you look at her pictures, compared to the rest of them, she doesn't bleed. There's bruising around her neck and that tells me she was probably strangled to death before she was taken to the warehouse. The bruises are already visible. It also explains why the silver didn't burn her the way it did the rest."

"Because dead girls don't fight back," Marcus concluded grimly.

Gray shook his head in the back seat. "All this time I was paying more attention to the other pictures for the simple fact that they were more violent. Kelsey comes in and proves that the least violent of all the kills is probably the one that will tell us who the killer is."

I took enormous pleasure at the pride in his voice. "He knew her. He liked her. He didn't want to kill her, but he had to."

If I was right, my list of suspects was somewhat short. I wanted to start with Professor Peter Hamilton.

"Did you have relations with that girl, Councilman?" Gray asked his question in that Western, all-lawman twang he got when he wanted the truth.

It was overkill. It was so weird that I was the soft touch between the two of us. That so rarely happened to me. "Gray, let up on him."

The vampire waved his hand to silence me. "It's all right, Kelsey. It's a legitimate question. The answer is no. I did not have sexual relations with Miss Taylor. I did, however, feed from her. I did so several nights in row, and now I understand why she sought me out."

"She looked for you?" I wanted to know everything about what she'd done while she was investigating.

"Yes," Marcus replied. "I thought she seemed out of place. By nature, the girls who choose to work the clubs are harder, tougher than Joanne Taylor was. Perversely, her very softness was alluring to every vampire who walked through the door."

"See, I don't get that," I said as the bright lights of the city flowed by. "That other vampire, Michael, thought I was soft and you agreed with him. You guys must have an entirely different version of soft than me."

Marcus had the temerity to chuckle. "You might be prickly on the outside, Kelsey, but on the inside you long. We can feel it. Especially myself, given my talents. You long for someone to take care of you the way your father never did. You long for someone to love you just the way you are, and you're not even sure of who that is, yet, but you want a man who will be willing to stand by you while you discover it."

I wasn't sure I liked being such an open book to anyone, much less a bunch of vampires. "How can you see that much when you barely know me?"

"Two thousand years of interactions with other human beings can refine your ability to see past defenses," Marcus said. "It's also one of my talents. Academics aren't the strongest so we adapted. We can sense what humans need. It makes it easier to feed. You are very resilient, *cara mia*, but there is such softness on the inside."

Gray frowned from the backseat. "Hey, I don't know what you called her but don't. It sounds awfully intimate. She is soft, though, and sweet when she wants to be. She can flay you alive when she thinks you've done her wrong."

I flushed because I really could. It was time to get back to the subject at hand. "So Joanne sought you out?"

The vampire nodded his agreement. "She seemed out of place with the others. She wore the clothes that were provided for her, but she took no pleasure in them. She was always trying to cover more of herself. I thought it odd that she covered a designer dress with a sweater. I asked her why she was there and she told me she needed the money. For three nights she allowed me to feed from her. I felt her distaste so I fed from her wrist. It's less intimate. On the fourth night, I simply offered to pay for her school. I wouldn't miss the money and she needed it. It was painful to watch her, but she turned me down and sought out another vampire. I decided it was her game. I was wrong."

What a dangerous game she'd played. "Did she ever ask you about Britney Miles?"

We were approaching the club and Marcus slowed down the Bentley. "She asked if I'd met her. I said I had. She's one of the girls I did bed. She was a hard girl, very aggressive. I told Joanne that she had moved on after me. She seemed to be working her way through the vampires. Before me she'd had Michael and several of the visiting vampires. After me she allowed Alexander to make an appointment with her."

"And he's seriously Jack the Ripper?" Gray snorted a little, a show of his suspicion. "Don't all you vampires claim some historical relevance?"

Marcus pulled to the side of the road, putting the car in park. He met Gray's eyes in the rearview mirror. "Do not doubt it for a moment, Lieutenant. He is everything that history claims him to be and so much more. He's incredibly clever. He's been careful for the last ten years. He knows that if he steps out of line even once the king will have him executed. If he's working again then he'll do anything to keep it quiet. I believe this is where you leave us, Lieutenant."

Gray sighed and made sure he had the keys to my Jeep in his hand. He leaned up and pulled me in for a quick, possessive kiss. "You be careful." His hand cupped the back of my neck. "I love you."

"I love you, too," I said, the words coming more and more easily to me.

He turned to the vampire, his expression turning forbidding in a second. "And you…"

"Will be horribly murdered if I so much as lay a hand on your lovely woman," Marcus concluded the coming threat with a jaunty wave of his hand. "I will take good care of Kelsey."

"See that you do." Gray hopped out of the car with his bag of equipment. He was going to watch the club from the parking garage I previously staked out. He was also going to get my car and pay for any tickets I'd gotten since he was the reason I'd had to leave it behind. I watched him quickly fade into the background as Marcus pulled away from the curb. He drove the last block and stopped in front of the huge row of Victorian townhomes I now knew were all connected.

Anticipation thrummed inside me, a beast who wanted out of its cage.

The valet hustled to open my door.

"Good evening, Ms. Atwood," he said solicitously. "Welcome to the club. Ms. Sears is looking forward to making your acquaintance."

I waited for him to take the keys from Marcus, who nodded briefly and joined me, his hand immediately finding the small of my back.

"Did I mention how beautiful you look tonight?"

"I believe you failed to do so," I replied, not recognizing the teasing vixen coming out tonight. I was enjoying Marcus's good-natured flirting. Gray had unleashed a monster.

The vampire smiled brightly. "Then let me tell you that you are stunning tonight, Kelsey. You look every inch the lady."

I wondered if that wouldn't actually be a problem. "Are you sure I'll fit in? I saw what Joanne was supposed to wear. I think I'm dangerously overdressed."

"You're perfect. As I said, you're a lady. You look like my mistress tonight. I'm a possessive man, a creature of my time. Anyone who knows me knows I would object to a woman of mine wearing what some of the club girls wear."

"I would probably spend the entire night worried something was going to fall out, so it's best I stay covered," I admitted as we walked up the steps.

The entrance to the club opened and a tall, statuesque blonde stood in the doorway. She didn't have my modesty problems. She was dressed to kill in a bright-red skintight gown with a plunging neckline. Her face should have been on a magazine cover and her chic platinum hair was cut short. I studied Stacy Sears and understood why Marcus thought I was soft. Anyone would look soft compared to her. She was beautiful and undeniably hard.

"Good evening, Councilman," she said with a deferential nod.

Marcus returned her nod, but I got the feeling he didn't particularly like this woman. "This is my new mistress. Her name is Kelsey Atwood. I expect her to be treated with respect."

"Well considering the calls I've gotten about her, how could I not?" The blonde put a hand on her hip. She was slender and her hands were elegant and obviously well taken care of. I wanted to hide mine. I didn't go to a manicurist. I bit my nails often when I was thinking through a problem. As though he knew what I was thinking, Marcus tangled his fingers in mine and gave me a reassuring squeeze.

Stacy continued her speech as she ushered us inside. "I got a call from Zack Owens threatening all manner of horrors should I allow anything bad to befall you. I've never heard him so concerned about anyone except his wife. Are you his long lost sister or something?"

"Nope." I took in the surroundings. I gawked pretty openly. The entire place was plush and very old world. The carpet beneath my feet was Oriental and the entire place looked like it was lit with faux gas lamps. It was easy to think I was walking into Victorian England. Alexander Sharpe must feel at home here.

"Then I get a call from Dev telling me to answer whatever questions you have," Stacy said. "And trust me, Dev Quinn doesn't call unless it's really important. So tell me, what does Marcus's mistress want with me?"

"I'm a private investigator," I explained. "I think you're missing some girls."

Her eyes got wide. "You mean those girls aren't slacking off? They're in serious trouble?"

Yeah, there was no soft way to say it. "They're dead."

The blonde sagged a little. "Shit. I'm sorry. I was being rude. Please come into my private dining room. Marcus, Henri asked me to tell you he's looking for you."

Marcus sighed. "I know what it is about and I need to speak with him. *Cara mia*, do you mind?"

"Not at all." I actually thought the blonde would talk more without Marcus around.

"Stacy, you will take care of her." It wasn't really a question, more like an imperial command.

"I'm not a monster, Councilman," the blonde said. "I don't leave humans to their own devices here."

Marcus's eyes narrowed. "I know one woman who would disagree with you. Understand, this is my woman. I will not deal with you in the same way the king did. You will find I have less compassion and I will not listen to my woman's advice when it comes to such a thing."

With that said, he turned and walked down the corridor.

"That sounded like a threat." I wondered what had set off the normally even-tempered vampire.

"That's because it was," Stacy returned, looking me over. "You're human, right? You're not one of those glowy companions, are you?"

I shook my head. "I make it a habit to never glow."

The blonde smiled, her first real emotion of the evening. "Good, I can't stand those bitches. Come on in and tell me what the hell is going on with my girls. Let me buy you a drink."

Yes, it was good Marcus was gone. She'd relaxed the moment he left. Now we could get down to business. "A woman after my own heart."

Ten minutes later, I was enjoying a margarita on the rocks as I filled in Stacy Sears. She seemed genuinely upset and I was beginning to understand that her emotions were reserved for a select few, her "girls" being in that small circle.

She sighed as she thought about it. "I doubt it was a vampire."

"I do, too."

"They wouldn't waste the blood and they would never bring anyone else into it. They're secretive. Even the ones who hate the king respect the law concerning keeping their presence hidden. I know that everyone's going to point a finger at Alexander, but why would he start up again after more than a hundred years?"

"You think he's a model citizen?" If Alexander Sharpe had an accomplice, it could be a woman. I doubted it, but I wouldn't refuse to consider it. He would likely have a lot of exposure to this woman.

Stacy laughed, a husky, almost masculine sound. "Hell, no. I have no doubt he still kills from time to time, though no one can prove it, and believe me they've tried. The king would love to execute him, but he doesn't have cause to order a righteous kill proclamation. That's my whole point. Alexander has learned to keep quiet. Why bring in others?"

I toyed with the crystal as I thought about what she'd said. It made sense, but I had to cover all my bases. If Alexander Sharpe wasn't involved then someone was trying to make damn sure it appeared he was. "Do you keep records of who sees whom?"

Stacy nodded and slammed back the rest of her drink. A well-dressed man came forward to refill it. "Of course. I can give dates, times, and room numbers. I'll have my books copied from the last several weeks and sent to your office. I keep records of what goes on in the club, but what happens after hours or off grounds is a mystery."

"You think the girls were seeing the vampires in places other than the club?"

"I would be shocked if they didn't. Look, I never meant to become the madam of the supernatural world. It just kind of happened. When the king took over, he freed the slaves. It was a naïve thing to do, and that's coming from a former slave."

"You?" I was surprised because looking at the proud woman, the last thing I thought was slave.

"Yes. I grew up in a vampire household in New York," she explained simply. "The vampire who wanted to see Marcus, his name is Henri Jacobs. He was my mother's master. As masters went, I couldn't complain. He was actually quite kind. He sent me to college for a business degree and got me the job running this place. The horror stories I've heard make me think I had it good. Anyway, the problem with freeing slaves meant there was a huge hole in who would feed the vampires."

"So I understand Dev Quinn came up with this plan."

Cool blue eyes rolled. "As if. I came up with this plan and I went to Dev and believe me that took some guts. I told him I could institute it and have the entire system up and running in six months. It took me three. It's a good system, damn it. The girls get cash and the vamps get fed. I'm not going out and forcing these girls to work. I put out the word that I was looking and I was willing to pay top dollar and they came in droves."

I could imagine. "So you set them up with clothes?"

"And taught them how to do their makeup and hair and made damn sure that they were strong enough to defend themselves if they needed to." I could hear the frustration in her voice. It was the sound of someone older and wiser watching kids make the same mistakes she had and not being able to do anything about it. "I also taught them to never take a vamp outside Ether or the Club where there are paid bodyguards to help them out if they need it. I taught them to not fall for their damn johns."

I was betting she had and that a wealth of experience caused her to be so adamant about the girls protecting their hearts. Somewhere along the line some vamp had broken hers. "Were the relationships supposed to be short term?"

She leaned forward, her elbows on the table, and she gracefully rested her chin in her palm. "I trained the girls to never sleep with the same vamp more than a couple of times and then put some distance between them. You know what it's like. I can't imagine how powerful it is with someone as old as Marcus. You know how they can pull you in. When a vamp really wants to he can make you feel like there's nothing in the world except him. In that moment, the two of you are all that matters. You would do anything for him and you get the feeling that he would do anything for you. It can feel like love. It can be the most potent high imaginable and you have to treat it like a drug. Fall in love with the drug, not the dealer."

"You think some of the girls fell for the same guy?" I didn't know how it felt, but it couldn't be better than when I was with Gray. What we had really was love. I told myself that. I didn't need a lecture because I had the real thing.

She sighed. "It was probably inevitable. I was naïve if I thought they would really listen to me. You know how young people are. They always know better. But I still don't see why a vamp would kill these girls. For the most part, vampires are protective of the women who feed them. They might not love you, but they tend to be grateful.

There's always the bad apple, but even Alexander minds his manners for the most part. I try to properly match him. I try to find girls who won't mind how rough he is."

"A girl like Britney Miles?"

Stacy flushed. "Yeah, a girl like her. I said I wasn't a monster…"

"If it hadn't been for you, there might have been a lot of violence. The vampires weren't going to go hungry. I'm not judging you."

Her eyes narrowed as she took me in and made a decision about me. "You aren't, are you? Most women do, you know."

The man who had been carefully refilling our drinks reentered the small, intimate private dining room. He approached Stacy and whispered something in her ear.

"And where is the Councilman?" she asked.

"I believe he is still with Mr. Jacobs," the young man explained solicitously. "I overheard them asking for a call to be set up in the conference room. I believe they are going to speak with the king about a business matter."

Ruby-red fingernails drummed along the solid oak table. "That's a problem. Well, please inform Mr. Sharpe that I need him to wait until such time as the Councilman can join us."

The young man looked ill at the thought of having to relay the message to the vampire.

It seemed that Marcus's meeting was going to give me an enormous amount of freedom. I likely should have been wary, but a confidence I'd never known had been flowing through my veins for hours. I was ready to take on anything. "I take it Alexander Sharpe is waiting to speak with me and Marcus is sadly preoccupied with business?"

"That would be the way of it," Stacy agreed. "And Alexander won't like waiting. If we take too long, he'll feed and disappear and you'll have to come back tomorrow night."

"As it happens, I have plans for tomorrow night." I didn't have firm plans, but they involved being with Gray. If I had to work tomorrow night, I wanted it to be on something he could be by my side at. I also seriously doubted he would be patient enough to let me get all dressed up and spend a second night with Marcus. "So, I guess I'll have to tackle Mr. Sharpe on my own."

"Seriously?" Stacy stared at me like I'd grown two heads.

"Is he going to attack me right here? Are you putting me alone in a room with him?"

She shook her head. "No, he's waiting in the lounge. There are at least twenty people in there, but it really is best if you have Marcus with you. You're…"

"Going to be a hit with the vampire crowd?"

"Oh, yeah, you're lovely and there's something about you that will attract them like flies to honey," she said simply. "I've been around them long enough to know. I can already see what Marcus sees in you. You know it's been forever since he took a woman as his mistress. He's absolutely the pickiest vampire I've ever met. Most vamps will do anything to keep a female with them, but Marcus prefers to be alone if he's not truly engaged."

"And what does Marcus like?" Though I was committed to Gray, I was still curious about my Italian escort.

She thought about it for a moment before answering. "He likes complicated women. He wants them lovely, of course, but mere beauty isn't enough for him. I wouldn't say he has a physical type, just lovely and complex. If you throw in a side of danger, Marcus will come panting."

I stood up. "Well, I'm certainly complex. I'm also not particularly good at following orders. Please take me to Mr. Sharpe. I want to get this interview out of the way."

"Are you sure? Marcus is likely to be mad."

"I can handle him." I knew something she didn't. Marcus didn't care about me the way she thought he did. He would probably be thrilled we could leave and he could get along with his evening. Now that it was clear I was happy with Gray, I was certain the vampire would lose any interest he had in me, if it had been there in the first place.

Perfect red lips tugged up in a smile, and Stacy Sears elegantly rose from her chair. "Then I suppose I can handle the fallout, as well. I like you, Kelsey. You aren't at all what I thought you would be. Can I give you a small piece of advice about the Councilman?"

I shrugged. "Sure."

"What I said to the girls goes for mistresses, too. He won't ever marry you. A vampire always wants a companion. They'll play around with humans, take good care of you and make you think they love you, but in the end, when a companion comes along, they'll leave you."

I felt for her. There was no way that bitterness hadn't come from experience. I could put her mind at ease about one thing. "Then it's a damn good thing I don't love him."

Stacy reached out and took my hand. "Make sure you keep it that way. Keep hold of my hand. The club is trapped. There are all sorts of strange magic in this place. If you're not with a vampire, you need someone who lives here to guide you through or you'll find yourself trapped. Once some dumbass vamp brought a human in and left her alone and it took us two days to find her."

She led me down an elegant hallway. I could hear the sound of music playing. It was getting louder and I decided the lounge area must be hopping.

A vampire smiled as he strode out of the lounge ahead of us. He stopped in his tracks.

"Stacy, is this a new girl?" he asked as he looked me over assessingly. "Because if she is then I'll take her. She's so different. She's...."

"Marcus's new mistress," Stacy finished for him.

"Damn," he cursed. "Don't guess you have a sister?"

Stacy ignored him as she pulled me along. "Get used to that. When it happens, tell them who you are and they should back off. Use Marcus's name like a blunt instrument. Trust me. No one here wants to cross him."

The lounge was lit with low lights, giving the place a private, intimate feel. My eyes adjusted quickly to the dimness and I could see couples swaying on the dance floor to the strong, seductive beat of the music. I recognized one of the girls, a wolf, from the school Liv taught at. She had been in the graduating class the first year Liv had joined the high school group. Though I'd promised not to judge anyone, I wanted to walk over, snatch her out of that vampire's arms, and escort her straight home. I understood the need and it didn't bother me on an intellectual level but seeing someone I knew...

"There he is." Stacy stopped and pointed to the man sitting in an elegant armchair watching the dancers with a blank expression on his face.

He seemed to be waiting, sitting utterly motionless, as though he could trick someone into thinking he was harmless, but I saw through him. He was a predator and a savage one at that. He was the first man I'd seen walk into the club the night I staked it out. I remembered that night well. It was the first time I'd laid eyes on Marcus and I'd thought he reminded me of a hawk. This man was something different. He was a spider, moving slowly, all his limbs a testament to delicate, graceful death. He would weave a gossamer web and then catch his prey and gleefully devour it. He would take his time, enjoying each bite. I swallowed as I watched Alexander Sharpe because I had no trouble seeing him as a serial killer.

"Mr. Sharpe," Stacy greeted the vampire.

He didn't get out of his chair, merely inclined his head and his dark eyes took us in. "Miss Sears. I take it this is Miss Atwood." His accent was perfectly British. Upper crust, without a hint of cockney to tarnish it.

"I am. I have a few questions for you concerning a series of murders."

His lips quirked up. "Doesn't everyone, dear?" He held his hand out. It was long and graceful, like the hand of a surgeon. "Please join me. I've been properly threatened into answering your questions."

I sank into the seat opposite him. The chairs were close. Our knees almost touched and I wished it wouldn't be so terribly rude to shove the chair back because I didn't want to accidentally have any contact with this man. I merely slid my knees to the side in a lady-like fashion.

"If you're all right here, I'll go see what's holding up the Councilman," Stacy said. "Remember what I said about the club. Stay here until I or Marcus returns for you."

Stacy turned and strode out of the room. I was alone with the vampire.

"So, dear, Marcus Vorenus has finally set aside his unrequited love for the luscious Zoey," the Brit drawled. His eyes slid across me as he appraised everything about me. I could feel it like a rabbit must sense a cougar. "Or has he? You'll forgive me, but you don't look like the mistress of one of the most powerful vampires in the world."

"Really?" I asked, trying for jauntily unconcerned. "I suppose I should be more beautiful."

His lips curled up and I feared I'd fallen into a trap. "I was referring to the fact that I happen to know the good councilman prefers to eat early in the evening rather than late and your neck is smooth. It's quite lovely and perfectly untouched. He likes it from the neck. I believe he thinks it's more romantic. You see, I make it a point to know the habits of those around me."

And there went our cover. "My relationship with the councilman is no concern of yours."

"So it is a ruse," he deduced with great satisfaction. "You're law enforcement?"

Vampire politics seemed to be a veritable minefield, so I chose to leave Dev Quinn out of my explanation. Quinn seemed to have made a place for himself in this world, but he had also pissed a bunch of people off. It was easier to go with a simple explanation. "No. I'm a private investigator. I was hired to find Joanne Taylor by her mother."

He sighed and there was pleasure in it. His hands caressed the plush velvet of the armchair as though he was touching a lover. "Yes, the lovely doe. Her eyes were wide and brown. It isn't often that graceful creatures allow us such delightful access to their charms."

I was a little nauseous at the thought of Joanne at this man's mercy. "The werewolves don't do it for you?"

He wasn't put off by the question at all. If anything, he leaned forward as though sharing an intimate secret with a friend. "The wolves are fine, but somewhat rough. It's difficult to shock a wolf, if you know what I mean. I like to see the surprise in their eyes."

Yep, he made my skin crawl. "You mean fear. You like to scare your lovers."

One shoulder came up negligently. "You consider it fear. I think of it as an arousing game. I never hurt the girls…too much."

"You met with Joanne." I didn't want to get into Alexander Sharpe's predilections. "Her appointment book stated she had a date with you shortly before she disappeared."

"Well, I wasn't about to let something so sweet and docile get past me. Unfortunately, she was more interested in the whereabouts of some other girl than she was in partaking of what I had to offer."

"She asked you about Britney Miles?"

"Only until I used enough persuasion to get what I wanted." The vampire was casual, as though rape was on the same level as a white lie.

"You took her by force." I was pleased that the question managed to come out somewhat civil. I wanted to shout. A low thrum of anger started in my belly. My skin began to heat.

The vampire's laugh was brittle and boomed through the room. "Silly girl, you can't force a prostitute. They know their place and if they don't, they certainly do after I'm done with them."

"These women are under the protection of the Council." I promised myself I would have a long talk with Dev Quinn when I updated him.

He was completely unconcerned with my threat. "Then they should complain to the Council. I'm sure Quinn put in some form of a system for situations like this. That faery is careful. I'm afraid you won't find a single working girl who'll stand up and protest. They like what I give them. Trust me, no one knows how to make a whore scream the way I do." He leaned forward and I forced myself to hold my ground. "Go on, Miss Atwood. Ask the question you really want to ask. Normally, I refuse to answer, but I'll tell you the truth. You intrigue me."

I should have avoided the trap, but I was far too curious. "Were you really Jack the Ripper?"

"Oh yes," he breathed. "I was. I am. Does something like that ever really die? I terrorized London, but they never understood. I was an artist. I killed, well, one often forgets one's first, fumbling attempts, but it was many more than the five they give me credit for. I was a doctor, you see, so I knew the disease those whores spread. I had to watch many a decent man suffer and die because he couldn't resist their siren call. I was doing the city a favor. My fatal flaw was a savage need for credit. I should have worked quietly, but it all turned out for the best."

"You were caught and killed, weren't you?"

He stared straight at me. "Yes, I was and by a clever girl much like yourself. You remind me of her. Something about the eyes. She put the pieces together and came for me one night. A little thing she was, but ferocious. She was stronger than she looked. I always wondered how the Council missed her. They're good at finding Hunters like her."

"I thought hunters hunted supernaturals for the Council." My grandfather had been one, but he didn't have any power beyond his natural strength and long practice.

"Are you serious?" He sat back. "Are you joking with me?"

Joking was the absolute last thing I was thinking about. "What do you mean? Why would I joke? I'm here on serious business, Sharpe."

A smile of pure pleasure broke over his face. It was a frightening thing to see. "I can see that. I can see that you're quite serious. Such webs they weave. Who am I to tear them down? Anyway, like I said, this girl had no training and no idea what power she possessed. I didn't know what she was at the time, either, which was why I underestimated her. It was my misfortune that she was an activist. You know the type. Wide-eyed idealist trying to save the world. Those instincts of hers took over when she found me and I was gutted before I could quite close my hands around her throat."

Something about the way he said "instincts" caused me to get goose bumps. It made me think of the way I had fought the wolves in the alley. I was also thinking about the way he'd talked about webs being woven. I had to wonder who was the spider and who was the fly. "You think she was a supe who didn't know it?"

He hesitated for a moment before continuing on. "Some humans are born with true killer instincts. I'm not talking about soldiers or even murderers. I'm talking about something else entirely. They remind one of wolves in the way they track their prey. The Council has always tried to find and train these humans, but this girl had gotten away."

"So she killed you and Jack the Ripper was relegated to the history books."

"Except I didn't die, not really. Unfortunately for her." His eyes lit at the thought of what had happened next.

"You killed her?"

"Oh, yes," the vampire said with relish. "After my training with the Council was done, I was allowed to settle in the United States, but not before I returned home one last time. I was the hunter then, and her screams still make me sigh. She had your eyes." Sharpe crossed his legs and his body relaxed into the chair like he'd related a pleasant story instead of confessed to multiple murders. "Tell me, dear, have you found Joanne yet?"

"I did. In Whites Chapel Cemetery." I watched him carefully.

"How very obvious! Please tell me you don't suspect I would do something so transparent." He looked horrified, as though he'd been accused of doing something socially awkward.

"No, but I wonder if you don't know who did," I said,

concentrating on every nuance of his expression. "Have you met a man named Peter Hamilton?"

He seemed to pulse with some strange form of joy, as though we were playing a game and he'd discovered he'd finally found a worthy opponent. "Very good, Miss Atwood. Yes, I have indeed made the mad professor's acquaintance. He accosted me one night outside this very club, though he'd left me a present the night before. It was the only reason I agreed to meet with the man. I found his gift…intriguing."

I could only presume what his gift had been. "What did he want from you?"

"Immortality, of course. Turns out the good professor has a brain tumor. He only has six months to live. It's made him quite mad. He believes I can cure him."

"He believes you can turn him."

"Yes. I didn't have the heart to explain the truth to the bugger. Besides, we all like to have our admirers, don't we? I think I could very much admire you, Miss Atwood. I find you endlessly fascinating."

The room got cold around me as the vampire smiled at me. I knew that no matter how this case turned out, Alexander Sharpe wasn't finished with me. I was on his radar and I couldn't even use Marcus's power to keep him away. He knew Marcus and I had nothing between us. He would enjoy toying with me.

Something behind me caught his attention. "Ah, it looks like he's left me another one of his trinkets."

One of the doormen walked forward carrying a small wrapped box. Alexander Sharpe held out his hands and then motioned the servant to exit. "Would you like to do the honors, my dear?"

I didn't want to. I had a suspicion, but I found myself untying the neatly placed crimson bow and lifting the lid off the box. Even in the dim light of the club I could plainly see the heart wrapped in tissue paper.

I shoved the box away and stood up with one thought in my head. He'd just delivered the package. He might be waiting to see if Sharpe would show up to acknowledge him. He might be standing outside, waiting eagerly to see if his god accepted the offering.

"Oh, I feel sorry for him," the vampire murmured, but I was already racing to get out of the lounge.

Chapter Thirteen

I rushed past vampires in the lounge who tried to catch my attention, but I stopped when I made it into the hall. I physically couldn't keep going. It was as though the walls themselves were threatening to close around me. They seemed almost alive and pulsating with menace. Whispers. I heard them coming from all sides, from the walls and the floors and the fixtures. Everywhere I turned something was beckoning, trying to lure me into the rooms. Traps. Stacy had mentioned something about traps. It looked like I was getting the full measure of one.

"Calm down and breathe through it." Alexander Sharpe's precise British accent cut through the panic I felt. He stood behind me, staring at me, curiosity in his cold blue eyes. He was long and lean, dressed in a conservative suit and tie.

What had she said? I needed a vampire to escort me or else the club would try to hold me. I felt it pulling at me. At first the whispers had been threatening, but they changed tactics. Now they soothed and tempted. They told me all the wonderful things that could happen if I opened the doors to certain rooms and stepped inside. When coaxing didn't work, it went back to fear. I would die if I didn't make it behind locked doors. It sent images of all the things that would come after me if I didn't leave this hallway immediately.

"Could you please get Marcus?" I wasn't about to hold his hand. I let my hand find the wall to steady myself because the magic was making me nauseous and the slightest bit dizzy. Touching Alexander would be worse.

"And stop this interesting test? Never. I think you're different, Miss Atwood. I would like to know how different you are. I begin to believe there's a reason a high-powered councilman is wasting his time on a woman he isn't fucking. He thinks you're a Hunter."

"What is that supposed to mean?" I practically snarled the question because I was getting damn sick of being left out of the joke. I took that deep breath Sharpe had advised me to take and tried to banish the nausea I felt.

"It means you can get the bloody hell out of here on your own if you try." He leaned casually against the very wall that threatened to close in on me. "Think about it; your prey could be getting away. He's probably standing outside, waiting to see if I will favor him with immortality's kiss. Bugger's been reading too many novels if you ask me. He's waiting, but he won't wait forever. How do you like the fact that he's standing out there and you're stuck in here?"

I didn't like it at all. It didn't sit well with me. If he was out there, then I wanted my hands on him. I wanted to run him to the ground and to feel him quake with fear when he realized I was after him. It started like it had with the wolves. The instinct started as a tiny ember in the pit of my stomach. It was a whisper at first, telling me I could break free of this magic.

Alexander Sharpe's bored voice sliced through my thoughts. "Then again, perhaps you're a silly little human. What's the fun in that?"

I growled at the killer and it was right there in the back of my mind that I could gut him like the first Hunter had, but this time it would be more permanent. I could end him and avenge my brethren. I wasn't sure where that thought had come from, but it was compelling all the same. There must have been something in my eyes because the vampire took a step back when I turned on him.

His dark eyes widened as though he was pleasantly surprised. Still, he kept his distance. "Yes, there you are. There's time enough for our game later. Right now, your prey is that way."

He pointed down the hall and suddenly I remembered how to get out of here. The voices were still calling to me. I didn't break through the wards or anything. I simply found it easier to ignore since I was completely focused on one thing—bringing Peter Hamilton to justice. He'd killed and tortured and ripped apart six women in an attempt to save his own pitiful life. He couldn't be allowed to get away with that. It was my job to see that he never did it again.

I slapped my left hand on the wall. If I kept in contact with that wall, I could make it to the front door. I wouldn't get lost if I didn't lift my hand. It was like a maze. I slipped off the three-inch heels. I didn't need anything to hinder me.

I ran down the hall, sensing the vampire behind me. He watched everything I did with an avid interest. I couldn't let that phase me. I almost ran into another vampire turning from the main hall down the one that led to the lounge. His eyes widened and he backed away from me.

"See, love, he knows instinctively what you are," I heard Sharpe saying as he jogged to keep up with me.

The carpet beneath my feet gave way to hardwood and I could see the front door. I felt a wave of triumph suffuse my body. I could see the end and I couldn't even hear those voices whispering. I'd beaten them. They couldn't hold me. I felt my power in that moment. It hummed through my veins.

The doorman caught a glimpse of me and then got the hell out of my way. My panic had morphed into pure predatory need.

I stalked into the night cautiously. If I ran, I might tip off my prey that something was wrong. The cool air hit my skin and I noticed that the moon was full. It hung huge in the sky, a perfect harvest moon. It illuminated the yard as I carefully looked around.

Sharpe came to stand beside me and that was all I needed.

He appeared across the street. He emerged from behind a line of bushes that ran the length of the parking garage I'd watched the place from a few nights ago. Professor Peter Hamilton stepped almost shyly from his hiding place, and his eyes were on the vampire. He walked across the street and entered the yard in front of us. He didn't even realize I was there. He was focused on the vampire. Hamilton's eyes were wide, his hands opened as if in supplication.

"Did you like my gifts, dark one?"

Yep, he was insane. It was there in his eyes and his manner.

"Well, they do tend to liven up one's day," Sharpe drawled

behind me.

Hamilton was almost hesitant, but he moved forward anyway. "What can I bring you to please you?"

The vampire laughed, the sound crackling like dead leaves. "I'll tell you what, Hamilton, I'll give you what you want if you can give me one more present."

"Anything," the college professor promised. His hands shook. He still wore his sports coat and slacks, as though he'd walked straight from a lecture to deliver a girl's heart.

Sharpe's smile was slightly demonic. "Deliver her heart to me and I'll give you what you want."

And of course, the bastard was pointing at me.

And of course, Peter Hamilton had a gun.

I leapt off the porch as the first bullet cracked into the door, narrowly missing my head. I landed in the soft grass below and rolled as he fired again. I wished I'd listened more to Gray when he'd taught me how to load and unload his gun earlier in the evening. He'd lectured me on how many bullets a gun held, but I hadn't really been listening. Hamilton had a pistol, but I couldn't be sure how many shots he had left.

Rolling into a crouch, I saw him stalking across the lawn. He didn't seem to think I would be any trouble at all after the way he'd handled those wolves. How had he handled them? The question floated over my brain as I dove behind a bush. He wasn't strong and he wasn't particularly fast, and his hands twitched dreadfully.

Then he fired again and the time for thinking was over. This one managed to graze my left arm. I hissed at the sting. Bullets freaking hurt.

"Asshole," I breathed as I started to bleed all over my god-awful expensive dress that Neiman's would never take back. "I've had the damn tag poking me all night long and you go and ruin it. Do you have any idea what this stupid dress cost?"

"I'll cut her heart out for you, Dark Lord," Hamilton promised, recklessly running toward me.

"Oh, I doubt that," came the silky reply.

Getting to my feet, I faced off against the man with the gun. Something happened to me in that moment. It was a lot like what occurred in Arkansas when I was sixteen, but it was more powerful. Instinct rose inside me, a hot rush of power flowing through my veins. Somewhere in the background, I heard someone calling my name, but it was a far-off sound.

The world narrowed to me and Peter Hamilton. My peripheral vision was still quite good. I could sense it waiting there in case I needed it, but I focused on him. A certain hyperawareness took over, and for a second I could almost feel time slow. I saw the fine tremble in his hand as he lifted the pistol. It didn't stop at his wrist. No, it quaked up his arm and into the muscles of his shoulders. Sound assaulted me, his heartbeat a rapid fire beat, so close together I thought the man might expire then and there.

And I smelled it. Death. It hung on him. He tried to cover it with colognes and soaps, but I could smell him rotting away on the inside.

Time sped back up, catching me almost unaware. His finger pulled back on the trigger. Instead of rolling away when he fired next, I dived low toward him. I hit the ground in a controlled slide and popped back up quickly before he could track me and get off another shot.

Thought fled and instinct took over. Like in the alley a few days before, I fought, the knowledge of how and where to hit flowing over me like a familiar wave. My foot kicked out, neatly catching him in the stomach. There was a huffing sound as all the air in his lungs was squeezed out and he staggered.

This time when he tried to fire, the gun simply clicked. Every predatory instinct I carried told me the fight was done. He couldn't beat me with his bullets. Now it was my time and all that was left was the kill.

Hamilton knew it, too. Somewhere in his filled-with-crazy brain, a survival instinct seemed to be taking over. He gulped air and managed to stay on his feet.

"Dark Lord, please help me." He backed away from me.

I was playing with him. Fear rolled off the professor, the smell almost eclipsing death. I liked the way his body jerked, as though his brain was so clouded with terror it had forgotten how to properly move. He should be afraid of me. I was going to kill him long before the tumor could.

Sharpe's laughter rang out. "Oh, I would never mess with that one. Well, not in any sort of a fair fight, that is."

"Kelsey!" Gray's voice threatened to break my concentration. Somewhere in the back of my mind, I registered that he was running from the parking garage. His eyes were almost certainly on my blood-soaked arm.

I didn't need him to protect me. The thought filled me with distaste. Maybe I should show him my power, prove my dominance.

I heard someone shouting in a foreign language. Italian it sounded like.

Ah, Marcus was here, too. Everyone had come to save poor little me. Sharpe responded and it seemed he knew Italian, too. I didn't care. It was time to show them I did not require their services.

I reached out and grabbed Peter Hamilton by the throat. I moved so fast he couldn't respond with anything but a tight gurgle. His neck felt nice in my hand. Warm flesh, but it covered blood and bone and I could take it all from him. Though I couldn't get his entire throat in one hand, I got enough of it to feel his Adam's apple begin to crush beneath the pressure I sweetly applied.

He was so vulnerable in that moment. In that moment, he was the prey and I the predator god who could set him free if I possessed an ounce of mercy.

I did not.

"Let him go, Kelsey." Gray was next to me, his hand on my arm, trying to separate me from my rightful prey.

I shoved at him with my free hand and he went flying away from me. I heard his surprised curse as he landed yards from his starting position.

"Kelsey, please, honey, this isn't you," he practically begged as he got up again.

"Oh, but it is," Sharpe replied.

"You shut up," Gray commanded.

"I wouldn't get close to her," I heard Marcus say.

With one hand, I picked Peter Hamilton up and tossed him to the ground. He was the tiniest bit taller than I was. Horizontal was a better position to watch him as he died, and I so wanted to watch the man. He was every man who had ever done me wrong. Every bullshit con artist wanna be player who tried to smooth talk me or my brethren. Every asshole who'd thought they had the right to our bodies.

And he was definitely every man who ever beat a woman or a child.

I found myself astride his chest. He was panicked, his eyes

begging me to spare him. I didn't feel like it. No, he deserved not an ounce of mercy from me. He deserved my vengeance. As I wrapped my other hand around his throat and started to squeeze, I felt more power flowing through me than ever before.

"Please, Lieutenant," Marcus's voice said. "Allow me. I have some experience in this."

Then Marcus's voice was inside my head. Calm. Cool. Like a wave of peace, his voice lapped at that rage in my brain. He told me to release my prey, to give over to him. He promised he could bring me peace, help me.

Foolish vampire. I kicked him out as I had the other two who'd tried that trick. Hamilton's throat was a toy in my hands and I shook him, enjoying the way his eyes had started to bulge.

Not so fast, cara mia, the voice in my head said calmly.

"Get out," I snarled. I attempted to push the vampire out again, but he wasn't budging. He was so much stronger than anything I'd encountered. He burrowed his way into my brain and then seemed to grow larger.

I wondered why he didn't take over.

I will leave when you are back to being yourself. It wasn't simply a voice though. There was a well of serenity behind the voice, willing me to join with it. He understood me. He could teach me. He tried to pull me back from the ledge I was on. Funny, I hadn't even realized how far gone I was until Marcus showed me.

Please, cara mia. Let him go and allow the lieutenant to dispense proper justice. It was like Marcus was petting my brain, soothing that part of me that wanted to kill. It felt good to have him there. So good.

My hold tightened because a war was being fought in my head and I wasn't ready to give up. "I am justice."

In that moment, I felt I was. I was born to hunt those like Hamilton who took advantage and hurt those weaker or less fortunate than them.

No, this isn't justice. This is vengeance. Tell me you aren't enjoying this and I will retreat. You cannot. You are receiving pleasure from hurting the human, and that is not who you wish to be.

A great wave of calm rushed over me and I was able to think again. Peter Hamilton was turning blue, his face a mask of agony. I was doing that to him and I was doing it because I liked it.

Shocked, I let go and stumbled to stand up. I felt arms go around me and Marcus pulled me away from Hamilton. Gray was walking toward me, his arms reaching out to take me away from the vampire, but Marcus protested.

"I will take care of her, Lieutenant." He nodded toward the professor. "You have a job to do. The wound is not serious."

"I'm glad she came to her senses. Baby, are you all right?" Gray had his handcuffs in hand. He hadn't heard mine and Marcus's dialogue. I'd spoken aloud, but quietly. He didn't know Marcus had been in my mind, easing me down from whatever the fuck had happened to me.

I'd almost killed a man with my bare hands. The need still thrummed through me. Nothing scared me more than the fact that I wanted to finish him off. That need warred with the need to curl up in a man's arms and let him hold me. I was so shocked that the man I wanted in that moment wasn't Gray.

I wanted Marcus's arms around me.

"I'm fine," I managed.

"I thought…never mind. I'll be back." He went about the business of arresting the professor.

I shook as I came out of the strange fog I'd been in. Marcus shrugged out of his suit coat and wrapped it around me as we sat down on the lawn. The peace he'd imparted to me with his mental powers seemed to be in his hands as well. Every second he touched me I felt myself calming. His presence was a balm to a wound I hadn't known I even possessed.

"It's all right," he whispered as he rocked me gently. "You didn't do anything you shouldn't."

"But I wanted to." I was terrified of what had happened. It had been like I was a separate person, and I was scared of what she had wanted to do. She was still there, still somewhere in my chest. That other part of me responded to Marcus. I gave in and let my head find his chest, briefly wondering how much better I would feel if we were skin to skin, no clothes between us. "What's wrong with me?"

His head dropped to lie against mine as though he enjoyed the contact as much as I did. "Do not worry about it tonight. I have questions that I will find the answers to, and I promise I will make sure you are safe."

"I'll hold you to that," Gray said, looking down on us. He looked as scared as I felt. For the first time since I'd met him, he seemed unsure. I wondered if he was having second thoughts about me. I couldn't blame him. I'd knocked him around like he was a rag doll. "I have to take him in and I have to write up the report. Would you mind taking her home?"

"It would be my honor to escort Kelsey home," the vampire said.

I shook my head. "No, it's a long way to Hurst. I'll take my car. I'll be fine."

Gray hauled me up, heedless of the fact that I'd been shot. Marcus protested the rough treatment but Gray wasn't listening. "Listen here, Kelsey mine, you will haul your sweet ass home, and by that I mean the home I bought for us because you were in my mind when I found it. You will get to our home and get in our bed and you will be waiting for me. Is that understood?"

Guess that answered my question. Now that he was here and I'd broken the connection with Marcus, I remembered who I loved. My Gray. I leaned into him and felt the first stirring of tears. I'd almost killed a man and there was something inside me I didn't understand, but I was going to have to face it. Gray's arms closed around me and I let go because I was safe there.

"It's going to be all right, baby," he whispered soothingly while his big hands rubbed my back as I sobbed. "I'm going to take care of you. I won't let anything happen, I swear it. Trust me."

I held onto him until he had to go and even then I let go reluctantly.

Gray leaned over and kissed me sweetly. "Get that arm checked out."

I'd completely forgotten about the bullet that had grazed my upper arm. Gray hauled the professor into my Jeep and I slipped off Marcus's coat as Gray drove away.

"I don't think you'll have any problems with that little wound, Miss Atwood," a menacing voice said behind me.

Marcus gave Alexander Sharpe a forbidding look and ran his hand up my arm. "Are you sure you were hit?"

"I guess not," I lied because the only evidence left of an injury was a small red abrasion. I'd bled profusely before. The bullet had heated my arm, scorching across it with violent fury, but I had next to no wound.

"I told you it wouldn't be a problem." Sharpe watched me with dark, interested eyes. "You should trust me, dear, I am a doctor after all."

"Come along, *cara mia*," Marcus said, taking my hand. "I need to get you home, but it would be best if you cleaned the blood off first." He began to lead me back into the club. I noticed most of the patrons had come out to watch the scene. My cover with Marcus was well blown. He stopped as we passed Sharpe. His voice was low but his threat was clear. "Whether or not she is in my bed, do not doubt she is under my protection."

"I think the king will have a say in that, Councilman." Sharpe grinned, a ghoulish thing in the low light.

"You stay away from her or you will deal with me," Marcus concluded.

"Of course," the vampire replied with a deferential nod, but as Marcus solicitously escorted me inside, I could feel Alexander Sharpe's eyes on me. He wouldn't give up his game, not when he'd finally found a worthy opponent. He would come after me. Sooner or later, he would come after me.

* * * *

Syl pressed a glass of wine in my hand.

"Here you go, mistress," the little demon said with great concern in his round black eyes. "Are you warm enough? Do you need me to draw a bath for you?"

I shook my head and downed the wine without thinking. He quickly moved to refill the glass. "I'm fine. Thank you, Syl."

"Well, I am certain my mistress is anything but fine." Syl's tongue clucked as he fussed over me. He reached out and drew the blanket up to my chin. "The master will have to learn to take better care of you. Imagine, allowing vampires into the house, much less letting one be alone with my mistress. You could have been bitten."

I enjoyed the demon's fluttering rituals of care and worry. After Marcus got me into the car, he'd been careful not to touch me again, though it had seemed as if his hands kept drifting my way. He'd utterly clammed up and wouldn't explain anything to me. I'd asked about why the king would have a "say" about me. He'd simply told me not to worry about it. He'd promised to take care of everything, but I wasn't sure I believed him. His shoulders had been stiff, anger evident in his posture.

I wasn't completely certain that anger hadn't been directed at me. Somehow, I'd been able to feel it. Marcus Vorenus had been one pissed-off vamp, but he gave me nothing more than a tight smile and a promise to fix things.

I didn't realize things were broken. Wasn't everything better now that I'd solved the case? The bad guy was going to jail and I hadn't separated his head from his body. I had to call that a win.

Still, something was buzzing in the back of my head. Something about the evening didn't add up. I shoved it aside, happy to be home.

This was my home now.

"Would you like for me to prepare a meal for you, mistress? After all the master has put you through, you should keep your energy up," Syl advised. "What is the world coming to when my mistress must deal with vampires and serial killers and all on an empty stomach? I can't imagine that vampire club had a good restaurant in it." He shook his head. I was beginning to understand Syl would have very old-fashioned notions of how marriage should work. In Syl's mind, Gray should provide for the household and I should sit around and let Syl take care of everything else.

"That sounds good, Syl," I said absently as I stared into the fire. I'd never lived anywhere that had a fireplace before. I'd never lived in anything even vaguely resembling the opulence of Gray's home.

Syl walked off into the kitchen, muttering about the plight of good servants, his cloven hooves clicking against the hardwood floors. I settled back further in the comfy chair and sipped the white wine Syl had brought me. It tasted sweet and that faint hint of peppermint that seemed to be in everything the demon served. I didn't mind. I was getting used to it, and I wondered if I could talk Gray into being a little more tolerant of the butler. He seemed so willing to help that it felt wrong to stop him.

I tried to concentrate on good things. I tried to think about Gray and what it would be like to marry him. I would have to change my name and that meant changing my business cards and redoing the lettering on my door at the office. It seemed like a lot of work, but I seriously doubted that Gray would be all right with me keeping Atwood. He seemed a possessive sort of man. What would we do now that the case seemed to be over? The way he'd talked earlier made me think he would want me to move in with him.

Was I ready for that? If I wasn't then I had better get ready for it because I wasn't ready to give up Gray and I didn't think he was going to allow me a whole lot of time to decide. He seemed to be interested in consolidating his victory now that he'd found me.

Syl served me an excellent meal and three more glasses of wine because he was worried about my nerves. Syl didn't believe in the newfangled medicines and found a good Sauvignon Blanc cured most things that ailed a person. When my stomach was full and my brain was pleasantly buzzed, he insisted I take myself off to bed. I climbed into a hot shower and when I emerged, Syl had left a T-shirt of Gray's on the sink and a towel he'd obviously warmed in the dryer. By the time I sank between the sheets, I fell asleep almost immediately.

For the first time in a long time, I had the dream. This was the dream from my childhood, the one I never, ever talked about around my father.

I am running, but on four legs instead of two. The moon is full and silvery on the sky. It hangs there, dominating the landscape and my life. I move to it and hear its call.

The forest is my home and I am the queen of it. It is simple to live here. I sleep. I hunt. I feed. I do each thing when I want and where I want. The world is suited to my needs. I stare at myself for a long time in the crystal water of the stream. I am brown and beautiful. My father runs beside me, showing me how to hunt and thrive. He is brown like me and he protects me in a way my human father never did. Large, he is the largest wolf I've ever seen, but he's so gentle.

I know that other wolves run in packs, but it has always been just me and my father. We like it this way.

Yes, this is my dream. The one that sustained me when I was young. And then it changes for the first time I can remember.

I stop when I feel eyes on me, and when I turn he is there in the dewy morning light. He isn't like me, but I know in an instant that he's mine. His deep blue eyes are kind as they look down on me and he holds out his hand and asks me to change so we can be together.

He is more than a friend or a lover or a husband.

He is Gray. He is my mate.

I love him with everything I have inside me. I change and walk toward him on two human feet, never forgetting the wolf inside me. She is a part of me, sometimes the better part. Gray is two natured as well, though not the same. He will accept my wolf and I will accept his second self. I walk to him and his arms go around me.

His lips meet mine and I am complete.

The world and everything in it is perfect until I hear a low growl. My father stands waiting. He peers at us, and I know that he will not allow this. He will never allow this. The enormous brown wolf that represented everything I wanted in a father shifts and suddenly he is a child. A black haired, brown-eyed child I had seen before.

"No," Lee Quinn says. "It's no good."

I woke up with a start. Fear hadn't been a part of the dream, but I had to force myself to breathe. It had been so real. I could practically still feel the ground under my feet, the air on my skin.

Why would I dream of Lee Quinn? In the dream he'd spoken with a deeper voice, the voice of an adult. It had rumbled out of his child's body.

"Hello, baby," Gray said lazily in my ear as he pushed up the bottom of the shirt I was wearing. "I'm making a new rule. No clothes in our bed. It's inconvenient."

With my pulse pounding, I turned toward him. He could banish the dream and the jittery feeling it gave me. I would stay away from wine from now on. It gave me weird dreams.

"Is it?" I lifted up for him to pull the bothersome shirt off my body.

His hands trailed up and tugged gently on my nipples. I sighed and he chuckled against my neck, trailing kisses even as his hands cupped my breast.

"Yes, it is. It is horribly inconvenient." He didn't bother to keep his weight off me. He pinned me down and took up all the space. "I might keep you naked all the time, Kelsey mine. If we're alone, I want you naked. When we eat dinner, I want you naked. When we sit and watch TV, I want you cuddling against me naked."

His fully clothed body rested against mine. I could feel the hard ridge of his erection against my thigh. He pumped softly in a preview of what he wanted to do to my pussy. "That's an awful lot of nudity for poor Syl to endure."

Gray's face hardened. His hands smoothed back my hair. "He won't be in our lives much longer. We'll have to get along without a butler. I want to be alone with you, Kelsey. I want it to be you and me. They're going to leave us alone."

I felt the intensity of his will and found I couldn't argue with him. "Did everything go all right at the station?"

A quick glance at the clock let me know Gray had been gone for hours.

He leaned down and kissed the bridge of my nose and then feathered kisses all over my face as he talked. "He needed some attention, but everything's handled."

Attention? "You had to take him to the hospital."

I'd put a man in the hospital. I'd held his neck in my hands and squeezed.

"Hey." Gray stared down at me. "Don't go there. He tried to kill you. You defended yourself. He's under guard and he won't ever hurt you again. How's your arm?"

"It was a scratch. I'm fine." I wondered if he would even notice I no longer had any kind of wound.

"I'm glad." He sighed and let his head sink to my shoulder, nuzzling my neck. "I was so terrified when I realized I wouldn't get to you in time. He could have killed you. I wanted to strangle the bastard, too."

"But you didn't. I did."

"Hush about that. There's no reason for you to feel guilty. You did a good job, baby. I'm proud of you. I'm happy that my woman can handle herself. Now look at me and get that guilt out of your eyes. There's no place for it here."

Not in our bed. I let it go because I wanted him and I didn't want to think anymore. Thinking got me in trouble. Being with Gray made me happy. "Yes, Gray."

The bathroom door was partially open, sending slivers of golden light into the room. I'd learned Gray didn't make love in the dark. He liked to see what he was doing. "I like the sound of that, sweetheart." His fingers toyed with my upright nipples. He rolled them back and forth between his thumbs and forefingers. "You'll go to the courthouse with me tomorrow and sign for our marriage license."

It wasn't a question. I was getting used to his bossy ways. I'd learned I could hold my own with him when I needed to, so it was fine to give him his way. "Yes, Gray."

"We'll get anything you need from your house and move you in tomorrow night," he explained. "You can do whatever you want, redecorate, repaint, I don't care, but you live here. This is your home. Our home. We're going to be here for a long time."

"Yes, Gray." I stretched my arms out. I was ready to move on to the "feeling really good" portion of my evening. I needed him. I needed him more than I wanted to admit. "Now, are you going to tie me up or what?"

Gray went still. "Are you sure you want that, baby? I don't have to. I love you. I'll make love to you any way you want."

"I want you. I want every perverted, kinky inch of you," I replied with a seductive smile. "Tie me up. Hands and feet. Make me completely vulnerable to you. Anything you want is yours. I love you." I'd never loved anyone the way I loved Gray. I would have given him my life much less my body.

He smiled as his hands went immediately to the nightstand. He came back with a couple of lengths of rope. "You amaze me."

"How?" I have to admit, I was ready to hear something good about myself. Something that didn't include how well I managed to bust a dude's windpipe.

"You should have worried." He ran the thin rope over my torso, teasing my skin with it. It was silky against my flesh, and he was already making me squirm. "Damn, baby, we were looking for a killer who was into bondage and had a beef with the Council. I should have been a suspect. You shouldn't have trusted me."

He caught my hand in his and started to tie me to the bed. I gripped the cool metal of the headboard. "I love you. You would never lie to me."

At the time, I didn't think about how out of character that statement was. I'd never once given it a second thought. What Gray did wasn't violent. It was consensual and loving and real for me.

Gray went silent and I thought he was processing what I'd said. He lowered his head for a moment and when he looked back at me, all the love he had was in his eyes. "I love you so much. You're everything I want, everything I need. I would do anything for you, Kelsey mine. Remember that always."

He was quiet as he finished tying my hands and then moved down. He slid his hand down my body as though I was a canvas and his touch the paint. He kissed my feet before tying them loosely. He explained about something called a spreader bar and how he would buy one and how he couldn't wait to get started on a playroom that would be only for our exploration.

I was completely open and vulnerable to him and I felt no fear or apprehension. He was my mate. Husband, lover, these were simple, small words to explain what I felt for him. He was…right. It was simple to give myself to him. It was natural.

Gray tossed off his shirt and ran his hand along his tattoo, as though placating the thing.

"You can still feel it?" My eyes were drawn there.

He nodded. "It hums around you. It didn't until you touched it. I've had it since I was thirteen and it's grown with me, but I never felt it like a presence on my body. I think you woke it up, but I don't feel anything more than the physical. It felt like it was trying to come off my damn body when you were in danger tonight. It knew before I did. It burned hot when you were in danger. I had to get to you."

"I'm fine. You can tell my dragon that." I longed to touch him, but I contented myself with the fact that I would get my turn. Tonight was about Gray. He'd been forced to watch as I fought. It went counter to who he was. He wanted to protect me. He was a possessive man, but he'd put it aside and supported me when I'd walked into that club as another man's mistress. He accepted me for whatever the hell I was. He was willing to make me his wife even though he knew there were many unanswered questions. We would face them all together, so I sighed and gave myself over to him.

He stood over me, a sexy smile on his face. "Your dragon?"

"Definitely mine. Everything about you is mine." I was possessive, too.

His hand rubbed against the dragon. "Even the demon parts?"

I nodded. I wanted all of him. "Even those."

He shucked off his pants. He was a gorgeous beast, every inch of his body covered in muscle. All mine. I was greedy and I wanted every piece of him, including the kinky parts, the demonic parts, the sweet parts, the frustrating ones. All of Gray. He leaned over and reverently kissed my navel.

"One day," he whispered, "I'm going to plant our baby right there."

"One day." In the future, I vowed, because I wasn't ready for that and I wanted some time with him before we even thought about having babies. There was so much we needed to figure out before we could consider it.

"But for tonight, I'm going to take out all of my frustration on your sweet body," Gray promised.

He tweaked a nipple and I just about came off the bed. Well, I would have if I hadn't been tied down. There was something about being completely at his mercy that made my heart race in a good way. Those ropes wouldn't hold me if I really wanted to get out, but they were a reminder that I didn't have to think about anything but him. I didn't have to do anything but let him please me.

"Do you have any idea how scared I was?" he asked, his voice thick with emotion.

I did. I know how I would have felt. "I'm sorry, baby."

His hands had sprouted neat claws. With infinite care and precision, he dragged them over my skin. Everywhere they touched I felt a spark. "I couldn't take it. I couldn't handle it if something happened to you. You have no idea how important you are to me, how alone I was before I found you."

Oh, I did, but this was his moment and I let him have it.

Gray reached over to the nightstand and brought back a brown paper bag. He smiled down at me, a sexy, sensual expression. "I went shopping on my way home."

It was two in the morning. "What kind of store was open on your way home?"

He shoved his hand into the bag and came out with a small, oval-shaped object. It was a pretty pink color and had what looked like wings on either side. He laid it right over my clitoris and grinned as he turned it on.

"Oh," I sighed as the vibrator went to work. I tried to squirm, but Gray had been very efficient.

"Feel good, baby? I thought you would like it," he drawled as he looked down on me. "It has a remote, you know, and straps to hold it on while you walk around. I'll put this on you when we go to a party or out to dinner and you'll come for me. I'm going to train you properly. I'm going to top you, sweetheart. You're going to be my sweet little bottom." His eyes were dark with arousal as he looked over my body, and I was surprised as his fangs had come out. I noticed in some ways his fangs seemed to be on the same wavelength as his cock. When his cock got hard, really hard, it was almost impossible for him to keep the curved fangs in check.

I hoped he understood just how hot those fangs were. They reminded me that no matter how nicely he dressed, there was a beast inside my man. My beast.

He moved to the side, his hands cupping my breasts as he leaned in.

"Kiss me," he ordered as he leaned over, and I didn't hesitate.

I'd realized that there was nothing at all truly violent about what Gray wanted from me sexually. He wasn't playing out rape fantasies. If I refused, he would untie me and turn over and go to sleep. What Gray got off on was my enthusiastic compliance. I opened my mouth under his and let my tongue play around those magnificent fangs of his. They were like Gray himself—dangerous if wielded improperly, but this man would never hurt me. I let my head fall back as he nuzzled my neck. He was my knight in shining armor and I wasn't a girl who believed in them. I did now. I believed everything he was offering me.

The butterfly hit the perfect spot and I started to moan. Gray's head came up.

"No. Not yet. Tonight you come with me. You come all over my cock or you don't come at all." He brushed the vibrator to the side and kneeled between my legs. "I have a lot of work to do with you, Kelsey mine," he promised as he fitted that big cock against my pussy. "I think you'll enjoy the training, though."

One long, rough thrust and he was in. He was so big that the fit was almost uncomfortably tight. He was on his knees, his hands cradling the cheeks of my ass as he ground himself into me. His eyes were on the sight of his flesh disappearing into mine.

"You're so beautiful, baby," he said reverently. "I love you." After a minute or two of long, slow thrusts he changed his position and placed the vibrator back on top of my clit. The exquisite tremors made me shake.

"Gray," I pleaded because he didn't want me to come but I didn't see a way around it.

He chuckled as he moved on top of me, his weight pressing the vibrator down, grinding it in time with his pounding thrusts. "You come now, Kelsey. You come all around my cock. Make me feel it."

I obliged, thrusting back against him as much as the restraints would allow. The whole center of my body convulsed. Every muscle seized almost painfully and then burst into pleasure. I screamed as I came and Gray's hands became almost savage as he held my hips in place and his desire took over. He'd seen to me and now he would let himself go.

He pounded into me, using me as roughly as he wanted because he knew I didn't care. I lay shaking beneath him as I watched him throw back his head and growl as he came. He bit into his bottom lip as he held his hips tight against mine, getting every last drop out, pouring it all into me. He finally fell over, exhausted. He let his head lay against my chest and his hands moved restlessly over my body.

"I reserved the room today," he said and I felt his smile on my skin.

I knew which room he was talking about. He was talking about the bridal suite at the downtown hotel where he'd first "seen" me.

"You were sure of yourself," I murmured. My body felt deliciously replete.

Gray's head came up and he looked seriously at me. His hand went possessively to my stomach. "I'm sure of us."

I smiled. "I am too, Gray."

He seemed satisfied with my answer and went about untying me, kissing each limb sweetly as he undid the knot. When he was finished with the task, he rolled over onto his back and pulled me into his arms. He cuddled me close, my head resting on his chest.

I was drifting off to sleep, secure in the circle of his body when he whispered to me. "I'm going to marry you and no one will ever take you away from me. I won't let it happen. Once we're married, I won't let you run away from me."

I shook my head because that was a strange statement to make. I hadn't tried to run from him when I discovered his parentage. I couldn't think of anything that would make me run from him.

I didn't have a very vivid imagination.

Chapter Fourteen

Peter Hamilton simply wasn't strong enough. The next day, I stood inside the courthouse trying to pretend to listen while Gray introduced me to some attorney he knew. The minute we entered the courthouse, Gray had been besieged with acquaintances. It had taken us twenty minutes to finally make it to the department that handled marriage licenses. We'd signed everything we needed to sign and now had to wait three days to get married right back here at the courthouse. I was supposed to arrange some sort of small reception afterward with my mom, brothers, and Liv. I'd received these instructions in between small discussions with coworkers who were shocked to discover Lieutenant Sloane was taking a bride.

I was supposed to play the dutiful fiancée and start moving into my new home, call the restaurant Gray wanted to have the reception at, and most of all contact Devinshea Quinn and give him back his check. That didn't seem particularly fair to me. I'd caught the killer, I deserved the money, but Gray had been extremely insistent that I have nothing further to do with the faery.

"We're getting married in three days," Gray was saying to John something or other.

But I was thinking about strength.

I'd felt Peter Hamilton's strength last night. It seemed to be an intrinsic part of whatever was happening to me. When that other part of me took over, I could judge my opponent's strengths. One thing had been certain. Peter Hamilton's body was breaking down. He'd found it difficult to properly aim the gun due to his advanced brain tumor. If he had trouble holding a gun, how had he managed to handle five werewolves and a shapeshifter?

That wasn't the only question running through my head.

"How did he know to send the letters to you?" I asked Gray as he walked me to my car. He held my hand in his and squeezed it lightly.

"Kelsey, it's not a secret that I'm a Texas Ranger." He was dressed in proper Ranger gear today. He had on a suit and tie, with expensive cowboy boots on his feet and a Stetson on his head. He looked delicious and masculine, and I had no idea how he brimmed with energy after the night we'd had when I could really use a nap. It was his fault. He was the one who woke me up at the god-awful hour of six a.m. because he needed sex before he went to work.

"I don't know." Nothing about the night before added up in my head, including the fact that I was just getting around to thinking about it. I'm suspicious by nature, but it hadn't really hit me until that moment.

"All he had to do was look on the website to find out what area I work for," Gray continued. "It's also no secret I've worked serial murders before."

"So have several of your colleagues. And I seriously doubt that it mentions your supernatural affiliations on the website." That was my issue. Unless Alexander Sharpe had actually been working with the professor, he had zero ties to our world.

Come to think of it, how had he figured out Alexander's secret? There were too many questions and not enough logical answers.

Gray took both of my hands in his as we reached the Jeep. "Kelsey, let it go. Hamilton's in jail. I'm going before the Council this evening to wrap it all up and then we can put all of this behind us. I'm going to work some normal cases for a while and we're going to concentrate on our honeymoon. I took two weeks off. We'll spend our wedding night here in Dallas and then we're going to Hawaii where we won't even discuss serial killers. So stop worrying about it."

"But why would Hamilton want to cause the Council trouble?

He doesn't even really understand how vampires work. How would he know about the Council?"

Gray's hands tightened around mine. "I don't know, Kelsey. Does it matter? We were wrong about him wanting to cause trouble between wolves and vamps. It was merely an unfortunate side effect. As for how he knew about vamps at all, I have to figure one of the students in his class told him. Joanne probably wasn't the only supe he taught."

My heart sped up. I knew there was a reason I wanted those class rolls. "You're right. If Joanne wasn't the one who told him, then maybe I could question the other students in his class. Quinn would probably know which ones were supes, or I could ask Marcus to take a look."

"No." Gray frowned as he regarded me. "You're out of this. If you absolutely have to work then go open your office, but this case is over. We caught him with the sixth girl's heart, Kelsey. He's guilty. Let it go."

Some part of my stubbornness must have shown through because he softened his stance.

"Sweetheart, is it so surprising I want my future wife to concentrate on our wedding instead of a closed case?" he asked, his voice cajoling me. He lowered his lips to mine and touched them sweetly. "Please, Kelsey mine, I want to be happy for a little while."

Put like that I couldn't refuse him. I sighed and kissed him back. "I'll call the restaurant."

"Thank you." He rewarded me with a brilliant smile. "Go on then, future Mrs. Sloane."

And I meant to. I really did. I meant to call the restaurant, but I got another call first.

"So, I had to hear from Marcus that you caught the killer last night?" Dev Quinn's smooth voice accused me over my cell phone as I drove west on I-30 toward Hurst. I needed to pack some things. I could figure out what to do with my furniture later, but my clothes needed to come with me now.

"He's in custody," I replied with as much professionalism as I could muster. I toyed with the travel mug of coffee Syl had handed me as I left the house earlier today. It was already empty. I needed a bigger mug. "I believe Lieutenant Sloane will be meeting with the councilman tonight to go over everything."

"But I didn't hire Lieutenant Sloane, Kelsey." Quinn's reply made me feel guilty. "I hired you. Marcus was surprised that a college professor managed this on his own."

Loyalty told me to keep my mouth shut. Honesty had me turning the car around. If I didn't at least look at those rolls, I would hate myself. I owed Helen Taylor to follow through, to make sure that the end was really the end.

"The Rangers are sure they have the right man," I replied even as I was estimating how long it would take me to get to SMU.

There was a pause, and even over the phone I found Dev Quinn intimidating. "What do you think, Kelsey?"

"I have some questions."

"Then find the answers," Quinn ordered. "Come to my office at five. I expect an update."

I was about to tell him I wouldn't be cashing his check, but I was met with a click as he hung up, obviously certain I would obey his command. Quinn and Gray had more in common than they would guess. Maybe it was why they didn't get along. According to the clock on the dashboard, I had plenty of time before it got dark. It was more than enough time to go look at the rolls and meet with Quinn. I would update him and then politely give him back his check. If Gray got upset I hadn't done everything he asked, then I would have to find a way to make it up to him.

My brain worked overtime the entire drive to SMU. I was willing to forgive myself for not seeing clearly last night. I'd been riding the adrenaline high of meeting Jack the Ripper and then fighting for my life. The beast that seemed to be inside me didn't think analytically. She seemed to run completely off instinct. If Marcus hadn't been able to talk me down, I would have gleefully killed Peter Hamilton and then I would have gone after Alexander Sharpe. It had been there in the back of my mind that I should kill the vampire before he tried to kill me. I would have dropped Hamilton's corpse and turned to start in on Sharpe. The need, the urge to kill had been a strong force. I hadn't even let Gray reach me. Marcus had helped me turn from it. I could still feel the peaceful push of his magic calling me back to myself. Marcus had known what to do. That vampire knew a hell of a lot more about what was going on than he let on, and I intended to get answers out of him, too.

The campus was already starting to look empty as I pulled into the faculty parking garage. I pulled up to the second level and found a spot in the back where hopefully no one would notice I didn't have the right pass. If I got a ticket I would have to deal with it. Before I got out of the car, I shoved the gun Gray had given me in my bag. I had been forced to shove it under the driver's seat of my car earlier because they don't let anyone but law enforcement carry in a courthouse. I doubted there was a metal detector at the admin building, and even if there was, I had a permit. I only cared about getting to the administration building and looking over those class rolls. Hamilton had promised to send them to me, but he must have forgotten in the midst of all his murders.

I hurried along the pathway, not paying any attention to what was around me. When I emerged into the late afternoon sunlight I saw that the last classes of the afternoon were starting to let out. I slipped into the door of the admin building and prayed that they stayed open until five. That would give me an hour to convince someone to let me look at the rolls.

In the end, it was a cinch. The news of Peter Hamilton's arrest on murder charges was all anyone could talk about. He was only being charged with the murder of Joanne Taylor, and the official story was that he had killed her accidentally in a fit of rage brought on by his brain tumor. Did Gray have an assistant who came up with that bullshit or was it the work of the Council? Whoever it was, they'd done me a massive favor. When I explained who I was and that I was merely tying up some loose ends for the victim's mother, the girl working the registrar's desk pulled up the rolls and started to print them out for me.

"Could I have everything from the last three years?" I asked as she typed. She bombarded me with questions and I answered because it seemed to keep her working.

"And you were there when they arrested him?"

I went into the whole story, albeit a highly edited version. If the Council could make up crap, then so could I. I kept talking right up to the point that I got the printouts in my hand. I thanked the girl kindly and then dashed off. I waited until I was out on the steps to take a look at what I had in my hands. The sun was low in the sky and I kind of hoped I wouldn't find anything. If I didn't then I could happily go along with whatever Gray wanted. I could tell Quinn that we were being paranoid, give him back his check, and get ready for my honeymoon. If I didn't find anything out from this line of questioning, that was exactly what I would do, I promised myself as I looked down at the lists of students.

But that wasn't how it worked out. Right there on page three, I found the one name I had sincerely hoped I wouldn't find because I was in serious trouble. I stood up, shoved the papers into my bag, and took off for my car because I was going to see Quinn early. The king had a much bigger problem than he could have imagined.

My cell phone in hand, I walked briskly toward the parking garage. I called Gray first, but it went straight to voice mail. It wasn't surprising since I knew he was scheduled to be in meetings all afternoon. I left a message and decided that maybe it was time to give some new friends a call. Gray might not be thrilled with the Council, but they served an important purpose, and if someone was trying to take down the king, then I had to try to stop it. I clicked the button to call that Zack guy I had met the other night. He told me to call him if I had any trouble, and he seemed pretty competent. He could also get a message to Quinn if I needed him to.

He answered on the first ring.

"This is Owens," a deep voice said expectantly.

"Zack?"

"Kelsey?" His voice went from professional to concerned in no time flat. He also had excellent ears since he knew my voice and we'd only met the once. "I'm so glad you called. How are you?"

"I'm fine. I need to talk to Quinn." I walked into the parking garage. It was far emptier than before. Faculty left at the first opportunity around here. A little like the students. "Tell him I know who the killer is and he's got some cleaning up to do."

"Kelsey, you're breaking up." The phone crackled and if he said something else, it got lost.

"It must be the damn parking garage." A deep chill swept over me. The hair on the back of my neck stood up, and I knew someone was watching. "Zack?"

"I can barely hear you," he practically shouted.

I spoke as clearly as I could. I wanted someone, anyone to know where I was because that feeling wasn't going away. "I'm in the faculty parking garage at SMU."

Out of nowhere a hand batted the phone out of my hand. It clattered to the ground. I spun from the force of that hand hitting me and looked straight into the cold eyes of Darren Castle.

"You had to keep looking, didn't you?"

I backed up. He'd been the name on the list. The one name I hadn't wanted to find because it meant I was knee deep in the mud. "You killed her and she was your friend."

"She was a pretty girl," Darren said, but I heard the hesitation in his voice. "Unlike every other wolf alive, I like some variety. I enjoyed chasing her. I would have enjoyed catching her if she hadn't forced us to kill her."

I needed to keep him talking. My phone was face up and the lights were on, indicating the call was still live. There might be some shot at Zack hearing the conversation. My heart was starting to pound. Gray was going to be so upset if I got myself killed three days before our wedding.

"No." I'd seen the way he treated her even after she was dead. "You loved her. You didn't want to kill her. You hated yourself for doing it. It's why you buried her separately, why you took care with her."

He stood there, blocking the way out of the garage. Even in his flannel shirt and jeans, he radiated power. His build was stocky and muscular and there was no doubt he was an alpha. He didn't lead any pack today, but he would someday. He would lead them by right of tooth and claw. He would lead them because he would be able to kill anyone who questioned his right.

"I accept her death," Darren said with a righteous tone to his voice. "And I didn't kill her. My father did. I haven't killed anyone, though I did watch a couple of times. He killed Jo because she saw Hamilton with that vampire. She was going to give up the entire game. Dad had to strangle her or she was going straight to the king with news that Sharpe wasn't the killer. Everyone would have known and then it would all have been for nothing."

I breathed, patiently waiting. He seemed willing to talk. If he wasn't lying, he hadn't actually killed anyone before and likely wanted to put it off. Just because he'd helped his father didn't mean he was ready to move up in ranks himself. Killing isn't easy. Not the first time. Not even when you're a predator. "What did you expect to get out of this?"

Now I had him on a subject he really liked. His face came alive with passion. "Freedom. Ever since McKenzie sold us to the vampires for a seat on the Council, we've been slowly becoming their slaves. We are wolves. We should rule ourselves. We shouldn't have to watch as our women become whores."

"Have some of the she wolves chosen to stay with the vampires for more than a night?" I thought about that couple I'd seen going into the club. They'd been together for a while, I would guess. That must upset someone like Joseph Castle to no end. It made me wonder what other rules the king had tossed out. Traditionally, the alpha of a pack was practically a god. He made all the important decisions for his group. "Does the king not allow the alpha to select mates anymore?"

Darren practically spit his answer at me. "We're allowed to make suggestions, but if a female chooses not to mate with our selections, then we have to back down. He can also shut down our business ventures whenever he pleases."

I bet he could. According to Gray, the king shut down a drug ring the wolves had been running. "So the king won't let you rape women or run drugs. You have it hard, man."

I should have watched my mouth, but I was starting to agree with the king more and more.

His eyes began to take on the predator inside him. His features elongated as he struggled to control his urge to change. "It will all be over once the Ranger finds your body. He'll have to believe it was Sharpe since the idiot professor is in custody. I've already written the note. When he raids Sharpe's apartment, he'll find traces of you everywhere. Dad's taking care of that. I have to bring you in and we can finally be done. When Sloane tries to bring in Sharpe and the king saves him, the rest of the wolves will finally see him for what he really is."

I saw a few problems with the scenario and wondered if the Castle men weren't every bit as crazy as Peter Hamilton. "What if the king allows the arrest?"

"He won't." Darren's hatred was thick in the air. "Vampires protect each other. They expect us to do what they tell us, but they only care about their own rules. Otherwise, why would they let some scum like Sharpe live after everything he's done?"

I didn't point out that they'd done the same things as Sharpe. I chose another tactic because I wasn't so hot on becoming victim number seven. "You're underestimating Lieutenant Sloane. He won't arrest Sharpe."

"Of course he will. He doesn't play favorites. He'll arrest anyone he thinks has done something wrong. Look how he fucked with Quinn last year. That was sweet. My dad laughed the whole time Sloane was hauling that pervert out. Too bad he couldn't make it stick."

"I assure you if he thinks Alexander Sharpe killed me, he will not arrest him. Sharpe will die and there won't be anything left to identify. He loves me. He won't leave it to the justice system."

"He's a Ranger."

"He's a man first. We're getting married," I explained logically. "Would you calmly arrest the man who killed your mate? If he kills Sharpe, then the king might have a problem with it, but everyone else will think justice is done."

That seemed to flummox the younger man. He frowned as he thought about it. I felt my back touch the concrete barrier of the small elevator that led to the second and third floors. Darren was thinking and generally growing more panicked as he considered the angles. I considered the angles, too. Even if Darren decided I was right, he couldn't call a mulligan and get a new hand. He had to play the one he'd dealt himself, and that included getting rid of the obnoxious PI who screwed everything up.

Very cautiously, I slipped my hand back and hit the button for the elevator. As I heard it start to ding, I reached into my bag and pulled the .45 Gray had given me. Without hesitation, I shot him squarely in the shoulder and watched as he was blown back by the impact. His entire left side flew around like he was attached to a chain someone had yanked. I threw my body into the open elevator and immediately hit the number *two* button and then punched *close doors* as many times as I could in the few seconds it took to work.

Even as the doors were closing, I watched Darren's body jerk up from where he'd fallen. He turned to the elevator and he growled low in the back of his throat. It started as a growl, but before the doors were fully together, it was a howl that shook the garage.

It was the single, longest elevator ride in the history of time. I'm pretty sure of that. The whole time I stood there, holding the gun and waiting for the doors to open, I fought the instinct that threatened to take over. It was stronger, possibly because I'd let it loose the night before. There was something inside me, like a caged wolf, clawing to get out. Adrenaline rushed through my system, seeming to feed it. I couldn't lose control. I'd been insane the night before, nearly unstoppable. Marcus wasn't here and I wasn't sure I could get control back without him. The first time someone had knocked me out with horse tranquilizers and the next time Marcus had been there. What if I went crazy? We were in a public place. No, it couldn't happen.

I needed to get to the Jeep and drive like the wind to Gray's office in Garland. I had the address. I would go there and dump everything in his lap. He would handle it and I wouldn't have to find out how far gone I was. I forced that twitchy beast down. I shoved it away with every ounce of will I had.

When the doors opened, I ran. I ran as fast as I could toward the dark blue Jeep that represented freedom and safety. I might have made it if a big brown and white wolf hadn't been between the car and me.

Wolves are way faster than elevators.

The force of stopping on a dime nearly set me on the ground. I managed to stop my fall, but the gun clattered to the floor. The wolf snarled and I wondered briefly if his clothes had ripped and torn around him or if he'd taken the time to unclothe before becoming the big, toothy predator in front of me. It's funny the things that go through your brain when you know you're going to die. Darren Castle was going to get his first blood and it would be mine. He wouldn't knock me out and take me to a convenient location. He was going to kill me right here and right now.

What was more important? Survival or keeping my conscience clean? It was no question at all. One way I died and the other I had a chance at staying alive and being with Gray. That was all that mattered to me in that moment. I wanted to see Gray again. As the brown wolf leapt through the air, I let down every defense and let the beast take over.

This time it wasn't a tiny ember that blossomed. It was a full-blown bonfire that raged through my body uncontrollably. Fear fled and in its place was a righteous certainty that I wanted to live.

The wolf flew through the air, his jaws opened wide. I felt the heat from his mouth as I kicked up and I shoved myself under the pouncing wolf, catching him in the chest and following through to shove him behind me.

Even before he hit the ground, I was up and looking. Through almost alien eyes, I took in everything in that sparse concrete-laden lot. During the times when I fully surrender to the beast, it's as though I'm rewarded with superpowers. My every sense heightens and any fear I felt flees. I can still feel emotions, but they're muted in comparison to the joy of the hunt, the anticipation of the kill.

There were only a few cars around at this time of day. Above me there was a wealth of pipes crisscrossing the ceiling and disappearing into the adjacent building. The wolf turned, growling in frustration as he got back up and began to run toward me again.

I leapt straight up, catching the pipe in both hands and swinging my legs back. The motion brought power with it and I timed it perfectly. I caught the werewolf in the jaw and was satisfied with the crack and the whimper as my opponent went down. I dropped down, knowing I had mere seconds before Darren recovered. My foot had caught him right across the jaw, but I hadn't felt the bone break. I was still fighting my instincts on some level, and there was a part of me that was screaming to give it up and let them take over completely.

Stop pulling your fucking punches and let a real woman do the job, a voice inside me growled.

Fighting to maintain some semblance of control, I searched around for a weapon. I ran from car to car, looking for anything I could use, but freaking college professors aren't big on carrying weapons. There was a lot of tweed and great literature, but nothing in the way of guns.

Darren landed on the late-model piece of crap I was searching and the hood dented under his weight. He snapped at my head and I leaned back before catching him in the snout with as much strength as I could put in my fist. I didn't look back as I moved on to the next car and finally hit pay dirt.

Somebody actually played a sport, and lucky for me it was baseball. Unlucky for me Mr. Shortstop remembered to lock his car door. I was desperate enough to rear back and shove my fist through the back door window. It cracked against my fist, the pain blossoming, but I was able to ignore it. Blood start to run. It reminded me I needed to fight. My fist closed around the bat as the wolf leapt onto my back. He bit down ferociously on my shoulder, close to my neck. The sharp, terrible sensation pushed me straight over the edge.

I roared, the beast in me firmly in control. I threw my body back in an attempt to dislodge the wolf. We hit the Volvo behind us and Darren foolishly let go as his spine hit the car. I took the opportunity to run and regroup. Behind me, I heard the elevator doors open.

"Oh my gosh, lady, do you need help?" a middle-aged man asked, taking in the sight of a young woman being assaulted by what I was sure he would describe as a big dog.

Darren growled at the man, but he walked bravely forward. "Shoo!" he yelled in a strong voice.

I turned and he got a good look at me.

That was when he ran.

I didn't have time to ponder that as Darren was running full throttle toward me. I took the proper stance, knees apart and a little bent. In my state, I grinned at the thought of letting one fly. My elbow was up in a perfect imitation of Jamie on the L. D. Bell High School baseball team. When Darren pounced, I swung and hit. This time I caught him full in the head and his whole body twisted with the force. He didn't whimper. He didn't moan. He just went down.

I was nowhere near satisfied with that. Rage filled me. He'd thought he could kill me? I brought the bat down again and again. His big body twitched a time or two, but after a while he didn't move anymore. Blood splattered, but I didn't mind. It was only right that I cover myself in it. He was my enemy and I'd won our game.

My heart raced and I felt disappointed the game was over so quickly. I hit the body over and over, trying to get out all my rage. He'd tried to kill me, to take my life, but I'd shown him what it meant to cross me.

"Shit," I heard a voice say behind me.

"Don't get close to her," another voice warned.

It was too late. Someone was reaching out to me.

"Kelsey," Dev Quinn said as his hand touched my shoulder.

I reared back, all instinct and rage. He'd come into my killing field and dared to interrupt me. Swinging the bat back, I hit him full force across the chest. His emerald green eyes registered complete shock as his body flew away from me. He hit the concrete with a thud and a low moan came from his mouth. This one wasn't dead yet. He needed another couple of hits before I could claim him. I held the bat over my head and was about to bring it down on the faery's head when an arm shot out and I looked into seriously blue eyes.

Dan held my arm in his hand, the threat obvious. He would break it if I didn't stand down.

"You don't touch him," he snarled around his really freaking big fangs. "He is mine."

But in my mind he wasn't. In my rage-addled brain, that faery was mine because he'd walked into my territory and tried to keep me from my rightful prey. Now the vampire was doing the same damn thing. He stared at me like he could scare me into backing down. Idiot.

I pulled my arm out of his grasp even as I kicked him straight on in the crotch. Vampires, I discovered, liked their privates uninjured as much as the human male. Dan went down with an outraged shout and I took advantage. I swung the bat straight down at his sandy blond head. My bat hit the concrete and split in two as the vampire nimbly rolled away in the nick of time.

It was okay. A broken bat becomes a handy stake.

"Daniel!" Quinn had managed to get to his knees. He pointed my way.

I rushed the vampire, the lovely pointed end in my right hand, his heart in my sights. Dan's handsome face registered shocked and he took a defensive stance. His fist reared back and it was just a question of who handled the impact best.

Or it would have been, if the world hadn't stopped on a single command.

"Sleep," a peaceful, familiar voice said deep in my brain.

My hand lowered and I saw Marcus running toward me as I began to fall. I was in his arms as everything went black.

Chapter Fifteen

"Well, it's been an awfully long time since I saw anyone put Daniel on his ass," I heard a voice say as I started to come out of the darkness. "It was worth the broken ribs for that sight alone. I'm glad I took the bat in the chest instead of what happened to you. If that had happened to me, we would never have any more kids."

"It's not a fucking joke, Dev," a low voice growled. "She nearly killed you."

I opened my eyes a smidge and saw them standing there.

"Oh, it wasn't that bad." Quinn had changed his shirt. He was back to masculine perfection in an olive-colored dress shirt and black slacks. "I've had much worse, though it has been a while since I broke a bone. I'll moan and complain about the pain for days and see how much sympathy sex I can get out of our wife."

A familiar voice chimed in, disapproval dripping. "It could have been avoided if Daniel had taken me with him as I advised. I can handle her. I am the only one who can handle her when she gets like that. You're lucky Zack drives as quickly as he does or you could have had a much bigger problem on your hands."

I lay perfectly still. I wanted to listen in as Marcus argued with Dan and Quinn.

"You think I couldn't have handled her, Marcus?" Dan asked

defensively. "Damn it. I held back because I don't like hitting girls. I took Dev because I thought he could help. He has a relationship with her."

"He spent ten minutes with her," Marcus complained. "I have a relationship with her. Devinshea tossed money her way and expected her to comply because of it. He knows nothing about her. Neither of you has ever met a Hunter before and you're proving it even as we speak."

"What the hell is that supposed to mean?" Quinn asked.

I felt a hand on my shoulder. "It means that she is awake and listening to everything we say. It's no use, *cara mia*. Open your eyes."

Dark eyes looked down into mine. He smiled, but I saw the deep concern in them.

"What am I?" I asked desperately, needing to know what the hell was wrong with me. It wasn't normal to have something primal inside waiting for a chance to get out.

The vampire smoothed back my hair and lifted me up. I felt weak against him. "Rest. I had to use an enormous amount of persuasion on you. The weakness will pass."

I couldn't rest when I wasn't sure of where I was. The room was painted a neutral color and I'd been placed on a comfortable bed, but the bars on the door didn't lie. "I'm in jail?"

"It's a holding cell." Dan looked at me with a mixture of guilt and wariness. "It's only a precaution. You were out of control. It's a good thing you're awake. The Council is ready to meet. You need to answer for the killing of Darren Castle."

"It was obviously self-defense." Zack slid his key card through the lock and the door swung open. "I told you that when I asked you to go save her. He attacked her. I heard the whole thing."

Dan sighed. "I know that, Zack, but you know as well as I do that the kill has to be declared righteous."

Marcus squeezed my hand. "Do not worry. It will be all right."

I shook the fog out of my head and turned to Marcus. He was the only one in the room I had any trust in at all. "His father killed those girls. Darren admitted it to me. He was the one who told Hamilton about vampires and led him to Sharpe. He was planting evidence against Alexander Sharpe. They were trying to make everyone believe Sharpe and Hamilton were partners, but Joseph Castle killed them all."

Dan shook his head. "Son of a bitch. If he'd succeeded..."

"The wolves would revolt," Quinn said.

Dan pulled out a cell phone and quietly called someone explaining that Castle needed to be found and brought in.

Someone had changed my clothes. I was wearing a too big *V-neck* sweater and a pair of men's Levi's. My feet were covered only in a pair of white socks. "Who changed my clothes?"

"Our wife and her friend." Dan shoved his phone back in his pocket. "You were covered in blood. I thought it best you didn't go meet the Council like that. I was going to change you myself." Dan grinned and rolled his blue eyes. "But Marcus there insisted on propriety. So we brought in Zoey and Neil. Devinshea and I left the room. No covetous male eyes saw you, I assure you."

I looked up at Marcus and saw he didn't care that the other two men thought he was ridiculous and old-fashioned.

"Thank you," I said quietly. His hands on me felt so good, though not necessarily in a sexual way. It was sensual, for certain. While I sat with his arms around me, I felt peaceful and calm, as though he could take the serene core of himself and impart a piece to me. I knew Gray wouldn't like it, but I needed it. I put my hand in his because I needed the support for whatever I was about to learn. "Now, will someone please tell me what's happening to me?"

Zack's open face broke into a huge smile. He knelt down beside me. "I would be thrilled to tell you."

"Boss," a heavily accented voice said from the barred door. It sounded Northeastern. "Her brothers are here and so is the witch. They want to see her before she goes in."

Dan inclined his head. "Thank you, Trent, show them in. I have some questions for them anyway."

"I'm sorry," I said quietly, looking at the two of them. I had tried to kill them. It wasn't so surprising I was in jail.

Quinn smiled broadly. He really was devastating when he smiled. "Not at all. It was very exciting. The only problem was we didn't bring Zoey along. It makes me long for the old days," he sighed and exchanged an intimate look with his partner. There was a whole lot of history between them. "We'd fight and almost die and then Dan would come in to save the day and we'd all go to bed and celebrate the fact that we survived."

Dan shrugged. "It's still a little like that. I celebrate every day the twins don't accidentally kill themselves or others."

"Kelsey." Jamie rushed into the room. Nate and Liv were behind him, but they moved more cautiously. Jamie pulled me out of Marcus's arms and I immediately felt the loss of his warmth. "I was so worried when they told me you were here."

"She's fine, Jamie," Nathan said solemnly. "Dan wouldn't hurt her. He's only trying to help."

Liv stood beside him, looking the slightest bit guilty and I knew. I just knew. "You two set me up."

Nathan swallowed before answering. "It wasn't like that, Kels."

Jamie let me go and glared at Nate. "What do you mean? Nate, are you trying to tell me you know what's been going on?"

Liv stepped up and reached out for my hand. Her lovely eyes radiated concern. "Kelsey, you know something's wrong. It has been for a very long time. The king came to me and asked if I would help you, and I couldn't turn him down."

"What does the freaking king want with me?" I practically shouted.

"Calm down, Kelsey," Nathan said.

"You calm down," I shot back at him with a growl.

"You better start explaining, Nathan," Jamie said in his best big-brother voice. "I want to know what's going on and why you felt more loyalty to these people than your own damn family."

"Loyalty?" Nate asked, his voice rising. "You want to talk about loyalty and family, Jamie? How about protecting our sister rather than passing her off to some fucking demon? How about that? You practically shoved her into bed with a Hell Lord. This is your fault, Jamie. And Liv's. Liv is the one who brought her back into this world. I wasn't on board with this plan until Liv shoved her back in. What was I supposed to do? She can't handle it."

"She can once she gets the training she needs," Liv shot back. "I sent Helen to her because Helen needed help and Kelsey needs to use her skills. You're the one who wants her to live a half life because you can't handle what she really is. You know she needs this, Nate."

"All of you stop." Marcus stood and reached for my hand again. The minute he touched me I sighed and felt the burgeoning rage slip away. "Can't you see how fragile she is? She has absolutely no control yet. Daniel, is this mockery of a trial absolutely necessary? It would be better if you allowed Zachary and myself to handle her."

"Sorry," Daniel said, getting up. "It is necessary and considering how we're all going to have to handle her, we should do this in chambers. Everyone, please follow Dev. The Council is ready, if Marcus will take his place."

Marcus sighed. "I don't think it's a good idea for me to leave her."

Daniel shook his head and held out his hand to me. "I've been watching. I think I can keep her calm until the last of the episode goes away. I know she should rest, but we need to settle things."

Marcus reluctantly placed my hand in Dan's. As I touched him, I felt his will. He pushed his persuasion at me. It wasn't as strong as Marcus's, but I felt it's soothing nature. Where Marcus's was warm, Dan's was cool, like a breeze on a hot day. The others filed out and I let Dan lead me even as certain pieces fell into place.

"You were the one who tested me in the alley," I said softly, thinking about the voice in my head. It had been his.

"Yes." Dan led me down the hall and up a set of stairs. "I had to be sure. I sent one of my vampires, an illusionist, to test you. Dev and I watched from a building across the street. You were never in any real danger, though Chad sure as hell was. He was very surprised. It's been a long time since anyone saw through his illusions."

And other pieces fell into place. It was daylight. Only two vampires currently living in Dallas could daywalk. My heart ached with the absolute betrayal of it all. Why else would Marcus, who was far older than Daniel, follow his instructions? "And did you find out what you needed, Your Highness?"

The King of all Vampire gave me a slight smile. It was tight and there was no real humor behind it. "I did. Don't blame Nate. I asked him not to tell you. I asked Olivia not to mention she knew me, either. I thought it would be easier if I got your friends involved. You came to my attention six months ago. When I took over from the last Council…"

"You mean when you staged your coup," I stated, needing to needle him.

His mouth tightened but he let it go. "When I became king ten years ago, I had all the old records brought over from France. It's taken me time to go through them. I learned a lot from those files.

One of the things I discovered was a line of genealogy dating back to Roman times. It was carefully kept by the Council. It concerned a certain type of werewolf."

"I don't see what any of this has to do with me."

"You are one prickly female," Dan said, his smile seemingly genuine. "It has everything to do with you. Do you know what a lone wolf is?"

I'd heard the term. "It's like a super wolf. It's not an alpha though. They tend to work and live outside packs. They tend to be drifters."

"Yes, they do. They also tend to be cantankerous and a bit lazy," Dan said with great affection. "The gene is recessive and very, very rare. There are only two loners in the whole world now. The Council kept track of them. They were watched closely."

"Because they're dangerous?"

"No, because the Council is always watching to see if the loner takes a human lover. It is rare, but some do."

"Why does the Council care who some loner sleeps with?"

"Because if the lone wolf manages to produce a child with a human, there is the slight possibility that child will be what they call a Hunter. A Hunter has many of the strengths of a wolf. It's like having the soul of the wolf, but not the body. A Hunter has strength and speed and instinct, but they aren't vulnerable to silver and they don't have to follow the moon. Some Hunters find, once they accept the beast inside, that they can change their hands into claws."

I stopped in the middle of the hall. "And you think I'm a Hunter. You're not the first person to call me that."

I thought about Syl. He'd said I was a Hunter, and it was who I was not what I did.

"Yes, I suspect many people have tracked you," Dan replied. "My coup, as you call it, saved you, Kelsey. The former head of the Council was a man named Louis Marini. Two days before he was killed, he signed an order to have one Kelsey Atwood brought to France under Council supervision. You would have been kidnapped, brought to the Council, and trained to do what you were born to do. You were sixteen and something had triggered your power a few months before. The Council watched you from the time you were born."

The night in the woods with my father had been the first time I'd felt the power. My fear and rage that night had been a catalyst. It had been a turning point. "And what was I born to do, Your Highness?"

The doors at the end of the hall opened, and Dev Quinn stood there impatiently.

Daniel wouldn't be rushed. "You were born to track and kill demons here on the Earth plane. It is what Marini would have trained you to do. It is what Hunters have done for millennia."

The room got cold as I realized the impact to Gray and me. How was he going to take the news? Would he be angry? And there was still one last question I had.

"Are you trying to tell me my father is a lone wolf? My father hunted and killed wolves. He hated wolves."

"All of those things are true about John Atwood," Daniel allowed. "But John Atwood was not your father as I will prove when we go before the Council and have your protection declared."

I stopped as he tried to lead me into the Council chamber. I didn't want to go in there. If I went in that room, everything was going to change. My whole life was going to change. "I want to call my fiancé. I'm getting married in three days. I want Gray here."

The king's face hardened. "He's on his way, but I don't think you'll like the reunion. He has a lot to answer for. Now it is time to go. Don't worry. It will all work out and you will be well taken care of. I promise you that." He pulled me along, and I entered the chamber where my life would change forever.

The Council chamber was a large, intimidating room dominated by a huge semicircle of dark wood that functioned as a desk. It's a little like a big old courtroom and five judges sit above it all. There was a place in the middle that was empty and plenty of seats in the back of the room. Nate, Jamie, and Liv were sitting in the gallery seats. Jamie was facing away from Nate, a sure sign he was pissed. Zack sat next to the blond wolf named Neil and his gun-happy Goth boyfriend, who I still kind of wanted to injure heinously. Dev Quinn sat next to the beautiful redhead from the photo in his office. She winked at Daniel as we walked into the room and then caught my eyes and smiled encouragingly.

I really didn't care. I wanted Gray. No matter what the king said, I wanted Gray here.

"Gentleman, madam," Daniel addressed the Council. "This is Kelsey…Atwood, for now. She's the woman in question. Kelsey, allow me to introduce the Council. You know Marcus Vorenus, of course. He represents Vampire. To his left is His Royal Highness Declan Quinn, Prince of Faery. Yes, it's his twin."

The man who looked exactly like Dev Quinn sighed. "Finally, Daniel, some interesting business. You're quite pretty. Whatever shall we do with you?"

"You'll have to pardon him. He's an ass," Daniel said, continuing the introductions. "John McKenzie, he's the alpha for the North American pack."

McKenzie was roughly forty-five and his face was as hard and unforgiving as one would expect from a man who led that many werewolves. His hair was cut in a military style and he had the bearing of a general. "Damn, Donovan. She's really his daughter. I can smell it from here. Wish the old guy was alive because I'd love to see him try to handle this one."

"Chris Hancock, he's the leader of the panthers and holds the shapeshifter seat," Daniel said as he moved down the line. "Esme Reynolds represents the witches, and Sir Ronald James speaks for human interests."

"Good evening," the older Brit said with a nod of his head.

"Now," the king began, "Will Jamie Atwood please stand?"

Jamie complied, standing readily, his green eyes confused and wary. "I want to know what's going on, Your Highness. If my sister killed a wolf, then she was defending herself."

Daniel nodded. He turned back to the Council. "I move to declare the killing of Darren Castle to be righteous. Ms. Atwood was defending herself. All in favor?"

There were five ayes and no nays. I was off the hook for the killing. It was quick and I probably should have been relieved.

My pardon was seemingly unimportant to the king. He had bigger fish to fry. "Excellent. Mr. Atwood, you are the oldest of your mother's three children."

"I am."

"Do you remember a trip your mother took roughly two months after giving birth to Nathan?"

Jamie thought for a moment. He would have been five at the time. "We went to visit her cousin. My father was on an extended hunting trip and Mom packed us up and headed west to see…I think her name was Gina. We stayed for two months and then Dad showed up and we went home."

I didn't even know Mom had a cousin named Gina. Dad had never let us leave the state without him.

"What city did Gina live in?" The king seemed to be enjoying his stint as prosecuting attorney. Or was he defending me? I couldn't tell.

"Las Vegas," Jamie replied.

That seemed to mean something to a whole bunch of people in the crowd. There were gasps of surprise, and the woman I now knew was the queen had a sheen of unshed tears in her hazel eyes.

"And Kelsey was born eight months after you returned home."

Jamie's face fell as the implications hit him. "Are you trying to say my mother had an affair and Kelsey isn't my father's child?"

"There is no doubt on that count," Daniel replied with a grin, as if he hadn't knocked my entire childhood on its rear. "Your sister donated blood at a blood drive two months ago. I took the blood and had a DNA test done."

I remembered that blood drive. It had been at Liv's school and she'd been so insistent that I come. She'd promised me dinner if I went and helped out. At the time, I'd thought she wanted to spend time with me, but now I knew. She was under orders.

Daniel looked at me with a smile like what he was saying was a good thing. "Your father's name was Lee Owens. He was Zack's brother. Zack is your uncle."

Zack smiled at me, but I still didn't feel a thing. A numbness had settled over me. "This Owens guy was a lone wolf?"

"Yes," Dan replied. He seemed a little surprised I wasn't thrilled to discover some werewolf I'd never met had knocked up my mom. "I'm sorry to tell you he died about ten years ago."

"Okay." What did they want from me? I felt vulnerable standing there in that big, intimidating room with all these powerful people staring down at me. I didn't even have a freaking pair of shoes on. They obviously wanted me to react in a certain way, but I couldn't. I only wanted one thing. "Can I go home?"

The vampire sighed. Things obviously weren't going according to plan. "Kelsey…"

The door in the back flew open.

"Kelsey!" Gray yelled, looking for me as he strode through into the room. His eyes widened as he took in the scene in front of him.

I didn't hesitate. I left the king behind and ran, flinging myself into his arms. Big, muscled arms wrapped around me and I tried to sink into his warmth.

"I want to go home, Gray," I said into his chest. There was nothing I wanted more.

"I'll take you home." He picked me up. For the first time all afternoon, I felt really safe. He glared at the assembly. "This woman belongs to me. You have no authority over her. Leave us alone."

He turned and started out, but the door was quickly closed and three big dudes with large guns barred our way out.

"I can't let you leave with her, Lieutenant," Daniel said. "And you know it."

Gray's jaw firmed stubbornly as he turned to face the king. "You into kidnapping, Donovan? Are you going to keep her here against her will?"

Quinn walked up and stood beside the king. "She'll stay here once she fully understands how important she is and what you've done to her."

Gray carefully put me down, but his arms stayed around me. He held me possessively and stared at the faery. "I have done nothing but love her and get her to fall in love with me."

Quinn frowned. "Did you? Tell me something, Kelsey. Did he tell you the truth about himself?"

"Yes, he did." I didn't get why everyone was so against me being with Gray. He'd been upfront and honest about his parentage and I'd accepted it. We were adults. It was our decision as far as I could see. "I know he's half demon. I don't see where it's your business. It's between me and Gray. Stay out of it."

He shook his head. "I can't do that because I don't believe he's told you the whole truth. Has he told you that he's been feeding you fertility drugs?"

Gray gasped behind me. "That's a lie."

"It's not a lie, Kelsey," Daniel said with sympathy. "Dev caught it this afternoon. All he had to do was touch you to know someone had been playing with your fertility."

"It was faint the night you came into the club, but it's quite powerful today," Quinn agreed.

My hands tightened around Gray's arms. I wasn't about to believe it. "I have that ring thing. I can't get pregnant."

Dev shook his head at my naiveté. "The drugs he has been using on you are far more powerful than anything a doctor can give you. That device is supposed to stop ovulation, but I promise you're ovulating right now." He turned his attention to Gray. "What did your father promise you if you produced a child with a Hunter? Was he willing to let you go in exchange for a powerful child?"

"I didn't give her anything," Gray said.

"It would taste like peppermint," Dev pointed out.

I turned and looked at Gray. "It was Syl."

"Kelsey, I didn't tell him to do that," he said, practically begging me to believe him.

I took a deep breath and reached out for his hand. I couldn't...wouldn't believe he would knowingly do that to me. He loved me. I knew he loved me. "I know, baby." I turned back to Quinn. "Am I pregnant?"

"No," the faery said, "But it wouldn't have taken him long. And you didn't answer my question. What did your father promise you for impregnating a Hunter?"

"Answer the question, Lieutenant. Don't bother lying. We know you met with your father." Dan gestured for a man to come forward. It was the guy with the Northeastern accent. He walked forward, several black and white photographs in his hand. When he held them up, I saw a picture of Gray in the T-shirt and sweats he'd worn the morning after we'd first made love. He'd gone jogging and stayed out for a long time. Now I could see plainly he'd met someone.

The man in the picture with Gray was powerfully built and dressed fashionably in a pinstriped suit. There was a vague resemblance between the men. They had the same build, the same nose, and similar strong jawlines. There were several pictures and Trent held them up for all to see. In one, the two men were arguing, but as the photos continued, Gray seemed to calm down and listen. In the last picture, Gray and his father were shaking hands.

"What do you do, Trent, follow me around?" Gray growled.

Trent shrugged. "It's a hobby. Stop stalling and answer the question. What did he offer you? You should know that I have tapes of the conversation. I could let her hear the whole thing."

Why wouldn't I want to hear it? It was plain on Gray's face that he didn't want me to hear it. Panic threatened and I could feel the beast...no, she's a wolf...I could feel her starting to twitch again. I turned to him and stared into those deep blue eyes. I loved those eyes.

He closed them like he couldn't bear to look at me anymore. "An extra thirty years."

Donovan whistled. "That's impressive. He must want that child very much."

"He thinks you're planning a war," Gray replied and I heard the pain in his voice. "He thinks you'll break off contact when the vampire/demon contracts expire."

"It's a good plan," Quinn admitted. "He takes out a demon hunter and perhaps gets one of his own to train. Maybe he could even convince Kelsey to play for your side. She would be extremely effective at killing vampires. It's a good call. Tell me, what were you planning to do if she didn't get pregnant?"

"I'm not on their side. I wouldn't fight beside my father. Never. As to the rest of it, I'm gonna find a way out," Gray stated with implacable will.

"There is no way out," Daniel argued.

"No way out of what?" I practically screamed. I was sick of all these men standing around talking about me and my future like my opinions didn't matter. I was invisible to them except as a pawn with which to hurt each other. I turned to Gray because he was the only one who mattered. I put my hands on his waist, needing to touch him, to reassure myself that we were together. "What are they talking about? What do you mean your father offered you thirty years? I don't understand any of this."

His breath hitched. His hands framed my cheeks and he stared for a long time, as though he was memorizing my face. When he spoke, his voice was like gravel. "I'm on a contract, Kelsey. I'm a legacy. My mother agreed to have me in exchange for money and power. Father chose her because she had certain psychic abilities he wanted bred into his son. I'm his second child. My half brother is an empath, but he doesn't have prophecy powers."

"What does it mean?" I held on so tight. I didn't want a family history. I wanted him to tell me it was all a mistake and we could leave and fly to Vegas and get married. If we'd done that in the first place instead of trying to make his vision come true, we would be married and making love right now.

"It means I was allowed thirty-five years on this plane before I have to go to the Hell plane and reside with my father permanently."

My hands fell to my sides as my world crashed down around me. "You're going to Hell?"

Gray's hands grasped my shoulders and he shook me lightly, but I could see out of the corner of my eye, Nate, Jamie, and Zack on their feet. "I am not going to Hell. I'm going to get out of it."

"You were going to marry me and leave me alone after five years?" My heart hurt and I couldn't look at him anymore. I hated the fact that everyone was watching us. We were entertaining them.

The wolf inside me howled.

"No, he wasn't going to do that," Quinn said with growing certainty. "The marriage was his ace in the hole. If he couldn't get you pregnant before his contract was up, he lost his chance. But if he married you…"

Donovan took up the train of thought. "Marriage is a contract. You vow to live with your husband. He was going to take you with him. Demonkind would honor the contract and you would be forced to follow him."

Jamie cursed as he rushed Gray, his fist reared back. Gray did absolutely nothing to avoid the blow or defend himself. He took Jamie's punch full on and staggered back from the force.

"How the hell could you do that to her?"

"I love her, man," Gray said, willing his friend to believe him. "I wouldn't take her with me."

"But you'll get her pregnant to buy yourself some time," Nathan accused.

Gray rubbed his jaw. "I'm buying us time. I will find a way out, damn it. I will not let them take my wife or my child. I'm going to save us." He turned to me. "Kelsey," he said desperately. "I am begging you to believe me. I love you, Kelsey mine. I love you so much. We can make this work. I swear I'll get us out of this. Come with me. Trust me."

I wanted to. I wanted to take his hand and slip it in mine and walk out. I came up with a hundred ways I could make it work. I could not marry him and force him to use a condom. I could take my five years with him. At that moment, staring down the possibility of losing Gray, I thought maybe Hell wouldn't be so bad. If we were together, maybe I could handle it.

"She isn't going anywhere with you." Nathan moved between us as though he could stop the demon from taking me.

"If you think for one moment that I'll let you anywhere close to my sister again, you're insane, Sloane," Jamie spat.

I saw something die in Gray's eyes. Jamie was his friend, probably the one human he'd ever told his secret to. He was so alone. How would he live if I walked away?

"Back off, Jamie. He didn't want Syl around me. I was the one who let Syl in. Gray asked me to stay away from him. He didn't know anything about it." I was about to take his hand and tell everyone to fuck themselves when Dev Quinn opened his mouth again.

"Kelsey, the fertility drugs were magical," he said carefully. "They would have the added effect of making you vulnerable to him. Did you fall in love quickly? It would be intense and unexpected. It would be out of character to feel so much, to trust so much in so quick a time."

I stumbled back, the shock making me fall into Quinn. He tried to steady me, but I didn't want him touching me. Was my love for Gray all a trick of some drugs? It felt so real. It felt like the only real thing in the world. How could it be false? I overcorrected and was about to fall to my knees when Marcus caught me.

He cursed up at Quinn, saying what I could only imagine was some truly filthy stuff in Italian.

"She had to know the truth, Marcus," Quinn defended himself.

I stood quietly, numbly in Marcus's arms, letting him hold me up.

The queen was on her feet. "You didn't have to do it in front of an audience, Devinshea. And you, Daniel, you should know better than this."

Gray looked liked someone had punched him in the gut. He stood silent for a moment, ignoring my brothers' growls and the crowd looking on. He focused solely on me and his eyes went red. His skin lost its color and I wondered if he was going to lose control of his form, but he didn't. He seemed to shrink instead.

"Don't lie to me, Quinn," he said in a voice that must have cost him so much. He was practically begging his worst enemy. "Is it true? Her emotions were affected by the drugs Syl gave her? She said she loved me."

Quinn had the grace to look sympathetic. "I'm sorry, but that magic is powerful. It can act like a love spell. She would fall quickly. In bed, she would probably be very submissive. I believe it had the added punch of making both her and her lover adverse to using anything that would stop the intended effect."

Gray shook his head. "I had a box of condoms in the dresser. I never thought to use them."

"And she wouldn't have thought to ask you to," Quinn explained. "If it's true you had nothing to do with giving her the drugs, then I'm sorry Lieutenant. You were tricked, too. Your father was determined to have that child."

Gray's eyes closed and I could see what it was costing him to survive these moments. I wanted more than anything to walk to him and take him in my arms and tell him I loved him. Instead, I stood quietly, allowing Marcus to hold me while the only man I'd ever loved turned and began to walk away.

He was at the door when he stopped. He didn't turn around. "Vorenus?"

Marcus didn't pretend to misunderstand. "I will take care of her. I promise."

Gray nodded and walked out.

Marcus's arms tightened around me. "I cannot believe you have done this, Daniel. I could believe it of Devinshea, but I thought you would have more compassion than to do this to her. She's fragile and you seek to break her."

"I didn't like it, Marcus, but it had to be done. I cannot allow her to fall into demonic hands." Dan sighed and braced himself. "If you didn't like that, old friend, then I doubt you'll approve of my next move." He turned to the Council. "I move to declare Kelsey Owens a ward of the Council. If you look in the packets Trent is passing out you'll find a schedule of her training and all protocols concerning handling the Hunter. When her training is finished, she will hold the office of sheriff."

"What if I don't want to be sheriff?" I asked, but no one cared.

Marcus was livid. I could feel it. I could practically feel the emotion pouring off him. "Nay. My vote is nay. We are not the old Council to come in and change a person's life on our whim, Daniel. How can you do this?"

The King of all Vampire crossed his arms and allowed everyone around to feel his will. Even I could feel it. "It must be done. She's a dangerous creature. She must be controlled or put down."

"Danny?" The queen breathed out his name, her eyes wide.

"Master, she's my niece." Zack put himself between me and the king.

Daniel stared at Zack, his lips in a sympathetic frown. "She's also capable of enormous destruction. You haven't read the files I've read. Hunters, when left to their own devices, always kill, and she'll do it indiscriminately. If I let her go, she won't be able to stop herself. She is completely undisciplined. She nearly killed Dev just for touching her when she was in that state. Tell me, Kelsey, do you want to be responsible for killing someone or perhaps many people because you can't control your power?"

"No. You should put me down." There was a hollow place inside me, an emptiness I was fairly certain nothing could ever fill.

Dan sighed. He walked up to me. "I am not going to kill you. I'm going to train you. I'll teach you to control the power inside you. You can use it for good, Kelsey. You can help people with it."

He was talking to the wrong girl. "I really don't care."

That wasn't the answer he was looking for. It seemed I was turning out to be a disappointment to the king. I didn't care about that either. "You will care. You're in shock. I'll give you time, but I want my vote." He turned back to the Council. "I move to recuse Marcus Vorenus from this vote. He's obviously emotionally involved with the female in question. As he holds the vampire seat, I invoke my right to vote in his place. Vampire votes aye."

And so did everyone else, with the exception of the witch. She voted nay and Donovan didn't have any convenient way to dispose of her. It didn't matter. It was one versus five, reaching the threshold in which, apparently, the Council can claim someone's life.

"Are you done with her, then?" Marcus asked, the rage in his voice barely in check. "May I take her back to the cell you intend to cage her in?"

There was a lot of yelling and arguing going on. The chaos was all around me, but I focused on Donovan and the sound of Marcus's voice. From what I could tell, Marcus Vorenus might be the only person in the world who hadn't lied to me or used me to further himself and his agenda.

"She can go and rest," Donovan said. "I'll make sure her new quarters are arranged for tomorrow."

"There will still be bars on the door, I suspect," Marcus replied.

Donovan didn't move. "Yes, but it will be more comfortable. She can have guests. She can have family with her. Olivia has offered to stay with you for a few days while you settle in."

"No," I said firmly with the only real emotion I'd had in hours. "No, I don't want to see her."

"Kelsey," Donovan cajoled. "She was worried about you. Don't blame her or Nate."

"Fuck them," I growled. "You can put me in a cage, Your Highness, but you can't make me forgive them."

"Come, *cara mia*." Marcus took my hand firmly in his. "I will stay with you. I won't leave you alone."

He began to lead me out. Donovan nodded and the man named Trent stepped out. He was apparently my security, well, everyone else's security from me.

Marcus turned as we passed the vampire king. His voice was low, but I heard him over the arguments going on around me. "And Daniel, call her by her proper title. Call her your *Nex Apparatus*. At least Louis was honest about what he was."

Donovan's blue eyes flared with what looked like shock and then he registered only a dull kind of pain. He turned and walked back to Quinn, who put an arm on his partner's shoulder, seemingly to comfort him.

Liv and Nathan were hot on our heels.

"Kelsey," Liv pleaded, trying to get me to turn around.

"Do you wish to speak with them, *cara*?" Marcus asked.

I shook my head. In that moment, if I never spoke to them again, it would have been fine.

"Go," Marcus said firmly.

Liv and Nate stopped. Their expressions went blank and they both turned and walked out the door.

I almost made it out of the Council chamber. I almost made it into the hallway that led to my little cell where I could lay down and try to shut out the world. I almost made it...

Joseph Castle burst through the doors, the same doors Gray had run through looking for me, the same ones he'd walked out of my life through.

"That bitch killed my son," he declared, his clawed finger pointing at me. "She killed my son and I will have my vengeance."

Chapter Sixteen

Marcus paced back and forth. I watched him from the cot in my jail cell. His long, elegant hand stroked his chin while he contemplated the problem of me.

"I'll be fine on my own if you want to go back." I almost hoped he didn't. I should want to be alone, but I found him comforting even when he was agitated.

His handsome face turned toward me. "They can handle Castle without me." He laughed bitterly. "Apparently I am not needed at all, *cara mia*. If the king doesn't agree with my position, he'll simply have me recused and vote in my stead." The vampire walked over and sank down beside me on the cot. "I would rather stay with you. Kelsey, you have not cried. It's fine to do so. I won't think less of you."

I shook my head. "I don't need to. I'm fine."

His fingers played soothingly with mine. "You don't have to be strong."

"I'm not," I replied. "I just don't care."

I didn't. Since that moment that Gray had walked out, I'd been blissfully numb. It hadn't hurt that Quinn had delivered a tea that he claimed would flush the drugs from my system. I didn't care about anything and I found it freeing. I'd always known that it wouldn't work out. I'd always known I would be alone. It turned out my father, well, the dude who raised me, had been right. I was a freak and a dangerous one at that. My friends and family thought I belonged in a prison under supervision.

I'd realized something important though. The king could put me in prison, but he couldn't force me to become the *Nex Apparatus*. I would sit here, ignore anything he wanted me to do, and there wasn't anything the king could do about it.

"I don't believe you," Marcus said. "You're in shock. When the time comes, you will cry and I'll be there for you."

I doubted that. It seemed to me the king and Marcus had some serious issues. I doubted Donovan was going to allow Marcus to stay with me for any length of time. He would handpick the people to be around me and I would ignore all of them. I would find it very amusing. The king would never know that the one person who might be able to convince me was the one person he would never allow around me.

The door opened and the king entered.

"We have a problem." The king looked tired, like the stress of the day was taking its toll. I didn't feel at all sorry for him. The door opened again and Zack strode through.

"This is not a problem, master," Zack was saying.

"It sure as hell is," Donovan shot back. "Castle is demanding full wolf rights."

"For what?" The question was merely curious. I didn't really care. "I thought the Council cleared me."

"They cleared you for the killing of Darren Castle. That's not what the alpha is demanding rights over. It's the accusation. It's a completely archaic law, but my lawyers claim he can do it," Donovan explained.

Marcus stood up. "You cannot expect her to do that."

The king shook his head. "We have no physical proof, Marcus. She's accused him and I believe her, but I can't convict him without proof. I would let him go and keep an eye on him, but he is pushing me. He won't relinquish the right. He wants me to prepare the arena for tonight."

"He wants vengeance," Marcus declared.

"Of course he does, but he has the right to face his accuser according to all wolf laws. If I refuse, Castle will use it as a rallying cry to gather the wolves to his side." He turned to me. "Kelsey, will you take back the accusation that Castle killed those girls? If you publically rescind the accusation, he won't have grounds to demand a fight. He wants to get you into the arena where he'll fight you. He has the right to demand tooth and claw. You'll be forced to go in without any weapons."

I shrugged. "He did it. I won't say otherwise."

Zack kneeled down to get eye level with me. I took in his brown hair and eyes. I could see it, the resemblance between us. I wondered briefly what my bio dad looked like and how he'd died.

"Kelsey, please," Zack said. "Castle is an alpha, a true alpha. He's got a hundred and fifty pounds on you. Rescind the accusation and I promise you, I'll make sure he sees justice. I'll do it quietly, but as painfully as you see fit."

"Zack," Dan warned.

"She's my niece." Zack glanced back at his master. "She's the only blood I have left."

"Do you think I don't know that, Zack?" Daniel said bitterly. "Do you think this isn't costing me? I know everything I owe Lee Owens. Even as we speak, Dev is trying to calm Z down because she is so pissed off at us she's threatening to kick us out if anything happens to her. Damn it, my son is named for her father. Do you honestly believe I want to hurt her?"

"Then allow me to take her place," Zack said.

"No." He had a wife and a little girl. I remembered him talking about her. I supposed she was my cousin. If this guy was such a badass, I wasn't going to let someone with a kid take my place. "I'll meet him."

"No, you will not." Marcus turned to the king. "Can you not see that she is devastated? She will use this as an excuse to commit suicide. She's at a delicate stage. I have more experience with Hunters than you do. They're emotional creatures. You dealt her a blow today that she hasn't even processed yet. If you allow this to happen, you are killing her."

"I have no choice," Donovan said with a sigh. "If she won't publically take back her accusation, I have no option but to allow the ritual. Kelsey, please, take back what you said. I'll put everyone I have on digging up evidence and then we can go after Castle. I promise you, I will bring him to justice."

In this, the wolf inside me and I were of the same mind. There would be no retraction. I wasn't going to lie. "No. He did it. If he wants to try to kill me, then good for him."

"You're so stubborn," Donovan cursed under his breath. "Do what you can to get her ready, Marcus. This takes place in two hours. Is there anything I can get you?"

I thought about it. There was really only one thing I wanted. "Bottle of tequila?"

Donovan rolled his eyes. "No. I won't send you in drunk."

"Then you're worthless to me, Your Highness." I sat back and closed my eyes. "I'm gonna take a nap. Wake me when it's time for my execution."

Donovan cursed again and I heard the door opened. "Fix her, Marcus. Zack, I need you with me."

The bed dipped again as Marcus sat back down. "Kelsey? Kelsey, is there anything I can do to talk you out of this?"

I didn't bother to open my eyes. "Nope."

I was ready for it to be over with. There wasn't much to look forward to anyway. I wouldn't see Gray again. Nathan and Liv had sold me out. The way I saw it, it didn't matter what Castle did to me. If Castle killed me, then I didn't have to rot in a cell so it might be a win for my side either way.

"I'm going to speak with the wolves. Perhaps I can talk some sense into McKenzie. I will return. Please reconsider."

The door hissed open and all was blissfully silent once more. I shifted and let my head find the pillow. Sleep seemed like a really nice thing to do, but it wouldn't come. I lay there thinking of Gray. I'd been so happy with him. He'd made me feel like I had something to offer a man besides a quickie. Nothing ever felt so right as lying in his arms. It was really hard to believe that it was a lie.

I went over every moment of our time together in my head as time passed. I remembered every touch, every glance, every time I made him crazy. Even though he'd lied to me, I wondered where he was. Was he as lost as I was? He wouldn't be waiting for me in the parking garage this time, or at least I hoped not. I wasn't going to come out of this place, it seemed.

I was going to die here. Would anyone tell him? Would he mourn for me?

The door hissed open and I sighed because I didn't want to listen to Marcus beg me again. I tried to pretend to sleep.

"Lady," a voice several octaves higher than Marcus's said.

I opened my eyes and Lee Quinn stood there holding a key card and a bottle. Despite the seriousness of my situation, I had to smile. "You're a good little thief, aren't you?"

He grinned. One of his teeth was missing. He was going to be a looker when he grew up. Now he was one sweet-looking boy. "That's what my granddad says."

I sat up and studied the kid. I should call his dads. Neither one of them would want their baby boy in here with me, but I found myself curious. No grand desire to pummel the child rushed through my veins, so I thought we were safe. "Who'd you steal the card from?"

He plopped down on the chair his dad had previously occupied. He was surprisingly self-possessed for a kid his age. "I swiped it off Trent. He can be easily distracted. I stole this from the bar down in Ether. I just grabbed it, though, so it's not tequila. Is rum okay?"

I laughed, the first amusement I'd found in anything all day. "What do you do? Eavesdrop?"

He passed me the rum, which would work nicely. I held it in my lap as he replied. "I snuck into the security room. Almost every room in the building has cameras in it. Lots of people say Papa is paranoid, but I don't know what that means."

"It means he's careful. It has to be getting late. Shouldn't you be in bed? Tomorrow is a school day."

Lee set his feet up on the coffee table and stretched his arms out behind his head. "Don't have to go. Got suspended."

He said it with no small amount of pride. His parents were going to have so much trouble with him.

"What on earth did an eight-year-old do to get suspended?"

"Punched a guy in the face," Lee admitted. "He called Mia fat and made her cry. Mia's my friend. I had to stand on a chair though. He was a lot taller than me. I'm in third grade. He's in fifth."

Oh, I liked Lee. "Sounds like you had good cause. Did he punch you back?"

"No, I was faster than him, but not faster than Mrs. Nichols," he allowed. "Actually, I am faster than Mrs. Nichols. She snuck up on me. Are you going to drink that? Papa always drinks when he gets really upset. He calls it Papa juice, but Mama drinks it, too. I think it's one of those things adults say when they don't want you to do something because you're a kid."

I nodded. "I think you're right."

He got very serious. "I'm named after your dad. He died saving my mom and my papa."

No wonder he was practically a saint to these people. "Lee is a nice name," I said because I didn't know what else to say.

"Are you gonna fight the alpha?"

"Yes. He did something really bad and I know about it. I could lie and then I wouldn't have to fight, but he would get away with hurting some girls."

Lee's little jaw firmed. "He killed them. He should pay for that. My dad thinks you shouldn't fight him though. Mama is mad."

"Sorry." I didn't much care about Quinn and Donovan, but I liked the kid. I didn't like causing him trouble. It was hard enough being eight. "I think she'll probably get over it."

"I don't know about that," a voice said from the doorway. I looked up and the queen stood there. A harried looking Trent started toward Lee, but the queen put a hand out. "Stop that. She's not going to hurt Lee." She gave me a wry smile. "Are you?"

"I think he's probably safe. He brought me liquor after all." I showed her my pilfered rum.

The queen held up her own bottle and I noted it was a damn good tequila. "He's not the only one." She walked into the room and affectionately ruffled her son's hair. "Go to bed, little ruffian. You might have gotten suspended, but Papa found you a tutor. He'll be here at 7:30 in the morning."

Lee sighed. I got the feeling he was used to being outmaneuvered by his mom. He stood up and walked to her. He threw his arms around her waist and hugged her tightly. "Night, Mama. I love you." He turned back to me. "Bye, Kelsey. I hope the alpha doesn't kill you."

The queen watched her son walk out of the room. "Trent, why don't you follow my baby boy and make sure he doesn't stop anywhere along the way?"

Trent eyed me like I would murder someone the minute he turned his back.

The queen arched a regal eyebrow and Trent sighed and walked out the door. She turned back and took a look at the bottle in my hand. She shook her head. "No, that won't do. Let's drink this."

The Queen of all Vampire sat down across from me and pulled the cork on the bottle of imported tequila. She didn't wait for me to tell her I didn't have any glasses much less an actual kitchen in my crappy cell. She took an extremely long swig from the bottle and passed it to me. She didn't look very queen-like in jeans and sneakers and a black sweater. It was similar to mine, and I figured out where I'd gotten the clothing from. She filled it out better than I did. Her auburn hair was pulled back in a ponytail.

I took the bottle and matched her. "You're not what I expected."

"I rarely am," the queen replied. "Let's talk, you and I. First off, I am so sorry my husbands are dipshits."

"I'm sorry, too," I replied, unwillingly liking the woman.

"Sometimes I think they make each other worse," she mused. "They have a mutual admiration society for each other's Machiavellian plots. They enjoy intrigue far too much. You should have been told what you are right off the bat. If I'd been doing it, I would have invited you to dinner, explained what you are, and offered you the training to control it."

"That probably would have worked better," I allowed. "If the dinner was really good, that is."

She smiled. "Oh, it would have been good. I know the way to a wolf's heart."

"I'm not a wolf." The denial was automatic. Even as I said the words, I knew I was lying to some extent.

She took another swig. "Not fully, but I think you'll find you fit in well with wolf society, probably much more so than you ever could with humans. If you give it a chance, you might be able to find a home here."

"I don't need a home." I felt surly. A couple of hours before I'd been moving into my new home, the one the man I loved had bought for me. Now I had a fucking cell.

"Spoken like a true loner," the queen said. "Your father would have said the same thing."

"Don't call him that," I shot back. I was starting to get emotional again. Twitchy. It was the only way to describe it. I couldn't help but think about the dreams I'd had since childhood. They'd been just that—dreams. I'd had no loving father. Apparently he'd been here, busy taking care of the queen. "He was some promiscuous asshole who knocked up my mom and went on his merry way. There are probably ten more like me out there."

The queen's hazel eyes narrowed dangerously. "I'll ignore that because I know what it feels like to be where you are, but understand your father would have loved you. He would have done anything for you had he known you existed. If Lee Owens had lived and discovered who you were, he would have come for you and nothing would have stopped him."

I wanted to believe it. I wanted to believe someone wanted me. "How did he die?"

The queen sighed and it seemed the memory hurt her on a fundamental level, but she talked about it anyway. "It was right before Daniel took over. We were betrayed by a demon. He gave up our location to the head of the Council. Zack managed to get Daniel out of there, but Dev, Lee, and I were left behind. The vampires knew Lee would never allow them to take us, so they filled him so full of silver he couldn't move. He fought so hard. I begged him to take vampire blood and save himself. I begged him to run, but he wouldn't. He said he couldn't. Are you going to use this fight with Castle to kill yourself?"

Sneaky queen. I was still thinking about the man who fathered me as I answered the question. "No. But if it happens, it happens. I won't take back the accusation, Your Highness. I'm right and he's wrong. If I die because of it, then I do."

The queen sat up and leaned forward, tears shining in her beautiful eyes. "He would be proud of you. I really hope you don't die, Kelsey Owens. I would really like for you to get to know my son."

The door opened again and I was glad to see Marcus walk in. The talk with the queen made me anxious. It ran across my nerves, bringing up all sorts of feelings. I'd managed to shut out so much of what I was feeling, but she and that boy were bringing it all up again.

I wouldn't have a son because Gray was gone, my mind raced. I didn't have a family anymore because they'd all lied to me, including my mother. Jamie hadn't lied, but I didn't feel like being fair at that moment. I didn't have friends because who would want to be friendly with some freak. I didn't fit anywhere. I wasn't a wolf and I wasn't human.

My eyes started to well with tears and my hands started to shake. Marcus cursed impatiently and crossed to me. His hand slid beneath my hair and rubbed the back of my neck gently. It was like someone had turned down the volume. I sighed and leaned against his hand.

"I do not leave her alone for more than half an hour and one of you is in here again, riling her up," Marcus said, looking at the queen.

She frowned. "I wasn't trying to hurt her. I just wanted to meet her. She's Lee's daughter. I was curious."

"Don't you think your family has done enough to her for one day?"

"Marcus, you have to know I had nothing to do with this," the queen protested. "This is one of those things Danny and Dev don't bother to tell me about. If I'd known, I would have stopped it. I understand she has to be trained, but it could have been handled differently." She stood up and paced as she thought. "I certainly would have brought her in before she got involved with that demon. That's what makes me crazy. Daniel knew, but he let it go on. She should have been brought in the minute he got that DNA test back."

"I believe he would tell you he wasn't sure she was a Hunter," Marcus explained. "She could be Lee's daughter and still have merely been human. According to Daniel, she's shown nothing of a Hunter's skills in the past few years."

"What's different?" Without really thinking about it, I leaned toward the vampire.

"I believe this case you have worked on pushed you over the edge. It triggered the instinct to burst forth. Meeting Lieutenant Sloane was also an emotional experience. The two combined have forced the beast into the open. Have you ever felt it before?"

I told him about the night with my father. I didn't candy coat it the way I had with Gray. I told him about running afterward and how I survived the cold. He took it all in with an academic nod.

"The killing of the wolves would have been a trigger," Marcus explained. "I'm surprised you managed to contain yourself then. It could have been much worse, Kelsey. You could have stood your ground and tried to kill any wolf who entered your territory."

"Yes, my territory. That's why I attacked Quinn. He came into my territory." I hadn't liked it.

Marcus brought my hand into his lap and rubbed it gently. "I can teach you to control that beast. I can train you to integrate the wolf into your personality. She's a part of you that you can learn to tap into and use for protection. Right now, the wolf is close to the surface because you're emotional. We need to keep you calm until I've taught you to control your instincts."

"You've trained a Hunter before?" the queen asked. Her eyes were on the place where Marcus held my hand. He'd taken one of my hands in both of his and was rubbing long strokes up and down my arm. It was a little like petting, and I knew I should stop him, but I couldn't bring myself to do it. It felt too good.

Marcus nodded. "I have, Your Highness. The Council trained Hunters long before I walked the night, and always it is an academic who handles the Hunter in the beginning. Hunters and academics have a long history of partnership."

"Because of the persuasion powers of the academic?" the queen continued her questions.

"This and the fact that academics are able to bond to females in ways the other classes cannot." Marcus's fingers almost absently tangled in mine. "Though we sleep, we do not go into a fugue state the way other vampires do. If a Hunter needs her mentor during the day, only an academic can be there for her, but it goes far beyond that. I can go into her dreams, as you very well know. I can sense her emotional state. If we…got close, I would be able to taste the food on her tongue, to sense when she's in trouble. An academic can have a very intimate relationship with a female. It helps the Hunter to bond with her trainer. It helps her trust him and allows her to form other relationships later on. Without training, Kelsey would more than likely be alone the rest of her life. She would push people away and never truly understand why."

"By close, I suppose you mean sleeping with her," the queen deduced with a wry smile.

His hand squeezed mine while he spoke to the queen. "It's where the relationship usually goes. It's difficult to stay apart when properly training a Hunter. You have to know her inside and out. Unless the female is simply ugly on the inside, you discover her true beauty. A certain affection will always spring from that." He looked down at me. "I would never force you into anything, *cara mia*. I doubt I will be allowed to train you. Please remember whoever the king chooses must respect your wishes concerning your own body. You do not have to share yourself with anyone."

"He's talking about Henri," the queen offered.

Marcus huffed and cursed under his breath. "You must talk sense into him, Zoey. Henri has never trained a Hunter before. He should allow Hugo Wells to try. Hugo is older than Henri and he's unmarried. For the first three months, she should not be allowed out of his sight, and that includes during sleep. She needs to remain in the room with him."

"I doubt Kim is going to like that." Zoey's eyes widened. I thought she wouldn't much like that.

I pulled my hand out of Marcus's. I better get used to trying to calm myself down. I wasn't letting some other vampire do that to me. Marcus was different. I'd felt a connection to him even before we'd met, but I wouldn't let some vampire I'd never seen before touch me and keep me like a pet he was trying to train.

"*Cara,*" Marcus began.

"No," I said, moving away from him, turning to the queen. "Tell your husband he can go to hell. I won't be treated like a dog. He can't order someone to adopt and housebreak me. I'll stay in this fucking cell or he can put me down humanely, but I won't go with that Henri person."

"You'll go with who I tell you to go with." Donovan opened the door with a wicked frown on his face. A shorter man in a suit came in behind the king. He stared at me, wariness on his attractive face. "I'm doing this for your own good, Kelsey. Don't you interfere, Z. If I allow her to walk into that arena and she gets killed, you'll never forgive me. Henri, persuade her to walk into the Council chamber and take back her accusation."

The blond guy named Henri narrowed his eyes as he concentrated his will my direction. A rush of power sizzled across my skin as he attempted to get me to do his will. He was strong, much stronger than Michael had been. He was stronger in this way than the king, but he wasn't anything close to Marcus. The impulse was right there. My legs wanted to move. I wanted to rise and do exactly what that voice ordered me to do. I would walk into the chamber and tell them I made the whole thing up.

My feet hit the ground and I saw the king relax. He thought it was going to be all right. That was what really did it. I pushed through because I didn't intend to give the king what he wanted. That slight smile gave me the strength I needed. I shoved back at the magic invading my limbs. I pictured that wall in my head and slammed it shut with everything I had.

"Hell." Henri staggered back. He put his hand to his forehead as I climbed back on my bed.

Just to piss the king off, I slipped my hand back into Marcus's.

"She shoved you out?" the king asked, frustration evident in his voice.

"Yes. That was very unpleasant," Henri complained. "I've never had that happen before. I would like to avoid it in the future."

"She's extraordinarily strong," Marcus said and I heard the satisfaction in his voice. "Don't feel bad, Henri. She almost managed to shove me out the first time I tried. With training, she will be able to."

"Fine," the king said, gritting his teeth. His Texas drawl got worse when he was angry. "Marcus, if you get her to take back the accusation, I'll let you train her."

"And she would never trust me again," the Italian replied, letting his arm wind around my shoulders. "I won't bend her to my will. I will, however, give her something to think about. You're good at invoking rights tonight, Your Highness. Perhaps I should invoke one of my own. I am the oldest vampire walking the Earth plane. You have placed her under the protection of the Council. I invoke my right to be Kelsey's patron."

The queen's jaw dropped. "Marcus, no."

The king let his head drop back and a groan came out of his mouth before he looked back at us. "This fucking night is never going to end. Hell, if you think it'll work, I'm willing to give it a try. I'm out of options. You're betting a lot on her, Marcus."

I pulled away from the vampire who, it seemed, claimed some right over me. "What does he mean?"

Marcus flashed a secret little smile. He reached out and gently touched my cheek. "He means I do not wish to live in a world that would grind you into dust, *cara mia*."

"He's your patron, Kelsey." The queen's perfect pale skin seemed whiter than before. "If you're killed, the alpha will demand Marcus's head and Daniel will be forced to give it to him."

"My fate is tied to yours," Marcus put succinctly.

"Motherfucker." I was going to have to kill another damn wolf.

Chapter Seventeen

"Take it back," I growled, standing on my toes to try to look the vampire straight in the eyes.

"No." Marcus smiled infuriatingly. He was enjoying this. I tried to remember that the first time I'd seen him I felt his terrible sorrow. Now, there seemed nothing but amusement and a willingness to see what happened next.

"I don't want you to be my patron," I swore.

"I don't want you to die in the arena."

"I am not taking it back, Marcus." That decision had been made in Helen Taylor's backyard when she'd asked me for justice. I'd promised. I had nothing left but my word.

He lifted a shoulder, elegantly showing me his lack of concern. "Then you will fight, but you will fight for my life as well as yours."

The door opened and we stopped the argument we'd been having for the last fifteen minutes. Once I'd started yelling at Marcus, the king and queen had taken it as their cue to leave. Now the king was at the door again.

"It's time," he said grimly.

I stared up into Marcus's beautiful, serene face. He didn't look like a man terrified of dying. He seemed like he would accept anything fate offered him. He'd tied himself to me in a fundamental way, and I knew I couldn't let him down.

"Maybe I'll decide two thousand years is plenty of time to live," I warned him, though I knew I was only talking tough.

"Not quite two thousand," he corrected with that mysterious smile.

He held out his hand for me. I wanted to reject it. I wanted to tell him to fuck himself, but I wanted his warmth even more than that. I'd listened to everything he said about trainers and Hunters, and while the idea of having Marcus be my personal Cesar Millan rankled, I also found it tempting. What if I could feel love without the presence of a love spell? What I'd had with Gray had been the best feeling of my life. It had been like seeing the sun after a lifetime of rain. I still felt it. I didn't know how long the spell would last, but I didn't want it to go away. Even if the pain was heartbreaking, it was better than the dull fog my life had been before it.

"The arena is covered in sand," Donovan explained as he walked us toward the elevator. "It's best you go in barefoot if you aren't used to fighting in it."

"Is Castle used to fighting in it?" I asked.

Donovan's blue eyes were hooded with concern or maybe plain irritation. I couldn't tell. Things hadn't gone according to plan, and I had the feeling not many things had the nerve to go against Daniel Donovan's plans. "No. The arena is where we train new vampires. Castle wanted the fight to take place in the wolf compound in Denton, but technically you belong to Vampire according to ancient laws concerning Hunters. Lone wolves aren't popular in the wolf world. It was easy for the previous councils to claim ownership of them. I have the right to determine where you will fight since he chose the weapons."

"Shouldn't I have been the one to choose where to fight?" I asked curiously. "Or Marcus? He is my patron."

"And I am your king," Donovan stated firmly.

I snorted. I really had to stop that. It was neither feminine nor pleasant, and yet Marcus always smiled when I did it. Donovan wasn't as amused.

We got into the elevator and Marcus's hand played with mine. "And where would you choose, *cara mia*?"

"Starbucks. I could use a Frappuccino." My stomach was grumbling. I really should have taken Donovan up on his offer to get me something. "And one of those little cookies. Maybe a bunch of those cookies."

Marcus chuckled. "I promise to feed you properly after you have defeated the alpha and, I suspect, the two betas." He slid a glance to the king. "Am I wrong, Your Highness?"

The king shook his head as the elevator plunged downward. "No. By accusing the alpha, she accuses the pack. Yes, he is insisting she fight him and his two betas. I didn't want to scare her."

No, because I hadn't been scared at all. "And I don't get any weapons?"

"I managed to negotiate with McKenzie on that point," the king said. "You'll be allowed to use cesti."

I had no idea what that was. "Yay me."

"It is a glove used by gladiators in Roman times," the king explained as the doors opened and I was assaulted by the sound of people chanting. We got off the elevator and we seemed to be backstage, so to speak. Above me, the ceiling seemed to rumble and shake with sound. The arena seating was over my head and from the sounds of it, the place was packed.

"Kelsey?" Zack Owens held a large box in his hands. His face was tight as he walked over to us. "It seems like every wolf in North Texas made it. I found what you needed in the armory. I got the smallest pair we had, and we'll still have to tape them on." He stared down at me and I wondered what he saw. I was a five foot six, one hundred twenty pound female in clothes that didn't quite fit and no shoes. I was sure I came off as pretty pathetic. Zack turned to the king. "Damn it, master. Let me take her and run. She'll get torn apart out there."

"It's her choice, Zack," the king said.

"Yes, now it is her choice," Marcus interjected with a bitter flair. He eyed the king. "You have given her no say in anything that is to happen to her up to this point, but it is her choice to fight the alpha. Perhaps you and Devinshea will get everything you desire, Your Highness. You will have quelled the wolf rebellion by allowing such a valuable asset to honor their traditions and, if she dies, you can get rid of me as well. Your precious family will be safe from me once I am gone."

The king shoved his hands through his short, dark blond hair. "Damn it, I am so sick of being in the middle of this. I have no problem with you, Marcus. I have no problem with any of it. You think I don't remember what I felt the first time I met Z? I was eight years old and I knew I was going to spend the rest of my life with her. I don't begrudge anyone that, but I can't get Dev to understand. I don't want you dead, Marcus. You've been my friend, my freaking father half the time. I can't stand having you look at me the way you have the last two years, but what do you want me to do? He's my partner."

I took a step back, not quite understanding the conversation, but feeling so wretchedly jealous of the queen I could hardly stand it. She had three men fighting over her it seemed. I only wanted one, but even he had been an illusion.

"I apologize, Daniel," Marcus said solemnly. "I don't agree with you on the way you have handled Kelsey. I also do not wish to put you in a bad position. I withdraw from the Council. Henri can take my place until another election can be held."

"Marcus," Donovan said, practically pleading.

"It's for the best. I will return to Venice," Marcus explained as my heart fell. "I have been gone far too long. If it helps, I have no intention of acting on any impulses I might have. Your family is safe."

He was leaving and I would be alone here. He'd promised to take care of me, but I'd learned that people only kept their word when it was convenient for them. No man except my brothers had ever offered to do so much as open the door for me. Except Gray...

"Evan might have something to say about that one day." The king stared at Marcus as though he could will the older vampire into doing his bidding. He finally shook his head. "This isn't over. I'm not going to let it be. Tomorrow we're going to sit down and talk this out. I have to go make sure everything's ready."

As the king walked away, I sat back on a bench and my uncle opened the box he was holding. Lying in the box was what looked like twin gloves with silver blades embedded on the back. The blades were long and wickedly curved. Cestus, Zack told me as he held them out for me. Claws, I thought dully as Zack started to pull them on me. They fit over my hands and up my forearms. He was right. They were too big.

Marcus sat down beside me. "You are all right?"

I sucked it up. I hadn't cried about Gray. I sure as hell wouldn't cry over him. I promised myself I would learn. I wouldn't let another one in. "I'm fine."

He sighed and his eyes had darkened, his mouth curving down. "I'm sorry, *cara mia*. You don't understand the situation. It's best for everyone if I remove myself."

"It's not best for her," Zack said under his breath as he wrapped tape around the cestus to keep it on my hand.

"The king will never allow me to train her," Marcus argued.

"Hey, no big deal." I concentrated on the feel of the leather on my hand as Zack went to work on my other hand. "I don't intend to let anyone train me. I intend to sit my ass in a cell until the king either kills me or lets me go. You weren't going to change that. I don't buy the crap you're selling, Vorenus. I never did."

"I do not want to leave you," the vampire insisted and I got the feeling he saw right through my defensive posturing.

Zack finished taping my left hand and I stood up, ignoring the vampire. The light from the arena glowed in front of me. I would go out there alone. A picture of Gray crossed my mind and I felt tears gathering. He would never have allowed it. I wondered what he would do if he knew. Would he rush in to save me or let it happen because he didn't want me anymore? I would have given anything in that moment to feel his arms around me one more time.

"No one fights for you, do they?" Marcus stayed close to me as I walked to the edge of the large entrance.

Even from where I stood, just outside the light I could see them. Some I recognized from various places like Liv's school or the clubs I'd been to the last few nights. Some were total strangers, but they had one thing in common. They'd all come to watch me die. All in all, it wasn't how I'd thought my day would end.

"I can fight for myself." The beast inside was starting to twitch again. She was starting to call me a whiny fucking pansy who deserved everything she got if I walked out there all pathetic and ready to die.

The beast inside me isn't polite. She's kind of a bitch, but she did have a point. Was I really going to give them what they wanted? Was I going to give them my life? Was losing Gray so overwhelming that my poor little heart couldn't take it?

"Let's make a deal, you and I. If you live, I'll take you with me," Marcus promised. "We will go to Venice and there is nothing the king can do about it. You'll like Venice. I will teach you. Anything else that happens between us is up to you."

"I don't need your pity, Vorenus." The floor was cold under my feet. I wondered if the sand would be warmer.

Marcus put his hands on my shoulders and spun me around. His face was savage as he looked down on me. "I have no pity for you. I have affection. I have desire. I have gratitude because you're the first thing that has made me feel alive in years. I'm not offering to take you with me because I feel sorry for you. I'm begging you to come with me because I'll feel the loss if you do not. Please, *cara mia*. Have mercy on a man. Come to Venice and allow me to soothe you. Come to Venice and allow me to teach you. Come to Venice and give me the chance to seduce you."

I nodded because there wasn't a place in my life anymore for turning down a good offer. I hugged the vampire, his touch immediately flooding my senses with his will. He wanted me to live. He wanted me to come to Venice with him.

He wanted...me.

I wasn't sure how I felt about the last part, but I liked the rest of it and I trusted him. He would never force me into anything. I could go with him and he would wait until I decided what I wanted. The thought of being far away from everything seemed like heaven. In Venice, I could find out who I really was. There would be no king, no Castle, no Nate or Liv to deal with. There would be me and my teacher.

Yes. Yes. Yes. The beast inside liked that idea very much. She longed to be close to Marcus. And all we had to do was kill three creatures who outweighed us by a hundred pounds of muscle a piece and had years more experience killing than we did. Yeah, she liked that idea, too. I never said she was smart.

"I'm supposed to take her to her room when it's done," Zack said to Marcus. He stared out at the arena, too. He handed Marcus a key card. "If Trent takes her instead, here's the key. Get her and take her out the back. I'll have a car waiting to drive you to wherever you want to go. I'd advise hiding out for a day or two and then heading to Houston. You can catch a flight to Europe from there. Daniel might look for you, but if I promise you'll come back after the initial three months, I think I can eventually convince him to let you go. He feels bad enough already."

"Zachary, you have never betrayed your master," Marcus said with sympathy in his eyes.

Zack's head shook, a firm negative. "Nor am I betraying him now. She'll come back. I know she will."

I wasn't so sure about that, but before I could answer I was pulled abruptly from Marcus and whirled around to face my brother.

Zack shook his head Jamie's way, surprise plain on his face. "How did you make it back here? We have a ton of security."

"I have my talents, too," Jamie growled at the wolf. "I'm taking my sister and getting her the fuck out of here and there's nothing you can do about it."

I dug my heels in. Not only was I fairly certain Jamie was overestimating whatever talents he thought he had, there were several reasons me leaving was a bad idea. "I can't go."

Jamie's fingers threaded through mine. "You sure as hell can. I'm sorry Nate sold you out like that. I don't know why he did it but it's obvious he cares more about his friends than his family. He can go to hell. We don't have to talk to him again."

I pulled away from him. "Jamie, stop it. If I let you take me, they'll come after you, too. I really am what they say I am. If I don't get this under control, I could seriously hurt someone. If I make it through…"

"If?" Jamie practically yelled.

"When," I corrected myself. The beast wasn't the only one who didn't appreciate my pessimism. "When I make it through this thing, I'm going to get help and I'll get this under control. Marcus is going to teach me and then I'll come back and we'll sort it out, Jamie."

I would have a lot to deal with if I lived. I could cut Liv out of my life even though it would hurt, but how did I deal with Nathan and my mom?

Marcus moved between my brother and me. He was taking control. Once he'd made the decision to take responsibility for me, everything changed. There would be no more asking permission of anyone. Marcus was in charge. "Mr. Atwood, your sister has to fight. There's no way around it. If she runs with you, the king will hunt you down and so will the wolves. Daniel has to because of the danger she poses. You're getting her emotional when she needs to stay calm. You will leave my student alone or I will dismiss you myself."

Jamie looked ready to explode. I intervened, firmly grasping

Marcus's arm to let Jamie know I wasn't being forced. "Jamie, I need him. He's the only one who can help me. Please. I'll be back in three months and I'll be better."

"I don't understand any of this." Jamie stared at me and I could tell he was completely lost. I wasn't the only one who had the world ripped out from under me.

Zack put a comforting hand on Jamie's shoulder. "I'll explain everything to you. You might not remember it, but we've met before. We played together a couple of times when my brother and your mom...met. Let me walk you through this. I know it's hard for you to believe, but I will do just about anything for her."

"I do remember," Jamie admitted. He closed his eyes for a moment and came to a decision. "Where can I sit? If she's going to do this, then I can force myself to watch."

I hugged my brother tightly, making sure I didn't poke anyone with the pointy end of my weird gloves. "Thank you." I needed something from him. I needed it more than anything. "Promise me something, Jamie."

"Anything."

"Don't hate him. Don't leave him alone."

He knew who I was talking about and his face hardened. "You can't ask me that. He lied to us."

"Did he?" Gray had been all I could think about for hours and I'd come to some conclusions. "He's been your friend for years. He's been loyal to you. He didn't feed me those drugs. He didn't tell us about the contract but...I don't know. I can believe that he would think he could get out of it. It's how he works. He gathers everything he needs around him and then he works the problem. I was something he needed. Hell, I don't know that I wouldn't have made the same deal in his position. Thirty years is a lot of time to work things out."

"He was willing to get you pregnant to save himself."

He wouldn't look at it that way. "He was willing to get me pregnant because that's often what married people do. He wanted a family. If it bought him a little time, he was already planning it anyway. We can't judge him. We don't know what it's like to walk in his shoes. I know I can't be with him, but Jamie, I can't walk in there knowing he's going to be all alone. He needs someone. Yell at him. Beat the shit out of him. I don't care. Don't leave him alone. I couldn't handle it if something happened to him."

"I'll try, Kels. But only for you." He turned to Marcus, giving him a forbidding look. "You better be everything they advertised or I'll be hunting a couple of vampires."

Zack led Jamie off and it was just me and Marcus.

He gazed down at me, his eyes deepening to a fascinating obsidian. They were so dark. I could lose myself in those eyes. His hands found mine, drawing them up to his chest. "Keep your hands on my body. We need connection. Listen to me. Let everything else fall away. There's only you and me in the whole world."

I breathed and felt his chest rise. His heart beat and mine found his rhythm. Slow and steady as the sun. I let everything slip from me but the feel and smell of him, the sight and sound of him.

"I want you to accept the beast that lives inside you. Clear your mind of everything except the coming fight." His hands moved up to cup my face, but mine stayed where he'd lain them. "Relax, *cara mia*. Let me in. I will be with you the whole time. You will not be alone for an instant."

Magic, soft and warm, was inside my head before I had a chance to defend against it. I wouldn't have. Marcus's magic was too seductive to throw a wall up against. He spoke to me with his eyes. I have no idea how long we stood there with him whispering in my head, making a place for himself deep within my brain, but a bond formed in those moments and I knew Marcus had become important to me. Necessary. He was a source of strength to tap into, a place to calm myself. I merely had to hold the thread that bound us together and he would be there.

"Is she ready?" The king's voice interrupted us.

Marcus leaned over and his lips brushed my forehead. "She is."

"Then take your place, Marcus," the king said. "I'll walk her out."

"I will be in the stands, *cara mia*," Marcus promised. "You'll be able to see me and I will join you immediately after you defeat Castle. When you are out there, relax. Let me and your wolf take control. We won't steer you wrong."

Even through the calm, I began to panic because it was all getting too real. The crowd was chanting, eager to get this started. The gloves on my hands felt wrong. "But I don't even know how to use these things. I...I've never fought like this."

"But I have," Marcus replied calmly. "Who do you think those belonged to? I fought many times using them. At one time, they were so familiar to me I felt naked without them."

"You were a gladiator?" Donovan asked, his eyes lifting in surprise.

"I wasn't always an academic," Marcus said with a small smile. "In life, I was a warrior. Well, I was a criminal because of my religion. I became a gladiator because I had no choice. I was much like you, Kelsey. And like you, I was terrified the first time I was tossed into the ring. But I won, as you will. I will tell you everything, Kelsey, all my stories if you allow me to help you."

"Your Highness." The big wolf, McKenzie, strode up to us. "We have to begin. Castle is accusing her of running. My people are getting riled."

Marcus gave me one final look and walked out to the stands. McKenzie followed him and then the king's hand was on my back, nudging me forward.

"Kelsey, I know you won't believe me, but I'm sorry it's come to this," the king was saying. "I never meant for this to happen to you. I only meant to find you and train you."

I doubted that. No matter how well-meaning he was, he was always a king and that meant he would always have an agenda. I simply nodded because I knew railing at him would do nothing but bring shame on Marcus. Somehow, in those moments, I'd truly become his student and he my mentor. There was a pact between us and I meant to honor it.

Even though I wanted to tell Donovan to stuff it.

We marched to the end of the walkway where the concrete met sand. The crowd saw me and began to howl. I could see three men pacing at the other end of the arena. I noticed all three men were naked, ready to change. Castle's head came up when he scented me.

The king stared at the wolf with distaste. "Kelsey, when you kill the alpha, take his heart. Carve it out if you have to. It's tradition. If they force us to follow their rituals, they can handle it when we cut out their hearts."

The king leapt up gracefully, holding onto the railing and pulling himself into the stands. I glanced behind my back and saw him taking his place on a raised throne. The queen sat to one side and Quinn on the other. The dark-haired faery leaned over to talk to the king, the duo always whispering, always plotting as though they were two halves of a whole. Jamie sat with Zack, both paler than normal. I took it all in, some voice inside telling me to look so I didn't get distracted later.

The arena was smaller than I'd imagined, roughly half the length of a football field. The sides of the arena were made from wood and there were various things sticking out. They looked like something you would find in a dungeon. I supposed the vampires used them for training purposes. There were wooden spikes in two places at the front and back of the arena, and on the sides there were places with hooks and long, probably silver chains attached to them.

There were, perhaps, two hundred people crowding the stands, most of them werewolves, but I recognized others. Nathan stood beside Liv, their bodies pressed to the railing. Liv had been crying, her face puffy, but she wasn't hiding it and she hadn't cared to reapply her makeup. Scott had managed to skip his Hooter's night. He sat back, watching with hooded eyes. He'd probably be happy to see me lose. The rest of the people were sitting except two.

I glanced into the stands and Helen Taylor calmly stood up, holding hands with her remaining child. After the briefest of moments, the party around her stood and I knew I was looking at the deer herd. They stood and stared down at me, calmly requesting I finish the job I'd been hired to do.

"Yes, *cara*," Marcus's voice said in my head. "You're their only chance at justice. If you die, no one will care about them. They're prey animals with no one to defend them. You are their champion."

I was, I realized as I turned to face the man who had killed Joanne Taylor because she'd had the audacity to stand up to him. He'd killed women to further his plot against the king. They'd been pawns to be used and discarded as he saw fit. He didn't care that they'd had dreams and plans. A righteous anger began to burn through me and I felt that beast rise. I didn't fight her this time. I melded with her, letting her rage mate with mine until we were one. My need for justice meshed neatly with her thirst for revenge.

I heard the king speaking, explaining the argument between us. McKenzie was there as well. This was a fight between Vampire and the Packs, he stated, and when the fight was over, the side that lost would accept the outcome. The beast inside me wanted to argue with that statement. This had nothing to do with Vampire. This was an internal quarrel. The beast inside me was a wolf and she craved acknowledgment. She would howl and fight and kill until those bastards acknowledged her dominance. The wolf understood only strength and I had that in spades.

The king asked the wolves if they were ready. Castle howled, the sound filling the arena with the promise of his will. My wolf responded with a surge of adrenaline. Inside me she paced and twitched, but I stood my ground, my feet sinking into the warmth of the sand. McKenzie asked if Vampire was ready and I did as the voice in my head urged. Marcus calmly explained what was expected of me. I was a gladiator, thrown to the wolves as Marcus had been thrown to the lions. I saw it in my head, the image as clear as day. My connection with Marcus was so much stronger when I opened my mind to him that I could read his thoughts as easily as he read mine. He was thinking about his introduction to the arena. He'd been thrown to the lions, but the predator inside him had risen that day and the lions hadn't had a chance.

"The wolves have no chance, either." Marcus chuckled in my head. "You are more wolf than any of them have met, *cara mia*. Prove it to them."

I held the cestus over my head as Marcus had when he'd fought as a full-fledged gladiator. It was the sign of a professional, cool and prepared. It made Castle stop his preening for a moment. He sneered at me across the sand that separated us and all was silent for a moment. The king gave the order and chaos broke loose.

The crowd screamed as the three wolves changed forms. The two betas knelt in the sand, their limbs flowing around them, changing shape in easy movements. They were just the preview though. Castle didn't need to kneel and think about his form. He began to run toward me. He started on two feet, running with powerful strides toward his prey. His change was so quick, so effortless, that one moment he was a man and the next he leapt through the air, a powerful pitch-black wolf coming for me. I stood my ground, waiting for the right moment. He came toward me, snarling through the air, my neck in his sights.

"Wait," the patient voice said in my head. "Wait," it said even as I could feel the heat from his body and see the spit in his mouth as he opened his powerful jaw. "Move!"

I leapt into action, rolling under the wolf and kicking up at the same time. The motion sent the big wolf scrambling as he hit the sharp wooden stake and it impaled him through the shoulder. I glanced up and knew it wouldn't take Castle long to get himself off that stake. He'd heal fast. I needed to move quickly if I wanted to gain the advantage.

It would be easier to fight Castle if I took out the betas first. I wanted to be able to focus all of my attention on Castle. While Castle writhed on the pike, the betas began to circle me. I had rolled to the center of the arena and the smaller wolves began to work in tandem. Smaller, I thought, didn't mean small. They were simply smaller than the enormous wolf Castle became. They snarled and growled around me, enjoying the play. They twitched their tails and snapped their sharp teeth toward me. I tried to keep them both in my sights, but it was impossible. They surrounded me and Castle was almost off the spike. I was running out of time.

"Shh," the voice said. Marcus's voice was starting to mingle with my own inner voice. "Calm yourself. You have them right where you want them. Stop trying to follow them with your eyes and open your other senses."

Breathing deeply, I let the instincts flow across me. I let the wolf inside take over completely. She was triumphant as she took hold of our body. I felt her will, her joy in this fight. I tracked the wolf in front of me with my eyes, but I knew where the other one was, too. I sensed him behind me and I felt the moment he decided to attack. Time seemed to slow as I moved into place. He leapt toward me and I turned at the last second, powering up to catch him in the gut. I felt the claws on my cestus sink into the soft underbelly of the wolf, and I drove forward like I was pulling a lever. That lever opened the wolf's belly and I felt the blood gush as I rolled away, yanking my hand out of the eviscerated abdomen.

The beta hit the ground with a thud and I knew he was dead before the sand had settled around him. The claws on the cesti were pure silver. It was why Zack had handled them with the greatest care. The silver would burn the flesh. It would damage the wolf's flesh so terribly that it died before the wolf's natural healing powers could kick in. He could, eventually, heal a cut to his arm, but I sank those claws deep into his belly. I had cut through flesh and into his organs. He hadn't stood a chance. The silver on my hands was coated in blood and I was perfectly satisfied with the metallic smell floating on the air. I felt Marcus's approval from across the arena. The vampire's dark eyes never left me. While the rest of the crowd sat on the edge of their seats or screamed their preference, Marcus was still, all of his energy, his will, poured into me.

One down, two to go. The crowd seemed to finally understand this wouldn't be an easy kill for the alpha. I wouldn't go easy.

Hell, I thought looking at Castle as he managed to pull himself off the spike, I wasn't going down at all. He was going down.

The second beta howled his displeasure at his friend's death. He lost his discipline and came after me with no thought but to get his jaw wrapped around my neck. Castle barked and I knew instinctively he was trying to order the beta to stop. He needed a moment to heal the wound in his shoulder. He wanted to face me two to one, but the beta was so far gone in his rage that he didn't listen. He pounced, his weight shoving me down into the sand. His claws sank into my shoulders. The pain was blistering.

"Forget it," the voice said. The pain didn't matter. I could deal with it later.

The pain receded and I used my legs to roll the wolf off and over me. My feet sank in the sand as I ran for the other side of the arena. The wolf nipped at my heels. I sped up, knowing exactly what I wanted to do. I reached the side of the arena where silver chains hung. The wolf was too close. I turned and he was coming at me. I reared my fist back and hit him straight in his snout. He whimpered as he went down. His big body hit the sand.

When I looked at the other side of the arena, Castle was changing. He took human form again. It would help him heal quicker.

"I am going to kill you, bitch!" Castle screamed across the arena.

I picked up the chain in my free hand. "That's what your son said." I couldn't help it. I really can be a bitch.

Castle's scream might have curled a lesser woman's toes, but I had other things to do. His wound was healing before my eyes and that beta was already getting up. I hefted the heavy rope and slung it at the downed beta before he could rise. The chain was thick and heavy, but I lifted it easily. I caught him across the legs. The flesh immediately started to smoke and the wolf howled. He tried to move, but the chain weighed a ton and the silver sapped his strength. The crowd roared as Castle changed again. Magic filled the air and knew

I had very little time before he reached me. I didn't need much.

I shoved my bladed hand across the wolf's throat and punched into it. I dragged it through his flesh with strength and will. The cestus on my hand didn't bother me anymore. I'd worn it many times before. In my mind, I thought about all the battles I'd fought and won, the cestus cutting through my opponents' flesh. My memories were meshing with Marcus's, but it gave me a confidence I wouldn't have had. It filled me with experience. I pulled my hand out of the beta's throat, but Castle was already on me.

The force of Castle's big body shoved me against the arena wall and my head slammed against the big silver hook. I saw stars for a minute and went on my knees. My peripheral vision started to get hazy.

"Kelsey!" I heard my brother yelling. Nathan was throwing one leg over the railing and I was glad to see Scott stopped him. He couldn't do anything…

"Get up," Marcus barked the order in my head and my legs didn't dare refuse. "Turn."

I spun around as Castle bore down on me. Despite the throbbing pain in my head, my right arm came up instinctively to block his gnashing teeth. The blades on the cestus cut into Castle's jaw and he jumped back. It gave me enough time to shake the cobwebs out. Castle's next attack went straight for my thigh. I jumped, but he managed to catch my left side and sink his powerful jaws into the meat of my leg right above my knee. The teeth burned as he sank them in and I knew if I didn't throw him off, he could break my femur and then I would go down. I didn't heal the way he did. If I couldn't run, I couldn't fight. I went for the softest part of him I could reach.

I shoved a blade into his eye.

He immediately let go and before I could blink, he'd changed forms. His left eye was a bloody, mangled mess. He stared at the blood pouring onto his hands then with a growl, he reared back and punched me straight in the face. I hit the side of the arena again, this time the back of my head smacking into the wood.

Castle pressed his advantage. He used his powerful fists in a way he hadn't been able to use his claws. He punched me in the face, the stomach, the chest. I felt like a body bag. I might have fallen over, but Castle kept me upright with the force of his blows. Pain as I'd never imagined ripped through my body. As I absorbed the agony from one blow, another landed. It seemed to never end. The crowd was chanting, screaming something, but it was a distant thing. Marcus was trying to tell me something, but even his voice was far away. I felt his panic. There wasn't a lot I could do about it.

Castle finally decided to let me hit the ground. I tumbled to my knees and I realized my right eye must be swollen because I couldn't see out of it anymore. My left shoulder screamed and was kind of stuck at a weird angle. It must have separated at some point. My whole body was on fire. The pain was so bad I started to hope Castle got this thing done soon.

I pitched forward and felt the sand against my swollen face. Marcus was pleading with me and the wolf inside was howling for me to get my ass up, but I thought about Gray. He was going to be sad when he found out. I wondered if he would blame himself. I wished I'd never gone after those class rolls. If I'd done what Gray had asked, I would be planning the menu for our reception. I would be arguing with Gray over fish or chicken, and when we got sick of fighting, he would take me to bed. If I'd chosen him over my stubborn instincts, I wouldn't be dying in this terrible place.

Castle was enjoying his fans. He kicked me a couple of times, but I hurt too much to even grunt. I've heard that when pain gets to be too much, the body shuts down and a blissful numbness takes over. I didn't get that. I got misery that seemed to never end.

Finally, he kneeled down and lifted my head up by the hair. From my angle, I could make out the queen weeping openly and pleading with her husband. Donovan looked like a man who wished he'd never put a freaking crown on. Zack and Jamie were moving toward the front of the crowd.

Castle leaned down. "I think I'm going to like killing you most of all, little girl. Do you know what I'm going to do when you're dead? I'll give it a month or so, but I'll kill every single bitch who works in those clubs and I'll pin it on a vamp. I'll have my war, you understand? You changed nothing."

He dropped my head and reared back to change. He would kill me in his wolf form. It was traditional. He took his wolf form and howled before he pounced, his teeth going for my throat.

I used every bit of energy I had left to flip my body over, ball my good hand into a fist and shove my right hand up. I saw the look on Castle's face when he realized what was going to happen. There was nothing he could do. He couldn't change course and his own heavy weight helped me. My claws sunk deeply into his chest. I fought to shove them in further even as his big body fell onto me, forcing my arm to go into an odd angle. He landed on top of me and he snarled as my claw found his heart. Even as the light went out in his face, he growled at me.

The arena hushed. Our final moments had been a close battle. I wondered if anyone really knew what had happened. The wolf lay on top of me, his snout in my neck, my hand in his chest. The crowd seemed to be waiting to see who got up.

"Very good, *cara mia*," Marcus whispered in my brain. He knew what had happened. He would have felt me die. "You've done well, but you must finish. Listen carefully. I want you to…"

He gave me the words to use. I had to follow both wolf and vampire traditions. Marcus talked me through everything. He let me know he would be with me after I finished, but I had to get through this part by myself. I rolled the wolf off of me, shoving his body to the sand with as much strength as I could muster.

There were shocked cries as the alpha of the Dallas pack slumped over in the sand and I struggled to get to my knees. I didn't feel that overwhelming urge to continue my kill the way I had before. Marcus gave me the strength to force my wolf to calm down. She gave me the strength to stay on my feet and do what I needed to do, but I was in control.

Some of the wolves began crying, but I saw many seemed relieved. I leaned exhausted over the carcass to fulfill the last of my duties. Donovan was on his feet, looking down on me with satisfied relief and something like respect. He nodded as I reared my good hand back and punched through Joseph Castle's chest. I had to work at it and it wasn't pretty, but I claimed the heart and managed to get to my feet. My left hand dangled. I couldn't see out of one eye. I saw the horror in Liv's eyes as I walked past her on my way to the king. I knew I must be really fucked up to get that look.

Donovan walked down the steps to the edge of the railing. He stared across the arena to where McKenzie sat. "The battle is done. I declare the killing of these wolves to be righteous. I need to know this is done, John."

McKenzie's low voice carried across the arena. "The Packs are satisfied that justice has been done. I will select another alpha after I speak to the pack. I'll choose carefully, Your Highness."

"And I will trust your judgment," Donovan promised and then turned his attention back to me.

I held the heart out to him and he took it with no hesitation. Daniel Donovan wasn't afraid of a little blood. I braced myself because it wasn't easy to stay upright. I gave him the ancient words between a king and his death machine. "Your Highness is satisfied with his *Nex Apparatus*?"

Donovan's face fell and then hardened. His words ground out of his mouth. "I am. You're dismissed."

Suddenly the queen was by his side and Quinn was close behind her. Their faces registered shock.

"Daniel," the queen said, putting a perfectly manicured hand on his arm. "You have to heal her."

Quinn shook his head. "She won't let him."

He was a good judge of character. I wasn't letting that vampire anywhere near me.

I began to turn to leave the arena when a small face caught my eye. He was trying to hide behind a pillar at the top of the arena, but when he saw me looking, he stepped out. Lee Donovan Quinn had avoided his bed again. He was dressed in pajama pants and a T-shirt. He looked down on me and smiled, holding his small hand up in greeting. I tried to smile back, but before I could he was gone again. The kid was fast.

Marcus's hand was on my elbow. "Brace yourself, Kelsey."

He held me tightly and shoved my shoulder back into place. I screamed as the pain threatened to take me under again. I could move my left arm, but I didn't particularly want to. Every muscle in my body ached, but I was going to walk out of that arena. Marcus seemed to sense it and took a step back.

"Marcus," Donovan shouted as I started to stagger out. "I'll send a doctor to her room."

He'd probably send Sharpe. It would be just like that bastard to send Jack the fucking Ripper in to examine me. I held up my good hand as I walked out of the arena and managed to give the king my happy middle finger.

Chapter Eighteen

Marcus held his hand out and I let him lead me onto the water taxi. It was private, of course. Marcus liked to have the best. I was rapidly learning that Marcus Vorenus was a legend in Venice. The minute we'd stepped off the plane he'd been inundated with admirers who were thrilled the vampire had come home.

They knew what he was. Venice is a tolerant city. I'd been promised many new experiences as he taught me about my power. I breathed in the air from the Adriatic Sea as the boat took off. We had no luggage with us. We were fugitives. I was wearing clothes Marcus had bought in New Orleans, where we'd hidden for two days before taking the plane across the Atlantic. Marcus had spoken to Zack several times and been assured that while the king was furious with us, he was calming down as Zack and the queen worked on him. They'd talked him out of hunting us down and dragging me back.

I went to stand with Marcus, who was gazing at the ocean over the cabin of the water taxi. He looked and felt so peaceful. I let my hands go around his waist. I was getting used to my desire to be physically connected to the vampire. It was an impulse between a Hunter and her trainer. Marcus didn't mind and it made me feel better, though not as good as his blood had made me feel.

We'd fled in the car Zack had left for us and driven immediately to a hotel in Fort Worth where Marcus convinced me to take his blood. I'd been hesitant when he cut a place in his chest and urged my mouth to it, but once I tasted it, I'd been ravenous. That blood was better than any drug I'd ever encountered. It healed me and made me feel warm and safe. It connected me to Marcus, who in the course of a measly few days had become everything to me. He was my teacher, my protector, my only friend in the world. He was not my lover, but that was my choice for now. I wasn't sure how long I'd hold out because I slept beside him at night. I started out on the edge of the bed, but before too long I'd rolled and tossed until I curled against him. He would chuckle and put his arms around me, pulling me close. He'd held me that first long night after the arena when I'd finally given in and cried. The experience had been purgative and healing and not possible without him.

The boat slid across the water and Marcus's dark eyes lit up as Venice rose like a jewel on the ocean. My eyes opened wide to take it all in. I'd never been out of the US before. Hell, besides Arkansas and Louisiana, I'd never been out of Texas before. Venice was a stunning sight, a beautiful, alien world, and Marcus seemed extremely satisfied to be home. He pulled my hand to his lips and kissed it firmly before holding it to his heart. This was our home for now.

I studied the man beside me and wondered what would happen between us. I wanted to open myself to him, but I hesitated and I knew why.

The drugs were out of my system. I was no longer under the influence of any spell.

I still loved Grayson Sloane.

It wasn't like before. My love for him was a wary thing. If I met Gray at this point, I would push him away. I would never let him in. I would find a way to sabotage any relationship we could have. I had to heal myself before I could consider even talking to Gray. I needed to discover who I could be. I wanted to be the woman Marcus was sure I could become.

"That is it," Marcus said, a wealth of satisfaction in his voice. He pointed to an elegant townhouse with a pier for his private boat. There was a line of servants waiting to greet us. "Welcome home, *cara mia*."

I smiled at him, genuinely happy to be alone with him. I would take this time to explore, to learn, to grow because I needed to become all I could. I had a new mission. I might not be able to be with Gray, but he was my client even though he didn't know it.

I would save Grayson Sloane if it was the last thing I did.

The boat pulled up to the pier and Marcus hopped out. He placed his hands around my waist and lifted me lightly onto the landing. He leaned over and kissed my forehead affectionately. The sun was going down. I slid my hand into his and walked into the night.

* * * *

Kelsey, Gray, Marcus and the entire Thieves gang will return in Addict.

Author's Note

I'm often asked by generous readers how they can help get the word out about a book they enjoyed. There are so many ways to help an author you like. Leave a review. If your e-reader allows you to lend a book to a friend, please share it. Go to Goodreads and connect with others. Recommend the books you love because stories are meant to be shared. Thank you so much for reading this book and for supporting all the authors you love!

Sign up for Lexi Blake's newsletter and be entered to win a $25 gift certificate to the bookseller of your choice.

Join us for news, fun and exclusive content including free short stories.

There's a new contest every month!

Go to www.LexiBlake.net to subscribe.

Addict
Hunter: A Thieves Novel, Book 2
By Lexi Blake
Coming Soon!

When Kelsey Owens returns home to Dallas, she is a changed woman. After months of training with Marcus Vorenus, she has more control over her abilities. She's ready to start her new job, even if it means dealing with the King of All Vampire and his partner, Devinshea Quinn. Her first assignment, however, will force her to face her past. Grayson Sloane is in trouble and she has to find him.

With the help of Gray's brother, a full empath demon, Kelsey tracks her one time lover down. Before she knows it, she's pulled into Gray's undercover operation in a demon sex club and sitting across from a Duke of Hell. Abbas Hiberna plans to use her city to test his new drug, Brimstone. It doesn't just give supernatural creatures a high. It also leaves them vulnerable to demonic persuasion.

When the king's own men begin to turn against him, even the royal family is in danger. Keeping them safe will put Kelsey in the duke's crosshairs and test her fledgling relationship with Marcus. With her new life crumbling around her, a dark secret about her former lover is revealed and Kelsey will have to choose between saving Gray Sloane and the revenge she's waited a lifetime for.

* * * *

Excerpt:
"Stop fidgeting," the demon ordered as the elevator began its climb. He'd told me to refer to him as Matt. It wasn't his real name. Demons jealously guarded their real names.

"You try having a piece of dental floss shoved up your ass, and we'll see how you like it," I grumbled back. I tried not to look at myself, but it was hard because the entire elevator was mirrored. I didn't like to think why they'd done that. I was just thinking about the fact that my ass was hanging out. We'd been allowed into the club when Gray's brother had explained he'd procured me for Gray. I could tell the bouncer wasn't that impressed. He'd looked at me differently after I walked out of the "dressing room." The demon had taken charge, briskly ordering me out of my nice clothes that covered me up and into lingerie. I don't even know if I could call it that. Marcus had bought me a ton of pretty, frilly things he liked to see me in, but they tended toward filmy nightgowns and beautifully made corsets.

I was dressed in a white lace demi-cup bra that pushed my boobs up and made them look a lot bigger than they were. There was the white thong currently stuck between my ass cheeks. I had on thigh-high white hose and four-inch stilettos. Gray's brother had brushed out my hair and placed a white mask over my face. I didn't know what I hated more, the shoes or the so-called underwear. I longed for my nice cotton bikinis and my comfy Uggs. Apparently both of those were a no-go in the house of sin Gray was currently residing in.

I was grateful for the mask as the elevator stopped on the fifth floor, and my heart started to race. I reminded myself that I was here on a case. I was just going to make sure Gray was all right. That was all. I didn't have any interest in him beyond the fact that he was my brother's best friend and potentially had information I could use.

So why was my heart thumping as loud as the heavy rock beat that filled the space as Matt led me out onto the floor?

There was a large man in a tuxedo standing at an elegantly appointed desk.

"My lord," he said deferentially. His eyebrows arched as he looked at me. "Trying something different tonight, my lord?"

Matt laughed. "Not at all, Kevin. Let Tristan know I'll be requiring his services. This one is for my brother."

"Very good, sir. Lord Sloane does like slender brunettes," Kevin said, nodding us in.

We walked past the security desk and into some combination of a strip club and a place for swingers. All of the women were dressed in a similar fashion to me, though they seemed to favor leather and dark colors. I was the only one in the room wearing white. Naturally every eye turned to me.

Behind my half mask, I studied the room. It looked like a grand ballroom. The floors were polished hardwood and the room was lit with chandeliers. The walls had those white panels favored in

European palaces. It had an old world feel to it, if one ignored the stripper poles at the far end or the various women and men tied up and being spanked across the room. There was also a bar, naturally, and several intimate spaces with antique couches.

"You do seem able to catch my little brother's attention, don't you?" Matt said, satisfaction oozing from his pores.

I turned and there he was. He was sitting on a couch, his big body lounging negligently. He was wearing tight black jeans and a dark shirt he'd left open as though he'd walked out of the bedroom without bothering to button his shirt. It left his perfectly cut chest on full mouth-watering display. The tattoo that covered the left half of his torso looked sexy as hell in the low glow of the room. His face was a tribute to masculine perfection. Marcus was the perfect European male, all fine lines and aesthetic grace, but Gray was an all-American hunk of masculinity. He screamed dominant male and for good reason. He was and made no apologies for it. He was the kinkiest man I'd ever met. He preferred to tie up his sexual partners and when I was that partner, I'd been happy to do it.

I was thinking about doing it right now.

His deep blue eyes were looking lazily around the room. He had a female at his feet, her head resting on his lap. He didn't seem terribly interested in her. He was talking to another man whose face I couldn't see. He was smaller than Gray, with almost white hair. Gray stopped midsentence when his eyes caught sight of me.

Gray sat up, and I noticed that his hair was longer than it had been when we were engaged. He used to wear it in a strict, military-style cut. It was a little shaggy now, reaching to the tops of his ears. It was thick and wavy. I had always wanted to run my fingers through it. I flushed under his gaze, unsure if it was just the outfit I was wearing or complete and abject shame that I had a man who cared about me, and I couldn't help but think about someone else.

He was the ultimate bad boy. Grayson Sloane was a half-demon who had lied to me, used me, and had potentially tried to trick me into going to Hell with him. And I was shaking at the thought of his hands on me. I was also resolute. No matter how much I was attracted to the man, I was going to resist because I knew the score. Marcus was good, and Gray was bad.

Gray was also observant. He stood up abruptly and looked curiously at the new girl, namely me. He stalked across the room just as another big man moved to intercept me. He was shorter than Gray, though he still towered over me. He didn't have great control over his form. His eyes gave him away.

"New girl, huh," the demon said. His shirt was off and he had a girl on a leash trailing behind him. She didn't look terribly upset to be on a leash. I wondered how much she was getting paid.

"This one is for my brother," Matt said, attempting to dismiss him.

"Oh, it's you," the man said. "I didn't recognize you, sir. His lordship has enough pretty brunettes, don't you think? This one looks practically angelic. That's really not his style."

"I'll decide what my style is, Kall," Gray snarled at the smaller demon. "Go away and don't look at her again or we will have a problem. Do you understand?"

Kall bowed from his waist and murmured, "Yes, my lord."

Kall slunk away, pulling his girl behind him. Gray's face was tight. "Explain yourself, brother. How dare you bring her here."

Matt looked perfectly innocent. "I thought you would be thrilled, brother. This is the woman who has caused you such distress, is it not? Here she is. I didn't even have to threaten her. The moment she heard you were in trouble, she was scrambling to get here to you. I think she still cares for you. You know I can't stand to see lovers kept apart. I know the feeling too well myself."

"I'm not in trouble." Gray spoke to Matt, but his eyes were on me.

The woman who had previously had her head in Gray's lap crawled across the room and attached herself to his leg.

"Don't leave, Sir," she begged prettily.

Gray looked down like he'd already forgotten she existed and wasn't pleased to be reminded. "Go. Now." He pointed to the elevators and she crawled off, her head hung low.

It was a disgusting display, and I wondered if that wouldn't have been me had I stayed with him. "Well, if you're not in trouble, then I'll feel free to get on with my life, Sloane. Matt, where are my clothes?"

The demon with the upper-crust British accent waved his hand. "Probably in the incinerator by now."

"What?"

He gave a negligent half shrug. "Well, they didn't suit you, dear. It looks like some old man picked them out, perhaps trying to de-tart his 'much too young for him' girlfriend."

"You asshole. How am I supposed to get home in this?" How was I supposed to explain being more than half naked to my trainer?

"That's your problem, dear. I've done my level best to help. You can't expect me to solve all of your problems." Matt's mouth turned up in a slow smile. "And now my date for the evening is here." A thin young man with curly blond hair and blue eyes was walking toward us. He kept his eyes downcast and sank to his knees when he reached us.

"My lord, how may I serve you this evening?"

"I'll think of something, Tristan. And tell the colorist your hair should be a bit lighter to get it just right," Matt said, turning the young man's face up toward him. "Come along, now. I know public sex is all the rage here, but I prefer a bit of discretion. I'm going to take my sweet, little puppy somewhere private to play our games." His face turned serious as he regarded Gray. "I'm making due tonight, brother, as I have every night for the last ten bloody years. The object of your affection is in your grasp. I suggest you don't let it go."

With that I was left alone with the man who had lied to me. I was left alone with the first man I ever loved.

"You're supposed to be in Italy," Gray said and he made it sound a little like an accusation.

"I just got back yesterday," I replied, wishing I had more clothes on. I noticed that the man Gray had been talking to was watching us now.

"So it only took you twenty-four hours to get into serious trouble," Gray complained.

It wasn't how I expected the reunion to go. I was the injured party. I was the one who had come to save him even though he'd treated me like crap. The least I expected was a little gratitude. "I'm on a case."

"That's your excuse for everything, sweetheart," Gray said flatly.

I hated the fact that I felt tears welling in my eyes. That mask was coming in handy. I should have been happy. He was making it easy on me. I could go home to Marcus and cuddle up and know that I was in the right place with the right man. The time I had spent with

Gray had been a huge mistake. "Then it can be my excuse for leaving. I can see you have everything under control here, Sloane. I won't bother you again."

His hand wrapped around my upper arm and drew me close to his body. "You bother me every second of every day, Kelsey mine, and it's far too late for you to leave." He pulled me into the confines of his muscular arms. His mouth went straight to my ear and he whispered. "I'm undercover, sweetheart, and now you are, too. You know how to play this role. Keep your mouth closed and look submissive. Do you remember?"

I nodded. I knew exactly what he wanted. I was capable of keeping my mouth shut when the occasion called for it.

"You're a sight for sore eyes, gorgeous," he said as he allowed his hands to slide along the curve of my hip. "I missed you, Kelsey mine."

You Only Love Twice
Masters and Mercenaries 8
By Lexi Blake
Coming February 17, 2015!

A woman on a mission

Phoebe Graham is a specialist in deep cover espionage, infiltrating the enemy, observing their practices, and when necessary eliminating the threat. Her latest assignment is McKay-Taggart Security Services, staffed with former military and intelligence operatives. They routinely perform clandestine operations all over the world but it isn't until Jesse Murdoch joins the team that her radar starts spinning. Unfortunately so does her head. He's gorgeous and sweet and her instincts tell her to trust him but she's been burned before, so he'll stay where he belongs—squarely in her sights.

A man on the run

Since the moment his Army unit was captured by jihadists, Jesse's life has been a nightmare. Forced to watch as those monsters tortured and killed his friends and the woman he loved, something inside him snapped. When he's finally rescued, everyone has the same question—why did he alone survive? Clouded in accusations and haunted by the faces of those he failed, Jesse struggles in civilian life until McKay-Taggart takes him in. Spending time with Phoebe, the shy and beautiful accountant, makes him feel human for the first time in forever. If someone so innocent and sweet could accept him, maybe he could truly be redeemed.

A love they never expected

When Phoebe receives the order to eliminate Jesse, she must choose between the job she's dedicated her life to and the man who's stolen her heart. Choosing Jesse would mean abandoning everything she believes in, and it might mean sharing his fate because a shadowy killer is dedicated to finishing the job started in Iraq.

* * * *

Jesse pushed through the double doors, his whole being surprisingly calm. This was what he needed. He'd been sitting in his office waiting for her to wake up, thinking about how he would handle this interrogation with some modicum of civility.

It was so good to know civility wasn't going to be required.

It wasn't so good to realize that the minute she'd opened that bratty mouth, he'd gotten hard as hell and he wanted to fuck her more than he wanted to figure her out. There was a little voice playing in his head that told him to just get inside her and all those secrets would open for him. All he had to do was thrust inside her tight body and the mysteries of the universe would reveal themselves.

Yeah, he wasn't going to do that. He was going to do his job and find out who she worked for and then he would walk away from her. He wasn't going to hold her tenderly or hope she could love him. No. It was time to grow the fuck up. How was it being through what he'd been through in Iraq hadn't managed to teach him what this one woman had? He needed to shut down and do his job.

But that didn't mean parts of his job couldn't be very pleasurable.

"Uhm, Jesse, don't you think you should handle this in the conference room? It's where Ian planned on keeping her." Adam Miles's voice was an unwelcome intrusion.

"No." He knew the old Jesse would have stopped, but this was between him and Phoebe.

"Adam, I can really explain. This is all one huge misunderstanding." Phoebe tried to bring her head up.

That was an easy move to counter. He brought his hand down on that sweet, sweet ass. Phoebe had the damn prettiest ass he'd ever watched for hours and drooled over, and now he had zero reason to not spank that gorgeous flesh. He heard that sound, that smack as his hand hit her, and he felt her shiver. She didn't scream. Nope. He'd thought if he smacked her good, she would call him a fucking pervert, but he'd been a dumbass idiot and this Phoebe just moaned a little as the slap went through her.

It wasn't the type of moan that would cause him to stop

spanking a sub at Sanctum.

Motherfucker. He knew he hadn't been wrong about her. He'd thought there was a submissive streak buried under her "I'm a good girl so don't fuck my sweet little asshole" exterior.

"The only explanation is I'm a dirty little spy and I need to tell my captor everything in order to keep him from slapping my ass silly." He couldn't be professional with her. It wouldn't work. It would only serve to put distance between them, and now he could see that distance was what she'd worked for the whole time. She hadn't let him do more than hold her hand and give her an awkward peck. She'd had him convinced he just wasn't her type, but he could smell her now. Yeah, that wasn't sweet or gentlemanly, but then that obviously didn't work for her. "She likes me slapping her ass. Take a deep whiff, Adam, and you'll be able to tell she's aroused."

She gasped and her whole torso came up off his. "Jesse!"

Yeah, she sounded like a pissed off girlfriend, but she wasn't his girlfriend. She was the woman who had played him and then nearly painted her initials on his chest. And he was the idiot who had stood there and almost begged her to do it.

He cringed at the thought of how stupid he'd been about her. He knew he was ping-ponging, caught between wanting to understand her and wanting to throttle her, but most of all, he wanted to get his hands on her.

He wanted to see just how much she'd lied about.

"You might want to think this thing through, Jesse," Adam began.

He was just about to tell Adam where he could shove his thought process when Big Tag strode out of his office. A thunderous look clouded his boss's face, but Jesse was ready to throw down with whoever he needed to. This was his op and his…fuck, he didn't even know what to call her, but Phoebe was his.

Ian stopped in front of them. "Take her to your office. Do what you need to do but keep it down. Apparently we're still having a baby shower and I have to attend or risk having my balls ripped off my body. I like my balls, Murdoch. Keep her quiet. Charlie's serious about this party thing. When did I fucking lose control? She's not even an employee here."

"No. I'm part owner," Charlotte said, her voice a sharp instrument. She was a beautiful woman with strawberry blonde hair.

She rested her hand on the bump on her belly that seemed to get bigger every day. "Eve and I own half this company, you know. And we have all the boobs so try getting around us. Phoebe, I swear to god if I find out you've done one thing to put this company and our people in danger I will take you apart myself. Is that understood? You better hope you can prove you weren't going to hurt Jesse. He's one of my men and I will deal with you."

Phoebe's head came up again. "Your men? That's a little presumptuous, isn't it? You treat him like a puppy you can pat on his head and send away. He isn't yours and if you think you can take me, you're wrong."

Charlotte's lips curled up and Jesse realized Phoebe had just fallen into a trap. "She doesn't like the fact that I said you're mine, Jesse."

Big Tag was frowning at her. "I didn't either."

She waved him off. "I meant as a friend and employee, but Phoebe's brain goes straight for the sexual. I wonder why. Li's right. You're going to owe him a hundred bucks at the end of this thing. She's all Stockholmed out. Who wants cake?"

Bound by His Blood
Jennifer August
Available now!

Investigative reporter Sheridan Aames is hot on the trail of a lethal drug flooding Boston. She never expects her snitch appointment to end in a hail of bullets...or to learn the sexy detective who rescues her is actually a vampire cop. It's not the fact he's a vampire which bothers her – it's realizing he's a Dominant. She doesn't want anything to do with that and doesn't mind telling him. Except she can't quite shake the compelling need pulling her toward him, the desire to kneel at his feet and see what comes of such an act. Logan McCallister knows there's something special about Sheridan from the moment he wraps his arms around her and mists them to the safety of his house. He's instantly attracted to her, drawn almost against his will to her spunky, vivacious nature. As a Dominant, McCallister is accustomed to subservience, instant obedience, and sensual submission. Sheridan's defiance stirs his excitement -- the more she resists her submission to him, the more he needs her, something he swore never to feel again. But as they battle their conflicting sexual desires, their investigation reveals a bigger — and more dangerous — threat to each other and mankind. Sheridan must find it within her to bend her knee...her neck...her heart...and submit to Logan to save humanity and herself.

* * * *

Boston, 1888
"Come on, Logan. It'll be a grand night. It's your eighteenth birthday. Time to become a man."

Logan McCallister gave Joseph Kilkairn a sour look. The Scotsman was bound and determined to drag him to a brothel. McCallister wanted to go. He really did. Fear held him back.

If Father finds out where I've gone...

His straight-laced father would have an apoplectic fit if he knew his first-born son, the one he'd been meticulously grooming to join the family shipping business, had left their stately Beacon Hill house to pay for sex. Boston Brahmins did *not* engage in salacious activities, nor did they cross class lines.

The fire in the hearth crackled and popped. Wood groaned as it shifted into ash. The big house in which he lived with his father, younger brother, and sister was as empty and personable as an ancient tomb. None of his family had stayed to celebrate his birthday with even a special meal much less gifts or well wishes.

Not that I expected anything different.

His father ran a strict household. Frivolities like presents, celebrations, and affections were frowned upon.

Logan set his jaw as a spurt of rebellion tempted him.

One night out of a lifetime of duty won't matter.

McCallister shifted the perfect knot of his cravat, brushed away non-existent lint from his custom-tailored jacket and nodded his head. "All right. I'm in."

Joseph chortled and thumped him on the back. "You're going to love it," he said. His dark blue eyes gleamed. "I was there last week, myself. Had a gorgeous dove named Claudine take care of me. Gor, she was something else."

Excitement thrummed in McCallister's veins, easily beating away any lingering fear. Following Joseph from the house, McCallister leaped into the waiting coach with a light step born of eagerness. As they bounced and jostled over the cobblestone road leading from Beacon Hill, the gaslights flanking each side of the street streaked past like falling stars.

They arrived at Desdemona's Palace a quarter hour later. McCallister climbed from the coach and stared at the elegant house in front of him. A full moon washed over the two-story building and graceful wrought-iron railings. Soft golden light flickered in nearly all the windows. A curtain moved on the upper right and he saw the perfect form of a woman outlined against the light. A taller male figure joined her and they disappeared from sight.

McCallister rubbed his hands together, suddenly eager to find and bed a woman with large breasts and a lusty appetite.

Joseph sprinted up the stairs and pulled the discreet gold chain near the door.

"Ready for the most incredible night of your life, McCallister?"

He grinned at his friend. "Absolutely."

The door opened and a tall man with shoulders wider than the entry looked down at them. Recognition flickered in his black eyes when he looked at Joseph. He stepped back and waved them inside.

"Madam Desdemona will be with you shortly."

He disappeared down the hall and McCallister looked around, trying to calm his racing heart.

A flight of stairs to their right led to the upper floor where he assumed the actual bedding took place. The entry in which they stood flared into a long and mostly dark corridor with a closed door at the end.

Sounds from around the house buffeted him. Throaty laughter and deep moans floated from above while from what seemed below, indeed under his feet, he swore someone sobbed.

He frowned. "Do you hear that?"

"Yeah," Joseph said. He rubbed his hands together. "Sounds just like Claudine when she was riding my cock last week."

The far door opened and McCallister straightened, all thought of the peculiar sound dispelled.

Desdemona was beautiful. Tall, raven-haired with a voluptuous and lush body revealed by the satin gown she wore.

A sheer robe hung over the gown and trailed down her curvaceous form as she glided toward them. Beneath the robe, her full breasts and wide hips pressed against the white satin. McCallister swallowed hard. Her nipples puckered visibly through her dress.

"Good evening, gentlemen." Her throaty contralto wrapped around his cock and held fast. He prayed he didn't disgrace himself.

"Madam Desdemona. You look ravishing as always." Joseph bent over her hand.

McCallister thought his friend overdid it a bit with the bowed head and near subservient posture but then she was an incredibly beautiful woman. Her eyes were a shade of blue he'd never seen before. They looked as though they were lit from the inside by flashes of lightning. Her mouth was full, lush and ruby red.

"Who have you brought me, Joseph?"

She didn't take her gaze from McCallister and he forced himself not to squirm.

Joseph made the introductions. "I was hoping you would personally see to his entertainment, Madam Desdemona."

Her small smile revealed a set of perfect, white teeth. McCallister found himself captivated by them. He wanted to feel them on his body – nipping, tugging, scraping. He licked his lips.

"I'm sorry, but I don't do that anymore. I'll be happy to set you up with one of our other girls, though."

Joseph leaned forward. "But Madam, it's his eighteenth birthday today." He tossed a wink over his shoulder at McCallister. "And he's a virgin."

"Damn it, Kilkairn," he snapped, embarrassment engulfing him like a ravenous beast.

The look on the madam's face changed dramatically. Her brows lifted and the lightning flashed in such quick succession McCallister had to look away. His head spun as the air leeched from his lungs, and his knees shook like the eagerness of a new colt.

The madam stepped closer and curled her long fingers around his forearm while nestling her breast against him. "Is this true, Mr. McCallister?"

He didn't want to admit to it, wanted to lie and claim he'd bedded dozens of chits. But he couldn't. Her blue gaze demanded only the truth.

"Yes," he said with a rasp. "I'm a virgin."

Her smile was like a gift and she squeezed his arm before letting go. "Joseph, I will send Claudine to you. Mr. McCallister, come with me."

Joseph hooted and pounded him on the back. "See you soon, you lucky bastard."

McCallister followed Desdemona down the hallway, his gaze glued to the sway of her ass and hips. His hard cock bounced with each step and anticipation made his balls tighten painfully.

She opened the door, stepped through then beckoned to him. "Shut the door, Mr. McCallister and let me take you."

McCallister carefully did as commanded, sucked down a deep breath and turned to face the beautiful whore.

* * * *

The whimpering woke him. Soft, pathetic sounds of despair bounced inside his head. McCallister frowned and struggled to open his eyes. They were gritty and painful.

Cold, damp cement pressed along his back.

He forced himself to keep his eyes open. The room was mostly dark but for a single beam of sunlight streaming from a narrow slit in the wall across from him. It took long seconds for his eyes to adjust to the shadows.

Something cold surrounded his throat. His arms were thrust over his head and manacled to the hard wall. Fear exploded in him.

Where am I?

He yanked at his chains and choked as the collar bit into his throat. The stench of piss and putrid water rose from the ground, gagging him. He continued to pull until sweat poured down his temples. His neck, chest and arms burned from the effort.

"It's no use," a weary voice said.

McCallister squinted into the darkness. Three men were chained to the far wall in similar fashion. One man with golden eyes that burned like candles stared back at him. The room was too dim for any other impression but fear again shuddered through him.

"What happened?" he asked.

"Don't know."

A sudden cacophony of noise, voices and movement assaulted McCallister. He groaned against the painful intensity. Just when he thought he would die from the sheer volume, it disappeared.

He fell back to the wall and sucked down a deep rasp of air, shaking and shivering like a newborn colt.

"Where are we?" he croaked.

"In that whore Desdemona's basement," the golden eyed man spat.

"Who are you?" He didn't know why he asked except talking seemed to help keep his burgeoning fear at bay.

"Leopold Caine. You?"

"Logan McCallister." He squinted into the shadows at the other two men. "Them?"

"James Robinson and Edward Fontaine."

Each man made small noises that could have been grunts of hello or pain, he couldn't tell which. Exhausted by the conversation, McCallister slumped back to the wall. "Now what?" he whispered.

The golden eyes flashed harshly in the dim light. "Now we wait."

The creak of wood and rusty iron sounded in the shadows. McCallister managed to turn his head enough to see a door open.

A familiar voluptuous figure was outlined in the doorway.

"Good. You're finally awake."

About Lexi Blake

Lexi Blake lives in North Texas with her husband, three kids, and the laziest rescue dog in the world. She began writing at a young age, concentrating on plays and journalism. It wasn't until she started writing romance that she found success. She likes to find humor in the strangest places. Lexi believes in happy endings no matter how odd the couple, threesome or foursome may seem. She also writes contemporary Western ménage as Sophie Oak.

Connect with Lexi online:

Facebook: https://www.facebook.com/lexi.blake.39
Twitter: https://twitter.com/authorlexiblake
Pinterest: http://www.pinterest.com/lexiblake39/
Website: http://www.lexiblake.net/

Sign up for Lexi's newsletter at:
    http://www.lexiblake.net/contact.html.

Made in the USA
Middletown, DE
27 January 2015